Praise f

"*As Dawn Breaks* is a riveting a............................oura-
geous heroines of the First Wo.............................munitio-
nettes played a vital role in Great Britain's war effort. Kate Breslin crafts
a multi-faceted story of breathless suspense, memorable characters, and
authentic emotional depth layered upon a canvas of war. Readers will
be captivated by this exquisite blend of historical intrigue and heartfelt
romance from one of the finest voices in inspirational fiction."

Amanda Barratt, author of *My Dearest Dietrich*
and *The White Rose Resists*

"Breslin's pen is masterful with brilliant strokes of romance, suspense,
and the search for courage written into every page. Dazzling with historical detail, *As Dawn Breaks* takes readers into the heart of the war effort
as women enter the factories as munitionettes, famously coined Canary
Girls, while the men are off fighting during the Great War. The characters
are complex and realistic as they speak to the human emotions of loss and
love. Another not-to-be missed tale from this amazing author!"

J'nell Ciesielski, bestselling author of *The Socialite*

"In *As Dawn Breaks*, Kate Breslin takes readers on a heart-pounding
journey across Great Britain with clandestine characters who are struggling together to stop a dangerous foe. Once again, Breslin has woven
together a brilliant mystery, romance, and World War I conspiracy that
will keep you riveted until the enemy is finally exposed."

Melanie Dobson, award–winning author of *Catching
the Wind* and *The Curator's Daughter*

"Riveting! With her trademark attention to historical detail, Kate Breslin
sweeps readers to a Great War home front full of intrigue, suspense, danger, and courage. For both the heroine and the war effort, the stakes could
not be higher. Through this cast of nuanced characters, we explore loss
and new beginnings, a longing to belong, and the meaning of home. Well
before the last chapter, you'll feel as though the family within these pages
is your own. An immersive, absorbing, and completely satisfying read."

Jocelyn Green, Christy Award–winning author
of *Shadows of the White City*

Books by Kate Breslin

As Dawn Breaks

KATE BRESLIN

BETHANYHOUSE
a division of Baker Publishing Group
Minneapolis, Minnesota

Published by Bethany House Publishers
a division of Baker Publishing Group
11400 Hampshire Avenue South
Bloomington, Minnesota 55438
www.bethanyhouse.com

Printed in the United States of America

Library of Congress Cataloging-in-Publication Data
Names: Breslin, Kate, author.
Title: As dawn breaks / Kate Breslin.
Description: Minneapolis, Minnesota : Bethany House Publishers, a division of Baker Publishing Group, [2021]
Identifiers: LCCN 2021031577 | ISBN 9780764237485 (paperback) | ISBN 9780764239335 (casebound) | ISBN 9781493433827 (ebook)
Classification: LCC PS3602.R4575 D39 2021 | DDC 813/.6—dc23
LC record available at https://lccn.loc.gov/2021031577

Unless otherwise indicated, Scripture quotations are from THE HOLY BIBLE, NEW INTERNATIONAL VERSION®, NIV® Copyright © 1973, 1978, 1984, 2011 by Biblica, Inc.® Used by permission. All rights reserved worldwide.

Scripture quotations labeled NRSV are from the New Revised Standard Version of the Bible, copyright © 1989 National Council of the Churches of Christ in the United States of America. Used by permission. All rights reserved.

This is a work of historical reconstruction; the appearances of certain historical figures are therefore inevitable. All other characters, however, are products of the author's imagination, and any resemblance to actual persons, living or dead, is coincidental.

Cover design by Kelly L. Howard

Author is represented by Hartline Literary Agency.

Baker Publishing Group publications use paper produced from sustainable forestry practices and post-consumer waste whenever possible.

21 22 23 24 25 26 27   7 6 5 4 3 2 1

To our families

Whether we are born to them, create them, or choose them
along the way, love and acceptance are what bind us.

For the women working in munitions during WWI

May their hard work and sacrifice in saving a nation
and their fighting lads never be forgotten.

By the tender mercy of our God,
the dawn from on high will break upon us,
to give light to those who sit in darkness and in the
shadow of death,
to guide our feet into the way of peace.

Luke 1:78–79 NRSV

Prologue

AYLESBURY PRISON
BUCKINGHAMSHIRE, ENGLAND
EARLY MARCH 1918

O nly by searching the bowels of hell would he find the devil. "The prisoner's cell is this way, Captain. If you'll follow me."

Marcus Weatherford pulled his gaze from the shadowy confines beyond the barred gate to glance at the uniformed warden. Then with a backward nod to his companion, the two men followed the warder into the gloom.

As they passed a checkerboard series of locked doors along the dimly lit hall, Marcus again prayed their mission wasn't in vain. Would the prisoner, only four months into a two-year sentence for forgery, be willing to cooperate? More importantly, were MI5 and Scotland Yard on the right track, or was this another fool's errand?

"Here." The warder halted in front of a door with a small, barred window. Marcus stepped forward to peer into the cell. "Unlock it and leave us."

"I'll need to remain just outside here, sir."

"As you wish." Once the door was opened, Marcus and his companion entered the sparse room. The inmate sat on the narrow bed, attempting to sew a button onto a plain white shirt.

The afternoon's gray light flooded in through a tiny window at the back of the cell.

Ashen and thin, the prisoner set aside the shirt and rose from the bench. Defiant blue eyes held his gaze. "Who are you?"

"Detective Quinn with New Scotland Yard." Marcus turned to indicate his companion. "And I'm none of your concern at the moment. We've come to make a deal *if* you have the right answers to a few questions."

The insolent expression thawed. "What questions?"

"Do you know a man called Thomas Brown?"

"Never heard of him."

"What about Rhymer?"

The blue eyes flared, and Marcus leaned in, his pulse thumping. "What do you know?"

The prisoner's head cocked slightly. "Why should I trust you?"

"Because you have little choice. Quinn and I can stay and hear what you have to say and perhaps make a deal. Or we can leave you to go back to your . . . buttons." Marcus nodded toward the crumpled shirt on the bed.

A breath expelled from the sullen mouth. "I had a brother Thomas, but the name Brown means nothing. He likened himself to Thomas the Rhymer, from an auld Scots fairy tale told to us as bairns." The eyes clouded. "Thomas died years ago, somewhere across the world."

"Perhaps not." Marcus fished from his pocket a small, frayed paper tag penned with a set of numbers. He held it up for inspection. "Recognize this?"

The prisoner's pallor flushed. "Where did you come by that?"

"An abandoned flat in Paris. It's stamped *Ezekiel House*, an orphanage on the outskirts of Glasgow. Is it yours?"

"Aye. The tags were marked with our room and case number. 'Tis how they identified us." The prisoner's eyes lifted. "You said you found the tag in France?"

Marcus almost smiled. Another puzzle piece fitted into place. The orphanage had verified there was a brother Thomas and, after combing through Glasgow's old police records, Marcus found the boy described as having dark hair and blue eyes, much like the prisoner. "If your brother *is* alive after all these years, what proof can you offer to make a positive identification?" He tucked the tag into his jacket pocket. "Otherwise, no deal."

Instead of answering, the prisoner's lips compressed into a flat line. Marcus struggled to hold on to his patience. They needed confirmation.

When the silence stretched on, he turned to Quinn. "I think we're finished here—"

"Wait." The prisoner stepped forward. "Thomas had a red birthmark above the hairline."

"Where on his head?"

The blue eyes gleamed. "Put me in the same room with him and I'll show you."

Marcus did smile then. The police report also described a port-wine birthmark. They now had their irrefutable witness. "Our deal is a full pardon in exchange for your help in identifying Rhymer, the man we suspect is your long-lost brother, Thomas."

"A pardon? Just like that?"

"Just like that." Marcus frowned. "But be warned: Any betrayal on your part will constitute treason to the Crown." He leaned in. "That means death."

The prisoner's nostrils flared. Marcus didn't back down. "Do you understand and agree to the offer?"

"Aye."

"I'll make the arrangements." His pulse thrummed. "Speak of this to no one."

He gave the prisoner a final warning glance and left with Quinn.

Now they could prepare for the next stage of the trap—capturing Rhymer, the saboteur MI5 and Scotland Yard had been working feverishly to find. And once they made an arrest, they would have the proof needed to arrest the real mastermind . . .

A man scheming to bring Britain to its knees by killing thousands of its citizens.

1

NOTTINGHAM, ENGLAND
MONDAY, JULY 1, 1918—FOUR MONTHS LATER

*H*er final moments of freedom. Like the rattling gasps before death.

Rosalind Graham's throat constricted as she surveyed her sanctuary for the last time. In a matter of days she would receive her sentence; a prisoner, denied the right to an opinion or to make her own choices. Fated to live out her life in bondage, concealed beneath the sanctified guise of marriage.

"Rose, you didna hear the whistle? Shift's over and I'm due back at the Mixing House before I can clock out. I want to speak with you before you go off and leave me forever."

Seated inside her small overhead crane, Rose gazed down at the jaundiced face of her co-worker, hailing her from the factory floor. Like most girls filling shells at the No. 6 Chilwell National Shell Filling factory, Tilda Lockhart had contracted the yellow skin and bleached hair of a "canary girl," as they were fondly called, from handling the explosive powder TNT.

Rose's job of moving the filled shells by crane onto railcars for shipment had spared her such physical consequences. Yet the grief in her best friend's upturned face matched the anguish in her own heart. "Wait for me, Tilly, I shall be down soon."

"I'll meet you over by the changing rooms."

Rose drew a deep breath once her friend departed, and gave her little world a last, lingering look. She stepped nimbly from the open crane and grabbed at the thick rope to shinny down to the factory floor. Her bruised arms ached with the burden of her weight—another reminder of Julien's private "talk" with her last evening on the kind of wife he expected.

She bit her lips to stave off a sob. Even now the church near Aunt and Uncle's estate in Leicester was being readied for Saturday's nuptials. In five short days, any and all freedom would become forfeit.

She'd imagined having more time—time to experience life and its wonders, to be able to seek out a man she truly loved and with whom she could start a family. Pity's sake, she wasn't yet twenty-one years old! What terrible sin had she committed that she must become the property of a man as much a bully as her uncle?

You know the reason, Rose. See no evil, hear no evil. She mentally shoved the maxim aside. What good was wisdom when it came too late?

Her boots soon touched the floor, and she trudged toward the building's exit to go and say good-bye to her friend.

The munitions factory had become her refuge, a place to hide from her uncle's watchful eye while she enjoyed her work in aiding the war effort. Here she could laugh and be easy with Tilly and others that she considered the salt of the earth—not like the silly, snide upper-class girls from her boarding-school days. And she was able to earn her very own wage.

Except you haven't a farthing now, have you? Stepping outside the building into the bright July sun, Rose shoved her hands into her pockets. She considered again the most recent betrayal by her uncle who was also her *guardian*, a word she'd once naïvely likened to angels when she and her little brothers came to live with the Cutlers after their parents' death.

But Sir Ridley Cutler of Cutler Enterprises, the second largest weapons manufacturer in Britain, was as far from being heavenly as his ruthlessness could take him.

And now he'd stolen all her savings. Her last hope for independence.

She blinked against the glaring light, still aching with the memory of awakening last night to discover Aunt Delia in her room, removing the money from Rose's secret hiding place in the closet. When she'd climbed out of bed, Aunt quickly turned, and the hurt and indignation had stuck in Rose's throat seeing the tiny woman's genuine fear. The wide, dark eyes seemed to say, *Please go back to sleep and say nothing or he will hurt me.*

Her pity had won out and she'd settled back into bed until after her aunt had quietly left the room. Rose had thought to confront Uncle Ridley this morning over his coercing Aunt Delia, but she dared not anger him, not after his recent threat against little Douglas and Samuel. They were only eleven and eight years old, for pity's sake! She shivered again at the notion Uncle would actually take them out of boarding school and ship them off to some orphanage overseas if she gave him trouble . . .

Marching across the cobbled paths between buildings, Rose headed toward the changing rooms. What a fool she'd been, playing up to his vanity months ago so that he would allow her to work at Chilwell. Likely her uncle knew her scheme even then but said nothing. After all, what better publicity for his weapons company than to have his own niece become a munitionette for the war? And then, on the eve of *her very last day of work*, he'd bullied her poor aunt into stealing her funds!

His theft only tightened the noose already around her neck. The same way he'd moved up her December wedding to Julien and then threatened the welfare of her brothers if she disobeyed.

Now you are good and trapped. Rose clenched her teeth. If she could only turn back the clock! Never would she have ventured into her uncle's library weeks ago and happened upon his dealings with Julien. . . .

"You're looking more angry than sad on your last day, Rose, but I'm glad to see a spark in your eyes."

Tilly stood outside the building, a clipboard shielding her eyes from the sun. "Let's go in where hopefully 'tis cooler."

Upon entering the shadowy interior, Rose paused once more to reclaim her sight.

A steady stream of first- and second-shift workers were entering and leaving through the changing room doors, the air an odd mix of fragrant soaps and powders from the women who had bathed and changed, and the pungent stench of sulfur clinging to those who had not.

Passing by the doors, the sounds of high-pitched female laughter rang from within as she and Tilly took up the bench seat just outside the room.

"So tell me, lass. After seeing you brood outside, can I hope you've decided to call off this farce of a wedding?" Tilly pulled off her work bonnet, revealing splotches of greenish-white hair. She wiped her damp brow. "'Tis time you came to your senses."

"Nothing so brave as that." Rose offered a weak smile. "I was just giving myself another good scolding. I should have hidden my money in a tree instead of a hatbox. Only a fool underestimates my uncle."

"Dinna blame yourself! 'Twas *his* crime, not yours. Sir lofty Cutler with his millions, and still he robs his own niece—and he makes your poor aunt do the dirty work!" Tilly shook her head. "'Tis shameful and I dinna care if he *is* knighted. He probably paid for that title."

Touched by the show of support, Rose reached to squeeze Tilly's hand. After today she might never see her dear friend again. "Promise me, you *will* be at the church on Saturday? I . . . I will need you there more than I can say."

"You know that only death would keep me away, lass."

Tilly's blue gaze had turned suspiciously bright, and while the words were meant as a fervent promise, Rose worried. Her friend's complexion of late had turned even more sallow.

Tilly Lockhart was the strongest woman Rose had ever known, but the ill effects from TNT exposure were taking their toll. "Are you unwell, friend? You *would* tell me?"

"Dinna fash, I'm more than fit. 'Tis just this devilish heat." She tugged at the neckline of her boiler suit, revealing a glint of purple and silver against the white shirt collar beneath.

Rose gasped. "Is that a brooch you're wearing? How did you slip it past the inspector this morning?"

"Not so loud!" Tilly cast out a furtive gaze. "I didna wear the pin during inspection."

"Then how . . . ?"

"I hid it in here." Tilly poked a finger into her greenish hair, which was pulled into a bun.

Rose frowned. "You take too many chances, Tilly. You will be fined or get the sack if you are caught wearing it. The rules are clear—"

"'No jewelry, hair grips, matches, or cigarettes.'" Tilly sighed. "Believe me, I know the rules and risks, and how easily one could light off this tinder house." Her brow creased, eyes turning somber. "But I . . . had my reasons."

"What reasons?"

"I wanted you to see it. 'Twas my mother's and my only memory of her since she died birthing me. I'll never be parted from it." She cast about another quick glance, then pulled back her neckline to reveal the lovely jeweled thistle of amethyst set into silver. "'Tis our national flower, yours and mine." She tilted her head. "You are Scots, after all, despite your fancy speech and all that proper Sassenach schooling."

Eyes fixed on the brooch, Rose refrained from comment. Tilly didn't know all of Uncle's conditions in allowing her to be here. He wanted no "peasant speech" in his home, nor would the Earl of Stanton, her future father-in-law. A slip in diction would cost her the job.

"The amethyst *is* beautiful." She glanced up at her friend. "But you could have avoided the risk and shown this to me at our lockers this morning."

Tilly shrugged. "Maybe I feel a bit reckless. You're leaving, so it doesna really matter what happens to me now."

"Do not say that!" Rose turned to face her squarely. "You will always matter to *me*." She reached for Tilly's hand. "I would have got the sack months ago if not for you. Do you remember? I fell off that silly ladder as I started climbing up into my first crane."

Tilly grinned. "I told the instructor it was because the rungs were oily and he should take more care."

Rose smiled. "You knew all along I was clumsy in those new boots. You even pretended to wipe away 'the oil' and then gave me a boost back onto the step."

"You were just nervous." Tilly shrugged. "'Tis quite a change coming from fancy dresses and boarding schools into a world of boiler suits and climbing ladders."

And finding my first true friend. Rose's eyes misted, recalling her first day at Chilwell. Seated alone on the bench beside her locker, she'd been nervous and afraid; the first whistle had already sounded and she was still finger-combing her hair after forgetting to put a brush into her toiletry bag before work. Being forbidden the use of metal hair grips, she couldn't seem to manage the thick unruly locks long enough to stuff them up beneath her work cap. With the clock ticking, she imagined failure before even starting her job—and being sent home to Uncle, who would mock her for thinking she could ever become a munitionette.

Tilly had appeared then, brush in hand, and after several brisk strokes deftly twisted and knotted Rose's curls into place so that they fit perfectly beneath her bonnet. The two had shared a smile before they rushed toward the changing room doors, laughing when they reached the timekeeper only seconds before the final whistle sounded. "You have been like a sister to me from the first day we hired on together," Rose said softly.

"Aye, we're the orphan twins," Tilly joked. "Though thankfully, *you* were saved from the streets." Suddenly her face crumpled. "Never forget me, Rose Graham."

"Never." Rose leaned to embrace her, and Tilly's grip on her was almost painful.

After a moment they sat back, and Tilly gave a loud sniff before she recovered. "The truth is, I'm soon to leave the factory myself."

"You?" Rose blinked. "Where will you go . . . Canada?" Tilly often spoke of sailing across the Atlantic to that country one day.

"You can still come along, 'tis not too late." Tilly's eyes searched hers. "Son of an earl or no, you dinna have to marry him. He's a brute by all accounts, and trust me, you canna ken what freedom is until you've lost it."

Her words only increased Rose's anguish at her upcoming nuptials. "I would go with you if I could, Tilly, but I must stay for Douglas and Samuel."

"You said yourself the lads are doing well at school. They have each other. But you, Rose, your life will become an iron cage."

"Please stop." Her hands curled against her lap. "There are things . . . I cannot change."

"All right then," Tilly said softly. "But when you *can* change things, come take shelter with me across the sea. You'll always be welcome."

Rose knew that day would never come. Still, she managed to nod.

"Now, you've distracted me from my other purpose." Tilly straightened. "As you seem determined to go through with this marriage on Saturday, you must have a proper bride's showing of the gifts. I went home at lunch, and all is ready. There's to be a party at my house after the shift, so you must come."

"A party?" Rose's eyes widened. "For me?"

Tilly nodded, her features determined. "Take my bicycle—'tis red now, since I found an auld can of paint in the shed, and you ride on ahead. Remember how to get there?"

"A block past Attenborough station on the right." Rose had visited Tilly's cottage only once before, when Uncle's chauffeur took ill and she was allowed to ride the forty-minute train in from Leicester.

"Aye, 'tis just a mile away. Once I finish here, I'll round up some of the lassies and we'll meet you."

Rose senses hummed. A real party with friends! Then she remembered Miles Luther awaited her outside in the Rolls and her enthusiasm dimmed. "Oh, Tilly! I wish I could, but Luther—"

"Och, dinna mind your uncle's sheepdog." Tilly handed her the clipboard with paper and a pencil. "Write Luther a note. Say you must work three extra hours. 'Tis for the lads at the Front, so he willna suspect and go tattling to 'Sir Cutler.' Tell him to come back and collect you at nine o'clock tonight."

Pencil in hand, Rose stared at the blank sheet. What if her lie was discovered? Luther might spot her riding the red bicycle toward Tilly's house. She didn't dare defy Uncle, not when Douglas and Samuel would pay the price. She tried handing back the clipboard. "No, I really cannot take the chance."

"'Tis your *last chance*!" Tilly frowned as she crossed her arms, refusing the offering. "Trust me, Rose. No one will find out. How long has it been since you've had an hour or two of enjoyment? We'll have ginger biscuits and tea and play cards. You can even fetch my brass tub from the shed and have a cool soak before the rest of us arrive."

Rose set the clipboard back in her lap. Tilly was right. Her last chance at freedom before Julien closed the door on her life. And with Douglas and Samuel away at school, there was no one else on earth with whom she'd rather spend this time.

She scribbled her note to Luther.

"I'm glad to see you're a brave lass after all." Tilly's tone had eased. "I'll have the dust boy, Jeremy, take the note to Luther at the front gate while you slip out the back."

Pulse racing, Rose returned the clipboard and note to her friend. Tilly's relieved smile matched her own. They could postpone their good-byes for a few more hours.

"One more thing." Tilly plucked from beneath her boiler suit collar the thin chain of spark-resistant brass that held her factory-numbered disk. A metal key also hung from the chain.

"Tilly, that key is—"

"Against regulations, aye." Tilly flashed a look of sufferance. "But you willna get into my cottage any other way . . ." She paused at the sound of approaching female voices. A pair of floor supervisors walked in their direction. "Here." Tilly pressed the chain with the key into Rose's hand. "Now give me yours, so I'll have a tally disk to show at the gate when I leave."

"Won't the gate guard know the difference?"

"Ha! Auld one-eyed Griggs pays no mind. He just writes down the number and says 'Pass.' Be quick now. I canna be late to meet my . . ."

Rose's hand shook as she quickly palmed Tilly's chain, then removed her own and gave it to her friend. Once the supervisors had passed, she caught up with Tilly's note of hesitation. "Meet whom?"

"Not important. Just a final task to finish." Slipping the chain over her head, Tilly stood as she tucked it beneath her uniform. "I'll be along with the others before you know it."

Her smile seemed at odds with her pale face and sorrowful eyes, and Rose's worry returned. "Tilly, there is something you are not telling me. Are you all right?"

"Dinna fash about me." Picking up the clipboard, she held it to her chest. "I'm too braw to be sick or put down easily. Remember, I grew up on the streets of Glasgow. Not even the cheeky London lassies I oversee in the Pressing Room dare to give me guff." She looked away. "If I seem sad, 'tis because I'm already missing you.

"But enough blethering." She drew in a breath and smiled. "We'll enjoy the hours we have left. Now go and have a soak in the tub, and dinna let Winston into the cottage. He's likely been in the neighbor's sty again, the daft dog."

Despite her misgivings, Rose grinned. "I'll see you there."

She watched her friend leave for the Mixing House, before entering the changing room where several first-shift factory girls still bathed and dressed. Swiftly, Rose peeled out of her boiler suit and, garbed in her chemise, padded barefoot into the washroom to join her co-workers, who would be scrubbing away the day's traces of chemicals before leaving the factory.

Even with all her current troubles, or perhaps because of them, her heart thrummed as she imagined the upcoming revelry. It was ages ago, during her childhood in Edinburgh, that she'd last had a real party.

The austere halls and grand rooms at Leicester were devoid of any such frivolities. No birthdays or balls, especially with the war on. Only at Christmas when she, Douglas, and Samuel were not at school did Uncle Ridley install a holiday tree, and only then so he could entertain his business associates. Her aunt would always slip Rose a pretty ribbon from her sewing box and give candies to the boys.

The bittersweet memory of those small tokens made her smile as she finished scrubbing.

Christmas was the only time Aunt Delia defied her husband.

Back at her locker, she dressed while a middle-aged co-worker rummaged through a locker a few feet away.

"'Ay luv, 'ave ye any Oatine Cream?"

Rose turned at the question.

The woman looked perplexed. "I 'ad a full tin 'ere, but I've searched and it's gone."

Oatine Cream was a popular face lotion, advertised to keep a munitionette's skin soft and healthy after being exposed to the harsh chemicals at the factory.

It also happened to give Rose hives. "I am sorry, I do not use it."

"Well, ain't that grand." The woman scowled. "I spend my earnin's on pricey cream so's it's get pinched from my locker. One o' those dodgy Scotch, no doubt."

Rose stiffened at the remark. It wasn't the first time someone had disparaged her northern heritage. Perhaps a lesson was in order. "I still might be able to help," she said. Tilly used the cream.

She went to her friend's locker and opened it—and drew back at the pungent fragrance. Roses? When had Tilly started wearing perfume?

Delving through the clutter, Rose located her friend's array of toiletries. "Here we are." Reaching for the face cream, she noticed beside the tin a small red box with French gold lettering. She leaned in for another whiff. Definitely roses. Did Tilly have a beau?

Closing the locker, she offered the tin. "You may borrow this."

The woman's face brightened, and when she took the cream, Rose smiled and said, "I'm certain my Scots friend will not mind."

The woman hesitated, eyes wide. "Thank ye."

At least she had the good grace to blush. Satisfied, Rose returned to finish her toilette and mulled over the possibility Tilly had an admirer. Her friend's earlier remark came to mind. *"I canna be late to meet my . . ."*

Sweetheart? Rose smiled at the fanciful thought. Tilly wouldn't keep him a secret. But the perfume?

She stared at her friend's locker. What if it was meant for *her*? The flower scent *was* roses.

Suddenly her eyes burned. Tilly's kindness and generous heart knew no bounds; she'd arranged a party tonight in Rose's honor, with tea and biscuits and other favors. Why should she be surprised that her friend also wanted to present her with the lovely French perfume?

And then all too soon we will part from each other. Her lips compressed as she leaned against her locker. Once she crossed a chasm of no return with Julien, her dear friend would cross an ocean. How could she face the miserable future without Tilly?

Closing her eyes, Rose prayed as she'd done so often in the past few months, asking for some sign of deliverance. *Lord, please tell me how to carry this burden.*

As if awaiting an answer, she remained still for several seconds. But only the echo of feminine laughter and the slam of a locker door met her ears.

She would beg Tilly to remain in England! With the war on, Julien's flights back and forth to France were frequent, and since Rose had accepted Uncle Ridley's edict to wed, his watchfulness over her would surely lessen. She and Tilly could still have their friendship.

Her hopes glimmered. She would speak with her friend tonight at the party.

Quickly, Rose finished dressing and left the changing room to head for the factory's exit.

The tall, grizzled Griggs stood heads above the many first-shift workers who were leaving through the back gate. Clad in his worn infantry uniform and wearing his black eye patch, he made entries in his ledger as the line moved slowly forward.

As her turn came, Rose tried to steady her breathing. Her fingers fumbled for the brass disk on the chain, and she held up the numbered ID.

Griggs gave it a glance before his single bloodshot eye focused on her. Seconds passed as she held the air in her lungs, and she thought she might suffocate. Behind her, workers bent on leaving grumbled impatiently.

Her hand with the disk began to shake. *Lord, please help me!*

A group of boisterous second-shift workers suddenly entered the back lot, and one of them called to Griggs in greeting. The old guard turned from her to raise a hand in their direction, then quickly scribbled her ID number into his ledger. "Pass."

Nervous laughter bubbled up, popping out as a high-pitched squeak before Rose was able to quash it. Keeping her head down, she dared not look at Griggs as she hurried past him and through the gate.

Tilly's red bicycle was easy to spot amidst the hundreds of black two-wheeled conveyances crowding the lot, and soon Rose was on her way riding toward the town of Attenborough.

She pedaled hard toward the railway station, the exercise releasing her pent-up anxiety. Luther must have received her note at the front gate by now. Would he decide to wait for her the three extra hours . . . or return to the estate?

As her bicycle flew past leafy green poplars and tall oaks, past the parched lawns and rows of brown-and-gray houses abutting the street, she couldn't help darting an occasional glance behind her. If he did discover her on his return to Leicester, the stocky chauffeur would haul her bodily into the car and take her home to face her uncle's wrath.

She shoved away the worrisome thought as she passed the rail station, heaving a sigh when Tilly's white cottage came into view. Riding up onto the dried lawn, she dismounted and leaned the bicycle against the wood siding.

Fishing the chain with the key from her blouse, Rose jogged in an unladylike manner up the short flight of steps to the porch. She crouched to insert the key—but found the door already unlocked when the knob turned easily. Tilly had forgotten to secure the cottage after lunch.

Rose straightened and began pushing the door open when a low growl sounded behind her, followed by a rapid staccato of yips.

Smiling, she turned. "You must be Winston . . . Ugh!" She held a sleeve to her nose. The dog was covered in awful-smelling mud. "You've been in the pigsty again, haven't you?"

The small terrier's pink tongue lolled to one side of a dirty mouth while his dark eyes gleamed with mischief. She held her breath as she raised the hem of her skirt, hoping he wouldn't jump up and soil her clothes.

Winston saw an opportunity—and darted between her feet into the house.

"Get back here, you rascal!" Dropping her hem, Rose whirled around and followed the dog inside, then spied his dirty paw prints trailing across Tilly's polished floors. "Oh no!"

Winston paused to look back at her, his muddy stub of a tail wagging as if daring her to chase him. Determined to outsmart the animal, Rose quickly scanned the parlor before spotting Tilly's white apron tossed over the back of a chair. She retrieved the smock and held it in front of her, creeping slowly toward the dog and talking softly. "There's a good boy. All you need is a thorough scrubbing, and I know where Tilly keeps the tub."

She waited to pounce as Winston gave a yip and another wag of his tail. He started back toward her, and Rose reached out with the apron to grab him—

The roar of thunder rocked the cottage on its foundation. Tilly's furniture danced around the room at the same instant glass shattered from the windows in all directions.

Rose flew backward, feeling the bite of the shards in her flesh as she crash-landed several feet away. She clutched for the frantic terrier, curling up with him on the parlor floor.

German Zeppelins? Blood pounded in her ears as she craned her head, looking toward the broken windows, but she could see nothing. Her arms hugged the squirming dog to her chest.

Breathless, she waited for the next attack, and after another distant explosion echoed through the cottage, there was silence. She managed to sit up, holding on to the dog lest he walk on broken glass.

Gradually, she became aware of more noises—whistles and people shouting. Scrambling to her feet, she rushed toward the open door and released Winston to run outside.

Dozens of Tilly's neighbors clogged the street, crying and pointing toward the station. Rose left the cottage, walking across the lawn to follow their direction—and stared in horror at the enormous black cloud billowing upward into the sky.

Not the train station.

She fell to her knees in the dry grass. The devastation at No. 6 Chilwell was glaring even from a mile away. The remnant of factory buildings and tall stacks became a dark blur amidst the gray-green smoke spreading outward and heading into the town of Attenborough.

Tilly. Rose joined the neighbors who had started rushing forward, praying as she ran toward the place that had once been her sanctuary.

All around them the toxic gray haze had begun to settle, casting shadows against the leaves on the trees and tiled rooftops of row houses facing the street. Her lungs filled with the acrid smoke, and as she began to cough, she fished the handkerchief from her sleeve.

Drawing nearer to the destruction, she and the others had to dodge pieces of the wreckage littering the street while other debris continued raining from the sky. Rose screamed as she recognized the unspeakable carnage landing near her feet, and she tried to run even faster. *Dear Lord in heaven, so many bodies . . .*

By the time she reached the factory she was faint, her lungs burning. The opened west gate provided access, and she and the others headed inside. Whistles and bugles blared behind them as local ambulances and police lorries sped past.

Desperate to find her friend, she plunged into the mayhem. Hundreds of panicked workers, many of them wounded, swarmed to escape the factory's complex. Fires burned unchecked as volunteers frantically worked to extinguish the explosive flames.

She cried out at the sight of a co-worker—a fellow crane operator—severely burned and being lifted onto a stretcher and taken into an awaiting ambulance.

Lord, please let me find her! Rose pressed on toward the Mixing House, where Tilly had said she must finish a final task before leaving. The caustic air tasted bitter, her burning eyes tearing up as she picked her way through the rubble toward her destination.

She hadn't gone far when she paused beside the damaged rail of a metal platform overlooking the factory. Her sudden, sharp breath stung her raw throat.

Over half of Chilwell was gone. Completely destroyed. And the Mixing House—

She grabbed for the steel rail, her watery gaze fixed on the patch of scorched earth—all that remained of the building where her friend had been. "*Nooo!*"

Viciously, she rubbed her eyes with the grimy handkerchief. But when she looked up again, she saw only the horrible empty . . . nothing.

Rose lowered her head and stared listlessly at the ground near her feet. A glint of glass caught her eye and she bent to pick up the debris. Dizziness swarmed her, noting the silver now covered in soot while the glass—a purple jewel—remained pristine.

Attached to the brooch was a charred piece of dirty white cloth. Part of a collar . . . *'Twas my mother's. I'll never be parted from it.*

A deep sob tore from her chest. She would never see Tilly again.

2

*T*he soft whimper awoke her.

Rose opened her eyes, blinking at the bright light flooding through the open windows. She lay huddled in a ball on the parlor floor much as she had before, though now a lap blanket protected her from the glass shards. She stared at the toppled furniture. *Tilly . . . ?*

Another high-pitched whine sounded beside her ear. "Winston."

The grubby dog rested on his belly, inches away from her head. He gave a soft yip, then crawled forward to lick her face. Rose raised herself to sit, every muscle in her body aching. Her sore throat and stinging eyes proof against the caustic haze still permeating the air.

She shook her head, trying to clear it. *What time is it?*

Her wristwatch was covered in sooty ash and she wiped the face clean, shocked to discover the hands read one o'clock in the afternoon. She looked back at the open window. Had she slept almost a full day since the explosion?

No. Staring at the grime on her blistered hands, the memories returned; the acrid stench of smoke, and the weight of an injured woman—a shell cleaner she'd dragged outside away from the burning building. The agonized cries of the wounded as dozens of frenzied, soot-faced workers pulled at a collapsed beam trapping those beneath. The eerie moan of twisting steel just before an overhead crane crashed onto a pallet of filled shells.

Her relief when the shells didn't detonate was short-lived, as the factory floor had rocked beneath her with another blast from the next building.

Rose rubbed her sore eyes as though to erase the horror, then opened them again, assessing her condition. Aside from burns on her hands, her filthy clothing reeked with the bitter smell of smoke and ash. How had she managed to find her way back to the cottage last night after leaving the devastation? It must have been a miracle, or someone . . .

"Tilly?" She climbed to her feet, heart surging. "Tilly, where are you!"

Shouting for her friend, she rushed through each room in the cottage, taunted by the memory of the brooch and the hours she'd spent afterward searching the ambulances, even the factory hospital, without success. Yet she prayed against the proof, and her own reason, that Tilly would suddenly appear from one of the rooms, whole and safe and smiling.

Her friend was nowhere to be found.

Rose stumbled back into the kitchen, desperate for a glass of water to slake her enormous thirst.

She noticed the decorations for the first time.

Her feet moved slowly toward the festive table and its covering of bright plaid cloth. With a finger she trailed an invisible line across the pretty blue teapot and rims of mismatched cups. A red cake tin sat beside the tea set, and ironically nothing seemed disturbed from the explosion.

Tilly had planned this party in her honor. "A showing of the gifts," she'd called it, to celebrate a bride's coming wedding.

Now her friend wouldn't be at the church on Saturday.

Her chest constricted as she fished into the pockets of her skirt and withdrew the thistle brooch, its silver still blackened, the attached fragment of cloth singed and dirty. Her plan to beg Tilly to stay in England—to continue their friendship despite the marriage and help Rose to cope with a future she dreaded—was gone.

She tried breathing in and out deeply to steady her hammering heart while her gaze swept the table. A white beribboned box sat at the opposite end, and she remembered the red box of perfume in Tilly's locker, heavy with the scent of roses. Another gift her friend would never get to present.

Setting the brooch on the table, she approached the box and with shaky hands untied the white ribbon and examined the contents.

The first keepsake was a snapshot, taken by the factory photographer at Chilwell's last May Day picnic. She and Tilly sat outside at a table, bonnets off and beaming for the camera.

Her throat ached as she studied Tilly's beloved face, her broad smile and dimpled right cheek as their two heads bent together. Some co-workers thought them related, both with "blue eyes and the brown hair of Lowland lassies," as Tilly liked to say. In the picture, her friend's hair had not yet discolored from the TNT. The picnic seemed ages ago. Had it only been two months?

She flipped the photograph, her lips trembling as she recognized the cleverly scrawled words on the back. *"R and T—Rose and Me—Sisters of the heart we shall always be."*

"Even in heaven, dear friend," she whispered, then carefully laid the picture aside and removed the next gift from the box.

A tiny cloth purse made from the same plaid as the table covering. Rose opened the clasp and withdrew a folded bank note. Her eyes widened. *Five pounds!* Nearly a month's wages for a munitions worker.

Had Tilly decided to help her gain her freedom despite Uncle Ridley's theft?

Rose withdrew the next item—a folded advertisement for a place called Nova Scotia in Canada. The painted illustrations revealed spacious green land surrounded by the sea and fishing boats nestled inside a small harbor. Beyond the beach stretched hills thick with tall pine and fir, and in the distance the gentle slope of a mountain.

The ad, a few years old, encouraged people to emigrate from Britain and homestead along Nova Scotia's beautiful shores.

Despite her pain, the irony made her smile. *She'd* been planning to convince Tilly to stay in England, while her friend intended to convince *her* to sail across the sea.

Now neither of them would get what she wanted.

Below the illustrations was a ship's price list advertising steep fares to depart from several different British ports. She set aside the paper and withdrew the last item from the box, a trade card with the name of a clockmaker in Glasgow.

She frowned and flipped the card, again recognizing Tilly's scrawl. *"Become a new person, Rose. If you have the courage."*

A new person? She narrowed her gaze, turning the card back. Who was this clockmaker, Mr. C. Liddle?

A disquieting thought began to take root. Was he someone who could do that? Make her a new person?

Gooseflesh rose along her skin despite the afternoon heat. Tilly confessed to growing up rough on the streets of Glasgow. Had she been acquainted with criminals? Someone . . . who could forge documents?

Her breath stilled. Had her friend imagined she would actually try and escape her wedding day to take on a new persona and sail to Canada?

The idea *was* insane, wasn't it? Her heart thumped. *Freedom.*

She thought of Uncle then and his punishment to the boys if she failed to marry.

Dropping the trade card onto the table, her agitated fingers reached for the chain still around her neck. She couldn't—wouldn't—jeopardize the lives of her brothers. Tilly had meant well, but she must go through with becoming Julien Dexter's wife—

Her fingers stilled on the chain. *Tilly's chain.*

An instant of horrifying clarity made her gasp; she'd forgotten to clock out yesterday in all her excitement, and then Griggs, the guard, had been distracted as he entered her ID number in his log. *Tilly's ID number.*

Shock waves coursed through her as she stared at the singed brooch lying on the table. It seemed certain her dear friend had been killed in the explosion, and likely—*Dear Lord!*—part of the carnage falling from the sky. That meant Luther, Uncle Ridley, Julien, the whole world would believe it was *she* who had died!

Rose reached for the kitchen wall to steady herself, grief and exhaustion mingling with a dangerous new hope. *Could* she become a new person?

She imagined her future as Lady Dexter, years of gradual decline into a beaten-down existence like that of Aunt Delia. And the boys—Uncle Ridley's threat to send her brothers to some far-off land by themselves if she didn't go through with the marriage.

But if the world thought she was dead . . .

Uncle would believe her gone to the grave and silenced forever. He'd have no reason to carry out his threat. But Douglas and Samuel, they would be devastated believing her dead. Surely she could not be that heartless.

What if she contacted them at their school? Told them she was alive—

The loud rumble of a car outside drew her attention. Quickly, she re-pocketed the brooch, along with the bank note and the clockmaker's card before walking back into the parlor.

A familiar black Rolls-Royce pulled up outside. Luther!

The car looked battered, the passenger windows broken out. Once the engine died, the door opened and the tall, middle-aged frame of Miles Luther emerged, the top of his head bandaged.

He walked around the front of the car and headed toward the front door.

Rose wasted no time. Heart pounding, she scurried back to the kitchen and rushed out the back door, scooping up Winston in her wake as she made for the shed. Once inside, she crawled beneath Tilly's overturned tub and prayed the dog in her arms would keep quiet.

Minutes passed like an eternity. Would Luther come out here

to look for her? Winston gave a soft whine, and she scratched him behind his dirty ears to reassure him.

Another minute and the car's engine roared back to life. When the sound faded, she waited a bit longer before creeping out from beneath the tub with the dog. Trembling, she returned to the kitchen.

Her decision must be made.

Tilly was dead. Rose had also noticed the black armband on Luther's sleeve. A sickening sense of reality cramped her insides.

The advertisement for Nova Scotia still lay against the plaid tablecloth. She stared at the paper as she leaned against the kitchen wall, sliding toward the floor.

Do I have the courage? A bone-deep cry escaped from her lips, and Winston climbed into her lap, licking her sooty hands. Yet she barely noticed, aching over the loss of her dear friend and mourning the sorrow she would soon visit upon her young brothers.

Because, as of this moment, Rosalind Graham was dead.

3

LONDON
FRIDAY, JULY 5 — FOUR DAYS LATER

*C*aptain Alex Baird settled into one of the study's leather chairs and looked at his copper-haired friend, who had taken the seat beside him. "Well, Simon. I've had a rest, and your bonny wife's fed us a fine meal, so would you and Captain Weatherford care to tell me why I'm here?"

Captain Simon Forrester turned from Alex to consider the imposing man who had commandeered the desk. "Marcus?"

"I have an assignment, Captain Baird." Weatherford clasped his hands on the desktop and scrutinized him. "Though I'm still debating whether or not you're up to this particular task."

Alex shifted in his seat. He'd been wary when Simon's telegram arrived in the south of France two days ago. A request to attend an "unofficial meeting" in London. It meant cutting short his furlough, and yet he was glad for the chance to see Simon and his wife, Eve, again, since the three friends often became distanced by the war. Their cottage here in Highbury was also more to his liking, rather than a billet at one of the air bases.

Still, he had dreaded this day. The man behind the desk held his darkest secret, and Alex suspected it was time to pay up for the pact they'd made. "What's this assignment that has you doubting my abilities, Captain? I cut short my stay in Biarritz to travel all the way back to London. That should show some initiative."

"Yes, I imagine leaving behind the sunny beaches of southern France *was* a hardship." Weatherford's mouth curved beneath his dark mustache. "What I'm most concerned about, however, is your ability to separate any emotion from your sworn duty."

Was this about his brother Ian? Alex frowned. "I gave you my word."

"I know you did, Alex." Weatherford spoke quietly. "But this is different."

Sensing Simon's curiosity beside him, Alex kept his attention on Weatherford. Apparently, the captain had kept their secret even from his friend. "Different how?"

"I need you to travel to an air base in the north and receive your medical discharge—"

"Hold on!" Alex leaned forward. "'Tis been twelve months since I took a furlough, so I may be a wee bit tired, but that doesna warrant a medical discharge." He straightened. "I can get back into the cockpit whenever you like."

"Rest assured, Captain, the medical discharge is merely a ruse." Weatherford reached for a file on the desk. "There is an important reason you will be in Scotland. Critical, in fact." His dark eyes leveled on Alex. "And before I say more, I'll need your oath of confidentiality."

"Scotland?" Anxiety rippled through Alex at the thought of returning home. A year had passed since he'd gone back with news of Ian's death. The pain and guilt still gnawed at him. He glanced at Simon.

"Take the oath, man, so we can get on with it."

Alex raised his right hand. "I swear it. Now please explain."

He caught the silent exchange between Weatherford and Simon before his friend turned and said, "On Monday there was an explosion at a shell-filling factory in Nottingham."

"I think I read about it in the newspaper when I arrived on the mainland." Alex frowned as he tried to recall the headline: "'60 Feared Dead in Midlands Factory Explosion.'"

"Aye," Simon said. "But with the war censorship, the real extent of the damage was kept from the public." He glanced back toward the closed study door before he lowered his voice. "Half the complex was destroyed, and neighborhoods up to three miles away received damage. Over a hundred and thirty souls perished and only about thirty could be identified." He shook his head. "Another two hundred and fifty were injured."

Alex went still, staring at his friend. In four years of war, he'd seen his share of death and destruction across the battlefields of France. How sadly ironic that here in Britain such carnage also existed, and with innocent civilians.

"Scotland Yard and the Admiralty believe it was intentional."

Weatherford's bald statement drew his attention. "Sabotage? You have proof?"

He nodded. "Months ago, the French Secret Service investigated an abandoned Paris flat, rented by the Greek arms dealer, Didymos Kahverengi. Among other aliases, Kahverengi is known to the press as the Merchant of Death."

Alex's thoughts raced. What did a medical discharge and Scotland have to do with him and an arms dealer?

"Kahverengi is suspected of selling weapons to the enemy. The French were looking for evidence." Weatherford withdrew a document from the file. "What they found was unexpected."

He held up a large photograph. "This is a picture of a charred scrap of paper the French discovered in the fireplace. It contains the names of four British munitions factories, and each has a number beside it. The first is the shell-filling factory, HM Barstow at Ludlum, with a number two. Then HM Factory Linworth at Devonshire with the number four. You already know of the third factory at Chilwell in Nottingham, marked with the number seven. And the fourth and last . . ." Weatherford gazed at him. "Moorside, listed with the number eight."

At his grave expression, Alex drew a shallow breath. "Where is this place, Moorside?"

Simon's hand came to rest on his shoulder. "*Moorside* is the government code name for the munitions plant, HM Factory Gretna—"

"No!" Alex jerked from his grasp. Gretna was home. The munitions factory . . . *Hannah.* "My sister works at that factory. She's just fifteen, a bairn!"

"Easy, man." Simon's voice held calm. "Scotland Yard and MI5 have been in Gretna, investigating for months—"

"Months? And you didna tell me?" Alex growled under his breath. "And all this time my family's been in danger."

"We hoped to catch the saboteur long before he became a threat to Moorside, Captain." Weatherford's mouth bowed. "We even had people in place at Chilwell. However, our plan failed and now we must do all in our power to catch him inside Gretna's factory."

"Tell me more about this arms dealer."

Weatherford offered him a dozen photographs from the file. Alex reviewed the faces of twelve different men. "Which one is Kahverengi?"

"Possibly all of them."

He looked up, startled.

"Each of those men in the photographs was in the company of an identified foreign agent of the Central Powers. We suspect illegal negotiations for arms. Kahverengi is known for using a variety of disguises."

"And he's the saboteur?"

"No, we believe he hired someone to do his dirty work. His agent is using either of two aliases, 'Thomas Brown' or 'Rhymer.' Both were written on the same charred list discovered in Paris."

"And that's it? You've nothing more to go on?"

"We have one key description from a reliable source," Weatherford said. "Our saboteur has a birthmark—a port-wine stain above his hairline. He also has blue eyes and possibly dark hair and would now be thirty-two years old."

"Who is this reliable source, Marcus?" Simon asked. "Can they provide my friend here with a few more details before he leaves for Scotland?"

"I'm afraid not. I can only say that the description is accurate." Weatherford turned to Alex. "As Simon already stated, Scotland Yard has been working for months at each of the targeted factory sites. They're interrogating all workers with either of the two names. So far, we've yet to come up with a person who meets the saboteur's profile."

"The numbers you mentioned listed beside each of the factories. What do they mean?"

"The month of the explosion."

Chilwell had been marked with a number seven. The explosion happened just days ago, on the first of July. "And Moorside?"

"Number eight."

August. Not even a month away. Alex stifled his agitation. "If this death merchant gets rich selling weapons, why would he want to blow up our munitions factories?"

"Why indeed?" Weatherford sighed. "We're fairly certain the Germans hired him to destroy the factories and upset the balance of power. The Huns are losing ground in the war, and the kaiser is keen to get it back.

"Kahverengi also owns shares in the largest oil, steel, and chemical companies in Europe, many of which supply raw materials for our munitions here in Britain. When a factory explodes and production is halted, his stock drops with the sudden loss of demand, though we've noticed he's the first to buy up any lower-priced shares. Once the factories recover and begin doubling their material output to make up for the loss, his stock—and his profits—soar."

Alex snarled. "So the scunner gets rich while good people die."

"Even more than that, I'm afraid."

"What do you mean?"

"He wants to keep the war going, Alex." Simon's attention shifted to Weatherford. "Marcus?"

Weatherford leaned back in his seat. "The German Army grows tired, Captain. With the Americans now in the fight, an Allied victory is within our grasp. God willing, we'll end this war before the year is out."

"And that's bad for business, pal." Simon grimaced. "Especially if you're an arms dealer."

Alex eyed them both. "How does Kahverengi manage to evade the law? The devil buys and sells stock and negotiates arms deals, but you're telling me he's not been arrested?"

"So far his dealings appear legal, Captain," Weatherford replied. "He's also got plenty of lawyers and agents to handle his affairs. As for his selling arms to the enemy, we have pictures but we need solid proof. While the French actively seek to corroborate that, *we* must catch his agent, Rhymer, in the act. Once he's arrested and made his confession, we'll have grounds to bring Kahverengi into custody."

"And that's where you come in, Alex," Simon said. "Because Hannah works at the factory and your family lives in Gretna Green, you're the best choice for this assignment. You can get inside and find the saboteur without drawing undue attention."

"And this sabotage could happen the first of next month?"

"Or any other day, Captain. Which is why we need to move on this now." Weatherford rose to his feet. "Trust me when I say that MI5 and Scotland Yard are working continuously at Gretna. Moorside is the largest cordite factory in Britain, with four different sites encompassing miles. Each site runs three shifts, and there are other agents already inside, but you'll be assigned to the site and shift we believe has the highest likelihood for sabotage. *Any* information you can glean will help our joint forces." His dark eyes bore into Alex. "Will you take this assignment and do your sworn duty, Captain Baird?"

Sworn duty. Alex let his gaze drop to the stack of photographs. One of these men—the devil himself—jeopardized all he held dear. Not only Hannah's life, but after learning the true extent of damage caused by the Chilwell explosion, his entire family was at risk. *"I'll watch out for Ian, Maw, I'll keep him safe . . ."*

The scars on his back throbbed with the memory of that promise. How could he protect any of them when he'd failed to save his brother?

He glanced up at Weatherford. Their bargain was sealed a year ago, along with his brother's secret. And for that Alex was bound by another promise, not that he'd refuse such a mission when it was his own family in danger. "When do I leave?"

"First thing in the morning. RAF East Fortune is your final reassignment." Weatherford pushed an envelope across the desk. "You'll be discharged from service by the base commander. As a civilian, you can obtain work at the factory."

He pierced Alex with a look. "Everything we do must appear by the book, understood? Until we know more about the intended sabotage, we cannot arouse suspicion. When you arrive at East Fortune, ask for Lieutenant Charles Stuart."

"Charles . . . Stuart?"

"Aye." Simon shot him a wink. "Marcus recruited the bonny prince himself."

"Stuart is working with MI5," Weatherford said, ignoring Simon's humor. "He'll be your liaison while you're working in Gretna. Once you arrive at the air base, Stuart will have your codebook so you can telegraph any information directly to him."

Weatherford collected his files and offered them to Alex. "I'm due back in Paris tomorrow, but you may borrow these tonight to study before your departure. If you have questions and cannot reach Lieutenant Stuart, Simon will act as my contact. Once you hire in at Moorside, you can also ask for any assistance from Mr. Arthur Timbrell." His eyes narrowed. "Remember, *by the book*. You must maintain security at all times."

Alex stood and reached across the desk. "You can count on me, Captain."

"Good." The two shook hands before Weatherford nodded to Simon. "I'll see myself out."

Simon also rose, and after their handshake Weatherford departed. Eve arrived at the study moments later with a tray of food. "I suppose Marcus didn't wish to stay for dessert?"

"Here, love, let me get that." Simon crossed the room and reached for the tray. After placing it on the desk, he helped his very pregnant wife into one of the leather wing-back chairs. "Where is Mrs. Kerr, wife? We hired her for good reason. I dinna want you exerting yourself, especially now."

Eve let out a satisfied groan as she settled into the chair. "She's running an errand for me, Simon. Please, you needn't worry. I'm fine."

"You say that, but if you're not careful, Evelyn Forrester, you'll have the bairn right here on the study floor instead of at hospital next month."

Alex noted the growl in his friend's tone and knew Simon fashed over his wife. Unlike most, he kenned the hardships the couple had faced over the war years, after Simon's plane went down and he was believed dead.

But God had given them both a second chance at love, and he hoped with the new bairn his two friends would find the happiness they once dreamed about.

Eve reached for her husband's hand. "Truly, Simon, I am well. Anyway, how heavy can a few small bowls of apple charlotte be?"

"We're taking no chances."

At Simon's scowl, she leaned to press her cheek against his palm. "All right. No more trays."

"That's better."

Alex had averted his gaze but looked up to see Simon give her a peck on the cheek before turning to him. "Tuck in, pal. Eve does wonders with rationed flour and a bit of fruit."

"I dinna doubt it." Alex smiled at her and took a bowl, the smell of apples and cinnamon filling his nostrils. But his appetite waned.

In less than twenty-four hours, he would arrive in Scotland to begin his mission: to find the saboteur and save his family.

He considered his years in France; the countless preparations before flying a sortie against the Huns's Jasta squadrons, then the incessant waiting to take to the air to strike and perhaps escape his own demons.

Yet these next hours before boarding the train would seem the longest of his life.

4

Seated in HM Factory Gretna's hiring office midmorning on Friday, Rose made knots in her gloves while she awaited the interviewer. The drab gray walls and dingy paned windows across the room's vaulted ceiling seemed a contrast to the warm gold of the polished oak desk and swivel chair in front of her. A matching oak filing cabinet stood sentry near the door.

She still couldn't believe she was here. It seemed like weeks rather than just a few days since the explosion and her decision to assume Tilly's identity and disappear into Scotland.

The office door opened, admitting a thin, dark-haired woman. "Good afternoon. I'm Mrs. Nash, chief supervisor for the women's workforce here at the Site Three complex. And you must be—" she glanced at the folder in her hand—"Miss Tilda Lockhart?"

Rose launched from her seat. "Uh . . . yes, ma'am."

Her pulse raced as the middle-aged woman advanced on her. "I see my assistant, Miss Childers, brought you tea." She offered a perfunctory smile as she extended a hand in greeting.

"She did, thank you." Rose accepted the proffered welcome, then blushed as Mrs. Nash looked to the floor where the knotted gloves had fallen from Rose's lap.

Her smile softened. "Let's get started, shall we?"

Mrs. Nash returned to the tidy desk where she took up the

swivel chair and donned a pair of eyeglasses. Sliding the rims up-ward along her hawkish nose, she reviewed what must be Rose's job application.

Collecting her gloves, Rose retook her seat, and it was several minutes before Mrs. Nash glanced up and removed the glasses. "I see you did not apply to us through the Labor Exchange, Miss Lockhart, which is irregular. Can you tell me what prompted your sudden decision to leave Nottingham's factory and come to HM Factory Gretna?"

Because I wanted my freedom. Rose pursed her lips against the truth and instead reached to finger Tilly's brooch, which she'd polished clean and now wore at her collar. The past few days were a blur of memories—fleeing her friend's cottage and taking the train north to Glasgow to visit *Mr. C. Liddle, Maker of Clocks,* a horrible man who had threatened to toss her bodily from his shop when she inquired about a new identity; then returning to her hotel to find a copy of the *Times* at the front desk and reading her own obituary.

Finally, her decision to pose as Tilly and leave Glasgow al-together after learning the munitions factory in Gretna was one of the largest in Britain, a place she could hide. "I know it all seems sudden, my coming here in person, ma'am," she said at last. "But I dearly wished to return to my homeland." *True enough.* "I've also lost someone dear to me when she died by . . ."

She'd almost blurted out Tilly's fate at Chilwell before thinking better of it. The *Times* had censored the truth, and it was doubtful Mrs. Nash knew the real devastation Rose had witnessed. *Black smoke and scorched earth. Carnage raining from the sky.*

She drew back her shoulders. "The truth is, ma'am, I need a fresh start. And I would like to continue my work for the war effort."

Her answer seemed to satisfy Mrs. Nash, who nodded in sym-pathy. "I am sorry for your loss, Miss Lockhart. This war has left many of us mourning our loved ones."

She slid the glasses back on and studied the application. "You state here that during your time at Chilwell, you supervised women filling shells inside the Pressing Room. How would you say they responded to you?"

"Remember, I grew up on the streets of Glasgow . . . not even the cheeky London lassies I oversee in the Pressing Room dare give me guff." Tilly's proud words, her smile, made Rose ache inside. Her friend had been so confident in handling her workers. Would she be able to do the same? "They respected me, ma'am." She shifted on the hard seat, voicing the words Tilly might say if she were in the room. "I believe in being fair, though I will not tolerate cheeky nonsense or misbehavior." From her own heart she added, "We all have our job to do, and the Tommies at the Front are counting on us."

"Excellent." Mrs. Nash beamed as she turned back to the application before her. "I see you are twenty-six years old." She looked up, her gaze thoughtful behind the spectacles.

"Is . . . that a problem?" Tilly had been five years older, and Rose worried about the disparity in their ages. Would the lie she'd told on the application be discovered?

"No problem. In fact, you're older than most of our girls here at the factory." She said no more as she continued reading, and Rose sagged against the seat. Did she truly seem older? The notion warmed her despite her nervousness.

"Your manner of speech also tells me you've been educated." Mrs. Nash nudged the spectacles farther up the length of her nose. "How was that possible with your background at the orphanage?"

Rose pulled absently at the knots in her gloves. "At Ezekiel House we all received daily lessons from the staff, and when I left there I secured a post with an Englishwoman, Lady McAllister of the McAllisters of Perth."

"Oh? And what was your position?" Mrs. Nash eyed her curiously.

Rose hesitated. Tilly had told her she was an upstairs maid, but such a post would never justify her own boarding school diction. "I was fortunate enough to become her ladyship's personal companion," she said, improvising. "Lady McAllister took me under her wing and educated me in the use of good English and in the social graces."

"You were indeed blessed, Miss Lockhart."

Rose smiled, tasting the acrid lie on her tongue. Still, she plunged ahead with more of Tilly's past. "Her ladyship held property in both England and Scotland, and we often traveled back and forth. A few months ago she died in Nottingham. I chose to stay on and find work at the munitions factory there."

Compassion returned to Mrs. Nash's dark eyes. "The lost loved one you mentioned?"

"Yes," Rose squeaked, her guilt pressing her with the weight of a 155mm shell. Tilly was who she mourned, and now herself as well, yet there was no going back. Only misery awaited any return to Leicester.

Mrs. Nash asked several more work-related questions, which Rose answered as carefully as possible. Her relief mingled with uncertainty when the hawkish woman finally rose from behind the desk. "Miss Lockhart, I believe your qualifications would make you an asset to this establishment. One of our Women's Welfare shift supervisors was recently forced to leave due to a long-term illness, so pending a routine health examination, I'd like to offer you the post."

Mrs. Nash continued to relay to her the duties of the job while Rose only half listened, her pulse pounding. She was to begin her new life.

"Most of our workers are quite young, many barely sixteen years of age," Mrs. Nash said as she came around the desk. "You'll be their chaperone of sorts during the shift, as well as keeping track of their work records and supervising their production on the factory floor.

"You should also be aware these girls come to us from all over the British Empire and from all walks of life." Mrs. Nash crossed her arms over her thin chest, her gaze earnest. "They range from naïve, homesick young girls away from their families for the first

time, to older, rougher girls from Dublin and London's East End."
She paused. "We do keep a factory staff of policewomen on each
shift to ensure order but pay particular attention to the more experienced girls. Make certain they do not abuse their break times,
hiding away in the washrooms or bullying the younger girls."

She smiled and relaxed her arms. "The pay is thirty-two shillings weekly with Sundays off. And as you've come from the factory in Nottingham, you know that the new hire paperwork process takes time. You'll receive your first wages two weeks from
today and then every Friday thereafter. Is this agreeable?"

Rose leaned back in her seat. Thirty-two shillings a week! More
than she'd earned as a crane operator at Chilwell. And the terms
were the same. "I gladly accept your offer, Mrs. Nash. Thank you."

"Splendid. We'll take a quick tour of the complex once you've
signed off on the necessary papers and made a visit to the clinic."

Rose watched her new supervisor retrieving documents from
the filing cabinet. Her dream—Tilly's dream—might actually
come true!

Once Mrs. Nash returned to the desk, Rose left her chair, and
after filling in the employment forms, she paused with the pen
over the place she was to sign her name.

She worried her lower lip with her teeth. Once the deed was
done, Tilly's life would become her own. *If you have the courage.*

Her friend's words were like a prayer in her heart as Rose
signed the paper. Before she'd left the cottage in Attenborough,
she made a promise to honor her dear friend—that she would earn
enough to secure ship's passage for herself and the boys, along
with seed money to start a new life in Nova Scotia. Once they
crossed the ocean, she and her small family would be free. She
handed the signed paperwork back to Mrs. Nash. "When should I
start?"

"The first shift begins tomorrow morning at six." She handed
Rose a booklet of rules and a tally disk similar to the one for Chilwell. "Use this temporary pass to enter and exit the factory. Your
permanent pass will arrive once your application is processed."

She smiled. "Now, let's go to the clinic, and on the way you'll get to view your work section. Later, I'll introduce you to your new charges."

Nerves tingling, Rose followed Mrs. Nash out onto the factory floor, where she began to relax at the familiar noises of machinery and seeing young women clad in khaki trousers, tunics, and bonnets. She also noted one or two of the policewomen her supervisor had mentioned.

Yet she saw none of the TNT shells she'd once loaded at Chilwell. "Where is your Pressing Room?"

"We do not fill shells at this facility, Miss Lockhart. We manufacture the propellant, cordite." Her voice exuded pride. "Our factory is the largest producer in Great Britain."

Rose observed in one area a series of shallow vats, waist-high and mounted on tables, and young workers standing and kneading by hand some kind of doughy mixture.

"The girls are mixing the cordite paste, popularly known around here as the 'devil's porridge.'" Mrs. Nash had followed her gaze as they paused to watch the process. "A combination of nitroglycerine and nitrocotton is used to make the cordite strands inside bullet cartridges." She glanced at Rose. "And this will be your new area, and your office is over there." She turned and indicated a closed door near the entrance into the section.

Her own office? Rose lifted a brow. It seemed already her life had changed!

As they continued on, Mrs. Nash indicated an opened roll-up warehouse door leading into another part of the site. "Both the niter stores and cotton stores are that way. Our girls use hooks with block and tackle to bring in five-hundred-pound bales of cotton to break them down for processing."

She pointed to a door on the opposite side. "You'll also oversee girls working in the Acids Room, where they mix the chemicals used to make the nitroglycerin and the nitrocotton for cordite. Both men and women test the finished acids for their proper weight and density." Her face sobered as she glanced at Rose. "Make no mistake, Miss Lockhart, this is very delicate work. Any misstep can be fatal, as you well know having worked in Chilwell."

When Rose blinked, Mrs. Nash said, "The newspapers were vague, but word spreads quickly among munitions factories." Her brown eyes softened. "It comes as no surprise why you would wish to have a fresh start."

Rose was grateful for her supervisor's understanding. Yet would she be able to handle such an important position?

"Your charges know their jobs, Miss Lockhart," Mrs. Nash went on, reading her concern. "They'll help you to gain your footing here, and I am always available whenever you need."

"Thank you."

They soon arrived at the clinic, and after a basic medical examination, Rose was declared fit. Pleased, Mrs. Nash led her toward the canteen. "It's break time now, so most of the girls on day shift will be having their tea."

Rose marveled at the size of the complex. "And this is all just one site?"

Mrs. Nash nodded. "We have three other site buildings, each with its own function to produce the finished cordite. They all interconnect through our own factory railroad system."

Certainly large enough! She followed her new supervisor into the canteen, noting rows upon rows of khaki-clad girls seated along either side of long wooden tables, laughing, talking, and enjoying tea.

"These young women work the day shift here at Site Three, but I'll take you to the table with the girls from your particular section."

Once they'd stopped at the farthest table, Mrs. Nash clapped her hands. "Ladies!"

A hush came over the canteen while hundreds of pairs of eyes turned in their direction.

"You girls in the nitroglycerin section, this is Miss Lockhart, your new supervisor. She will start tomorrow, and I want full cooperation and your best work for her, is that understood?"

Some of the girls at the table nodded and gave her friendly smiles while the rest looked on in curiosity. Each wore the same styled bonnet and uniform, and Rose's heart raced at wondering how she would begin to supervise so many of them.

Her breathing eased when only five rose from their seats. Sarah, Jane, Dorothy, Millie, and Hannah introduced themselves, and Rose noticed each girl spoke a different dialect.

Mrs. Nash had said they came from all over Britain. Rose smiled. "I'm very pleased to meet you, girls." But as she spoke, she became aware of the three workers nearest her at the table, glancing up at her, then at one another and sharing a smirk.

Were these the rougher girls Mrs. Nash warned her about? Relieved she wouldn't have to deal with them, Rose returned her gaze to the five girls still standing. None of them looked over the age of seventeen, and most had Tilly's same sallow complexion. "I look forward to our working together, ladies, and I will appreciate your help in learning more about your section and the work each of you accomplishes here."

One of the three workers at the end sniggered. Mrs. Nash frowned. "Miss Gladys Dunham, you will cease with your rudeness or I'll fine you for misbehavior." She stared at the other two. "Miss Colleen Shire, Miss Betty Pierce, that goes for you as well."

With their wages threatened, all three looked up at Mrs. Nash before turning to reassess Rose. At length the one called Gladys smiled tightly. "Miss Lockhart."

Were these three under her supervision then? "I hope we shall all get on well together," Rose said, and prayed it would be true as she kept her smile in place.

Finally she turned to Mrs. Nash. "Can you tell me what kind of housing is available?"

"Oh, I apologize, we should have covered that in the office. There is a current shortage for supervisory staff housing, and most of these girls live in Timber Town, the wooden barracks-styled huts you saw coming in on the train. They were built for our factory workers." She hesitated. "You might try in town, or if you wish, I can make arrangements for your temporary use of one of the girls' hostels."

Her strained smile suggested Rose think twice about moving into the same dormitory with her new charges. Nor could she, considering her present circumstance. "Thank you for the kind offer, but I do have a suitable room at the Gretna Hotel." Though now she worried how long she could remain there. Between four nights of hotel accommodations—two in Glasgow searching out that wretched clockmaker and then last night and tonight here in town, along with travel and meals—she'd already spent half of Tilly's generous five-pound note.

Mrs. Nash had said she wouldn't receive her first wages until Friday after next. That was two whole weeks away. "Perhaps I shall find a cottage rental in town."

"That's certainly possible." Her supervisor brightened. "And I will let you know of any vacancies for staff housing at once."

After completing the rest of her orientation, the lunch whistle sounded. Mrs. Nash bid her farewell, with Rose's promise to arrive for work promptly at six o'clock the following morning.

She soon departed the complex and stood on the platform with others who waited for the special factory train to return them to town.

Rose was excited to begin her new job and her new life. She just prayed she could measure up to Tilly's courage and strength enough to succeed.

5

"Miss Lockhart? May I join you?"

Standing on the crowded platform, Rose glanced at the amber-eyed young woman who seemed hesitant to approach. She couldn't quite place the girl, who looked pretty in her pleated white blouse and clean but worn charcoal skirt that complimented her reddish-blond hair.

She shifted aside to make room. "Of course."

The train arrived then, and the two quickly stepped aboard and took their seats. The girl sat across from her, offering a shy smile. "You likely dinna recognize me without my uniform. I'm Hannah Baird."

"Hannah, yes, I remember you from the canteen." Rose paused. "Are you already finished with work?"

The girl shook her head. "I sometimes take my lunch at home." She wore a soft blush. 'Tis only ten minutes from the Gretna platform, and my maw and da get a break from the wee 'uns when I'm there."

A thoughtful girl. Rose smiled. "I am certain your mother and father appreciate it."

"I suppose." Then she burst out, "Och, I'm so glad you're the new supervisor, Miss Lockhart! Mrs. Finch was our last, and she was auld and strict and she never smiled. She wasna modern atall."

Hannah appraised Rose's costume with admiration. "Your jacket is just the color of heather and cut so fashionable, and your matching skirt shows off your ankles. 'Tis so modern!"

"Thank you." Rose hid a smile. "How old are you, Hannah?"

"Fifteen, but my birthday's in a couple of weeks. I was just promoted to work inside the factory. Before that, I cleaned the workers' rooms in Timber Town."

"Do you still live at home?"

"Aye." Her ebullient mood faded. "Maw and Da say they need me at the house, but I want to live at the huts with my friends!" She pushed out her lower lip. "I'm not allowed to do anything on my own and I'm tired of being treated like a bairn." Her earnest gaze sought Rose. "I'm almost sixteen. And I have an important job inside the factory!"

Rose nodded, understanding Hannah's growing pains. Hadn't she experienced her own at that age? Always under the eye of the boarding school mistress, or at Leicester with her uncle and his paid spies, like Luther, his latest "sheepdog."

In the years since her parents died, neither she nor her brothers had ever been allowed to waver in their behavior—always proper, polite, resigned. Never recognized as the lost children that they were.

Rose pulled at the knots in her gloves. She had been the instrument of her uncle's power, groomed as wife to a man of his choosing. It still seemed impossible she'd broken free. If she hadn't, tomorrow she'd be walking down the aisle to meet Julien.

"Miss Lockhart? You look a bit peely-wally, white as Maw's washing. Are you well?"

"I'm fine." Rose shoved away her morose thoughts, relieved when the train began moving. Once she returned to the hotel, she'd ask at the front desk for any recommendations of rentals to suit her circumstances. She eyed the pretty girl across from her. "Tell me about your family, Hannah. You mentioned little ones. You have brothers and sisters?"

"I'm the only lassie, but I've got two younger brothers at home. Fergus is ten, and James is just six."

Douglas and Samuel were close to the same ages. Rose swallowed and said, "Being the eldest, I imagine that you stay busy with them."

"They're a handful." Hannah grinned. "But I've an aulder brother—well, he's my half brother from Da's first marriage. Alex is twenty-eight and he's handsome and a captain with the RAF, fighting in the war."

"A real hero, then."

"Aye, he's a hero and I love him so much!" Her radiant face clouded. "We also had another brother, Ian. He'd be twenty-two next month if he hadna died when his plane went down in France last year."

Not much older than me. Rose's heart went out to her. "I'm sorry. I lost both of my parents when the city bus crashed. I was just fourteen, near your age when your brother died."

Hannah leaned forward, rapt with curiosity. "Do you have brothers and sisters?"

Realizing she'd slipped into her own history instead of Tilly's, Rose averted her eyes to the train's open window. Tilly's mother died birthing her, and her father perished in a Glasgow dock accident when she was still just a child.

So what do I do now? Rose pursed her lips, turning back to the girl. It was too late to change her story. She'd have to muddle through. "I had a brother . . . once, but he died very young, and so I was sent to the orphanage . . ."

Why in heaven's name had she said that when Tilly's brother had died long after their parents, somewhere overseas? *Because you don't want Hannah asking you any more questions, that's why.*

"Your brother died and so did mine."

Hannah's commiserating tone stabbed at her conscience. Rose started to agree, then stopped herself. Even she couldn't bear to commit such hypocrisy.

"So . . . you've no family left atall, Miss Lockhart?"

Rose shrugged as more guilt pressed her. "It is not so terrible being alone."

"Och, now I'm certain my decision was the right one."

"What decision?" Rose hoped their current topic was at an end.

"I confess, Miss Lockhart, I had a reason to meet you on the train. When Mrs. Nash told you there was no staff housing, I wanted to . . ." The girl fidgeted with her work-roughened hands. "We've an extra room at our house. I'm sure Maw and Da would welcome you to stay with us."

Rose's hopes lifted at the girl's generous offer. Already she'd planned to settle her hotel bill, at least through Saturday, and then pray she could find something workable. Still . . .

"Hannah, truly, I am grateful for what you propose, but I would not wish to be a burden on your parents—"

"You wouldna be a burden!" Hannah's head shot up, color rising in her cheeks. "What I mean to say is . . . we'd welcome a boarder."

The girl's family needed the funds. Rose wavered. It *was* imperative she find an affordable place to live as soon as possible, but there was her particular circumstance to deal with. She laid a hand over Hannah's. "I would be very glad to speak with your parents about an arrangement, but there is something you must see before I agree."

The train had slowed as it drew up to the platform, and minutes later the workers disembarked, some of them heading in the direction of Timber Town while the rest dispersed toward Gretna's village. "Follow me," Rose instructed once they alighted, and they struck out in the direction of the hotel.

"Where did you work before, Miss Lockhart?"

Rose glanced at the girl, careful to weigh her words this time. "A few hours south of here by train."

"England then." Hannah sighed. "I wish my maw and da would let me go to England—or any place besides Gretna." She cast a beseeching look at Rose. "Some of my friends from the factory got permission to take the train into Carlisle tomorrow night. On Saturdays, the cinemas there have exciting, romantic films, not like the dull pictures shown here."

Rose offered another sympathetic nod, while a sudden yearning caught her unaware as she realized the care and protection Hannah's parents exercised over their only daughter. They wanted her living at home rather than apart from them in the hostels; and because of her tender years, they showed prudence in limiting her freedom to run about the countryside unchaperoned.

She'd once known that kind of love. Rose and her baby brothers, basking in the doting affection of their parents, all living cozy in the small Edinburgh flat above Graham's Drapers and Haberdashery. A lifetime ago.

Reaching the hotel, she turned her thoughts to the possibility of living with the Bairds. Rose imagined she would like Hannah's family. "My room is on the second floor, so we'll take the stairs."

Arriving at her door, she fitted the key and as she turned the lock, a familiar yip greeted her. "You've a wee dog!" Hannah said, rushing inside to the crate on the floor beside the bed.

"Hannah, meet Winston. The reason that I doubt your parents will agree to have me as their boarder." Rose was grateful the hotel proprietor had indulged her, letting her keep Winston in the room for a few days.

"He's braw!" The girl crouched beside the crate, and when Winston issued a growl, she scurried back to land on the floor.

"Winston, you will show some manners." Rose marched over to collect the dog, then sat on the bed with him.

Hannah rose to her feet and took a hesitant step forward. "Will he bite?"

Rose shook her head. "Winston likes to think he is fierce, but just hold out your hand so he can get your scent. Then give his ears a good scratch and he'll be your friend forever."

Soon Hannah was cradling the dog on the bed. "His fur is so white and soft," she murmured. "Have you had him long?"

"Just a short while." Again the memories lanced her heart—arriving at the cottage on Tilly's bicycle and finding Winston, muddy and stinking of pig slop as he sped past her into the house.

Her quick pursuit and then being tossed in the air as the explosion changed her world.

It had been a mistake to bring the dog. Caring for an animal was an added burden when she had no idea about her own future. Yet beneath her logic was a need to hold on to Tilly. Her friend would want her to care for her beloved companion.

Even Winston had sensed her waffling. Shortly after his bath at the cottage, his very soft and white self sat up on hind legs, his pink tongue lolling to one side of his mouth. His appeal had charmed her then, but the dog soon became a balm to her loneliness and grief. She'd clung to that last remaining thread connecting her to the sister of her heart.

"You'll make a fine friend to the laddies at home."

Hannah's crooning drew her back, and she smiled watching the girl scratch behind one furry ear and then the other while Winston grinned up at her.

No doubt he'd charm the Bairds, too. "Have you any pets at home, Hannah?" Even if the girl's family agreed to lodge her and the dog, how would Winston interact with another animal?

"We had a small collie, Tinker. He was Da's dog and followed him to work each day at the train yard. Tinker was ten when he ran to catch up with Da and got hit by the water truck." She gazed up at Rose. "That happened three weeks after my brother's memorial." She bent her head, scratching the dog's ear. "So I think Winston will be a welcome member to our family."

Her soft words held sadness but with a perception that impressed Rose. There was more to young Hannah Baird than her shy smile and adolescent frustrations. "Then shall we go and speak with your parents, so you can return to work?"

"Aye." Hannah rose from the bed and set the dog gently back inside his crate.

They soon set a quick pace along the dirt track leading back toward the Green. As they walked, Rose continued to harbor doubts over the Bairds' reception of her and Winston.

To fifteen-year-old Hannah, everything in life held possibility.

Rose had experienced the same sense of promise near that age until she'd lost her parents. Yet even after Aunt and Uncle arrived to collect them in Scotland, hiring a nanny to take her baby brothers in hand, Rose grieved her loss and still held hope their lives would be all right. That under their aunt's tender care they could eventually become a family again.

She'd been so wrong.

"There it is!" Hannah pointed to a large white cottage trimmed in black and nestled among a narrow woodland of leafy birches and pines. The house sat back a good distance from the road, and as they trekked down the long dirt drive, Rose prayed Hannah's instincts were correct and that she and Winston would be welcome.

❧ ⁓ ❧

"Och, ye may have the extra room, of course." Mrs. Baird's broad smile matched her husband's as Rose took tea with the couple in their comfortable parlor.

Hannah stayed long enough to introduce "Miss Lockhart" and tell her parents she was orphaned, newly arrived from England to take a job as shift supervisor, and in need of housing. Then the breathless girl grabbed an apple and a potato pasty from the kitchen before dashing back to work.

Seated beside Hannah's mother on the large blue couch, Rose reached toward the table for a jam biscuit and her steaming cup of tea. "I am grateful to you both for the offer, but are you certain about Winston? I would not wish to cause any difficulties."

"Yer wee dog is welcome." Mrs. Baird's amber eyes, so much like her daughter's, glowed from her pleasantly rounded face. She turned to her husband seated in the chair across from them, resting his hands on the top of his cane. "'Tis long enough since our own Tinker's passing, and the laddies will love having another dog to chase them around."

"Winston and I have not been together long, but he has proven to be housebroken and very smart. He likes to growl upon first meeting, but once he knows you and you reward him with a good scratching, he's as gentle as a lamb."

"Sounds a bit like our Tinker." Mr. Baird chuckled, glancing at his wife. He turned a warm smile on Rose. "I'm sure you both will be a fine addition to the family."

Family. Rose liked the inclusive words he spoke and the way he eyed her with a fatherly expression. A sense of warmth and rightness settled over her as she sipped her tea, and the hope she could afford to stay with these good people.

"Please excuse the brew. 'Tis a bit watery." Mrs. Baird looked apologetic. "What with the war on and having to ration here in Scotland."

"The tea is fine." Rose smiled. "And they ration down in England too."

Mrs. Baird's expression eased, and Rose set her teacup back onto the table. She looked to Hannah's father. "Mr. Baird, what do you normally charge your tenants?"

He chuckled. "You're the first, lass. We've not had one before." He looked at his wife. "Mairi?"

Mrs. Baird paused with her teacup halfway to her lips. "The room belongs to our auldest son, Alex. He's still over in France with the war, so he willna be home anytime soon." Then without taking a sip she set down the cup, her features pinched.

Hannah had told her that their younger son, Ian, died a year ago in France. Certainly, Mrs. Baird worried for her stepson.

Rose remained silent, allowing them a private moment of grief. She absently reached for the thistle brooch at her collar before she finally cleared her throat. "What would you propose then as a monthly fee? I will pay whatever you think is fair and what I can afford, of course." When the couple shared a bemused look, she stood. "I'll give you a few minutes."

Rose walked outside onto the front porch. As she scanned the fields beyond the woodland, she observed green pastureland, with a few dark cattle grazing openly and a herd of sheep on the next farm over. Most of Gretna was flat that she could see, unlike her childhood city of Edinburgh, built upon hills. And the heat wasn't nearly as intense here as it was in Nottingham days ago.

When Mrs. Baird called her back inside, Rose thrilled to learn the couple had settled on an amount for room and board that she could afford. "I can pay you for half the month now, and the rest once I receive my wages on the nineteenth. Would that be acceptable?"

"Aye, 'tis just right." Mrs. Baird smiled. "And I can send my lad, Fergus, along to help with yer luggage."

"That is kind, Mrs. Baird, but I can have the hotel bring me around in the carriage." After the explosion, Rose had little in the way of possessions—nothing more than the filthy clothes on her back and the thistle brooch. She'd packed Tilly's valise with a few of her friend's clothes, including the Sunday jacket and skirt she'd worn to the interview—and Tilly's birth certificate. Of course, Winston too, after she'd given him a good scrubbing.

Once she paid the funds from her small purse, Rose offered Mrs. Baird her hand. "I shall return this afternoon. Thank you both again for taking me in."

"We're glad to have you, lass." Mr. Baird leaned on his cane to rise to his feet, and he and Mrs. Baird walked her to the door.

With a backward wave at them, Rose returned to the hotel, eager to collect Winston and settle into her new home.

6

*H*e dreaded going home.

Alex's gut tightened as he stared from the train's open window at the familiar terrain of Scotland's East Lothian valley. He again considered his meeting with Weatherford and Simon last night. Though he was impatient to hunt down the saboteur who had threatened Moorside and his family, what would he say to his maw and da when they all finally came face-to-face?

He'd been devastated, witnessing his brother's burial in France last year, but then coming home to Gretna to watch his family grieve at Ian's memorial had nearly crippled him. He had absorbed their suffering, as he must for what he'd done—or rather, what he'd failed to do. His parents, oblivious to anything but their own sorrow, barely acknowledged his presence, while Hannah sobbed uncontrollably and Fergus and James looked more lost than aggrieved to know their brother was dead.

You shouldna have hunted him down. Better to have let him go. His gaze fell to the RAF uniform cap in his hands, and he ran an absent finger along the starched seam.

He and his brother had both been fascinated with the idea of man-made flight. Ian enlisted in the Royal Flying Corps when he was of age, and with Alex's help received his flight training at Dover. Afterward he joined him at Saint-Omer Air Base in northern France, where as a flight commander Alex could keep an eye on his younger brother.

With turnover rates high and pilots in constant demand, Ian found himself called up to engage in one sortie after the next, yet he'd proved his mettle, taking down a total of five Jasta fighter planes in the short time before his death.

With those five, he'd reveled in attaining his status as "flying ace." He also found an adoring audience in Paris on furlough weekends, where he'd spend his pay gambling and buying drinks for questionable women. Women like Olivia Charles.

The muscles in Alex's neck tightened. If Weatherford ever managed to find the traitorous witch, it would be his own good pleasure to sit in on her trial and execution.

Seducing his brother for her own gain, she'd been the one to cause Ian's disgrace. And she didna work alone; that scunner, Dexter, put her in Ian's path, then helped his brother with his naïve and deadly plan . . .

The train slowed, and Alex glanced toward the window as the station platform came into view. At 1730 hours, the air was warm, the afternoon sun still hovering high above the trees.

On the nearest side of the station building, a man in the new olive-green uniform of the RAF stood beside a military truck as if awaiting his arrival. Was this his MI5 contact, Lieutenant Charles Stuart?

Disembarking minutes later, Alex replaced his cap and saw the man hailing him.

Not a lieutenant.

"Captain Baird!" The young airman approached and offered a smart salute.

Alex returned it. "Cadet . . . ?"

"Patrick Donovan, sir. 'Tis an honor having ye here. A real honor." His boyish face flushed with color as he reached for Alex's valise. "I'll drive ye tae the base in a shake, Captain. Our commandant's waiting tae meet ye."

Alex raised an amused brow at the red-faced lad. "Lead the way, Cadet."

Once they boarded, the truck set out and minutes later arrived at the gate into RAF East Fortune. Alex caught the briny smell of the North Sea blowing in off the coast, and he surveyed the expanse of landing fields, flat green pasture mown short for the planes.

An array of tents and brown Nissen huts stood at the far side of the landing field, and beyond the buildings to the north were three enormous canvas structures.

"Those house the big airships, sir." Donovan followed his gaze. "We've been using them tae clobber the Hun U-boats swimmin' out at sea."

"I was told this airfield's now a training base for pilots?"

"Aye, sir. For planes and airships." Again, his fair complexion colored. "I'm just a pilot in training right now, but I've got meself some grand plans."

Alex cast him a sidelong glance. "Perhaps a wing command of your own one day, Donovan?"

"Indeed, sir!" His shoulders straightened as he wheeled the truck past the gate.

Alex smiled at his enthusiasm, recalling the thrill of his own flight through the ranks. "I wish you the best of luck, Cadet. And remember, always keep a steady hand on the stick and your eyes everywhere."

"Thank ye, sir!" Donovan gazed at him wide-eyed as though Alex had just shared with him some ancient world secret. The airman parked the truck in front of a green block building and killed the engine. "This is HQ, Captain, and the place we call home. If ye'll follow me, sir, I'll take ye tae see the colonel."

Donovan grabbed up Alex's single piece of luggage and led the way into the RAF squadron offices. Inside at the first doorway, a young corporal sat transmitting messages on his telegraph machine. Farther down the hall, in another makeshift office, a woman in uniform clacked away on a typewriter. Passing two more rooms with closed doors, Alex and his guide arrived at the office of the base commandant, Lieutenant Colonel Landon.

The aulder officer sat at his desk. He glanced up from his paperwork and rose to his feet. "Ah, please come in, Captain Baird. We've been waiting for you."

"Colonel." Alex nodded. He cast a quick glance at Donovan. "Of course, sir, you know the reason I'm here—"

"That will be all, Cadet Donovan." The colonel raised a gnarled hand toward Alex to stay any further conversation. "Do be sure to close the door on your way out."

"Aye, sirs."

Once Donovan left, the colonel turned sad eyes on Alex. "I was heartily sorry to hear that I'm to be the one to sign off on your discharge papers, Captain Baird. Especially when we are in great need of skillful, seasoned pilots such as yourself." He picked up a file from the desk. "I confess the proof of your fine reputation as an ace and a flight commander has preceded your arrival."

Alex bowed his head, shifting his stance. "Thank you, sir. Leaving the RAF . . . 'tis not a situation I'd expected."

"No, of course not." The colonel nodded. "However, I understand this aeroneurosis business to be quite serious and requires much rest." He smiled beneath a salt-and-pepper mustache. "And you, my boy, have done more than your share to deserve the chance to heal." He reached for another set of papers. "Once our typist finishes up the final forms, you and I shall sign them, and you can be off whenever you like."

Alex didn't like one wee bit of it. Nor did he care for the aeroneurosis malady Weatherford had cooked up. He'd been tired lately, aye, but not with the headaches or jitters typical of pilots who had flown in one too many dogfights.

"Everything by the book." Weatherford's orders. And so he must be seen to leave the service before seeking out a civilian job at Moorside.

"While the paperwork is being readied, Captain, I imagine you'd like to freshen up after your journey. You shall have a temporary billet in the instructors' tent, which is at your disposal until you can depart for home. In Gretna, correct? Of course it is." The colonel's brows knitted together as he nodded, having answered his own question. "I suspect it's why the RAF brass wanted you discharged here at East Fortune."

"Actually, sir, I'm also here to see a . . . a pal. Lieutenant Charles Stuart? Can you tell me where I might find him?"

"Ah yes, Lieutenant Stuart. He's the new chap we are expecting tomorrow."

Tomorrow? Alex frowned. "I'd hoped he would be here by now."

"My office received a call earlier. The lieutenant had to arrange a flight over from France this afternoon and missed the last train out of Victoria Station. He plans to get a lift on an early morning supply train, which should arrive—" he checked his watch— "about midday tomorrow. In the meantime, you're welcome to remain at the base."

More delays. Alex worked his jaw. "Thank you, sir."

"I shall ring for Cadet Donovan to take you to your billet." He picked up the telephone, then paused to regard Alex. "Since you will be here a while longer, Captain, once you've settled, please come to the mess hall for supper. It's 1800 hours, so most of the men should be there."

Again he thanked the colonel, and once Donovan arrived, Alex walked with the cadet toward the instructors' quarters, his mood wavering between impatience to track down the saboteur and relief at postponing his homecoming.

Either way, he must wait. Stuart had the codebook, and Alex wanted to glean from his new MI5 liaison any added information about his quarry at Moorside.

They neared the tents, and once more his gaze swept across the RAF post. Standard-sized plane hangars stood across the field from the airship structures, and beyond them Nissen huts likely used to house fuel or weapons and the airfield's repair facilities. East Fortune was set up much like his former base at Saint-Omer in France, only on a much smaller scale.

Inside the canvas instructors' tent, Alex was relieved to find the place empty. Donovan set his valise on one of the lower bunks and stepped back. "I can wait, sir, and take ye over tae the mess." He stood at attention, his face once more a rosy hue. "All the lads heard ye were coming in today and they're keen tae make yer acquaintance."

Despite the invitations to sup, Alex was in no humor for company. Still, he didna have the heart to refuse the cadet. "Just point me in the right direction, Donovan. I'll be there. What's tonight's fare?"

"The same as every night, sir. Tinned beef with neeps and tatties." Donovan made a face. "We call 'em turnips and potatoes in Ireland, but they taste the same wherever ye go."

"Too bad the tinned beef isn't haggis." Alex smiled. "Then every night could be a meal my fellow Scots Rabbie Burns would approve."

"Aye, sir." Grinning, Donovan relaxed his stance, then pointed back toward the tent opening. "Ye'll take a right once ye return tae the green building, and the mess is the Nissen hut around back." Excitement lit his face. "I'll let the lads know ye'll be stopping by."

After the cadet went in search of his supper, Alex put his valise on the floor and flopped down onto the thin mattress. Staring into the upper bunk's framework, he anticipated his meeting tomorrow with Stuart. How much could the man tell him about Scotland Yard and MI5's efforts to identify this saboteur, Thomas Brown or Rhymer?

Weatherford believed both names were one and the same man working for the death merchant, Kahverengi. And with a common name like Thomas Brown, the joint investigation must have already interrogated hundreds of men in the factories, checking each for a red birthmark. A slow process to be sure, and one that made him more anxious to get inside Moorside to begin his search.

He checked his watch. Fifteen minutes had already passed. His stomach rumbled, and so he rolled off the bunk, cleaned up a bit at the washstand, and headed over to the mess.

"Captain Baird!" Donovan beamed, rising from his chair at a long table filled with cadets. Alex nodded, then glanced across the room to the instructors' table with Colonel Landon at its head. The colonel smiled and waved him toward the young lads staring at him as though he were some god.

Alex fetched his food and returned to the cadet's table, where Donovan quickly pulled out the empty chair beside him. Settling next to the Irishman, he was amused and humbled at the battery of questions he received from the cadets. Some were fresh young lads, while others were aulder officers who had transferred in from other military branches to become pilots.

They asked about his flight career, how many kills—thirty-five—and how the fighting was going in France. As he responded to each question, he considered them, knowing once they left East Fortune as "finished pilots" and went overseas, very few would return.

Colonel Landon had said it earlier—the RAF was desperate for experienced pilots, as they were always in short supply. These lads not only risked death during training accidents, but if they made it as far as France, only the best and bravest would survive the Huns' experienced Jasta fighters.

And Ian. *Yours was such a senseless loss, brother.*

"Captain Baird, will you be instructing us now that you're here?"

Alex turned to a young lad dressed in the auld khakis of the Royal Flying Corps. "Well, Cadet . . ."

"Peterson, sir."

"I willna be here long enough to do any instructing, Peterson. I'm going home to see my family tomorrow."

Peterson's expression fell, and the table grew quiet.

Alex surveyed the downcast faces. "But if I was ever to train with you lads, I'd be honored." Satisfied at the return of their smiles, he chose the moment to stand and leave them. "Then I'll see you all in the sky?"

Several heads nodded as they wished him well, and he strode toward the colonel, who waited for him at the door.

"The typed forms are ready whenever you are."

Alex followed him back to the office, and once all was signed, the colonel gave him his walking papers. "Good luck to you, Captain Baird. I hope that by returning home you can make a complete recovery. And when you do, and if this blasted war continues, we would be pleased to have you return and instruct our cadets."

"I appreciate the offer, Colonel."

"You must be tired. If you wish to return to your billet, you'll have a chance to meet the instructors, perhaps some of whom you may have known in France."

Back as his tent, Alex did recall two of the pilots. Captains Carlson and Murphy had served out of the same airfield at Saint-Omer and flew sorties with his squadron. The three regaled one another with tales of various dogfights until it was finally time for lights-out.

Alex stared into the darkness, his head throbbing with exhaustion. Was the aeroneurosis Weatherford put into his file a possibility? He began massaging his temples, and minutes later, blessed sleep overtook him.

Both planes flew at high speeds, and adrenaline pumped in his veins. Gripping the stick, he angled his Sopwith Camel to come up around behind the single-seat Sopwith Pup streaking across the sky. He pushed the throttle to inch his plane forward, then alongside the left wing of the Pup—before he ducked, quickly easing back as the sun glinted off the steel revolver aimed at him from the other plane. A shot fired.

Ian, did I not tell you that woman was bad business? You're going to die, lad!

Still he kept his brother in his sights as they neared the Belgian border. He prayed they didna meet up with an enemy squadron of Jastas before he could get Ian on the ground.

But fail or succeed, his brother was dead to him. Desertion, a court-martial offense, meant a military tribunal. A firing squad.

He ground his teeth, perspiration beading along the edge of his flight cap despite the freezing wind. Dear God, why had he not stopped seeing her? Now Ian had gone too far.

Suddenly the Pup made a dive, trying to shake him off. He pushed the stick forward, and the nose of his plane followed like two enemy pilots ready to dogfight. Nearing the ground in the northwest corner of France—territory still heavily occupied by the enemy—the Pup continued downward while he wrenched back on his stick to level out.

Ian, pull out! He watched, helpless, as the plane spiraled out of control. The Pup crashed in a clearing surrounded by trees, and he ruthlessly jerked on the controls, bringing his plane around to make a sketchy landing near the wreckage. His wheels touched down on uneven ground, the plane bouncing back and forth, and he struggled to keep control. When he finally came to a stop, he vaulted from the cockpit, running toward the blaze with every scrap of air in his lungs.

He knelt beside the still form, his brother's flight cap gone and exposing his dark hair. Pulling off his own leather jacket, he grabbed Ian, shielding himself from the flames as he pulled his brother from the fire. He staggered with him several feet before the fuel ignited in a final explosion, knocking him and his burden to the ground.

Seconds passed while he struggled to rise, and then he tried to rouse his brother. Wake up! Wake up . . .

"Wake up, Captain."

The gentle nudge at his shoulder jolted Alex from sleep. He lay on his back, his undershirt soaked through with sweat.

"You look as if you've been to the devil's house and back, Captain Baird."

Again the low voice beside him. Alex blinked and turned to the shadowy figure crouched alongside his bunk. Then he recalled where he was and rose up on an elbow to face the stranger.

"Lieutenant Charlie Stuart, at your service." His whisper held an edge of humor.

"What time is it?" Alex glanced at his wristwatch.

"'Tis just 2200 hours, Captain. I canna say much for your night life, sir." His teeth flashed white in the darkness. "But I ken your meaning. I was able to hop a ride with a military train heading up to Auld Reekie tonight. The good lad here, Cadet Donovan, drove the twenty miles to fetch me and bring me back to the base."

Alex grunted. So Stuart had arrived earlier than expected. He cast a glance beyond him at Donovan's tall, thin silhouette. And it explained how he'd found his bunk.

The cadet shifted. "The colonel sent me to pick him up—"

"Keep it down over there!"

One of the instructors had awakened to grumble for silence. Alex started to rise. "Give me a few minutes, Lieutenant. I'll meet you in the mess and we can talk there."

"Aye, Captain." Stuart sketched a comical salute from his crouched position and then rose to lead young Donovan from the tent.

Quickly and quietly, Alex exchanged his undershirt and donned his uniform, the nightmare still fresh in his mind. Each time he was visited by the dream, he tried to change the outcome, and each time he'd failed. Now as a civilian and with the lieutenant's arrival, he was ready to begin his assignment. Yet if he would succeed—save his sister and all the innocent lives working at Moorside—he must rid himself of these ghosts.

Minutes later, his mind clear, Alex entered the mess and was relieved to see only Stuart inside. His MI5 liaison had also thoughtfully poured him a cup of coffee.

The lieutenant rose to his feet, tall and solidly built in his impeccable olive-green RAF uniform. In the lamplight of the dining hall, they assessed each other. He noted the lieutenant's wavy blond hair and dark-blue eyes and estimated the bonny prince's ruddy features to be close to his own age.

"As you were, Lieutenant." Alex moved to the table and took a seat while Stuart sat across from him. "Captain Weatherford said you have a codebook?"

Stuart nodded, the hint of a smile on his lips. "The years have passed, Captain Baird, but you're much the way I remember you."

Alex stared at him. "How do you know me, Lieutenant?"

"'Twas back in Reekie. You and my aulder brother Donald knew each other. Do you remember him from primary school?"

Alex tried to recall the years he and his family lived near the Princes Street station in Edinburgh. His maw had been alive for a part of that time, and he'd been just a wee lad. Still, the name Donald Stuart seemed familiar. He offered an apologetic shrug. "'Twas a long time ago."

"To be sure," Stuart said. "You and Donald were about six. I wasna more than a bairn myself, but I remember watching you lads from the window, playing football in the street."

The childhood memory suddenly returned, and Alex smiled. "Aye, a few of us joined several of the aulder lads from school, and on weekends we set up team fields along opposite sides of the road." He chuckled. "We'd dare one another to try for a goal and punt the ball across just as a carriage or a grocery cart passed by." He glanced at Stuart. "Where's Donald now?"

The lieutenant's features tensed. "My brother was killed two years ago aboard the HMS *Invincible*. The ship exploded and sank during the Battle of Jutland." He stared down at his coffee. "Only six men survived."

Alex bent over his own steaming cup. "I'm sorry."

Stuart raised his head, blue eyes somber. "Condolences to you as well, sir. I ken you lost a brother of your own last year." Bitterly, he added, "Seems we've all lost someone precious in this godforsaken war."

Alex nodded, then sought to change the subject. "How did you end up in MI5?"

"That took a bit of jam." Stuart drew a deep breath and leaned back in his seat. "I joined the Forty-third Squadron out of Stirling, and we stationed at Avesnes-le-Comte in France. When I returned to London on furlough late last year, I ran into an auld pal who worked for the Admiralty. He knew of my language skills and recommended me to his chief while I was there."

At Alex's questioning look, he smiled. "Before the war, I built oil derricks for the Shell Company and worked throughout Europe and parts of Asia. New languages come easily to me." He shrugged. "So I go wherever I'm sent."

"And now they sent you here as my liaison."

He nodded. "I'll also be working as a flight instructor for these cadets." He removed a small, soft-covered booklet from inside his tunic. "I'm certain you'll recognize this, Captain."

Alex took the codebook, quickly thumbing the pages. "A simple substitution cipher. Easy enough. We used the code during reconnaissance flights." He glanced at Stuart. "How should I contact you here at East Fortune?"

"Use the telegraph office in Gretna. And unless you have information worth sending, you can update me every other day." He paused. "Any questions, sir?"

"You ken anything more about this agent, Thomas Brown, or Rhymer? I wasna given much to go on."

Stuart shook his head. "I've been told about as much as you, Captain. Scotland Yard is still interviewing suspects, and I was called in at the last minute to act as go-between with London." He tilted his head. "Is your paperwork in order with Colonel Landon, sir?"

"Aye." He slid the codebook inside his tunic. "So when can I leave?"

"Tonight, if you like." Stuart reached for his coffee and grinned. "Tell me, Captain. How does it feel to be a civilian again?"

7

*M*aw, please! Tonight the cinema in Carlisle is showing *The Perils of Pauline*, starring the famous American actress Miss Pearl White! My friends from work got passes to go and the train leaves in an hour!"

Rose smiled from across the supper table as Hannah pleaded her case with her parents. She knew the girl badly wanted to go, for it was all the factory girls had talked about today during their breaks at work.

As for herself, she was relieved "Miss Lockhart" had managed to get through her first day of work as the new Women's Welfare shift supervisor. Rose's co-workers had seemed friendly enough, and most of her charges were respectful and helpful.

She was also grateful to be making a good wage, especially since Tilly's bank note was almost completely spent. By working twelve-hour days six days a week, as she had at Chilwell, she could hope to save quite a bit of money. And what she did receive would be her own from now on, not subject to her uncle's thievery.

Still, as she'd shrugged out of her jacket, she was glad for Sunday tomorrow. She definitely planned to sleep in!

"Miss Lockhart, please tell Maw that since I'm working at the factory, I'm auld enough to go to the cinema!"

Rose reeled in her thoughts and focused on Hannah across the table. Mrs. Baird sighed while Mr. Baird only shook his head. "Hannah, your parents love you and only want what is best for you."

"But I can *be trusted*!" Again she turned to her mother. "You dinna believe me, Maw?"

Another mother-daughter discussion ensued, and Rose flashed a quick smile at Mr. Baird, who winked at her.

She thought warmly about last night, settling into her new room with Winston. The Bairds had seen to her every comfort: pressed sheets and the Baird tartan coverlet turned back on the bed. A washstand at the ready with fresh lavender-scented water and even a small vase filled with sprigs of the same fragrant flowers, placed beside the lamp on her nightstand.

Hannah's parents had sat with her in the parlor last evening after the Baird children went to bed, and they waited patiently for her to explain more about their daughter's breathless summary of "Miss Lockhart's life."

Rose was careful this time, making certain her explanations matched those she'd already told the girl, yet even now the memory of those lies made her squirm. These were good, honest people and she was still bemused over their wholehearted reception of her—Hannah and Mr. and Mrs. Baird, as well as their two young sons, Fergus and James, who sat to her left.

She cast the boys a sidelong glance and observed they were too busy feeding cooked peas to Winston to pay much attention to their older sister's dilemma. The terrier had growled and bared his teeth at them at first, just as he did with Hannah, but then soon took to the rambunctious boys, especially when he was sure of receiving food.

Rose nearly chuckled as she watched them glance at their mother and father, then grin conspiratorially before slipping another handful of peas under the table. Her aching heart throbbed anew with the pain of the past week. How she missed her own "Duggie" and Samuel!

Six-year-old James turned to her then, and she had to school her features when she noticed he'd lodged a pea into each nostril. Then he let out a burst of laughter, and the green round projectiles launched directly onto her plate.

"Good heavens!"

Hannah's bid for the cinema was forgotten as Mrs. Baird reached across the table to grab her youngest son's arm. "James Robert Baird! What are ye thinking to act like that at the table? Shall I tether ye to the post outside so ye can graze on weeds like a sheep?" Her stern expression suffused with color. "Ye'll apologize to Miss Lockhart right . . . this . . . minute."

James bent his reddish-blond head to Rose. "Sorry, Miss Lockhart."

Fergus gave a snicker, but Rose kept her eyes on James. "Before I accept your apology, you must promise me never to do it again."

"I promise, no more peas."

"All right then."

His mother gave her an appreciative glance before glaring at her other son. "That goes for ye as well, Fergus. Yer aulder and ken more than yer wee brother, and ye shouldna be encouraging him."

The boy dropped his head. "Aye, Maw." To Rose, he said, "I'm sorry, too."

Across the table, Hannah's cheeks flared. "Och, you . . . you silly bairns! You've ruined everything!" Tossing her napkin onto the table, she left her chair and stormed toward her room.

Mrs. Baird issued another sigh and, with a quick glance to her husband, excused herself to go in search of their daughter.

Mr. Baird glared at his two youngest offspring. "You two hooligans have hurt your sister's feelings. 'Tis time you cleared the table and rinsed the dishes to make up for it."

"Aye, Da" came their sullen replies as each stood and picked up the empty plates and cups and trudged with them into the kitchen. When they were out of earshot, Mr. Baird smiled at her. "Was your brother ever full of such mischief?"

Rose thought to tell him about one Christmas when she and the boys were home from school and she'd walked in on them having a rousing pillow fight, feathers flying everywhere, until Uncle had put a stop to their "uncouth behavior." But oh, how they'd laughed with each other!

Humor edged her lips, though she kept her mouth closed. She couldn't tell Mr. Baird the truth about her own brothers, and she had no idea what kind of boy Tilly's brother had been.

He must have sensed her reticence, as compassion replaced his humor. "I've been thoughtless, Miss Lockhart. He was a wee lad when he passed away, aye?"

"Yes." Rose hated lying. Yet she offered him another in order to set him at ease. "But even so, he loved to tease me. I think it must be built into boys."

Chuckling, he nodded. "I was the same as a lad. And as a parent, I've come to appreciate the love and patience of my own maw and da." He hesitated. "What do you remember most about yours, Miss Lockhart?"

What should she say? Already they knew she'd been fourteen when her parents died. And Tilly had never known her mother, nor had she really spoken of her father.

"My mum . . . she was a seamstress." She could tell him the truth at least about her own parents. "She had a lovely voice and always sang 'The Water Is Wide' while she worked on a piece of cloth. My dad was soft-spoken and loved telling me silly stories about our ancestors while he wove tartan cloth on a big loom." She held out her hands. "I remember his palms, always red and chafed from working so much with the wool." A sadness pierced her, recalling the memory, yet she smiled at Mr. Baird. "They were good to me."

He had leaned back in his chair, his arms crossed as he listened, his expression kindly while he occasionally nodded his understanding. In him Rose saw her own dad, both men so completely different from her uncle. Sir Ridley Cutler was a man who demanded silence during evening meals when she and her brothers were at home, and whose wife cowered at the opposite end of the long formal dining table, too afraid to speak.

"Miss Lockhart?"

She glanced up to see that Mrs. Baird had returned to the dining room. "I've a favor to ask . . ." Her voice held uncertainty. "Hannah mentioned ye might be willing to take her into Carlisle tonight so she can see this film with her friends?"

Rose blinked. Was Hannah's mother willing to trust her with the welfare of her daughter? The family had only known her a day. "I . . . I do not know what to say."

Mrs. Baird reached for the back of her chair. "Och, I shouldna bother ye with this, lass. Ye must be weary after a full day's work. She can go another time."

"No!" Rose quickly stood. "I mean . . . I will accompany her to Carlisle, if you're certain you would wish me to."

"Of course." Mrs. Baird looked to her husband, who nodded. "After all, we trust ye with her welfare twelve hours each day at the factory. I wouldna request such a thing during the week, but tomorrow's Sunday and yer day off, so ye can have a nice sleep in and recover."

Rose's heart thrummed. The cinema! "How far is it to Carlisle?"

"Just ten miles by train, and the next one leaves in three-quarters of an hour." Mrs. Baird's amber eyes gleamed. "Bless ye, lass. 'Tis hard enough raising a daughter *without* a pack of wild laddies living in the same house."

At that moment, the loud *clank* of dishes sounded from the kitchen. Craning her head, Rose glimpsed James and Fergus standing at the sink, rinsing and stacking plates.

She turned to Mrs. Baird. "If you would like to tell Hannah, I will get ready."

Mrs. Baird smiled her relief. Rose hurried from the table toward her room, her excitement mounting as she remembered the last time she'd been to the cinema. It was her thirteenth birthday when Mum and Dad took her to see *David Copperfield* at the new Haymarket Theater in Edinburgh.

Ages ago now. And a year after that, her life had changed.

Uncle Ridley had decided films were in poor taste for his niece and any other proper woman, and she could still see her aunt's face, filled with such pathetic hope each time Rose begged for an outing.

Both then and now, she wondered how much of Aunt Delia's old life had been cut away and disposed of by Uncle Ridley. Delia had shrunk from the responsibility of her own sister's kin, leaving Rose and her brothers to fall prey to Uncle's strategy—shipped off to year-round boarding schools with only those precious Christmas visits giving them a chance to rekindle their affection for one another. And once, Rose had overheard the servants' whispers of how her aunt had become a shadow of herself after the asylum.

Entering her room, she was greeted by Winston's happy bark as he lay sprawled on her bed, his appetite sated with cooked peas. She breathed in the lovely scent of lavender and glanced toward her nightstand and the purple bouquet Mrs. Baird thoughtfully provided.

Moving to the closet, Rose also detected faint traces of leather, mustiness, and sweat. A man's room surely, evidenced by the blue-green tartan plaid on the bed and the wood-paneled walls. A brown cowskin bag full of golf clubs still sat propped against the wall, and a football rested on the floor beside the oak dresser.

Apparently, Mrs. Baird had decided to leave intact the remnants of her eldest son's presence. Perhaps having his things in here kept him alive for her during his long absences at war.

Their younger son, Ian Baird, had been dead a year now. Did any of his personal items remain to mark his memory . . . or had they been removed as being too painful to look upon?

Last night in the parlor, the couple made no mention of him, yet Rose had sensed a sadness beneath their kindness and warmth. How could she not when she herself understood loss only too well?

Removing the mauve jacket and skirt from the closet, she turned her mind back to the memory of her parents, having told Mr. Baird about them. Fragments she'd clung to, their lives never to be forgotten. While six years had lessened the pain, her sorrow would always remain.

She grabbed up her toiletries from the dresser and went before the washstand mirror to ready herself for the evening. Unpinning her hair to brush and re-braid, she caught the faint sound of a dish breaking in the kitchen and couldn't help smiling. Then recalling young James with his nose full of peas made her chuckle. A handful, indeed!

Mr. Baird had said it was to be expected of boys that age, and reminded of the pillow fight long ago, Rose hoped Douglas and Samuel enjoyed a bit of mischievous fun at their school.

Her hand trembled with the brush. While she'd reasoned that her "death" would ensure their safety . . . were they safe? Her memorial was set for the day after tomorrow, so she didn't dare yet call the school to find out how they fared, as they were probably in Leicester.

Rose ached as she imagined her brothers alone and grieving within the somber halls of the estate. No one to comfort them, nothing like this bright, warm place filled with a loving family who had already made her feel welcome.

Next week, she must find a way to make contact with the school. Though even if they *were* safe as she prayed, until she could get them out of Britain, the boys remained under their uncle's influence.

She stared into the mirror as new anxiety filled her. Douglas, at nearly twelve, was already growing distant and aloof. Last Christmas, when Samuel tried to goad him into a playful wrestling match, he'd coolly refused. When she questioned him later, he informed her such behavior was undignified for a young gentleman.

What was happening to her Duggie? And how would young Samuel change?

Her chest tightened as she dropped the brush, her fingers working quickly to gather and repin her hair. "Work steady and save every penny," she told her reflection. "And God willing, before the first snow falls, you can all start a new life across the sea." She added, "For Tilly."

Once she'd dressed, Rose secured her hat and went to the parlor to join Hannah. The girl wore the same charcoal skirt and white blouse of yesterday, and across her slim shoulders a pretty blue-green plaid shawl light enough for a summer evening. A straw hat similar to her own perched at a jaunty angle against her loose hair.

"Och, such a pair of bonny lasses!" Mrs. Baird touched a hand to her lips as she came upon them. She removed several coins from her skirt pocket and handed the money to Rose. "For the train fare and cinema tickets. And a wee bit extra to buy yerselves tea and biscuits."

"Mrs. Baird, that is not necessary . . ."

"Her father and I insist." She laid a hand on Rose's arm. "Yer a good lass to chaperone our Hannah tonight, and we trust ye as we would an aulder daughter, if we'd had one."

Humbled by her testament of faith, Rose's eyes burned. "Thank you," she whispered.

Mrs. Baird patted her arm and turned to her daughter. "Consider this an early birthday present, dear. And if ye mind yerself with Miss Lockhart this evening, we'll talk about more films in the future."

"I promise, Maw. Thank you!" Beaming, Hannah suddenly twirled in place, the hem of her charcoal skirt swirling. "Och, and Gladys and Colleen will be so surprised when I show up with Miss Lockhart!"

Gladys Dunham and Colleen Shire? Rose's buoyant mood sank. She doubted her arrival at the station with Hannah would be welcomed by the two factory girls whose mocking attitudes she'd already witnessed. And they hardly seemed suitable company for young Hannah.

At the girl's joy, however, Rose held her tongue. She'd ensure nothing went amiss tonight for her charges. "Miss Lockhart" was their supervisor, after all.

"You lassies had better not miss the train." Mr. Baird appeared from the kitchen and made to shoo them off with his cane. As Rose and her young charge headed toward the front door, Hannah was the first to rush outside. Rose followed, then turned to say a last good-bye and noted both parents' worried looks. "Is something wrong?"

"Och, no." Mrs. Baird wiped her eyes. "I meant what I said. We trust ye with our lass and wish ye both a lovely time." She glanced at her husband, who reached to put an arm around her shoulders. "'Tis just that we lost one of our bairns a year ago, and I . . . I tend to be a mother hen who canna stop clinging to her chicks."

Impulsively Rose returned to grasp both of Mrs. Baird's work-worn hands. "I promise to watch over Hannah and the other girls as if they were my own. Trust me, nothing will happen."

❖⟶ ⚯ ⟵❖

If only the earth would swallow her up and be done with her.

Gritting her teeth, Rose hardly knew which hurt more—the cramps in her stomach or the fact she'd been hoodwinked by two of the young women in her charge.

And the worst of it—she'd failed to keep her promise to the Bairds.

She sat hunched over in the lorry's open bed, her nausea increasing with each rocking motion of their bumpy ride back to Gretna. In the dark she could barely make out the weeping Hannah, seated beside her angry-faced father. Mr. Baird had been forced to hire his farming neighbor to drive him into Carlisle and liberate his daughter and her two friends from police custody. Gladys and Colleen sat on Hannah's other side, their heads bent and silent.

Her stomach lurched as the lorry hit another divot in the road, and she pressed the handkerchief to her mouth before she abruptly turned to retch over the side.

Rose couldn't recall a time when she'd ever been so ill. At first, she feared she'd contracted the influenza circulating among some the factory workers, but later when Mr. Baird arrived, she discovered the brazen pair with Hannah had slipped ipecac into her tea at the film's intermission.

If that wasn't awful enough, while she remained completely

indisposed in the ladies' lounge, Gladys and Colleen swayed Hannah to join them in a public house a short walk from the cinema. *And* they bought her a drink! The policewoman on patrol discovered the underage girls and took all three to the Carlisle jail to be held, while the Bairds and Mrs. Nash at the factory were contacted.

Miserably, Rose eyed the pair beside Hannah, giving each girl as stern a look as she could muster. But it was already near midnight, and the sliver of moon made it doubtful they could see her anger.

Abruptly there was another lurch, and Rose thrust her head back over the edge. Oh, how she longed for her revenge . . . just as soon as she could stop feeling so sick!

The trip back to Gretna seemed to take forever, and she almost cried as the farmer's lorry pulled up next to the train station platform in town and the driver killed the engine.

She glimpsed Mrs. Nash standing next to the station office, awaiting their arrival. "Miss Lockhart, are you all right?"

Rose slumped against the edge of lorry's bed. "I'll . . . be fine . . . tomorrow," she choked out, her response muffled against the handkerchief.

Gladys and Colleen quietly climbed down from the back, and Mrs. Nash took them in hand. "You two will answer for this."

Even in the shadow of the station lamp, Mrs. Nash's hawkish face radiated anger.

"Miss Dunham, Miss Shire, I'm not letting you out of my sight. I will escort you back to your hostel and let Matron deal with you." With her back ramrod-straight, Mrs. Nash led the pair in the direction of Timber Town and the huts. Again the truck's engine roared to life, and the farmer drove the remaining half mile to the Bairds' cottage.

After thanking his neighbor, Mr. Baird hobbled on his cane toward the front door. Rose struggled to keep pace while his teary-eyed daughter stormed ahead of them both.

Stumbling along beside him, Rose said, "Mr. Baird . . . so sorry to . . . let you down."

His sober face turned to her. "'Tis no fault on your part, Miss Lockhart." He reached to gently pat her on the shoulder. "You just concentrate on getting well."

She nodded into her handkerchief, grateful for his pardon, though she had yet to face Hannah's mother.

Arriving inside, they found Mrs. Baird in the parlor. She was clad in her nightclothes and holding her crying daughter. Her sad gaze sought out Rose. "Och, Miss Lockhart . . ."

Rose paused in front of her, intending to make her apologies. But a gentle nudge from Mr. Baird sent her off in the direction of her room. "Time enough to sort this tomorrow, lass. You go and get your rest."

Exhausted, her stomach roiling, Rose gladly obeyed. Once she'd reached her room, she peeled out of her clothes, dropping them where they lay before she pulled on her nightdress and collapsed onto the bed. Grabbing for the plaid coverlet, she wrapped herself in the soft wool, vaguely aware when Winston jumped up to lie down beside her. She cuddled him while her eyes drifted closed, and her last thought was gratitude—that God had given man Sundays off.

Because she had no intention of leaving her bed all day.

8

*A*lex bounced the beam of his flashlight from his watch to the curtained window of the cottage. He'd been surprised at Stuart's offer to drive him the two and a half hours into Gretna, but since his discharge papers were complete, he'd agreed.

He glanced back down the long drive toward the road where Stuart dropped him off. The man insisted he would stay at the Gretna Hotel before returning to the base in the morning.

Alex focused his light on the front porch and the top sill where Da always kept a key. His family would be asleep. The perfect time to steal inside.

Is that because you dinna want to wake them at this late hour . . . or because you can put off having to face them? He remembered the cadets in the mess hall at supper, surrounding him, hanging on his every word as if he were some legend and not an ordinary man.

If they could see you now, lad. He scowled and reached above the sill for the hidden key. Silently he unlocked and opened the door, then switched off the flashlight, grabbing up his valise. He'd slip into his room tonight and surprise them all at breakfast.

Moving stealthily through the house, he paused at Fergus and James's room, a set of bunk beds along the far wall. As his eyes adjusted to the shadows, he could make out their two small shapes beneath the blankets, snoring softly.

He turned toward the empty single bed along the opposite wall—Ian's bed—and a familiar ache seized him. Quickly, he moved down the hall, passing his sister's room and her steady breathing within. His pulse quickened as he imagined greeting them all in a few hours to announce he was home to stay after so many years of war. And he'd shoulder his burden each time he gazed into their faces.

With his parents' room at the other end of the cottage, he relaxed as he reached his own bedroom door. His exhaustion had returned, and it seemed impossible that seventy-two hours ago he'd been on a beach in Biarritz, France, a decorated RAF captain and flight commander.

Now he stood in his childhood home, a civilian ready to take on a saboteur who threatened to kill thousands. Without a doubt, the past several hours had changed his life.

Noiselessly he turned the knob, entering the room where he'd grown up during his boyhood years. As he softly closed the door behind him, he caught a faint whiff of lavender.

Maw must have dusted. Smiling, he crossed the floor toward the nightstand lamp when a low growl coming from the bed brought him up short. A dog?

Dropping his valise, he switched on his flashlight—and barely ducked in time to avoid the nine-iron flying toward his head.

"Get out, you thief!"

What the . . . ? He'd barely recovered his balance when the low growl turned into loud, excited barking.

"I said get out . . . or I'll scream!"

Reaching for the bedside lamp, Alex flipped it on and stared at the woman in white, kneeling on top of his blankets. She still held his golf club poised above her head.

"I dinna think screaming is necessary," he shouted, glaring at the white ball of fur on his bed. "Wheesht, you wee mutt, or you'll wake my whole family!"

"Hush, Winston!"

Keeping her grip on the club, she scooped up the dog and held it to her chest. The barking stopped, but the little white beastie bared its teeth at Alex.

He glowered at them both. "Who are you, and why are you here?"

"You must be Alex."

Despite her irascible tone, she blushed like a field of red poppies. She seemed to him to be vulnerable somehow, her angular face emphasizing the bruised half-moons beneath large blue eyes, while her long dark braid had unraveled, adding to her tousled appearance.

"Captain Alex Baird." He crossed his arms against his chest. "Now answer *my* question."

She tossed her head. "This happens to be *my* room now, and you are trespassing."

"That bed is mine, woman, and so is the club you tried to bash over my head!"

Immediately she dropped the nine-iron onto the bed. Leaning back on her heels, she emitted a soft groan and grimaced as though in pain while she clutched the dog. "For your information, I am renting the room from your parents." Chin raised, she reached to swipe away a drooping lock of hair from her eyes. "I would appreciate you leaving and closing the door behind you. I must . . . make myself presentable."

That could take some time. Despite his annoyance, he held his tongue. Instead he asked, "Why would you be renting my room—?"

"Alex?"

His maw had opened the door. "Son!" she cried, flying at him in her night-robe while tears streamed down her cheeks. His chest tightened as he enfolded her in his arms, his earlier fears melting. It had been too long since he'd been home.

She finally pulled back to look at him as if she might find something wrong. "We didna get word ye were coming. Why would ye not tell us?"

"A last-minute decision." He smiled gently. "I'd planned to steal in quietly and surprise you in the morning." He glanced at the woman on the bed. "It looks as if I'm the one who got the surprise."

"Och, where are my manners? Ye've not met our new boarder, Miss Lockhart. She works at the factory with yer sister." She glanced toward the bedraggled woman on the bed. "This is my son, Alex. He is a captain in the RAF and has been fighting in France." She turned to him, pride in her voice. "And now he's home!"

Alex forced a smile for his maw. So this crazed woman . . . Miss Lockhart . . . had been telling the truth, after all. Why did his parents need a boarder?

He started to ask Maw before she nudged him toward the door.

"Come, lad, let's leave poor Miss Lockhart to get her rest. We can talk in the morning. Meanwhile, ye'll be comfortable enough sleeping in with Fergus and James."

Back in the hall, she led him to his brothers' room. "The bed's all made so ye can slip inside and get some sleep," she whispered and reached for his hand. "'Tis so braw having ye home, Alex."

He swallowed past the knot in his throat and gently squeezed her fingers. "I'm glad to be here, Maw." *In more ways than one.* "Now, I'll be fine. You go back to bed."

Her soft chuckle reached his ears. "I canna think how I'll ever manage to sleep."

"Well, you can try anyway." He leaned and touched his lips to her warm cheek, then waited until she'd gone. Standing at the door to his brothers' room, he stared into the shadows at Ian's empty bed. Then he stowed his valise on the coverlet and made his way back to the parlor. Grabbing the quilt from his da's chair, he stretched out on the couch.

There were some things he still wasna ready to face.

❧⤙⤚⦿❧⤙⤚⦾

"Poke him and see if he's awake."

"No, ye do it. If he's not awake, he might get mad."

"Fraidy-cat. I dare ye."

"Yer a fraidy-cat, Fergus."

Awakened by the childish whispering above him, Alex pretended to sleep as he lay a moment under the blanket, holding back a smile. Suddenly with a loud roar, he threw off the quilt and vaulted from the couch, grabbing up both brothers in their nightclothes. "Who dares to awaken the great lion in his den at this early hour?"

Squealing their laughter, they clung to him as he swung them around in a circle and then plopped with them down onto the cushions, one lad on either side.

Fergus looked up at him, dark eyes shining. "We heard Maw tell Da ye were here, Alex. When did ye get home?"

He pulled them into a huddle and spoke in a low voice, "I stole into the house during the night, silent as the ghost that hovers over Blood Pond on Mr. Greene's farm." He leaned back against the couch and grinned at them. "And you both slept like wee bairns the whole time." He turned to James, then Fergus. "Have you lads been minding yourselves?"

"Aye!" they said in unison, and James wedged a small hand behind Alex's back before reaching to hug him tightly at the waist. "How long will ye stay this time, Alex?"

What should he say? Gazing down at the tousled reddish-blond head of his youngest brother, he reached to brush back a few tendrils. "How long would you like me to stay?"

"Forever!" cried Fergus, and James tightened his hold.

Alex's chest constricted as he slung an arm around Fergus, drawing him close. "Forever's a long time, lads," he said. "But I can stay a lot longer than I did the last time. How would that be?"

Fergus nodded, his eyes bright. "Are ye still flying planes?"

"Aye, and one day I'll take you both up in the air to soar the skies."

James looked up. "But . . . we willna die, will we, Alex?"

Alex smiled at his brother, his throat as tight as his chest. "No, laddie, we'll go up after the war." He changed the subject. "When did you two get so braw, anyway? I swear you've both grown since I saw you last."

Fergus nodded. "Maw says if we want to be tall as ye, we must eat our greens."

"Maw's right, and you should listen to her."

"Except when we're feeding the dog," James confessed. "Winston likes our peas at supper."

Alex's humor faded, recalling the noisy ball of fur baring its teeth at him last night. "You shouldna be feeding that animal from the table—"

"Hannah, I'll hear no more excuses! You showed poor judgment last night, and your maw and I have decided your punishment."

The sound of his da's angry voice from the kitchen made Alex pause. Fergus looked at him. "I think Da's mad at Hannah. Did she do something bad?"

"You lads never mind. Go and get dressed. Maw will be cooking us a fine breakfast soon. Quick with you now, go!" Both boys bounced off the couch and raced toward their room.

"B-but, Da, my friends, they swore they were taking me to meet Miss Lockhart! I didna ken it was a trick until I was inside the public house and they gave me a drink!"

His sister . . . drinking in a pub? Alex leaned forward, straining to listen.

"Did Miss Lockhart tell you to meet her there?"

"N-no . . ."

"And once you realized it was a trick, you didna leave as you should?"

"I did try, I swear it! And when I was about to give the drink back, the policewoman . . . she came up to me and demanded to know my age. I couldna lie to her!"

Alex heard Da's heavy sigh as he continued.

"Surely you ken our circumstances, lass. I had to pay for the petrol in Mr. Greene's truck to come and get you in Carlisle. And Miss Lockhart. Och, the shame of it!"

A long pause ensued before his da passed sentence.

"Your maw and I willna trust you again anytime soon. You must stay here in town so we can keep an eye on you."

There was a loud scrape of a chair, followed by his sister's teary voice.

"It wasna my fault! And I have an important job at the factory now and I earn a good wage, so how can you still treat me like a bairn? 'Tis so unfair!"

Hannah burst from the kitchen, eyes red from crying. Rushing through the parlor, she stormed toward the entryway, oblivious to Alex as she slammed the front door in her wake.

He stared after her. What the deuce was going on?

As he turned back toward the kitchen, he saw Da standing in the doorway. Tension and weariness were etched in his face before he saw Alex and smiled warmly. "Good morning, son. Maw said you'd arrived in the wee hours. I'm happy to see you home."

As he ambled toward the couch with the help of a cane, Alex fought to mask his shock. His da looked years aulder and so frail. Quickly he stood and closed the distance between them, gentle with his embrace. "Da? What's happened to you?"

"Let's sit, Alex." Da hobbled over to his favorite chair while Alex sat on the couch.

"'Twas a clumsy accident. I was at the rail yard to oversee the off-loading of a new shipment of ties for the track. Someone called to me, and I shouldna have turned at that moment, because the stack shifted and a tie came loose. Knocked me right to the ground." He shook his head. "I injured my back and I've been laid up since winter."

Winter? Why wasna he told? "Maw wrote to me, but she never said—"

"Because I asked her not to tell you." Once more Da's tone held a steel edge, but then his expression eased. "You had enough on your mind in France just staying alive. I didna want you to fash about us. We've done well enough. These days I help Fergus and James with their schooling, and your maw takes in mending from the factory workers. Hannah's job earns a fair wage, and up until now anyway 'tis helped."

Alex gazed at the man who had raised him by himself for a time after Alex's real maw died. An experienced yardman for the Caledonian Railway, Da had worked for the railroad from the time Alex wore nappies. But now . . .

He was a shadow of his former self. "What about work? Can you go back?"

Da bent his head, revealing a thinning shock of silver that hadna been there the last time Alex was home. "My job at the railroad . . . I canna sit or stand for very long, so I had to give it up." He lifted his gaze. "I do receive a small pension."

But not nearly enough. Alex worked to smother his ire. How could his parents keep from him the fact they were struggling? He'd been sending home a portion of his pay over the years, but had he kenned the situation he would have done more. "That's why you took in a boarder."

"Aye." Da straightened. "And now with your sister's trouble, 'tis a blessing Miss Lockhart is here."

"I heard you and Hannah in the kitchen." He leaned to rest his hands on his knees. "What was Miss Lockhart doing in Carlisle with Hannah and her friends?"

"We asked her to chaperone your sister to the cinema." Da reached up and tunneled his fingers through the sparse thatch of hair. "Hannah's been restless since last year, and especially now that she's auld enough to work inside the factory instead of cleaning huts. It was a big step up for her and with a better job and better pay . . . well, you heard her. She thinks it makes her all grown up now."

"How is Miss Lockhart qualified to act as a chaperone?" Again he envisioned the wild woman who nearly thrashed him with his golf club last night—and her noisy cur. "She obviously failed in her duty, and now the consequences will affect you all."

"I did not shirk my responsibilities, Captain Baird."

Alex turned to find Miss Lockhart standing at the arch between the hall and parlor. Instead of her nightclothes, she now wore a wrinkled pink jacket and skirt, but the pale features and dark bruises beneath her eyes remained.

"There were . . . circumstances beyond my control," she said primly. "The two young women your sister calls friends tainted my tea with a compound, which left me . . . indisposed." Again she thrust her chin at him. "I was unable to return to my seat in the theater, otherwise I would have discovered Hannah's absence."

Her prickly nature irritated him further. "Maybe you're a naïve young woman yourself, Miss Lockhart. You let three young lassies get the best of you. Not what I'd call a good candidate for a chaperone—"

"Alex." Da cautioned him with a look. "You dinna ken the circumstances last night. Miss Lockhart was quite ill."

"Your father is right."

She started to approach them, and Alex noted her measured steps were a bit unsteady. "What was this compound in your tea?"

She paused beside the couch, then moved toward the padded chair next to his da. Once seated, she raised her bruised eyes to him. "If you must know, it was ipecac."

He coughed to cover his amusement. A few months ago, some of the lads in his squadron pulled the same trick on a fellow pilot about to go on furlough for the weekend.

"And contrary to what you may think, I am not naïve." She tipped her head back, trying to look down at him. "In fact, I was recently hired as a Women's Welfare shift supervisor at HM Factory Gretna, and I believe I am doing a good job."

He smiled his sarcasm. "Actions speak louder than words, Miss Lockhart."

"Indeed, Captain Baird." Her color rose. "But words are powerful too, and yours seem to indicate a man who enjoys finding fault in others *and* you judge based on your own assumptions. Neither trait being a reflection on your wonderful parents, of course."

She smiled toward his da, and Alex stiffened. He opened his mouth to deliver his next salvo, when Da's glance pierced him.

Alex kenned the look and leaned back against the couch. Perhaps he *was* being unfair in his conclusion without getting all the facts. And the effects of ipecac had likely made her retch for hours.

He let out a sigh. In truth, he was more angered at coming home to find his family in such dire circumstances that they had found it necessary to take in a perfect stranger to live *in his room* and act as his sister's chaperone—with disastrous results.

And it didna change the fact Miss Lockhart *was* naïve. He kept that thought to himself, however. "You said you recently hired on at HM Factory Gretna?"

"That is correct."

"And how many workers do you supervise?"

"I have quite a few young women in my care, including your sister."

"And her two friends . . . ?"

She looked away. "Yes."

"Well, as a flight commander for two years, I can speak from experience. You're in for some troubles ahead, make no mistake."

9

The arrogant man! Rose started to frown in displeasure, then closed her eyes at the incessant pounding in her head. Why had she decided to leave her bed this morning? Surely not to subject herself to Captain Baird's inquisition and assumptions!

Her stomach gurgled and she pressed a hand to her middle, longing to retreat to her room. *His* room, she qualified, gritting her teeth. This morning she'd crept out in the small hours to find him fast asleep on the couch. Her guilt at taking his room would have prevailed if not for her pride now, and she determined to show him she would not crawl away like some chastened schoolgirl.

He had some nerve telling her she was doomed to failure, though his words made her pulse jump. She simply could not fail. The stakes were too high.

"Och, 'tis good to see yer all up and about."

Mrs. Baird appeared from the hall clad in her white apron. "And Alex, ye've had a chance to visit with Da and to better acquaint yerself with our Miss Lockhart." She beamed, oblivious to the silent hostility. "I'll have breakfast out in a few minutes. Has anyone seen Hannah?"

"I'll help you, Mrs. Baird." Eager to escape her tormentor, Rose stood and then grabbed for the arm of the chair as another wave of the lingering nausea passed.

"Lass?" Mr. Baird eyed her with concern.

"I'm all right." She gave him another smile, then darted a backward glance at his son as she headed toward the kitchen.

Mrs. Baird put her in charge of making porridge, a task she'd not performed since she was a girl living at home with her parents.

"How are ye feeling this morning, Miss Lockhart?"

Rose paused in stirring the oat mixture. "Better, thank you. I would appreciate an aspirin if you have one to spare."

"Of course!" Mrs. Baird reached into a cupboard and retrieved a bottle of white pills. She handed them to Rose, who thanked her and took a tablet with a glass of water.

"Mrs. Baird, I'm . . . very sorry about last night." She held out the aspirin bottle. "I broke my promise to you." She looked down, averting her gaze. Captain Baird had been right about her gullibility, especially with Gladys and Colleen. She'd known before leaving the house last night those two might be trouble, but still thought she could manage them. Tilly certainly would have kept them in hand.

"'Tis not yer fault, lass." Mrs. Baird clasped her hand along with the bottle. "I'm just grateful that ye both are home safely." She returned the aspirin to the cupboard. "Mr. Baird tells me Mrs. Nash from the factory was waiting at the station when ye returned?"

"Yes." Rose had the vague memory of her employer's presence last night.

"Aye, well, I suppose she wasna happy with any of them." Mrs. Baird turned to her, worry in her eyes. "It might even cost Hannah her job."

Remorse intensified Rose's headache. Already the Bairds had financial difficulties, and because she'd allowed herself to be duped by two teens, their daughter could get the sack and lose much-needed income for the family. "I cannot make any promises, Mrs. Baird. But I *shall* speak with Mrs. Nash tomorrow."

A relieved smile lit her face. "Bless you."

Because it was Sunday, the Baird family readied for church after breakfast. Since the food appeased Rose's head, and Mrs. Baird's mint tea soothed her stomach, she accepted their invitation to join them.

The family arrived at the church a few minutes early. "We usually stop at the headstone and say a prayer for Ian before we go inside." Mrs. Baird gazed at her eldest son.

Rose caught the faint color in his rugged face. "You go ahead, Maw. 'Tis getting close to time, and I want to save our seats."

He strode off into the church while Mrs. Baird looked after him, fresh grief in her eyes.

"I'll come with you and the family, Mrs. Baird, if that would be all right?"

She smiled. "Of course, lamb. 'Tis this way." They went into the churchyard and stood before the stone slab erected in Ian Baird's memory. While all heads bowed as Mr. Baird said a few words, Rose couldn't help but wonder why the captain had refused to join his family.

Once they went inside, she found herself squeezed into a front pew between Hannah and her older brother. Rose glanced at the spacious surroundings and recognized a few faces from the factory. The congregation consisted of mostly women and children, as the men were likely still in the war or dead.

She tried to relax in the seat despite her nearness to Captain Baird. Since feeling more like herself, she'd taken the time to notice his physique. He was quite tall and lean, and his muscled arms and broad shoulders suggested years of hard work. He smelled faintly of the leather she recognized from his room, along with a spicy scent; and with him seated so close, his body radiated heat like a furnace.

How long did he plan to be in Gretna? And would he continue to hold a grudge against her for Hannah's mishap? She should probably apologize, yet his accusations still stung.

As the preacher climbed toward the pulpit to speak, Rose recalled her boarding school days, when Sunday service was a requirement of all the girls. Many times, however, she'd visited the chapel on her own with only God to dry her tears and listen to her misery at being alone in a new and uninviting place. She'd missed those comforting hours. For unlike her parents, bless them, who had nurtured her spiritual upbringing, once she and her brothers became wards of her aunt and uncle, there was no more talk of church or of God, just the rules Uncle Ridley set down for their behavior.

Leaning forward, she anticipated the preacher's sermon. Would he speak about forgiveness? If so, then she would make the effort to amend her attitude toward Captain Baird, if not for herself, then at least for the sake of keeping harmony within his family.

"Nothing remains hidden from God's all-seeing eye!"

Rose shot up straight in her seat at the preacher's words. When he continued to expound on the perils of lying, he seemed to look right at her. She plucked at the tips of her gloves and darted a quick glance at Captain Baird, who appeared unfazed by the admonitions. Her gaze then swept across the entire congregation, and she noticed they remained rapt and motionless.

Was the preacher directing the message at her? *Oh, Lord, what are you trying to tell me?*

⋯⟶ ❧ ☙ ⟵⋯

Later at the house, Rose continued to flog herself with the preacher's words as she sat with the Baird family out on the back porch. *She* knew that *God* knew what she'd done nearly a week ago, but she didn't believe He blamed her for her actions. In fact, it seemed preordained that she be given this second chance at life, even though at a terrible cost to her dearest friend.

She leaned back against the wicker seat. Tilly was gone now, and Rose could not bring her back. She must live out her friend's dream, and at the same time save her brothers from Uncle Ridley's unscrupulous influence.

"Looks like the lads are getting as much exercise as your dog, Miss Lockhart."

Mr. Baird had made the remark, and she turned to find him smiling as he indicated with his pipe the scene playing out in the grassy yard.

The July day was sunny yet cool, and Fergus and James were chasing after Winston, who was much faster than both boys and possessed in his mouth the ball Mrs. Baird fashioned from tying two ends of a wool-stuffed stocking together. "Winston seems to be enjoying himself. I imagine all three will be exhausted by tonight."

"Aye. The lads willna have the energy to chatter away at nonsense until the wee hours." Mr. Baird glanced at his oldest son. "You'll get a peaceful night's rest, Alex, if that's the case."

Rose swiveled her attention to Captain Baird, who stretched out lazily in the wicker chair beside his father. His chestnut hair, cut short in military fashion, shone coppery in the sun.

He swung around toward his father, the green eyes pausing on her. "'Tis my hope too, Da. Those two are like magpies at dawn."

Rose thought the comment odd, as she'd seen him asleep on the couch last night. Mr. Baird smiled, however, and taking a puff on his pipe he turned his attention to his daughter.

Hannah sat off by herself on an old stump, watching her brothers at play. Alex angled his head in that direction. "My sister's still not talking?"

"I think she's waiting to know her fate tomorrow."

As if on cue, both men turned to Rose. Mr. Baird's face was creased in concern while his son's stretched taut with distrust. She in turn averted her eyes to the young girl on the stump and silently renewed her vow to speak with Mrs. Nash about Hannah first thing in the morning.

"Refreshments when yer ready. Our Sunday treat." Mrs. Baird appeared at the back door bearing a tray of jam biscuits and lemonade. Setting the fare on the wooden table, she resumed her seat on the other side of her husband and picked up the pair of men's trousers she'd been mending.

The couple smiled as they looked on at their youngest sons. Fergus had finally managed to get close enough to grab for the stocking in Winston's mouth, but the little dog dodged him at the last moment and the boy landed empty-handed in the grass.

His parents chuckled, and even Captain Baird smiled at their antics. Meanwhile, her little dog gripped the stocking ball in his teeth and wagged his stubby tail while watching James tackle his felled brother. The two boys giggled as they tussled on the ground.

Once again their laughter made her yearn for her own little family, and the merry sounds triggered in Rose another fond memory—Douglas and Samuel carousing in the snow one Christmas Eve in Leicester. She'd watched them play leapfrog with each other until both fell together into a laughing heap, much like these boys now. Such precious memories . . .

"Where are you from, Miss Lockhart? You sound English."

She turned to the captain and found him staring at her. "I . . . actually, I was born and raised in Glasgow—"

"Miss Lockhart's an orphan." From her place on the stump, Hannah turned to join in their conversation. "Her parents died in a bus accident when she was just fourteen."

"Aye, poor lamb." Mrs. Baird paused in her sewing to glance at her eldest son. "And she lost a brother as well."

"He was a lad and died before her parents did." Hannah left the stump to approach and take a chair. "How did he die, Miss Lockhart?"

"Hannah, dear! Mind yer manners." Mrs. Baird's tone held mild censure. "If Miss Lockhart wishes to share her personal life with us, let it be by her choice." She turned to Rose and smiled. "Only if ye'd like to, dear."

With all eyes upon her, Rose moistened her lips. "He . . . it was unexpected." She frowned, her mind racing to keep her stories straight. What a mess of things she'd made!

Her gaze darted back to Captain Baird, his attention still fixed on her. She couldn't afford any more mistakes. One misstep would send her packing, and it could mean going back to Leicester.

She shuddered to think of what Julien might have in store for her punishment. "I . . . I apologize." Pulling her attention from the piercing green eyes, she turned to Mrs. Baird. "I realize it was a long time ago, but my brother . . . I still find it painful . . ."

"Of course ye do, and we'll speak no more about it." Mrs. Baird left her chair and came to give Rose's shoulders an affectionate squeeze. Then she set to work passing out the refreshments, and Rose gratefully accepted the glass of lemonade and a biscuit.

"I imagine you'll remain here in Gretna for some time, Miss Lockhart?"

Rose had started to take a sip of her drink when she paused at the captain's question. "I plan on it, yes. And you?"

Instead of the cynical retort she'd expected, he looked at his parents and his sister. "I'll be staying as well."

"What!" Mrs. Baird nearly dropped the refreshment tray before setting it down.

Mr. Baird held his pipe to his chest, staring at his son in bemused delight. "You ken that I'm happy beyond words, lad. But . . . is the war over?"

"For me, aye." He hesitated. "The RAF gave me a medical discharge."

"You're unwell?" Mr. Baird scrutinized him.

"'Tis all right, Da. Just battle fatigue. Nothing that a good long rest willna cure."

"But how do you feel, son?" Mrs. Baird searched his face with a worried look.

"I'm fine, Maw, a few headaches now and then." He smiled at her. "And since I'll be home for some time, I thought I'd see about getting work at the munitions factory. I served as an airplane mechanic during the first year of the war, so maybe they can use someone to keep the machinery running smoothly."

"God be praised, Alex, 'tis the best news I've had in a long time!" Mrs. Baird rushed to her son and hugged him while Hannah shrieked her joy and vaulted from her seat to join them.

"Miss Lockhart, did you hear? My brother will be working with us at the factory. Is that not grand?"

Rose managed a smile. "Yes, grand indeed." Then she saw Mr. Baird's eyes glisten as he watched his family embrace, and she chided her lack of enthusiasm. Captain Baird could be irritating, but with the grief his family had already suffered in losing one son to the war, this was the best news for them all.

Love flowed between them like water—mother and son, then daughter and father, and soon Fergus and James, who had sensed good news and came rushing up from the lawn to clasp their small hands around the waists of their sister and mother.

So much affection. Rose averted her hungry gaze, the ache in her heart palpable. In six years' time, she'd shared only a handful of hugs and kisses during the holidays with her younger brothers. And poor Aunt Delia, too afraid of her husband to show more than an occasional brush of her hand.

It hadn't been nearly enough. And now *she* had become the intruder here, and with their son home, he would certainly wish to have his old room back. That meant searching out a new living arrangement.

Rose stared out at the yard. Winston stood poised, observing the activity on the porch. His tail wagged uncertainly while his mouth still held the stocking.

The pain in her chest rose to her throat. She must surrender the dog if she was to find quarters with another supervisor or stay temporarily in the hostels.

"Miss Lockhart, would ye like another?"

Rose snapped her head around. Mrs. Baird now stood beside her, holding the plate of jam biscuits. Hannah had retaken her seat on the porch while the two small boys stood beside the table, gulping down glasses of the lemonade. "Yes, thank you."

Taking a biscuit from the tray, she looked up at the kind woman. "I wonder if you and Mr. Baird would consider taking over Winston's care when I leave?"

"What are ye speaking of, lass?"

"Since Captain Baird . . . your son, will remain in Gretna, he'll want his bedroom. I shall find another place to rent."

"Nonsense! We're glad to have ye with us, lass. Besides that, we promised a full month's room and board, and so ye shall have it. Alex, yer happy to sleep in with the lads for now, aye?"

"Aye, Maw."

He seemed hardly keen on the idea, and her memory flew back to his slumbering on the couch. She said nothing, however. Better to make peace with him, especially if they were to be in the same company for the next month. "Thank you, Captain."

Mrs. Baird leaned in and added in a low voice, "And we appreciate ye speaking on Hannah's behalf tomorrow."

The girl must have heard her mother; Hannah's glowing face dulled as she rose quietly from her chair and took up her earlier perch on the stump. Rose sympathized with her, and with the family. She *would* get on her knees and beg Mrs. Nash if that was what it took to save the girl's job.

Turning back to those on the porch, her gaze collided with the captain's look of condemnation, and guilt warred with her dislike of him.

Of course he still blamed her. In his mind, *she* was responsible for letting herself be drugged by those brash girls and left to suffer in the cinema's lounge. But his sister still had much to learn about being accountable for her actions, including her choice of friends.

She arched her back, giving him equal censure. Was a truce between them even possible?

He barely nodded, as though taking up the challenge, while a smirk played along his lips.

Rose fought against her anger, an emotion she'd learned to control over the past six years. Truce or not, for the next month she *must* persevere despite his prejudice, and if he got a job at the factory tomorrow, it would mean suffering each other's company day and night.

10

His hunt for Rhymer had begun.

Alex stood with clipboard in hand the following day, observing two forklift operators carefully maneuver the five-hundred-pound bales of cotton inside the factory stores.

He'd accompanied his sister and Miss Lockhart into Moorside that morning, having no idea that when he applied for the job as a machinist mechanic, he'd instead receive a position allowing him full access to the site and the means to search for Kahverengi's agent.

It was Weatherford's doing, of course; especially when the interviewer introduced himself as Mr. Arthur Timbrell, site superintendent and Alex's contact at the factory.

Timbrell barely glanced at his application before assigning him the job of inspector for Site Three, where highly explosive nitroglycerine and nitrocotton were produced to make cordite. It made sense that Rhymer would choose this area to create his destruction. Alex was pleased that his new post gave him the flexibility to find his quarry, *and* that his sister worked in the same complex so he could do all in his power to keep her safe.

That is, if Hannah still had a job.

The lunch whistle blew, and Alex signaled a halt to the forklift drivers. "Fine job," he called to them once they'd killed their engines. "Have your dinner and we'll finish up when you return."

Two young lassies dismounted, each touching the brim of her bonnet to him before walking toward the ladies' canteen.

He should probably do the same. Workers gathered at lunchtime would be his best opportunity to scan faces for possible saboteurs without arousing suspicion. His stomach rumbled loudly then, and determined, he started off in the opposite direction toward the men's canteen.

"Alex!"

Pausing, Alex turned as his sister waved to him.

"You'll never guess!" she said, rushing forward, her eyes shining. "Miss Lockhart spoke to Mrs. Nash early this morning, and we all get to keep our jobs!"

"That's good to hear, lass." Admittedly, he was surprised—and pleased—with Miss Lockhart's sense of justice.

"And now you are working in the same building with us, aye?"

"I'm one of the inspectors for this site."

"Well, that means I'll get to spend time with you here as well as at home!"

He grinned. "So you willna tire of seeing this auld face every day?"

"Never." Her young features sobered. "You've been away far too long for that to happen, dear brother." She glanced behind her. "I've just an hour, and Maw said if everything got sorted, I could stay and eat dinner with the other girls today." She leaned up to give him a peck on the cheek. "I'll see you after."

Just like a butterfly. Alex smiled as she flew off to join her friends. No doubt Miss Lockhart was already in the canteen, being much celebrated by her workers for saving their jobs.

He shook his head and continued on toward the men's canteen. In his view, she was still somewhat gullible, but she'd made his sister very happy.

❖⤙❦⤚❖

Sand . . .

Rose sat in the ladies' canteen with a mouthful of gritty sandwich. Looking wildly about for a place to get rid of the food, she glanced down the long table toward Mrs. Nash, speaking with another of the Welfare supervisors, and seeing they were engaged in conversation, she pressed her napkin to her lips and pretended to cough, spitting out the fouled morsel.

She grabbed up her glass of water, taking several gulps, but the granules still crunched between her teeth. A soft moan escaped her as she peered into her lunch bucket. The rest of her food— the fresh raspberries and wedge of Dunlap cheese Mrs. Baird had packed for her—was coated in sand as well.

Heat flooded her face as she glared toward the next table, where Hannah and most of her co-workers sat eating and chattering. It made sense now why Gladys and Colleen stole glances her way, and every so often leaned in to whisper to one another, then laugh behind their hands.

Gripping the glass of water, she took another cleansing drink. Not only was their prank completely inappropriate but it also ended with a shameful waste of food. She hadn't yet received her wages and relied completely on the struggling Baird family to provide all her meals.

Did the two girls have no shame?

Rose began to regret having asked for their pardon. This morning, she'd begged Mrs. Nash to let all three girls keep their jobs. Her supervisor had agreed but insisted each pay a hefty fine for the ill-treatment Miss Lockhart received in Carlisle.

Only young Hannah had shown remorse for Saturday night, and she'd been grateful to Rose for saving her position. The other two, still laughing together over this latest insult, seemed to think it was a game of revenge.

The plea for their mercy had stemmed from her desire to protect Hannah from appearing favored, as Miss Lockhart was living in the Baird home. Her own years at boarding school as Sir Cutler's "poor Scots relation" taught her the painful lesson of being an outcast among her peers.

She'd also hoped that by giving the girls a second chance, they might change their ways.

Still crunching the grit between her teeth, she replaced the lid on her lunch bucket. Gladys and Colleen had obviously mistaken her kindness for weakness.

She closed her eyes. If Tilly were here, she'd likely exact her revenge on the two troublemakers to ensure they behaved themselves. But Rose knew her own leadership skills were sorely lacking. Unlike her dear departed friend, she was several years younger and not nearly as hardened by life.

Her stomach growled then, and she set the offensive lunch bucket on the floor beside her. She might not be twenty-six years old or have Tilly's background, but she could learn to be tough, couldn't she? And now that Gladys and Colleen had taken their petty revenge for the fines, hopefully life at the factory would resettle and the girls return their focus to working instead of causing trouble.

11

So much for wishful thinking.

Rose sat at supper with the Bairds the following evening, pushing her food around her plate with her fork. Not only was she weary after the long twelve-hour day, but she also felt frustrated at once again being the target for revenge.

You are so naïve, Rose. She stabbed at the piece of cooked turnip. Hadn't Captain Baird warned her she would have more trouble? No doubt the man would crow if he knew the truth.

Beneath the table she wriggled her toes inside her greasy stockings—a hurtful reminder of the machine oil *someone* had poured into her rubber work boots that morning before she'd arrived at work.

"So how do ye fancy yer new job as site inspector, son?" Mr. Baird had asked the question, his dark eyes shining as he gazed at the captain. "Quite a bit more responsibility than what you'd imagined when you hired on yesterday?"

Rose half listened while the captain explained to his parents his work duties at the factory. She'd noticed that since his return, no one had broached the subject of the war in France or his experiences there, likely to avoid resurrecting any painful memories, especially about the son they had lost.

She was still curious about Sunday and the captain's reluctance to visit his brother's gravestone at the church. And the fact he continued to sleep on the couch at night instead of the bed in Fergus and James's room. Obviously, he too had been greatly affected by his brother's death.

And what of your own brothers? Rose stared blindly at the food on her plate. According to her obituary last week, the quiet memorial service was held yesterday in Leicester. How were Douglas and Samuel coping with her death? Were they still at the estate or back at school? Or worse—had her uncle made plans to send them off to some orphanage overseas?

A knot settled in her chest. Just a few more days, once it was safe to call, and she'd find a way to contact the school.

"What is your opinion of the scheme, Miss Lockhart?"

Wrenched from her silent misery, she turned to the captain, blinking. Scheme . . . had the topic of conversation shifted? "Pardon?"

"The official Rationing Order to be signed this month."

"Oh . . . yes, that." According to the newspaper, ration cards were soon to be issued to each household in Britain. "Well, we have already been rationing unofficially for some time, so I believe the new law will ensure fairness. Everyone should receive the same quantities of food at the same cost, rather than this food profiteering only the wealthy can afford."

"Aye, well said, Miss Lockhart." He tipped his head to her, his green eyes warm.

Inexplicably pleased by his approval, she added, "Since I am renting from your parents, I plan to apply for my own rations card and contribute to the family while I am here."

"How kind of you, lass." Mr. Baird beamed. "We can always use extra food with these growing lads."

"Most generous, Miss Lockhart." Once more the captain nodded his approval before his gaze narrowed. "You seem a bit preoccupied tonight. Anything happen at work?"

Rose shook her head, offering a weak smile as her toes again squirmed inside the greasy stockings. "Just tired after a long day."

A half-truth was better than a lie, wasn't it? And he could hardly prove her wrong since she'd refused to give satisfaction to the alleged troublemakers at work by making an issue of it. Instead, she'd pretended all was well today while she walked around in the squishy boots.

Her feet were wrinkled as prunes.

"I wondered why ye only picked at yer food." Mrs. Baird's eyes held concern. "A good night's rest will make ye fit and ready to face another day."

"I am certain you are right." Rose prayed more than believed that tomorrow would dawn without some new prank waiting for her. "Thank you for supper, Mrs. Baird. Even with rationing, you make such wonderful meals, and I am only sorry to be more tired than hungry tonight."

She rose then, ignoring the captain's steady gaze. "If you will excuse me, I've laundry chores before bed." She glanced at Mrs. Baird. "May I heat water in the kitchen?"

"Aye, the kettle's on the stove, though I'm happy to wash yer clothes if you like."

"No," she said, unwilling to explain the greasy stockings. "Thank you, but I can see to the task myself." Heat flushed her face, and Mrs. Baird made an "ah" sound. Clearly, she assumed Rose meant undergarments—which was fine, so long as there was no more probing into this latest humiliation she'd suffered.

Minutes later, Rose took the kettle of hot water to her room. She grabbed the bar of Tilly's lavender soap, and after making a sudsy bath in the washstand basin she peeled out of her shoes and greasy stockings, then washed her feet—they were indeed like prunes—before putting the stockings to soak in the soapy water.

She eyed herself in the mirror. "You tried doing right by those girls yesterday, but what good did it serve?" she asked herself. "Now they think you're a namby-pamby."

But how was she to manage them without going to Mrs. Nash? Rose could ill afford to have her supervisor think her unfit for the task. It might cost her the job and destroy her plans for her and the boys' future.

"Where's your courage, Rose?" She frowned in the mirror. "As long as you continue to be weak, the bullying will not stop." Hadn't she learned that from Julien and her uncle?

Heartbreaking sobs from the next room suddenly drew her attention. Rose put her ear to the wall. *Hannah?*

The pitiful wails continued, and she glanced at her bare feet, then tiptoed from her room down to the next door. She knocked softly. "Hannah dear, are you all right?"

The door flew open, and the teary-eyed girl grabbed her arm and drew her inside. Rose immediately noticed the feminine furnishings, so unlike those of the captain's room.

"Och, Miss Lockhart!" she cried. "The factory's Mixed Club dance was tonight at Border Hall, but Maw and Da said I couldna go!"

Rose embraced the weeping girl. Having been made aware of the various social activities available to young factory workers at Gretna, she again berated her own naïveté with Gladys and Colleen Saturday night—and then today with the oily boots!

"There now," she said gently. "It may seem like the world has ended, but your parents *will* come around. Meanwhile, you must be on your very best behavior."

"I will." Sniffling, Hannah straightened. "But I dinna even ken how to dance!"

Once again the tears flowed and Rose recalled her own days as a wallflower, before Uncle arranged her marriage to Julien and then insisted she attend finishing school before becoming his wife. "Dancing is easy."

The girl wiped her reddened eyes. "Would you . . . teach me?"

Her watery gaze held such hope. Rose couldn't refuse. "I can show you a few steps."

Hannah hugged her again, then said, "Wait here!"

She soon returned with the portable gramophone from the parlor and a few records. "My friends dance the Ragtime Waltz and some of the animal dances like the Turkey Trot and the Grizzly Bear!"

Rose chuckled. "Let's start with the waltz. We'll do it without the gramophone."

After showing the girl the basic steps, Hannah was eager to put what she'd learned to music. "I've got a recording of the Military Waltz, so we can try that first. Then I want to learn the ragtime dances, because my friends say they play that music at all the socials."

Soon the fluid notes of the popular waltz echoed through the room. Rose held out her hands for Hannah, and as they began the initial steps, the girl's sturdy shoe came down hard on Rose's bare toes. "Ouch!" Immediately she let go to reach for the offended foot.

"How clumsy of me! Miss Lockhart, are you all right?"

Rose tried to smile while her toes throbbed. "Let's try once more, but this time pay close attention to your feet until you learn the steps."

* * *

Alex reentered the cottage from the back after surveying the grounds and making a mental list of necessary chores. Because of Da's injuries, his childhood home was in some disrepair and the yard needed trimming, though someone had weeded the garden— likely his sister.

He passed through the parlor when the sound of music reached him from the hall. He recognized the waltz, played often back at his airfield in France.

He found the source as he approached his sister's room. With her door ajar, he leaned against the wall to listen, reminiscing about his auld squadron and the men still fighting against the Huns. He missed them, but for now he had a more important mission close to home.

"Owwww!"

He straightened at the cry of pain.

"Och, not again! Can you still walk, Miss Lockhart?"

Alex nudged open the door to find their boarder bent over, clutching the toes of one bare foot while his sister stood wringing her hands. She glanced up at him. "Alex, I'm glad you're here! I canna seem to get the steps right for the waltz!"

Miss Lockhart straightened then and turned to him, her face rosy as she tried pulling at her skirt to hide her bare feet.

He fought his humor, certain she'd scurry back to her room. "So, Miss Lockhart is teaching you to dance?"

His sister looked forlorn as she nodded. Her face suddenly brightened. "Brother, you must ken how to waltz. Will you not dance with Miss Lockhart and show me how 'tis done?"

Admittedly, he'd enjoyed watching their prickly boarder change color and decided to add a bit more wood to the fire in her face. "Well, Miss Lockhart?" he said, approaching. "Would you care to show my sister by example? I promise I willna step on your toes."

She tilted her head up to him, and her blue eyes narrowed as he held out his hand. It was a moment before she gave him hers while placing her other against his upper arm.

Once he'd settled his other hand against her slender back, Hannah restarted the music until soon he was guiding the woman in his arms across the floor, the rich notes of the waltz resonating through the room.

His mood softened knowing she'd been helping his sister learn to dance. Heaven knew that with the war on and their da hurt, Hannah had been pressed into work at an early age and had missed much about being young and carefree. He imagined she was eager to attend one of the chaperoned factory dances as soon as Maw and Da would allow it.

Whirling with Miss Lockhart around the room, he caught the faint scent of lavender soap, and beneath his touch, the warm, delicate outline of her shoulder blade. The top of her dark head barely reached his chin, and he was conscious of her touch, feather-light, against his arm.

Her other hand in his grip was damp, a sign of how nervous

she must be while she kept her back arched stiffly, and he almost smiled. Prickly, to be sure.

His amusement faded, recalling her distraction during supper. Despite her assurances, *was* she having difficulties at work? After the stunt those two hooligans had pulled on her and his sister, Alex had no doubt the pair was trouble. For Miss Lockhart's sake, he hoped the lassies had apologized and then thanked her for saving their jobs.

"You both look so bonny dancing like that!" Hannah cried, clapping.

As he watched Miss Lockhart turn a deeper shade of pink, shame filled him. He'd been rough on her last Sunday, and all because the life he'd once known here at home had changed. It wasna her fault, and if she was to stay with them through the month, he'd need to make more of an effort to get along.

The final notes of music had begun to fade, and as they came to a halt, Alex hesitated before releasing her. "Thank you, Miss Lockhart. You dance very well."

"As do you, Captain." She averted her eyes from his.

"Where did you learn to dance the waltz?"

She looked at him then, her mouth slack, before the music started blaring again and his sister rushed forward with arms outstretched. "'Tis my turn, Alex."

Miss Lockhart's shoulders eased. "I see your dance card is now full, Captain." Her blue eyes gleamed. "If you will excuse me." Turning to leave the room, she called back, "As you've been a flight commander, I am certain you will avoid trouble, keeping your sister's feet aloft so that she cannot step on your own."

She'd used his words against him. Then Alex caught another glimpse of bare toes as she opened the door and disappeared into the hall. A smile edged his lips.

Aye, he'd make an effort to get along with their new boarder.

12

"Are you familiar with the game of football, Miss Lockhart?"

Rose glanced up from her ledger notes to see Mrs. Nash standing beside her desk. Quickly she rose to her feet. "Football, ma'am?"

Her supervisor nodded. "We have several girls' teams here at HM Factory Gretna, and they not only compete with one another but also with other munitions factories in Scotland. Unfortunately, your predecessor, Mrs. Finch, lacked the constitution to participate. But you are young and fit and . . ." She beamed. "I want you to coach the football team for your section."

"Me?" At Chilwell, she'd once observed a group of female munitions workers practicing football on the west-end field. They'd worn bright red jerseys, red stockings, leather running shoes, and shorts that exposed their bare knees. Secretly, she'd admired their daring as she watched them play and had imagined herself in such a costume—before dismissing the idea knowing her uncle's reaction. "Thank you for the honor, Mrs. Nash, but I have never played football, nor do I know the rules."

"Rest assured, Miss Lockhart, you'll do fine. Most of the girls are amateur players, and I'll provide you with a playbook of instructions. Since many in your work area have already been on one team or another, you should catch on to the game fairly easily."

She placed her hands against Rose's desk, dark eyes gleaming behind the spectacles. "Your team will need plenty of practice—at least three days a week. Competition for the Challenge Cup is fierce, and the top Gretna team will play Carlisle at our Summer Sports Day on Saturday the twenty-seventh of this month. All factory workers receive a half day off to attend."

Rose's pulse raced. Coach a football team? "When should I start the practices?"

"Saturday after your shift." Mrs. Nash straightened and smiled. "That gives you a couple of days to prepare. Your team will consist of your eight girls plus three from the niter stores. They may choose their own team name and pick up their uniforms from the factory's Athletic Association.

"The practice field is nearby at Baxter's Farm." Her thin face sobered. "With the Challenge Cup championship just two weeks away, I'm counting on our day-shift teams to play well." She turned to leave. "Come by my office after your shift tonight. I'll leave the door unlocked, and your playbook, a whistle, and a coaching jersey on the desk."

Stunned, Rose barely nodded before her supervisor departed. She slowly returned to her seat. Her own jersey! Hopefully she could learn the rules of the game quickly, and since the factory players were amateurs, how difficult could it be?

Then she considered Monday's oily boots and, closing her eyes, pressed her palms together on the desk. *Lord, please help me to offer guidance and encouragement to my charges. And please let them appreciate my efforts.*

She opened her eyes to stare at her clenched hands. Especially those brash girls.

Special bird to arrive Monday. Keep in your sights.

Taking the train back into work, Alex continued to mull over Simon's cryptic note. He'd traveled into Gretna at lunchtime to send his report to Stuart and discovered the London telegram awaiting him.

Who was this "special bird," and why would they require his surveillance?

Could it be Rhymer? The possibility kicked up his pulse. In the four days since he'd hired on at the factory, Alex had explored every room in every department of the Site Three complex. On the pretense of inspecting both the quality of work and the equipment, he'd visited warehouse bays, cotton and niter supply stores, and the production of the cordite in each of its phases. And in that time he'd put to memory dozens of faces of men who might fit the saboteur's profile, watching for any irregular behavior in the work areas and at their leisure in the canteen.

So far, he had little to go on.

As the train pulled up to the factory platform, Alex considered telephoning London from Timbrell's office. He hesitated. Weatherford had been adamant about maintaining security, which meant avoiding the risks of someone eavesdropping. Besides, if this special bird *was* Rhymer, then Simon—or Stuart—would have advised him further.

He drew a deep breath and exhaled as he entered the factory. Unless an emergency came up, he'd wait to see this special bird's arrival on Monday, though it wouldna stop him from wondering *who* he was to expect.

What had she got herself into?

Seated alone on the porch after supper, the playbook in her

lap, Rose rubbed at her temples as she tried to memorize the football rules of engagement. There were strange terms like *pitch* and *penalty area* and *dribbling*. And which players were *halfbacks* and *backs*, and for goodness' sake, what was a *winger*?

Surely her team would think her daft if she failed to comprehend how the game was played. And she refused to ask for help from them, especially after learning her brash girls—Colleen, Gladys, and Betty—were to be the captain and her star players.

She frowned. A person could take only so much humiliation.

She'd retrieved the book, jersey, and whistle that Mrs. Nash had left for her in her office, and while she was there, Rose also made a telephone call to her brothers' school in Hertfordshire.

She'd used Aunt Delia's name and kept watching the door, terrified her supervisor would return at any moment. However, the call had gone through quickly, and Rose was relieved to learn Douglas and Samuel were back at school, though guilt preyed on her at having caused them so much anguish.

Yet they were safe for now, and she renewed her determination to succeed at her job, earning the money necessary for their freedom. And that meant she must learn the game of football, as Mrs. Nash was counting on her to take her team to victory.

The girls still needed to decide on a team name. Rose wondered what they would choose. The three from the niter stores had also played before, so hopefully the team would require little guidance from her, since at this point she had absolutely nothing to offer.

"Have you ever played football, Miss Lockhart?"

She looked up to see the captain's tall frame appear as he stepped out onto the porch. And for what seemed like the umpteenth time, her mind drifted back to their recent waltz together in Hannah's room.

His power and grace in sailing with her across the floor easily rivaled Julien's abilities, but unlike her fiancé, the captain's hold on her had been gentle and she quickly lost herself in the dance, the melody and motion swirling and soaring her spirits high into the air.

Her musings quickly plummeted back to earth when the captain nodded toward the playbook in her hands. She snapped the cover closed. "I have not played, Captain, but I've enjoyed watching the game." *Once*. She averted her gaze, then recalled the football in his room and looked up at him. "You have played before?"

"Aye, as a lad and then in college."

He stood before her, balancing those same strong hands on his hips, and while she took in the wide set of his shoulders and lean torso, she imagined that power and grace from the waltz as he ran the ball down the field in his jersey.

Should she ask him to help . . . or would he refuse?

His condescending words of Sunday came back to her and she hesitated. *Courage.* "I wondered if you would mind terribly . . ."

"Explaining the game?" His hands dropped to his sides. "I heard you were going to coach Hannah's team." His green eyes held a glint, causing her spine to stiffen. Was he inwardly laughing at her?

"Of course I'll help," he said, as if reading her thoughts. "In fact, we can have a real football match here tomorrow after supper. You, me, Hannah, and the laddies. Just for fun. 'Tis the best way to learn how the game is played."

Her eyes widened. "But I . . . I have no proper clothing for football."

"I'm sure you can borrow a factory uniform." He glanced toward the backyard. "I'll set up the goal boxes tonight." He turned back to her, his brows raised. "Well, Miss Lockhart?"

Her excitement warred with the propriety ingrained in her over the past six years. Yet gratitude at his willingness to teach her the game quickly melted away her hesitation. She smiled as she rose from her seat. "Thank you, Captain. I look forward to your instruction."

And perhaps with his help, she would gain the respect of *all* her charges.

13

*H*er moment of proving herself had arrived.

Rose left her office for the changing room at the end of the Saturday shift, her nerves on edge. After quickly washing and changing into her blouse and skirt, she withdrew from her locker the new red football jersey she'd worn for last night's backyard practice game. Captain Baird had been correct: playing a match helped her to make sense of the rules and terms she'd pored over in the playbook.

Now she would put that knowledge to the test.

Pulling the jersey on over her blouse, she then donned a borrowed khaki bonnet. Hannah had told her the "Gretna Glycerin Girls," as the team now called themselves, wore the same as part of their uniform. While Rose had demurred from wearing the uniform shorts, she would show her support in matching her team with the rest.

She reached for the whistle, tethered to a long ribbon Mrs. Baird had donated from her sewing basket. Slipping the length over her head, the action triggered a memory—Tilly, handing her the chain with the key and factory disk that would change Rose's life. Had it really been just two weeks since the explosion and her friend's death?

Swallowing past the knot in her throat, she closed the locker door, then considered the whistle in her palm. Never had she had a whistle before, and her uncle thought the devices too vulgar for her little brothers. She scanned the changing room—only a few workers remained—and then raised the whistle to her lips. Perhaps just a test to make sure it worked.

She puffed gently—and a white cloud of chalk erupted in her face. "Ugh!" She blew the bath powder away from her eyes, along with any hope for success in the coming team practice. Another prank! Would they never end? *Oh, Tilly, how I wish you were here!*

Retrieving a washcloth, Rose wiped her face, then rinsed out the whistle before exiting the factory. Fiercely she blinked back tears. As with the oily boots, she refused to give those awful girls any satisfaction in their ploys to humiliate her.

Hopping the train, it was a short distance to Baxter's Farm where their practice was to be held. Hannah had invited her brother to attend, and Rose was much relieved to have discovered the whistle prank *before* she arrived on the field, especially in front of the captain!

Mrs. Nash had given her directions, and once the train pulled into the next platform, Rose disembarked and made the short trek through town. As she walked the tree-lined streets, she observed the neighborhoods of compact cottages housing the married factory staff and supervisors, while in the distance stood rows upon rows of the dark wooden huts that comprised the factory's Timber Town.

When she arrived at the farm, she immediately recognized the goal boxes placed along either end of the pitch. Why hadn't the playbook simply called it a field?

Hannah and most of the other girls were doing stretches, while Gladys, Colleen, and Betty stood to one side. As if sensing her presence, the trio looked up at her and then covered their mouths, likely laughing over their latest stunt. Rose said a quick prayer that she would not fail.

The captain watched from the sideline, and his presence gave her confidence. He'd been patient with her during their practice match last night, showing her various player strategies and what to watch for in the opposing team. And just as Rose had imagined, his agility and speed down the field had equaled the grace and power in his waltz. She smiled as she remembered how he'd let her steal the ball near the goal, and she'd made her first point while Winston barked and tried to run circles around them.

Still smiling, she raised a hand to him. When he nodded, she turned back to her players and blew the shrill whistle as loud as she could—to the shocked and disappointed faces of the trio standing apart. "All right, Glycerin Girls. Take your places and let's get started!"

⋄→·ᘐ ᘒ·←⋄

Coaching a football team hadn't been nearly as terrifying as she'd first imagined.

Rose's spirits were still high the following morning as she and the Bairds arrived for church. Once they'd entered in from the churchyard to take up seats the captain had saved, she again found herself wedged in between Hannah and the man to whom she owed a debt of gratitude.

She warmed at the memory of last evening when the captain had stood watching as she coached her first team practice. Thanks to his tutelage, she'd surprised her star players with knowledge of the game, and she prayed it would be a new beginning for all of them. *Oh, Lord, I hope this is a sign that my being here in Gretna is a part of your plan!*

Stealing a quick glance at the man responsible for her optimism, Rose's mood suddenly ebbed, as the captain's stiff posture and the crease along his brow conjured for her a more recent memory— when he'd stalked into the church only minutes ago while she accompanied the rest of his family to Ian Baird's memorial in the small church cemetery.

She eyed the tautness in his rugged face. What could be haunting his conscience enough to keep him from remembering his brother? It was as though the captain were trying to escape his demons . . .

Rose could certainly sympathize. When Mr. Baird had begun the prayer at the stone marker of his younger son, she'd closed her eyes and imagined Duggie and Samuel's solemn faces as they'd stood before her grave. Heart aching, she'd prayed not only for Ian Baird, who had died on the battlefield in France, but also for forgiveness from her own brothers.

"'Forget the former things; do not dwell on the past.'"

Rose turned her head toward the pulpit as the preacher continued his reading of the Scripture passage.

"'See, I am doing a new thing! Now it springs up, do you not perceive it?'"

A new thing! Once again, her hopes took flight. Was this not the sign she was looking for?

"'I am making a way in the desert and streams in the wasteland.'"

Her head angled slightly as she leaned back against the seat. Perhaps it meant she *would* have difficulties while she was here, but that God was with her, clearing a path for the future of her little family.

Rose prayed that she was right.

❖➤ ⚬ ⚬ ◄❖

Forget the former things. If only he could.

Alex sensed the slender woman beside him shift in the pew, and turning his head slightly, he gazed at her. Yesterday, Miss Lockhart had run her team through their first practice, and none of the lassies, save his sister, would guess that just the day before she'd kenned nothing of football.

During their backyard match, Miss Lockhart had stumbled down the field as she attempted dribbling the ball, confused between a gallery kick and being offside. Yet she'd been determined, to the point of obstinacy, to learn the basics of the game so as not to be defeated.

You could take a lesson from her, lad. Her courage came in trying to master a weakness—her ignorance of the game—while he, Captain Alex Baird, a flying ace in the war, couldna bring himself to stand with his family beside his own brother's memorial. Even knowing how his refusal hurt his maw and da, the guilt and pain were still more than he could bear.

He looked toward the altar. His faith had taught him God forgives all; yet until he could forgive himself, he'd never see the dawn break upon his soul.

New anguish filled him, and he bent his head, closing his eyes while his hands clenched into fists. *God, please help me to let go and rid myself of these ghosts so that I can find peace.*

14

GRETNA
MONDAY, JULY 15 — NEXT DAY

*I*t seemed his ghosts refused to leave, despite his prayers.

"Why are you here, Dexter?"

Arms crossed against his chest, Alex hid his shock the following morning as the dark-haired RAF lieutenant approached him outside the factory inspectors' office.

Pain from the past flooded him; visions of Ian, waving farewell as he followed this scunner into Paris for another furlough weekend of gambling and loose women—the last of which led to his brother's death.

Dexter's brown eyes glittered. "I should ask you the same question, Captain."

Simon's cryptic telegram now made sense—the special bird he'd been told to watch. Yet it didna prepare him for this. "I work here. What's your excuse?"

"Ah, there you are, Captain Baird!"

Mr. Timbrell rushed forward, somewhat winded. "I was delayed and sent Lieutenant Dexter and his publicity team on ahead, but I see you've met them."

Publicity? Alex relaxed his arms and glanced at the two men standing behind Dexter. The first—a short, stocky man in rumpled linen suit—held a notebook and pencil, while the other aulder man sported a brown barge cap and carried a tripod and camera.

Alex turned to Timbrell. "What's this about, sir?"

"A press tour, sanctioned by the War Office and the Ministry of Munitions. They hope to boost patriotism and support for the munitions industry."

Why would Weatherford allow the press to visit Moorside of all places . . . and in the company of Lieutenant Julien Dexter? "Mr. Timbrell, you're certain . . . ?"

"Orders from the top." Timbrell handed him a document, and Alex scanned the sheet. The order had been signed by a member of the Ministry Council. He frowned, recognizing the name. Dexter's father, the Earl of Stanton.

"All three have been properly cleared," Timbrell went on. "No coin, jewelry, or other flammables, and that includes flash powder." He turned to the photographer. "Make certain to keep your distance in the restricted areas." Then to Alex, "The lieutenant and his crew will be with us two days, Captain. I want you in charge of their factory tour."

Alex reread the signed document, his anger simmering. Already he'd been on the job a week and knew the site's layout, but why would Simon want him playing nursemaid to Dexter and his two-man band when Alex had a saboteur to catch?

Abruptly, Timbrell snatched the sheet from his grasp. "I'll leave you to it, Captain."

Alex blinked, watching the superintendent rush off.

"Since you work here, Captain, you must have been discharged." Dexter sounded amused. "RAF cleaning house?"

Clenching a fist, Alex longed to wipe away that smug look. He couldna speak of the medical discharge, as it was part of his assignment—not that he'd ever tell Dexter. "How is it you're here peddling publicity for your father, the earl? I thought the RAF needed their uniformed *lackeys* back in France."

Dexter shrugged off the insult. "My father is on the Ministry of Munitions Council, and since I'm a decorated pilot in His Majesty's service, what better delegate to lead this tour—"

"And spread your propaganda manure to all corners of auld Blighty?"

Dexter grinned, unfazed. "You haven't answered my question, Captain. How did you end up getting ousted from the RAF?"

"An auld injury. I couldna fly any longer." He told the lie as he locked eyes with the slightly shorter Dexter. "Too much scar tissue from last year's burns in that . . . unexpected crash."

Dexter's aristocratic features colored slightly. He turned toward the man in the rumpled suit. "Mr. Underwood is a war correspondent for the *Times*, and this is his photographer, Mr. Holden." The aulder man touched the brim of his cap.

"Captain Baird, you 'ave an idea where we should start?" Mr. Underwood asked.

"Gentlemen," Dexter said, "did you know the captain was an ace pilot in the RAF? He and I flew together in the same squadron in France."

"You don't say . . . blimey, that's it!" Underwood scribbled away on his notepad before he glanced up, his pudgy face animated as he swept a hand across the open space above him. "I can see it now! The slogan for my article: 'The Military and the Munitions Man— Working Together to Save Our Tommies.' Brilliant, ain't it?"

"Indeed." Dexter flashed a smirk. "I say we get some pictures, Captain, before you take us around the factory. Holden, why don't you set things up?"

It took less than thirty seconds to assemble the tripod. "Forget it, Dexter," Alex growled as the photographer stood with his face hidden behind the large camera. "I'll escort you and this circus around the factory, but I willna pose like some freak in your sideshow."

"Not even for the good of Britain and her patriots?" Dexter moved to stand beside him. "It's also orders from the Ministry and the War Office."

"Ready!" Holden called out.

Dexter flashed his teeth just before the click of the camera.

"Take another, Mr. 'Olden," Underwood suggested.

"Capital idea." Dexter slung an arm across Alex's shoulders. "Be sure to smile this time, *Captain*."

Alex bared his teeth. "Get . . . off . . . me."

Instantly, Dexter dropped his arm, and Alex fought another impulse to plant a fist in the arrogant face. Now that would make a picture.

"I'd like to get a few more shots before we move on."

Dexter was obviously pleased with Underwood's decision, and while the camera's shutter clicked away, Alex stood rigid beside the man he'd once threatened with death. There was no doubt the lieutenant enjoyed being the center of attention *and* knowing Alex had little choice but to endure the farce.

He held his temper. Simon's instructions were clear, and despite his own animosity, he'd keep his eyes on Dexter and his press tour at Moorside. Not that he trusted the lieutenant any more than he would a Hun.

Relieved when the pictures stopped, he led the trio on a tour through Site Three. They headed first to the niter stores, where lassies worked to shovel caustic potassium nitrate into railcars to be taken to process with other chemicals in making nitric acid.

From there they visited the cotton stores and then across the breezeway to the cotton preparation room.

"Your father must have pulled some strings to get you this tour." Alex glanced at his nemesis while the four observed the lassies breaking down and shredding the enormous bales.

Dexter gave him a sly look. "It wasn't my father's influence at all, Captain, despite what you may think. My exemplary service record got me *invited* by the War Office to participate."

Alex snorted. "Exemplary service record?"

Dexter's dark gaze challenged him. "As stated in my military dossier."

Alex's jaw tightened. It was bad enough Dexter believed himself "a decorated pilot in His Majesty's service," but his preening about the other couldna go on. "I'm sure your 'exemplary service' was a slip of the pen. After all, we both know the truth."

Dexter ignored him as they continued their tour to the nitroglycerine section. Upon entering the first door into a dim room, they watched several men in white coats—all chemists, Alex told them—processing glycerin with nitric and disulfuric acids in lead canisters to make the highly dangerous nitroglycerine used in cordite.

"Is it safe in here?" Dexter glanced at him, eyes wide.

"These lads know their job and take every precaution to keep the area safe, although"—he raised a brow, unable to resist—"an accidental bump to one of those canisters could send us all flying high without a plane."

Dexter hurried to exit the room, and Alex smirked as he followed with the other two men.

They entered into the next open door marked ACIDS.

"Good grief! What *is* that stench?" Dexter wrinkled his nose as he fished a monogrammed handkerchief from his pocket and held it to his face.

"'Tis the acids used in nitroglycerine. Much like those also used for making the nitrocotton, the other component in cordite." Alex, like most of the factory workers, had grown accustomed to the caustic odors in this section of the complex.

"I see only women here. Are they mixing the acids themselves?"

Alex followed his gaze. Several uniformed lassies worked with laboratory equipment at the tables. "No, but they measure the pressure and temperature of the acids and also adjust the strength of the nitroglycerin solution before 'tis added to the nitrocotton."

"Some of them look sickly." Dexter leaned in for a closer look. "Should they not be placed elsewhere? Their carelessness could cause an explosion."

Despite the man's ignorance, Alex sobered as he eyed the young faces looking a bit jaundiced. "'Tis sulfur from the acid," he said and glanced at Underwood, scribbling away on his notepad. "Canary girls they're called, because of their yellowed hair and skin."

The journalist glanced up. "Does the yellow ever wear off?"

"Aye, but it can take weeks or even months before it fades once they're no longer in contact with the chemicals."

Nodding, Underwood went back to his notes. Alex turned again to the lassies. Now that Hannah worked in this section of the factory, would she change color as well?

From there he led the three men into an open, well-lit area with a half-dozen round tables, each housing a shallow vat. Four lassies, including his sister, stood at each vat kneading by hand the nitroglycerine with the nitrocotton to make the cordite paste.

"Blimey, I know what this is!" Underwood halted, pointing to the vats. "Sir Arthur Conan Doyle 'imself wrote about these ladies in the *Annandale Observer* a few years ago."

He glanced at his photographer, Holden, who watched the process with quiet intensity. "He called it 'mixing the devil's porridge.' Now ain't that a grand line?"

Holden merely nodded and began setting up his tripod and camera.

"They ain't wearing gloves either, poor doves." Underwood turned to Dexter. "What do you say to posing with one of 'em, Lieutenant? Maybe kiss 'er hand?" His pudgy face lit up. "What a grand shot that would make for the paper!"

"Surely you jest." Dexter eyed him with disgust. "They're probably claws by now. In any case, white gloves wouldn't induce me to risk being poisoned by that 'devil's porridge,' as you call it."

Alex curled his lip at the man's arrogance. He'd seen his own sister's rough, reddened hands, while Dexter had never known a hard day's work. When his lordliness ran out of money, usually by gambling, his father the earl extended his son's credit. And when Alex had threatened to shoot him out of the sky after Ian's death, the earl again bailed him out, arranging his transfer to Orly Airfield in Paris and a cushy job flying dispatches between France and London.

He should have taken his revenge when he had the chance.

Already a year had passed, yet he wouldna forget Dexter's part in bringing that spy, Olivia Charles, into Ian's life.

"Mr. 'Olden's all set." Underwood approached. "A few pictures in front of the vats, Lieutenant? And 'ow about you, Captain?"

Alex scowled in response, leaving Underwood to scurry back to his photographer. Soon Dexter stood poised beside one of the empty vats while Holden snapped a picture.

"Alex?"

His sister had finally looked up from the farthest table and smiled as she wiped her hands of the paste. Leaving her post, she approached while the other lassies watched with interest.

Miss Lockhart was not among them. "Where is your supervisor, Hannah?"

"She should be back soon. Sarah suffered acid burns, so she took her to the clinic." Hannah surveyed his companions. "What is this?"

He glanced toward Dexter and his press team. "Publicity for the war effort."

"Excuse me, can I get your name for my article, miss?" Underwood made his way back to Alex, pencil in hand as he smiled at his sister.

Hannah blinked. "Why . . . I'm Hannah. Hannah Baird."

"This charming creature is your sister, Captain?"

Dexter had strolled over as well. Alex glared as the man bowed to his sister and introduced himself. "I've had the pleasure of speaking with both your brothers, Miss Baird, and I daresay they did not exaggerate your beauty."

"Save it, Dexter. My sister's off-limits."

But Hannah ignored his words, blushing bright pink as she ducked her head. Peering back up at Dexter, she said softly, "A . . . pleasure to make your acquaintance, Lieutenant."

Dexter looked beyond Hannah to the others kneading the paste. "Fair ladies, the Ministry of Munitions appreciates all the work you do here to aid in the war effort."

They all giggled amongst themselves.

Alex chafed at Miss Lockhart's delay. She should be here, returning order to her lassies. Or would she too be taken in by Dexter's pretty speech and good looks?

He narrowed his eyes. Pretty speech or propaganda, the scunner knew how to spread his share of manure.

15

*S*urely it could not be . . .

Rose halted at the sound of familiar laughter, a chill crawling up her spine. Then the deep, distinctive voice—and she ducked behind a wide concrete post a few yards from where Hannah and the other girls were kneading cordite paste in vats.

Praying fervently, Rose peered out from her hiding place. Seeing his face, she hurled herself back against the post, her heart beating wildly. It was him! That . . . monster had found her. *Lord, please help me!*

Her feet urged her to escape, but instead she pressed against the concrete, nails digging into her palms as she struggled to steady her breathing.

She peeked around the post once more to observe the scene.

Captain Baird had his back to her while he, Julien, and another man—a short, disheveled fellow with a notepad—conversed with Hannah. A few feet away, a photographer stood with his tripod and camera ready to take a picture.

She cringed at Julien's charming overtures to the red-faced Hannah as Millie, Colleen, and Betty approached to join them. How did her fiancé know she was here?

"Captain Baird and I served as pilots together in France."

Her ears perked at Julien's statement. So they knew each other? "They're also good chums."

The man with the notepad made the comment. Rose pressed herself back against the post. The captain and Julien were . . . friends?

That camera . . . she *had* caught a glimpse of the captain an hour ago, near the inspector's office. He'd been standing beside someone in uniform while having their pictures taken.

Because poor Sarah received such severe burns, Rose was too concerned with her crisis to take notice of the man *in* the uniform. And now he stood in her section, speaking with her charges.

Rose spun around and swiftly retraced her steps. Gritting her teeth to contain her panic, she forced her feet from doing an all-out run that would draw attention.

She could not let Julien find her!

Avoiding her own office—surely they would look for her there—she walked blindly toward the other end of the building, uncertain of her direction, knowing only that she couldn't hide in the factory for long. She pressed at her cramping middle, the lunch she'd so carefully guarded from any tampering now rebelling in her stomach.

With her nausea in mind, she made two more sharp turns to Mrs. Nash's office. Making apologies to her supervisor with an excuse of tainted mutton for lunch, Rose returned to the clinic where she'd taken Sarah and obtained a sick pass of her own. From there, she dashed off to wash and change and exit the factory as quickly as possible.

Once aboard the train, she stared at the building entrance, fearing that Captain Baird and Julien might emerge at any moment. But as the wheels began turning to distance her from the factory, she settled in her seat, watching as long as possible for any signs of them.

The train chugged toward Gretna's platform, giving Rose time to rationally consider the ramifications of Julien's presence in Gretna. The image of him and the captain together in front of the camera burned in her mind—and the fact they'd flown together in the war.

Was this a personal visit, then? *Oh, Lord, why of all the people in Scotland did Captain Baird have to be Julien's best friend?*

Did the captain know the truth about her? Julien could have shown him a picture. It might explain why they waited for her at the vat tables, since she'd told Hannah she would return soon.

The train pulled up to the platform, and Rose eased out a breath as she disembarked. Lifting the hem of her skirt, she half ran the entire distance to the Baird cottage, every so often glancing back for any sign of the captain and her fiancé.

She was breathless by the time she arrived to open the front door and step inside.

"Och, are ye all right, lass?" Mrs. Baird sat on the blue couch, looking up from stitching a piece of collar lace onto a snowy white blouse. A basketful of mending rested near her feet. "Yer face is as red as raspberries, and yer lungs are pumping much too hard!"

Putting aside her sewing, she stood and came to lay a motherly hand against Rose's forehead. "No fever that I can tell. What's happened to ye, lass?"

My worst nightmare. "I-I feel ill, my stomach . . ." She hated having to lie again, but she was desperate. "I think it was the mutton . . . a co-worker shared her sandwich with me at lunch."

"Poor dear." Mrs. Baird clucked. "When mutton's a bit off, it can make ye feel queasy." Her soft touch slid to Rose's cheek. "What ye need is a lie-down, so off ye go. Mr. Baird is out back having his pipe while the lads play with the dog, so ye'll have peace and quiet. I'll bring a nice cup of my mint tea, since it worked so well last week to settle yer stomach."

Rose smiled faintly and stumbled off to her room. Mrs. Baird could offer her a gallon of mint tea, but she wasn't leaving her sanctuary tonight even if it meant going hungry. The mere possibility the captain would invite Julien home for supper made her shudder.

Mrs. Baird brought the tea, and afterward Rose changed into her nightdress and slid into bed. Sipping at the fragrant brew, she contemplated her future. She would have to leave Gretna—tomorrow, once Hannah and her brother left for work. But where could she go . . . and with what? She had no money left. Nor would she receive her first wages until Friday, and that was four whole days from now.

Could she hold out in this room until then? And how would she slip into work to collect her pay?

A chill rippled through her as she imagined getting caught and being dragged back to Leicester. Shackled as Julien's wife, doomed to a marriage of convenience. And perhaps like her aunt, sent off to some asylum.

No! She set the rattling teacup and saucer sharply onto the nightstand. Never would she return to that horrible life; she'd bar herself in this room, feign the plague if she must.

There had to be another solution!

Sliding down beneath the covers, she tried to clear her thoughts, and eventually the tea did its work to soothe her nerves. Soon she found herself dozing. *Lord, surely you haven't brought me this far just to fail. . . .*

❧ ❦ ☙

Rose started awake a few hours later to the soft tapping on her door.

"Miss Lockhart?"

Hannah. "Yes?" she whispered across the room, fearing Julien's presence in the house more than the fact she was feigning her own illness.

"Maw wants to know if you'll be out for supper." Hannah's voice was muffled through the door. "She said she'd bring you more tea and a tattie scone, if you like."

"That would be lovely, Hannah. Please thank her for me. I'm still too unwell to leave my room."

"Och, I'm sorry, Miss Lockhart. And you missed all the excitement!"

133

Rose sat up, catching the word *excitement*. Had something more happened with Julien after she left? Curiosity made her slip out of bed and edge toward the closed door. "What kind of excitement?"

"Alex brought his friend, Lieutenant Dexter, and two newspapermen over to our work area today. They even interviewed me and the other girls! Can you believe it? The photographer took our picture too." Enthusiasm bubbled in the girl's voice. "Lieutenant Dexter also told us he and Alex flew together in same squadron in France."

Nerves on edge, Rose listened again to what she already knew. "Is he . . . the lieutenant . . . staying to supper tonight?"

"No, he's gone to the Gretna Hotel with the reporter and photographer. Tomorrow they'll finish their tour of the factory and return to London."

Rose closed her eyes and sagged against the door, making the wood creak.

"Miss Lockhart, are you all right?"

"Y-yes, only I must . . . return to bed. You go and have supper and I will see you later."

As Hannah's footsteps faded, Rose fell to her knees and said a prayer of thanks. Julien was leaving Scotland tomorrow! Perhaps his visit was merely a coincidence and he didn't know she was alive or in Gretna after all.

But how could she be certain? What if the captain had been instructed to . . . to apprehend her once she made an appearance?

Rising to her feet, she began to pace the room, only vaguely aware of his boyhood memorabilia still cluttering the floor and shelves. She didn't want to believe that Captain Baird—the same man who had danced the waltz with her and taught her the game of football—would stoop to such a despicable action. But what lies had Julien told him?

And yet, if it was not a trap and her fiancé's presence here merely chance, the captain might have no idea she was Rose Graham.

Hope flickered. Since his homecoming, he'd not asked her

any questions pertaining to Julien. And he wasn't acting more strangely toward her than usual.

Did she dare to believe her secret was safe?

Rose kept to her room the rest of the night. In the morning, when Hannah knocked softly at her door, she asked the girl to advise Mrs. Nash that she was still too ill to come into work and would need another day to rest.

Hearing the captain's deep voice as he questioned his sister in the hall, Rose moved to the door once more and listened as Hannah relayed the conversation to her brother. His only comment was that he hoped Miss Lockhart's condition wasn't severe enough to warrant a doctor.

She released a gust of air when the pair finally departed for the factory. Slipping back into bed, she awakened hours later, again to a soft rap on the door.

"Lass? 'Tis noon and I've a nice pot of Scotch broth on the stove. Can I bring ye a bowl?"

Huddled beneath the covers, she listened to Mrs. Baird's kind offer while burning shame blistered her conscience. Hannah's mother had done so much for her already, believing her ill, when Rose's true malady stemmed from fear and keeping too many secrets.

Her mouth watered remembering her own mum's delicious meat-and-barley broth soup. "I am sure some broth would make me feel much better, Mrs. Baird, thank you."

⇌ ⚬ ⇌

By midafternoon, Rose had decided to become "well" and emerged from her room wearing Tilly's white shirtwaist and blue skirt. She carried her empty soup bowl to the kitchen, and while setting the dish in the sink, Mr. Baird's gentle voice floated in from the adjacent dining room. Listening a moment, she realized he tutored his young sons in mathematics. How grand to have a loving father teach his own children in such warm, familiar surroundings. So different from the months of isolation at boarding school.

She left the kitchen quietly, venturing into the parlor. Mrs. Baird sat in her usual place on the couch, the basket of sewing at her feet.

She looked up. "Are ye feeling more yerself, lass?"

"Much better, thank you. Your soup was just the thing, and I am sure yesterday's tea was most helpful."

Mrs. Baird beamed. "My own maw believed a good Scotch broth could cure anything that ailed a body." She pushed aside with her foot a damp, shredded wad of newspaper on the floor and patted the empty cushion beside her. "Yer welcome to join me, lass."

Taking a seat, Rose picked up the wet newspaper, a sinking feeling in her chest. "Where is Winston?"

"Mr. Baird put him on a long rope beside the porch where there's plenty of shade and a bowl of water. The dog was up to a wee bit of mischief with his newspaper."

"I am terribly sorry! Winston has never done that before." Though Rose couldn't possibly know since she'd only had him a short time. "Can I replace it?"

"Och, dinna fash, 'tis already forgotten. Anyway, the lads are doing their extra lessons now and having the dog underfoot would only distract them from their numbers."

Rose smiled her relief. "Winston has found two best friends in Fergus and James."

"Aye, and they'll all get their time to chase one another after supper." She leaned to sift through the mending basket. "Now, where did I put that piece of lace . . ."

"I could help you." Rose surprised herself at the offer but was glad she'd done it. Over the past couple of weeks, she'd noticed the constant mountain of mending and it was the least she could do, considering the care Mrs. Baird had given her.

"Mr. Baird did say yer maw was once a seamstress." Mrs. Baird eyed her intently. "What kind of work did she do?"

Rose bit her lower lip. The more she tangled her own past with Tilly's, the greater risk of her blundering and being found out. But

it was too late to recant what she'd already told them. "My mum
. . . she was a dressmaker and made the most beautiful clothes."

"And so ye learned at her knee?"

"I did." She smiled, wistful. "Mum taught me to cut cloth using
a drawn pattern and how to sew the lengths together on a machine.
I also learned how to stitch the finer pieces by hand, especially
when a customer wanted lace, jewels, or even tiny seed pearls."

"I'm sure ye were a fine help to her, and being just a young lass
near Hannah's age." Mrs. Baird's soft words matched the warmth
in her gaze. "Ye must miss her fiercely."

Rose could only nod against the knot in her throat. She'd never
stopped yearning for her mum and dad and now her brothers, and
the life they all once shared together.

Mrs. Baird handed her a needle and thread and the partially
finished lace collar. "I miss my Ian, too," she said quietly, reaching
back into the basket for a torn stocking and the darning ball. "I
wish ye could have met him, Miss Lockhart."

She sat back and threaded a new needle. "Ian and Alex were
always close and full of laughter and mischief, just like my Fergus
and James."

At that moment, one of the boys—James—giggled loudly in the
other room, and Rose and his mother shared a smile. Mrs. Baird
fitted the darning ball into the sock and sighed. "Seeing my Alex
now, though, I think the war and Ian's death have taken their toll
on him." She glanced at Rose. "He's no longer the lighthearted
lad I once knew. I'll admit to ye now without shame that I'm glad
he's home with us again and out of danger."

"There is no shame in wanting someone you love to be safe."
Rose looked up before dipping her head to begin work on the lace.
What was her son . . . Captain Baird . . . doing at this very moment? Still leading Julien around the factory and learning more
about Rose Graham?

"'Tis hard losing those ye love."

Mrs. Baird's sigh followed her words, pulling Rose from her
musing. "I . . . yes, it is."

"I imagine it must be doubly hard being without yer family."

Instead of a lie, she held in her mind the image of Douglas and Samuel, still grieving at school. Her guilt and the longing to comfort them. "It can be." She glanced up from her stitching. "Still, I've managed all right."

"Of course." Mrs. Baird settled a hand on her shoulder. "Yer a brave lass."

So brave I hide in my room and pretend to be someone else. Rose forced a smile. How she hated deceiving this kind, generous woman and her family! Yet she had no choice, especially not with Julien close by.

Rose sought to change the subject. "Does your family always keep you this busy with mending?" She nodded toward the basket. "I cannot imagine that basket has shrunk since I arrived."

Mrs. Baird laughed. "I should hope not. After Mr. Baird's accident, I started taking in mending from the factory workers. I can assure ye, there are enough of them to keep me busy for the next hundred years."

Her skin flared. Of course! Why hadn't she realized the family would need the extra income? "Well, I shall help you as much as I can to shrink this basket down to size."

"I'm grateful, lass, especially that yer willing to finish the lace on that collar. 'Tis part of Hannah's upcoming birthday present. I've spent weeks making the green jacket and skirt in between all my regular mending. I ordered buttons from the haberdasher last week, and I pray they'll arrive by Saturday."

"If I can help in any way, I am happy to do it."

"See there? Ye have a fine hand at stitching." Mrs. Baird seemed pleased, and the two worked in companionable silence for most of the afternoon, listening to the children's voices or Mr. Baird's as he gave them instruction in the dining room.

The old mantel clock struck the hour of half past five when Mrs. Baird finally put aside her mending and rose to her feet. "Alex and Hannah will be home in an hour, so I must see to supper."

"Would you like help in the kitchen?"

"I'm grateful enough for the help ye've given me this afternoon, lass. Look at that."

Rose followed her gaze to the basket. The mountain of clothes had been reduced to a mere hill, easily tackled. "I shall keep working."

"Only if ye feel up to it?" Mrs. Baird gave her a searching look.

Rose started to rise. "I'm much better, thanks to you. Though I'll first go check on . . ."

"Winston!" Fergus and James shouted as they bounded from the dining room and raced through the parlor toward the back door.

"I think the lads share your concern." Mrs. Baird gave her a wink. "I'll fix the dog a bite to eat."

"That is more than a fair deal." Smiling, Rose resumed her efforts to eliminate the basket's contents. It was no wonder the poor woman found it difficult to keep up. The clothes seemed to multiply like the biblical fishes and loaves, with no end in sight. And each day she faced more of the same in order to help make ends meet.

Mrs. Baird was right—Alex being home and out of danger was good for their whole family. And because he'd secured a decent paying job at the factory, his wages should help ease their financial burdens.

She'd nearly finished mending a pair of trousers when the front door burst open.

"Maw, you'll never guess!"

Heart thumping, Rose glanced toward the entryway. How had an hour passed so quickly?

The needle in her hand stilled as dread clawed her insides. What if Julien had decided to stay after all, despite Hannah's assurances? Would he and Alex enter the parlor together?

At the sound of approaching feet, she tucked the sewing aside and rose from the couch, blood pounding in her ears. She could still make it to her room.

"Miss Lockhart, 'tis good to see you looking well!"

Hannah burst into the parlor. She was alone. "And you'll never guess!"

"Guess what, lass?" Mr. Baird ambled into the parlor on his cane and went to his daughter. Giving her a kiss on the cheek, he took up his usual chair. "You've good news, aye?"

Smiling, Hannah drew back her shoulders. "I found out this afternoon that when I turn sixteen, I'll get a pay rise. An extra five shillings a week!"

"Such fine news, lass. Is it not, Miss Lockhart?"

Rose had retaken her seat on the couch, fanning herself with the wet newspaper. "That is the rule, Hannah, and grand news indeed." She gave a feeble smile before glancing toward the door. "Where is your brother?"

"Alex said he had an errand in town."

Rose gripped the newsprint. "With Lieutenant Dexter?"

"No, the lieutenant left on the noon train to London with his pressman and the photographer." She sighed, her expression dreamy. "All the lassies in our work area thought him so braw in his uniform."

Hannah glanced at her father, then grinned at Rose. "I invited him to come back on Saturday for my birthday. He said he would try, but that he's needed in France." She sighed again. "Perhaps I'll invite him when he gets his next furlough. I'll be sixteen by then and much more grown up than I am now."

Beneath her smile, Rose's jaw tightened at the mere thought of sweet Hannah falling into the clutches of a man like Julien Dexter.

She would pray the innocent young girl had seen the last of that scoundrel.

16

LONDON
TUESDAY, JULY 16

*H*ow typical of his father to choose a backwater town like Gretna, Scotland.

Julien Dexter resettled in the club car's cushioned seat and gazed out at the passing hills and trees and distant steeples as the train headed south. Surely the old man couldn't have known he would encounter his longtime rival, Alex Baird.

A bitter smile touched his lips. The two-day excursion was hardly enjoyable, thanks to the captain's hostility. Though Julien did have the satisfaction of seeing equal shock on his face when they confronted each other, then witnessing the captain's misery at having to chaperone their tour.

"The Military and the Munitions Man—Working Together to Save Our Tommies . . ." Julien almost snorted with laughter at the pathetic catchphrase. His gaze darted to its author, the pudgy Underwood seated across from him, still looking as if he'd slept in his clothes.

Alex Baird nearly bolted at the newspaperman's suggestion the two pilots pose together for the camera. Of course, Julien had planted the seed, offering Underwood that rubbish about their days of flying together in France. As if they'd been chums, when in truth Baird would have gunned him down like a Hun if he'd had his way.

Clearly, he hadn't forgotten or forgiven the mess with his brother and Miss Charles.

Reaching into his pocket, Julien removed a gold cigarette case. He regretted the day Kahverengi introduced him to that blasted woman. With the war on, the back-alley cafés of Paris had become a haven for gamblers and he'd been unable to resist. He'd found Miss Charles charming and attractive, but during his next furlough with young Ian Baird in tow, she'd zeroed in on her new target.

He'd been relieved to dodge those amorous claws, though Alex Baird's little brother never stood a chance.

Taking out a cigarette, he tapped it against the slim case. Because there was nothing to be done or said to alter the past, he'd endured two days of Alex Baird's persecution in order to do his duty to the War office and to his father. Julien's mouth hardened. He should demand a commendation for his suffering!

He dug in his pockets for a match, then looked up to see the quiet Holden reaching out with a lighter. "Thanks."

Leaning back in his seat, Julien noted the photographer made no response. Why should that surprise him? Throughout the entire tour, the man said less than a dozen words, all of them "Ready!" before snapping his camera. Unlike Underwood, who never shut up . . .

"Once we get to London, Lieutenant, will you fly back to France right away? I imagine you're ready for a jolly time after Gretna. I 'ear they 'ave fine restaurants in Paris if you've got the quid, or maybe you like some o' those music halls?"

Speak of the devil. Julien drew on his cigarette, blowing the smoke toward the window. He stared at the unkempt journalist. "As if my plans were your concern, I'm leaving after I make a stop in town to visit my family."

Underwood leaned forward, his fleshy features alive with curiosity. "Ain't that grand? They'll be glad to see you. And when 'is lordship the earl reads my article in the *Times*, 'e'll be a proud papa."

Julien took another drag, letting the smoke ease from his lungs.

It was more probable his father would be disappointed. To the world, the Earl of Stanton and his two sons were a stable, loving family; yet behind the façade, Julien awakened each day caught between his hatred for the harsh, unloving earl who had sired him and a piercing guilt at having ruined his brother's life.

"Your mother passed away years ago now and you 'ave a sibling, ain't that right, Lieutenant?"

Had Underwood read his thoughts? Julien eyed him sharply. "Why do you ask?"

Underwood blinked. "We always collect background details before writing up an article, Lieutenant. An older brother, in a wheelchair?"

"Percy." He struggled to form the single word as he took another pull of smoke and stared out the window. Criminy, they'd been mere children, playing in a tree house behind their country estate. Percy said something to make him angry—Julien couldn't even recall what it was—and he'd shoved his older brother backward, never intending he should topple off the platform and fall several feet to the ground.

After Percy lost the use of his legs, their father accused Julien of wanting to hurt his brother, making him a cripple for the rest of his life.

He'd suffered from the incident as well; the years of self-loathing and his father's silent condemnation had ground away at his conscience. At every opportunity, the earl reminded him that he'd ruined his older brother's chances for a suitable marriage and the funds necessary for improving Stanton's coffers.

Dark humor caught in his throat. Perhaps his only saving grace was that dear Mother died of cancer and not in birthing him, or Father would consider him more of a pariah than he was.

"You were recently engaged to be married, ain't that right, Lieutenant?"

Julien snapped his head around, glaring at the fat-faced journalist making notes. "Do you not read your own newsprint, Underwood? Her obituary was in the *Times*."

Underwood's neck colored. "My condolences, Lieutenant, and the same to Sir Ridley Cutler and 'is wife. Will you be seeing them again? I imagine you all became close."

Julien ignored him, though Underwood's meddlesome questions conjured memories he'd rather have buried permanently. Like his failure to secure a fortune by marrying Cutler's niece.

Miss Rosalind Graham had been pretty enough when he'd met her last year at Cutler's Christmas party in Leicester, but her breeding was far beneath his station. And she'd been too naïve for his tastes; not the soft, willing European women he'd grown accustomed to.

He and his father had argued about the match, and as the earl always did, he threw Percy in his face. And each time afterward, when Julien flew dispatches into London and stopped by the house in St. James to check on his brother, if the earl was home, the marriage argument resumed.

It was Kahverengi who had changed his mind about taking Miss Graham to be his wife. While Julien argued with his friend that the earl planned to give her dowry to Percy as heir, Kahverengi suggested Julien demand stock in Cutler's munitions company, shares put into his own name so neither his father nor Percy could touch them. The earl wouldn't be around forever, and by marrying into the household, Julien could induce Cutler to share his wealth.

And so he'd engaged himself to Miss Graham, and Cutler gave him the first half of the shares with the promise of the balance after the wedding. A wedding that never took place.

The train drew into London, and Julien observed the green valleys and forested hills had given way to small boroughs, then clusters of multistoried buildings and factories, signaling their imminent arrival at the station.

He stamped out his cigarette in the tray and thought ahead to what he must do. With Miss Graham dead and the loss of that future revenue, he'd had to resort to other means. And while Cutler had handed over to him the rest of the company shares for his "intent to marry," Julien knew his generosity stemmed from greed. The wealthy munitions magnate wanted to continue their arrangement, profiting by means of clandestine exchanges . . .

The train's blaring whistle drew his attention. He and the other two men glanced out the window to see the train had slowed considerably, about to enter Victoria Station.

"I hope ye enjoy yer family visit, Lieutenant."

Julien turned in surprise to the photographer Holden. "Thanks again for the light."

He gazed at the slovenly newspaperman, and his mouth twitched with amusement. Wouldn't the snooping Underwood kill to know that once he arrived at his father's town house in St. James, he planned to enter the study and pick the lock on his desk. Since Tuesday evenings were the earl's standing engagement at White's, and with Percy reliably upstairs napping in his room, Julien could take his time photographing any new munitions information his arrogant father brought home to keep in his files. Information quite profitable when shared with the right clientele.

His smile broadened. "Gentlemen." The train finally stopped, and he rose and grabbed up his bag from beside the chair. "I am certain I shall enjoy myself immensely."

17

Peacock routed back to you today. Nothing to report.
Alex scanned his response to Simon and then handed the coded message to Mr. Wylie, who had manned the post office in Gretna for as long as Alex could remember. Once it was sent, he offered another, this time to Lieutenant Stuart at East Fortune.

One benefit from the press tour was having access to the other sites at Moorside, and while he'd kept his eyes on Dexter and his crew, Alex also watched for any potential suspects. It could be a long shot, but a couple of names were now en route to Stuart at the airfield.

Having finished his task, Alex struck out for home. Relief at ridding himself of Dexter continued to grapple with his anger. He could still envision the lieutenant preening in front of the camera while the newspaperman recorded every word out of his mouth. Peacock surely fit.

Alex had also taken exception when the dodgy man slipped in beside Hannah and the other lassies to have his picture taken. Then last night at supper, listening to his naïve sister wax on about the "braw lieutenant" and remembering her soft eyes on Dexter when he'd tossed her a few pretty words.

A growl rose in his throat. For two days he'd suffered Dexter's company *without* being able to settle the score for what the scunner had done to ruin Ian's life.

After Dexter had introduced his brother to the so-called Frenchwoman, Ian returned to Paris every furlough anxious to see her. Then Miss Charles began writing letters to him at the air base about marriage and Alex grew uneasy. Part of his responsibility as flight commander was to censor his pilots' outgoing letters, and he'd confronted Ian when his brother wrote back accepting her plan that they leave France and marry in neutral Holland.

He'd reminded Ian that desertion was a death sentence. They'd even come to fisticuffs over the letter, but his love-sick brother refused to listen. *"'Tis already too late for me, Alex . . ."*

Increasing his stride, he tried to outrun the memory of those last words. After the plane exploded and he stumbled and fell, he'd tried to revive his brother, gazing for the last time as Ian's dark eyes opened slightly, his ruddy good looks smeared in soot and twisted in pain as he whispered his guilt before succumbing to his burns.

Alex stared blindly at the road ahead. So many casualties he'd witnessed during the war, yet a part of him died that day watching his brother perish. Knowing he'd been the cause.

Dexter's claim of ignorance about Olivia Charles's true intent or where she could be found had nearly pushed Alex over the edge, and sweet heaven, how he'd wanted to have the earl's son arrested and court-martialed for treason.

But not if it meant implicating his own brother.

Alex rolled his shoulders, trying to ease the painful scar tissue. Never would his family learn the truth of what happened that day on the field, or the packet he'd discovered on Ian's body. Papers from *her*, written in German and hidden among some French stocks and bonds. Incriminating documents he'd been tempted to toss back into the flames.

But duty had won out. He'd met with Weatherford instead, and in exchange for handing over her letters to Ian, her photograph, even the documents, the captain agreed to ask no questions and promised his silence and an honorable burial for his brother. And in return . . .

The assignment at Moorside.

His spirits lifted at the welcome sight of home, and as he finally reached to open the front door, he let out a sigh. Dexter was gone, and despite loathing the man, Alex had done his duty as ordered.

He entered the cottage, and his thoughts turned to food as he inhaled the delicious smells coming from the kitchen. He headed in that direction, warmed at the sight of his maw, clad in her apron and making bannock bread in the skillet.

She looked up at him, her smile full of love. "Alex, 'tis so fine to see ye coming home to us every night, son. Did ye have a good day?"

"Aye." He smiled, forcing all thoughts of Dexter and his press team out of his mind—except for seeing their backs when they left the factory. "And the sight of you making me another home-cooked meal is like finding an extra guinea in my pocket."

"Och, ye rascal." She chuckled, removing the skillet bread from the stove. "'Tis almost time for supper, and everyone's in back. Will ye go and help yer brothers come in and wash up?"

"For your bannocks? No need telling me twice." He winked at her and left the kitchen, heading through the parlor for the back door.

Alex paused to see Miss Lockhart seated on the couch, her dark head bent over a jacket as she deftly worked her needle to repair a sizable tear in the sleeve. "Glad you've left your sickroom, lass. I trust you feel better?"

Her head shot up, the blue eyes wide in her startled face. "I . . . I am much improved, thank you, Captain. I think it was bad mutton in the sandwich I had for lunch yesterday. Your mother said the spoiled meat could certainly have made me ill."

Alex nodded. More than once he'd suffered the effects of tainted food while eating outside the air base in France.

He angled his head, observing her smooth ivory skin now rosy with color, much the same as when he'd waltzed with her in her bare feet across his sister's floor. She was a picture of health, a far cry from the whey-faced woman who had wielded his golf club during their first meeting. The memory filled him with warm amusement. Then it struck him that just a day after her ipecac mishap, and no doubt still feeling poorly, she'd gone into work to save his sister's job.

And now she helped his maw with the burden of sewing. His tone softened. "Supper's almost ready, if you'd care to join us tonight?"

"Why . . . of course, Captain." Surprise lit her features. "I need to finish mending this jacket. It will only take a few minutes."

With a brusque nod, he continued toward the back door and called in the rest of his clan.

Minutes later, while he supervised his brothers' handwashing, Alex replayed the conversation with Miss Lockhart in his mind. She had danced with him and they'd played a bit of football together, and while he was pleased they seemed to be getting along, she had yet to call him by his Christian name as everyone else did. And for some reason it bothered him.

He could still see the large blue eyes gazing up at him from the couch, much like a doe's before the hunter's strike. She seemed to him in that moment vulnerable, and tender . . .

Och, you've no business going there, man. Moving behind Fergus and James, Alex corralled them toward the dining room. His purpose was to find a saboteur who intended harm on his family, including Miss Lockhart, and that meant no distractions.

Dexter's sudden appearance had been enough to steer him off course; now that he and his press team were gone, Alex could resume his task. He only hoped the names he'd sent to Stuart tonight would produce results.

Why had the War Office sanctioned the tour at Moorside? Dexter and his newspaper pals had done nothing noteworthy.

Or had he missed something?

"Sit down, everyone, or this food will get cold before 'tis on yer plate."

Alex directed his brothers into their chairs, still mulling over the strange decision to showcase Moorside for the press.

He frowned as a possibility struck. A play for power?

Prime Minister Lloyd George was once the minister of munitions and now head of the government. With Moorside the largest cordite factory in the country, had this so-called tour been his way of flexing Britain's muscle—showing off for her people *and* for the enemy with their prized war machine?

But that kind of vanity might discourage Rhymer from stepping foot inside the factory. Their saboteur could decide to choose another target altogether, and they'd be back to where they started.

"Alex, will you say grace?"

As Miss Lockhart had joined them, Alex looked to his da and nodded. Then, bowing his head, he had a last thought before reciting a prayer of thanks: to tell Simon to keep the politicians out of his way so he could do his job.

❖⟩─❧❧─⟨❖

"You should have seen him, Miss Lockhart! He had ribbons and medals on his uniform and he was so charming! And when he smiled, Betty Pierce nearly fainted onto the floor!"

Rose set down her spoon, her own smile fixed while Hannah babbled on about the past two days of the monster's visit to the factory. Their meal of skillet-fried bannocks and Cullen Skink—Mrs. Baird's version of the haddock soup—was delicious, but Rose couldn't manage a bite through her clenched teeth.

Barely had she sat down and the captain said grace before the girl began a litany of praise for Lieutenant Julien Dexter—so much that Rose had been tempted to excuse herself and run to her room.

"Hannah, my lamb, 'tis obvious ye were impressed with the lieutenant, but ye did share all this with us last night at the table. Have a care for Miss Lockhart, and let's talk of something else."

Rose gave Mrs. Baird a grateful smile, but the mother's words were no match for her daughter's passion. "'Tis why I'm retelling the story, Maw! Miss Lockhart took ill yesterday and didna sup with us last night, so she doesna ken all that went on at the factory or how kind the lieutenant was to me."

Hannah glanced toward her brother at the end of the table. "Tell her, Alex. Lieutenant Dexter is your friend, and you both flew in the same squadron."

Sensing the captain's eyes on her, Rose stared at her half-eaten bannock while fear knotted her insides. She'd overheard yesterday's conversation at the factory but pretended interest. "Is that so?"

She looked up at him then—and quailed at the taut lines bracketing his mouth, the green fire in his eyes. *Did* he know the truth about her?

They stared at each other until Hannah said, "Well, brother, if you willna tell her, then I will." The girl drew Rose's attention. "Alex was his flight commander in France, and they fought the Huns side by side for over a year before the lieutenant transferred to Paris."

"Over a year?" Mr. Baird glanced at his son. "So he knew . . . Ian?"

Rose ventured another look at the captain. His mouth hardened as his glittering eyes sought hers. "Aye." He bit out the word. "They were of the same rank."

He turned to his sister, and Rose eased back in her seat, dizzy over their silent exchange.

"Lieutenant Dexter is the son of an earl, Hannah, so you can forget your romantic ideas. Not only are you entirely too young"—his gaze narrowed—"but Dexter will marry for money, not love. And I doubt he'll be coming back to Gretna anytime soon."

"But I thought . . ." Her expression fell. "My birthday. He did say he would try to be here."

"I also heard him tell you his duty is back in France. There's a war on, remember?"

She pushed out her lower lip. "I know it. I work at the factory too, *remember*?"

"Anyone for marmalade pudding?" Mrs. Baird rose from the table, her concerned look bouncing between her eldest son and daughter.

"Thank you, Maw, but I'll have my share of the sweets later." The captain shoved back his chair. "We've some timber in the back, so I'll work off your fine meal chopping wood. Best to get it cut and stacked now before the winter months." He nodded at Rose. "Miss Lockhart."

Once he'd left, Hannah sat looking unhappy while her mother

brought in a tray of the orange bread pudding. Rose took her cue to leave. "Dessert looks delicious, Mrs. Baird, but I would like to go outside and check on Winston and get a bit more mending done before bed."

"Ah, lass, yer a blessing." She smiled.

Leaving the dining room, Rose headed through the parlor and then paused at the basket of unfinished clothes. Why not take the mending outside? The evening was mild, and she would spend some time with her little dog as well.

She carried her sewing out back, placing the basket beside her wicker chair. Walking to the end of the porch, she caught sight of Winston lying in the grass and looking as dejected as she felt at the moment, especially after listening to Hannah's chatter about Julien.

There was also the captain's glowering at her all through supper. And what about his warning to Hannah? *"He's the son of an earl . . . when he marries, he'll do it for money, not love."*

He'd been right to caution his sister, but was there more to his meaning? Did he know her uncle was wealthy and that Julien had intended to marry her . . . and perhaps did still?

Despite the warm July air, she rubbed her arms and descended the steps to the grass. She lifted her little dog and cuddled him close as an overwhelming sense of loneliness engulfed her. She longed to see the little brothers she'd left behind, her own family.

As soon as she received her wages, she must make plans to leave this place. Her pay would be a bit scant as she'd missed two days of work, yet it would buy her a train ticket and a few nights in a hotel and food until she found work in a city where no one knew her.

What kind of believable excuse could she offer Mrs. Nash for leaving? She'd need a referral letter from her supervisor if she was to find another decent paying job.

The loud *crack* of splintering wood caught her attention. Rose glanced toward the far end of the backyard, where the tall captain wielded his ax. With a powerful downward thrust, the blade split the large chunk of wood in two, the halves tumbling off either side of the chopping block.

He paused, taking up the pieces to toss them into a pile before he grabbed a fresh piece of wood and, with the ax in hand, began chopping anew.

Rose moved onto the porch with Winston, and after releasing him she settled into her seat and resumed her mending. She occasionally looked up to watch the captain and found the cadence of his motion, combined with the sounds of the ax, oddly calming.

Even in her lulled state, however, she couldn't forget the real issue. Did he know her true identity, and if so, had Julien instructed him to spy on her?

Where would she go now? With limited wages and the clockmaker forger now an impossible situation, she couldn't return to Glasgow. Perhaps farther north or to the west? She'd heard about Nobel's factory at Ardeer.

The steady chopping continued, and Rose gazed at her dog, who seemed intent on watching the captain from the porch. He looked up at her then, furry ears perked, and her eyes burned. "I must say good-bye to you soon, my little friend. I cannot take you with me this time." She leaned to scratch him behind an ear, and the dog rose to his feet, emitting a soft whine. Rose looked away from him, blinking back tears.

The ax paused again, and she glanced over to see the captain had sunk the blade into the block and was pulling his shirt up over his head, revealing an expanse of toned, bronzed skin that made her blush.

Rose stared at his broad chest outlined in muscle, the ripples of strength across his belly. He seemed oblivious to her as he retrieved the ax and continued hacking away at the new wood, the corded power in his shoulders and back flexing with his raising of the ax . . .

She drew in a sharp breath at the patchwork of scarred, discolored flesh along his upper right shoulder and back. *Dear Lord, what happened to him in the war?*

He twisted around then and spied her on the porch as though he'd heard her gasp. For several seconds, they stared at each other, the stillness of the evening air between them.

Finally he retrieved his shirt and shrugged into it. He glanced at her again before resuming his task, this time wielding the ax with an intensity she did not understand.

Rose returned to her sewing, repairing a torn seam in a blouse. Yet she found it difficult to concentrate, not only because of the sheer beauty of him but also the wounds that, despite his scars, seemed slow to heal.

Alex took out his fury with the ax for another half hour before he turned toward the porch to find Miss Lockhart gone. His relief mingled with disappointment at her leave-taking, and he again took up the blade, letting the wood absorb his guilt and his rage much the way he'd made her bear his frustration at supper.

By immersing his anger in those cool blue eyes, he'd endured the foul repetition of last night, his sister's endless blethering about Dexter. He'd also been able to answer Da's questions about the lieutenant's relationship with Ian, revealing none of his own pain, or the regret that threatened to crush him, and kept him away when his family prayed at Ian's grave. *Dear God, please help me with this burden. I dinna think I can carry it much longer . . .*

He lowered his head, his chest aching. And again he remembered those eyes, holding his gaze, keeping him steady and silent about secrets he could never reveal.

But now she'd seen his scars. Would she mention them to his maw? He loathed having to explain the wounds to his family.

Lifting his face to the sky, he cursed his stupidity. Then he seized another chunk of timber for his blade and commenced chopping with a vengeance.

They would never forgive him. Any more than he could forgive himself.

18

*H*aving left the train station, Julien arrived at the impressive Georgian home near St. James Square and circled around back toward the servants' entrance. Because most of the staff would be at their evening meal, he intended to slip inside unnoticed and avoid old Ames at the front foyer, instead using the servants' stairway that led into the main house.

"Yer lordship! Ye half scared me t'death!" The chubby maid clutched at her ample bosom as he nearly collided with her when she exited the workroom off the servants' hall. "I thought ye were a robber stealin' in 'ere, and still the light o' day!"

"Ida." Julien smiled, mentally cursing the interruption. "Why are you not at supper?"

"I was jus' on my way." She gazed at him with those cow eyes, reminding him of their last dalliance. "Why are ye here, m'lord?"

"Because I *do* want to steal something," he said and leered at her. "But not here." He glanced down the length of the hall, relieved it was empty.

Red-cheeked, she placed her hands on her wide hips, her tone saucy. "An' what d'ye plan on takin' this time, m'lord?"

He drew her toward the back stairs leading up to the main floor and, after guiding her up the first two steps, turned her around so that they were eye to eye. "Now, what do you think?" He leaned in and gave her a quick kiss, and when it was done she covered her mouth in a giggle. He held a finger to his lips. "Promise you won't tell?"

She nodded, the dark curls bobbing below her mobcap. "I swear, m'lord. Not a word."

"Good girl." He went around her to climb the staircase.

"Will ye be wantin' another . . . later, m'lord?"

Turning on the steps, he sighed. "I wish I could stay, Ida. But I'm needed back in France." He reached out and touched her on the nose. "Hold that thought for the next time."

Again her plump cheeks suffused with color and she gave another giggle, this time revealing several missing teeth.

He turned his back on her, heading quietly up the stairs. An unexpected delay, but the drab little bird *would* keep his secret.

Making his way across the main floor, he was glad most all the servants were downstairs. He avoided the entryway, where Ames the butler took up his post, and cut through the drawing room instead, heading toward the library and his father's study.

To date, his forays had been quick and undetected. Afterward, he'd look in on his sleeping brother, then take an evening flight out of Kenley back to Paris where he would process the film before his planned meeting with Kahverengi.

He did enjoy the Greek arms dealer's eccentricities. They always met privately and most often in cemeteries around the city. Kahverengi would send him the name of the graveyard and a particular tombstone, along with two sets of numbers: a day and a time for their rendezvous.

The next was one week from now—the twenty-third—at dawn.

He was passing by the carpeted stairway leading up to the bedrooms when the new valet, Darby, descended. "Good evening, Lord Julien."

"Ah, good evening, Darby. Settling in all right? Everything shipshape?"

"Aye, m'lord, though his lordship your father took ill this morning. He's resting quietly upstairs."

That was a near miss. Julien's pulse thumped at his throat. His father wasn't at White's this evening. "How ill is he?"

"I believe it is the arthritis, m'lord. Quite painful. The doctor has seen him and given him a sleeping draught."

Julien's shoulders eased. His father would sleep for hours. "Thank you, Darby."

"Will you need assistance later, m'lord?"

Julien shook his head. "I'm only here for a short while. I'll look in on Lord Percy."

"Very good, m'lord." Darby gave a slight bow and continued on, no doubt heading belowstairs to have his supper with the rest of the staff.

Once he was inside the study, Julien pushed the door closed with his heel and strode over to the desk. He withdrew his gold cigarette case and removed the tiny set of picks. Crouching on one knee, he inserted them into the lock, moving the tiny tools around until he heard the familiar click and was able to open the drawer.

He spied the top file marked CONFIDENTIAL and grabbed it, setting it on the desktop. He stood and opened the folder to the first page. Seeing the recent date stamp, a thrill rushed through him knowing the new information would reap him a fortune.

Of course, it had been Kahverengi's idea when he'd hinted at this particular means of revenue, insisting that any inside information on munitions would be extremely valuable to the right buyer. Julien had needed no further explanation. With his own father on the Munitions Council, thinking the sun rose and set on his service to the minister, it was easy enough to discover a gold mine of intelligence tucked away in the earl's desk. Detailed plans for the future of Britain's armaments industry for which Kahverengi paid him well.

Until recently, Julien had limited his operation exclusively to his friend. He owed the arms dealer a great debt after that final evening at *Dés Chanceux* in Paris. The popular café had been his regular gambling haunt during weekend furloughs, where booze and women flowed freely and he'd nearly paid with his life for a rather long streak of bad luck.

His debts reached a level that even his father the earl couldn't afford to pay. As Julien left the Paris club that night, the house thug had confronted him, threatening to take what was owed in blood. Then suddenly the man Kahverengi was there, settling his huge sum and taking him under his wing.

How would he react knowing Julien had started sharing the same information with Cutler? To what degree did their financial paths cross?

He reflected on his most recent dealing with the weapons magnate, when the niece, Julien's future bride, had walked in on their negotiation. He'd thought by roughing her up a bit to scare her into obedience, but that failing, he'd planned to make arrangements after they wed. Though it was 1918, and having one's wife put away was a difficult and dirty business. In the end, it was a relief knowing she was gone and could tell no tales.

Cutler had paid him quite handsomely too, nearly as much as Kahverengi for the same information. Miss Graham's wealthy uncle seemed obsessed with competing for Nobel's share of the munitions market.

Julien scanned the information on the first page as he withdrew a small camera from his tunic pocket. More than once he'd considered telling Kahverengi about Cutler's desire for the information— test the waters, so to speak. But what if his Greek friend forbade him? Cutler's money was too good, and he didn't want to have to stop dealing with the man.

He raised the camera, checking the lens before he was ready to snap a picture.

"Julien?"

Blast. Quickly he closed the file. Apparently, he hadn't completely shut the study door. Why wasn't his brother napping? He pocketed the camera as he slowly turned around. "Percy, how did you get down here? I saw Darby headed belowstairs for supper."

"He forgot my stained shirtfront, so he returned and I asked him to carry me down."

His brother's long torso seemed to overshadow the wheelchair the servants kept at the foot of the landing. Percy's pale features creased as he inclined his head. "Why are you here in London?"

Julien positioned himself in front of the closed file. "I came to see you, Brother." He nodded back toward the desk. "I wanted to write a quick note to Father first. I heard he has not been well?"

"His joints again." Percy used his muscled arms to maneuver the wheelchair forward, coming to halt beside the desk.

Julien's pulse pounded, wondering how much of the file his brother could see.

Percy made no mention of it. "How was your press tour in Scotland?"

"It went well. Quite a few ladies working for the war effort there, and lots of pictures were taken. I believe the *Times* shall do the event justice." As he spoke, Julien glanced at his watch. Just thirty minutes to catch the last train to Kenley Airfield, and it would take him half that long to walk back to Dover Street for the tube to Victoria Station. He tried to quell his impatience. "How are you doing, Percy?"

His brother shrugged in the chair. "I have my usual aches and pains, but my stamp collection takes my mind off things and keeps me busy."

"I imagine you've got quite a collection by now." He fought another urge to look at the time.

"Yes, quite." The subject seemed to enliven his brother. "I've just acquired a rare stamp from Spain and one from Norway. I find it fascinating to see how other countries determine their designs."

"Indeed." Julien's chest tightened. *Dear brother, you could go to those countries instead of collecting idiot stamps, if I hadn't crippled you.*

His guilt intensified as Percy sucked in air through his teeth, raising himself up before resettling into the wheelchair. "I read Miss Graham's obituary in the newspaper two weeks ago. Were you able to attend her memorial service in Leicester?"

"Sadly, no." Julien desperately needed to escape. "I was stuck in France. Which reminds me—" at last he glanced at his watch—"I need to catch the last train if I'm to make it into Paris tonight."

"Of course, you must not be late." Percy eyed the desk, then his brother. "Shall I give your note to Father?"

"Unfortunately, I did not get that far with my letter." He offered a weak smile. "I'll send a postcard from Paris. Please give him my regards."

Percy nodded and backed the wheelchair away from the desk. "I'll just wait outside the door and then see you out. Ames is getting a bit feeble."

Julien could only nod, guilt and shame coursing through him.

While his brother hovered outside, he slipped the file back into the drawer. He hadn't expected this enterprise to sour. He'd promised Kahverengi the information, but now he must meet with him empty-handed. There was no way he could chance returning to the house before next week to obtain copies of the documents. Would his friend be cross?

Departing the study, he followed Percy to the front door, where they said their good-byes in front of the surprised old butler. Once outside, he again debated whether or not to stop his dealings with Cutler. The money was exceptional, and with Miss Graham out of the way, their arrangement could go on smoothly without any strings.

Both of his patrons had so far paid him well, and when Cutler's investments grew, Julien's stock value increased. He dreamed of the day he could walk into the house and toss a wad of banknotes into his arrogant father's face. He also planned to take care of Percy, so his brother needn't worry for anything the rest of his life.

But that was the future; at present he could ill afford to end up on the wrong side of things, and if Julien must choose, he'd be taking far more risk to incur the arms dealer's revenge.

19

*W*ell, so much for our efforts, Quinn. Seems this latest plan failed."

Sunlight streamed through the tall windows in Marcus Weatherford's Admiralty office as he hung up the telephone and gazed across the desk at the swarthy detective with Scotland Yard's Special Branch. "I just spoke with Captain Forrester. According to Captain Baird's telegram yesterday, our lieutenant made no attempt to contact anyone while at Moorside."

Quinn frowned as he scratched at a red, scaly patch of skin near his right temple. "Any possibility Lieutenant Dexter caught wind of the ruse?"

"I doubt it." Marcus leaned his elbows on the desk. "There was no way he could have known the press tour was just a ploy. No one at the factory knew, including Captain Baird. And Underwood assured me his cover as a journalist was convincing. On their return trip to London, he made a point of asking the lieutenant about his family and his relationship with Sir Ridley Cutler of Cutler Enterprises, whose niece—before her untimely death at Chilwell—was Dexter's intended bride. He even asked about Dexter's activities in Paris, yet he claims the lieutenant didn't strike him in any way as being suspicious." He paused, giving a slight smile. "Just full of himself."

Quinn tipped his head. "You never told me why you suspected him in the first place. Maybe he's just not our man?"

"You could be right, but when we saw the name Moorside on the charred munitions list Paris found in Kahverengi's flat, we suspected a leak high up in government. That code name is not public information." He clasped his hands. "MI5 is surveilling all members of the Munitions Council and their family members. The list includes Lieutenant Dexter, since his father, the Earl of Stanton, is on that council.

"A few days ago, I returned from France with a report that the lieutenant was seen weeks ago at the Montparnasse Cemetery in Paris just after dawn. There was another man with him, believed to be in one of the photos we have on the arms dealer. We suspect Dexter met with Kahverengi to barter information obtained from his father, though I doubt the earl is involved."

"Why rule it out, Captain? It would not be the first time someone from the peerage stooped to selling secrets."

"True, but I'm well acquainted with Stanton. He and his younger son have a rather strained relationship. I cannot envision them in league with one another."

"Stranger things have happened."

"Indeed they have," Marcus agreed. "But you asked why I suspected Dexter and it was because of the French report. If he does have dealings with Kahverengi, then it's likely he's also connected with his agent, Rhymer. I arranged with the site superintendent Timbrell to have Captain Baird accompany the lieutenant on his press tour, hoping Dexter would try to make contact with our saboteur." He paused. "If we'd been successful, it could have saved countless hours of manpower and protected thousands of workers in that factory."

Again the detective scratched at the red scab at his temple. "Has the lieutenant returned to France?"

"Yes, he flew out of Kenley last night. MI5 recently installed a man in the earl's home, surveilling for any possible security breach. So far, he's had nothing to report."

"So we just stand by and wait?"

Marcus nodded. "The MI5 agents at Moorside's other sites have nothing to report, though Captain Baird took Dexter through those facilities and came up with two names he sent to his liaison in Scotland. We'll have to see if anything comes of it." He sighed. "I still regret that Miss Lockhart slipped through our net. It's obvious she failed to fulfill her end of the deal, despite all our planning. She never met with Rhymer."

"What if she did meet with him?" Quinn's dark brows drew together. "I checked her work locker afterward. The package he sent her was empty, which tells me she delivered into the factory the dummy charges we'd replaced for his bombs. Perhaps Rhymer never trusted Till . . . Miss Lockhart, and he went ahead and planted his own explosives."

"I find it too coincidental that she fled from the factory just *before* the explosion." Marcus opened his file, skimming the report. "It states here she left by the factory's rear gate at 1840 hours that evening, enough time to get away before the blast."

He looked up at Quinn. "I think she changed her allegiance and tipped Rhymer off to our plan. Kahverengi has millions. If he's funding this sabotage as we believe, he could easily afford to send Miss Lockhart to live in luxury wherever she chooses."

"We have circulated her photograph at all our offices, Captain. Also with the major ports, here and in Scotland, in the event she tries to leave the country."

"That will help." He closed the file. "In the meantime, I'd like you to retrace her steps, including her history. Start at the orphanage in Glasgow and work forward, including her past contacts. Whether she's guilty or innocent of the Chilwell explosion, we need to determine her whereabouts." He narrowed his eyes on Quinn. "She's still our key to finding Rhymer and putting Kahverengi out of business."

20

Gretna
Friday, July 19

*E*xcuse me, Mrs. Nash? Did you say I have no wages coming?"

Rose stood at her supervisor's desk, heart thumping. She'd already missed two days of work after barely starting a new job because of Julien. Was she about to get the sack before she could even resign her post?

Any hope for a recommendation letter now seemed lost. "I am terribly sorry about my recent absence—"

"It's not what you think, Miss Lockhart, and I'm relieved that you've recovered from food poisoning." Mrs. Nash left her chair and came around to stand beside her. "The truth is . . ." She nudged the spectacles farther up her beaked nose. "According to our pay office, there is no Miss Tilda Lockhart."

Rose took a step back, the breath stuck in her throat. Had she been found out? "I . . . I do not understand."

"How could you?" Mrs. Nash crossed her skinny arms and leaned against the edge of the desk. "I only found out myself after lunch. You've been using the temporary factory disk I gave you when you hired on, and so I called the main office about your permanent one. That's when I learned the employment paperwork had simply vanished."

She shook her head. "The documents were sent by courier to the files office after you hired on, but the clerk in charge of processing was suddenly taken ill. Another stepped into his place, and somewhere in the interim, your paperwork never resurfaced. As a consequence, I'm sorry to say your name was never forwarded to the paymaster in the Wages Office."

Rose sat down in the hardwood chair across from Mrs. Nash, her mind boggled at the maze of details her supervisor had relayed. Yet one fact stood out: The secret of her identity, at least at the factory, was still safe. Her chest eased. "So . . . I will receive my wages?"

"Yes, of course, but unfortunately not until Monday. A copy of your documents is being hand-walked to the main office now." She pushed away from the desk and laid a hand on Rose's shoulder. "I'm very sorry this has happened, Miss Lockhart. I know you've already had to wait two weeks. If you are in desperate need of funds, I would be happy to make you a small personal loan after the shift today, just come and find me."

"Thank you." Rose struggled to inject gratitude into her words before she left and walked back toward her own office at the far end of the building.

Misery loomed over her like a dark shadow. It seemed the week only determined to get worse. First there was Julien's sudden appearance; then at football practice on Wednesday, her brash girls were back to being secretive and laughing behind their hands. And yesterday, Rose discovered the reason why—when she'd donned her work smock and discovered *someone* had put live earthworms in both pockets.

Fortunately, Dad had taken her fishing on a few occasions; otherwise when she'd plunged her fingers into the nest of squirming creatures she might have screamed—giving those brazen girls plenty to laugh about.

Today, their tricks found her at break time in the canteen when she'd purchased a cup of watery tea with Tilly's last coin. After adding to her drink the small amount of precious sugar Mrs. Baird had spared from her rations, Rose took a sip—then nearly spit out the bitter brew as the sugar in her locker had been replaced with salt.

With Gladys and Colleen conspicuously absent from the usual table of girls, Rose had no doubt they were off crowing over their latest prank. What could she expect? Her own absence Monday and Tuesday had simply given those rotten girls more time to devise new tortures!

Slowing her steps, she blew out a sigh. She was in over her head—with this job and with trying to coach a football team. Certainly not equipped to supervise others, not like Tilly. And what about her future in Nova Scotia? Since sharing with the Bairds about her mum and dad, Rose had started to consider opening her own dress shop. But what if she had to instruct employees?

And now this . . . this . . . latest disaster with her pay! Frowning, she resumed her pace and soon arrived at the nitroglycerine section where her charges should be *working*.

Instead of going to her office, she marched toward the Acids Room. Enough was enough. She had to stand up to them today. If not, Mrs. Nash *would* discover her laxness and Rose could not hope to receive a good referral when she left.

Chin set, she fortified her nerve with Tilly's words: *"If you have courage . . ."*

"Ye stupid lot, if ye can't do the work right the first time, then get out!"

Rose paused as she neared the Acids Room, the angry male voice coming from inside.

"That's why we don't need no females doin' a man's job! Go home to yer mams and yer little 'uns where ye belong, so we can get our work done!"

Hannah and the girls from the vats huddled beside the door, trying to look inside. Rose nudged them back and crossed the threshold into the caustic-smelling room.

A tall barrel-chested man in brown barge cap and leather apron stood waving his fist at her charges, his meaty face contorted in anger. Behind him stood three other male workers, each wearing similar garb and looking on with smug smiles.

Instantly her mind conjured Uncle Ridley as he towered over her frightened aunt. Rose barged in on the scene. "What is happening here?"

The furious man turned at her approach. "Who are ye supposed to be?" He started toward her, and she instinctively took a step back, then halted. *Courage* . . .

Anchoring her feet, she raised her chin. "I should ask you that very question, sir, and then you can explain to me why you are threatening my girls."

"Ye oversee this lot?" The ogre laughed, glancing back at his three cohorts. "Why, yer no more 'an a girl yerself." He flashed an ugly smile. "The name's Dobbs and I'm with the union." He held up a piece of paper. "Our pal nearly died because of *yer girls*!"

He pointed to Gladys, Sarah, Jane, and Dorothy, who stood at the gauges table clutching their measuring equipment. Seventeen-year-old Jane tried to muffle her cough while sixteen-year-old Sarah, her face blistered from the acid burns, visibly trembled in place.

"One of these here got the pressure too high on the nitroglycerine tank yesterday, and this morning it sprung a leak. When our Joe tried plugging it up, he got drenched in the stuff and had to get a wash down. He's got bad burns, and it's lucky ye lot didn't kill us all!"

Rose took a step forward. "Mr. Dobbs, I can certainly understand your reaction, but in future, if you have a complaint about the work, you will bring it directly to me."

"Bah! Ye don't belong here, either. This is a man's work and no place for yer kind."

Jaw tight, she was too incensed by his narrow-minded bullying to be cautious. Her feet inched forward a few more steps until she faced him squarely. "Mr. Dobbs—"

He grasped her arm.

In that moment, she relived her last encounter with Julien—fingers digging into her flesh as he pressed her up against a wall, instructing her on *her place* as his wife and how *he* expected her to behave. Never what she could expect from him or what she wanted.

"You will unhand me." Her raw voice, barely audible, reached his ears and he quickly released her.

She straightened the sleeve of her smock with trembling fingers and gazed up at him. "You are right, Mr. Dobbs, we should not be here. However, since most of *your kind* are off fighting in France and need munitions to survive, we women must fill the gap and do our bit to keep them alive. That means risking *our* health, *our* families, *our* livelihoods, and *our* peace of mind for your benefit as well as theirs and the rest of the nation.

"Furthermore." She crossed her arms to keep from shaking. "What proof do you have that it was my girls who over-pressurized the tank?" She glanced at the paper in his hand. "Is that the incident report?"

When he nodded, she held out her hand. "May I see it?"

He seemed reluctant so she grabbed hold of the sheet, her eyes narrowed. "Mr. Dobbs?"

He released the paper, and Rose scanned the report. "This states the leak was in tank number four. Is that correct?"

He scowled. "Like I said—"

"But, Mr. Dobbs, my girls have never worked with tank four. I can certainly check the work rosters to see who did, but I know number four is tested and operated on the night shift—by some of the men in your union, I believe? My girls work the day shift and have for some time." She thrust the paper back at him. "So you are quite mistaken."

He fisted the paper, his mottled face turning white. "Why, ye uppity piece—"

"Is there a problem, Dobbs?"

Heart pounding, Rose whirled at the sound of the familiar male voice. Captain Baird had entered the room and now stood behind her, feet braced apart and staring at the giant.

Relief at seeing him threatened the last of her composure. Knees wobbling, she locked them in place. She dared not wilt now. "There is no problem here, Captain." Again she managed a steady voice, returning her attention to the ogre in front of her. "Is there, Mr. Dobbs?"

He glared at Alex a moment, then at her before he finally took a step back. "I dunno why I waste my breath. Nothin' around here will change. C'mon, lads, let's get back to work."

Hannah and the other girls outside scurried off as Mr. Dobbs and his cronies pushed their way toward the exit.

Once they'd left, Rose eased out a breath and turned to the captain. His face held concern as he lifted a dark brow in question. She offered him a faint smile, and he nodded before retreating back into the factory.

Rose approached the workbench, where her charges stood looking dumbfounded. "Back to work, ladies. I would not wish to give that horrid Mr. Dobbs any other reason to find fault with us. He will never understand that you are the best thing that has ever happened to this war. Do I make myself clear?"

"Yes, Miss Lockhart." Sarah, Jane, and Dorothy wore relieved smiles while Gladys, a stunned look on her sallow face, slowly nodded.

As they resumed their work, Rose decided to postpone speaking with the troublemakers. Because of Mr. Dobbs and his nastiness, her head hurt and her heart raced and she needed a few moments of calm.

Once she'd checked on Hannah and the others mixing cordite, Rose sought out the washroom for some cold water and was relieved to find the room unoccupied.

Bathing her face, she stared into the mirror at her reflection. She didn't seem any different from this morning. The same dark-brown strands peeked out from her work bonnet, and blue eyes too big for her face still peered back at her.

She angled her chin. Perhaps it wasn't as weak as it appeared earlier? Had she truly stood up to that clod of a man?

Thank goodness the captain intervened when he did. Otherwise she'd feared Mr. Dobbs was about to grab more than her arm in his angry tirade.

Rose pressed her lips together as she tucked in the errant dark wisps. She didn't fool herself; what transpired minutes ago could not compare with what Julien would do to her once he found her. Captain Baird had come to her rescue this time, but would he do the same where his friend was concerned?

Blotting her face with a clean towel, she took a seat on the padded washroom bench against the wall. She had to leave Gretna—though she dared not resign or ask Mrs. Nash for a referral letter until she received her wages in hand on Monday. That was three days from now. And tomorrow was Hannah's birthday.

She pressed against the dull throbbing in her head. Hopefully, the captain had been truthful with his sister, telling her Julien wouldn't return anytime soon. It would mean, at least for another day, Rose would be safe.

21

*W*hat would it be today? A snake in her work boot? Beetles in her hand lotion?

Rose cracked open her locker door at work the following morning, exhausted after a fitful sleep. She'd awakened several times during the night, always from the same dream: Julien, his hands full of earthworms, facing off with her inside the factory. All eight of her charges, clad in their football uniforms, looked on as they giggled behind their hands, while Mrs. Nash stood shaking her head at Rose in disappointment.

Captain Baird had been in the dream, too. Siding with his friend, he'd stood beside Julien, arms crossed and wearing his barge cap while he shot Rose a smug smile.

Then in a fit of rage, Julien threw the worms at her—except it was acid, burning her flesh as he announced to all that when they married he'd send her off to the asylum to join her dear aunt, and no one would see her again.

She jabbed a thumb at her forehead as if to shove the nightmare from her thoughts. No doubt her skirmish with Dobbs yesterday and then Hannah's chatter at supper last night were the cause. The girl had regaled the family with every detail of Miss Lockhart's "heroic sacrifice" for her girls, "putting her own life at risk" against Mr. Dobbs, the "meanest scunner to draw breath" while she stood up to him.

Rose had sat at the table, enough heat in her face to rival the steaming plate of mince and tatties Mrs. Baird served her. When finally she'd ventured a glance at the captain, he seemed amused with his young sister's theatrics.

Mr. Baird then asked his daughter what happened next, but Rose quickly intervened to say his son arrived in time to diffuse any real confrontation. She'd been thankful at that point when the dinner conversation ended.

Today, however, as the captain and his sister rode in with her on the train, Rose was conscious of the steady green eyes on her. She hadn't forgotten his glaring at her over dinner a few nights ago, or his hostile look when she'd seen him chopping the wood. So different from the graceful man who swept her up in the waltz and patiently taught her the rudiments of football. But that was all before Julien's arrival. Was the captain now watching her and making mental notes to pass along to his friend?

She swung open her locker door, relieved when nothing jumped out at her. Exchanging her shoes for the rubber boots—after checking them first—she then removed her wristwatch, the only jewelry she wore into the factory. Afterward, she fished from her skirt pocket the five shillings Mrs. Nash had loaned her yesterday.

Rose had already considered avoiding Hannah's birthday supper at the Bairds tonight—and any risk of meeting Julien—by taking her evening meal at the Gretna Café in town. But Mrs. Baird had been effusive in her thanks after Rose finished the lacework on her daughter's present and insisted she join in the celebration.

And in truth, she dare not spend the borrowed money. Who knew what her future expenses might be while she searched for work in a new city? *Lord, please do not let that monster show up at the birthday party tonight!*

After stuffing the coins and her watch into one of her shoes, she narrowed her gaze on the clean, white work smock. Her other hung freshly washed on the clothesline at home after she'd emptied the crawling contents into Mrs. Baird's garden.

Plucking the smock from the locker, Rose held it away. She absolutely detested crawling insects. Had those bothersome girls got the idea to use spiders this time?

Taking hold of a pocket, she cringed as she drew back the cloth to peer inside.

Flowers?

Carefully she withdrew the posy of purple heather tied with a pretty gold ribbon.

The same gold ribbon Gladys had worn in her hair to the Carlisle cinema.

An identical posy lay tucked inside the other smock pocket, tied with more of the gold ribbon. Rose eased her shoulders as she leaned against the row of lockers. It seemed the battle—with Gladys, anyway—was over.

Admiring the purple blooms and pretty ribbons, she was caught unawares as her throat grew tight. It had dawned on her the true value of the twin gifts, especially coming from a girl who likely grew up in the harsh poverty of London's East End.

Gladys Dunham, one of the toughest of her charges, wasn't so different from Tilly or even herself. They all needed love and acceptance, despite their backgrounds or the hardships they'd endured. Perhaps the struggles are what made it even more important.

Her own boarding school days had been long and painful being spurned as an outsider. The snide remarks and cruel words still had the power to wound her young girl's heart; and the ache of that loneliness often returned when she was frightened or despairing of her future. Perhaps no one had ever stood up for Gladys before.

Mutual respect was the answer. Tilly had managed her girls at Chilwell because she knew them; she'd been brought up rough like them. She *understood* them.

Rose had failed to find common ground with her girls—much the way the pedigreed debutantes at school chose to remain distant from the daughter of a Scots tradesman.

She could imagine how Gladys might view her, as one of those pretentious types with her education and boarding school English. Yet Rose was probably more like her charge than both of them realized. *"You are a Scots after all, despite your fancy speech and all that proper Sassenach schooling . . ."*

Fresh grief washed over her, and Rose blinked back tears. Tilly was right. In the past six years, she'd forgotten who she was and where her roots lay, hiding in the shadows until yesterday when she was empowered to stand up to Dobbs, not only for her girls but also for herself and every insult and injury they'd all suffered.

She placed the flowers in her locker and donned her smock and cap before going through inspection and out onto the factory floor. "'Love thy neighbor as thyself,'" she murmured, recalling the Scripture verse Mum had taught her. Striding toward her section and the girls she supervised, Rose remembered one Easter at school when the pastor relayed the story of Christ washing the feet of His friends. He'd taught them a lesson in both humility *and* love.

Entering the Acids Room, she took heart as Jane, Sarah, and Dorothy glanced up from their worktables and beamed. "Good morning, Miss Lockhart!" they chorused before Jane had a fit of coughing. As the girls returned to their tasks, Rose sensed Gladys's dark eyes on her. She turned and smiled, patting the pockets of her smock to indicate she'd received her gift.

The girl's eyes held relief and she returned the smile, pink rising against her yellowed cheeks. Rose bowed her head before she briskly departed to check on the others working at the vat tables.

A truce, then.

22

A lex left work a few minutes early that night, stopping first at the haberdasher's to pick up Maw's package, then at the post office to collect the telegram Mr. Wylie held for him.

"East Fortune, Alex," the aulder man said as he handed him the missive from behind the counter.

"Thanks." Heart thudding, Alex tore open the envelope as he walked outside.

Two birds bore no fruit. —Bonny Prince.

So the names he'd given to Stuart after Dexter's tour amounted to nothing. Alex fisted the telegram. He'd been inside the factory two weeks now, surveilling the men working in each area, and still the saboteur eluded him.

Last night he'd sent Stuart the name of Dobbs as a possible suspect, or at least involved in some kind of subversion. Alex learned from talking to others that the union steward was an instigator and liked to make trouble. No surprise, considering yesterday the man had threatened Miss Lockhart and frightened her workers.

Alex also sent the lieutenant the names of Dobbs's three friends, so Scotland Yard could do a thorough investigation on all of them.

Tucking the crumpled message into his jacket pocket, he struck out for home. He could only hope this time Dobbs or his cronies could lead him closer to finding Rhymer.

Until then, he'd continue surveillance of the union men. He'd noticed today they remained in their work area, steering clear of Miss Lockhart's team.

She had surprised him yesterday when he walked in on the confrontation in the Acids Room. Dobbs's foul blethering had been loud enough to be heard in Glasgow, but Miss Lockhart proved her mettle as she stood up to the man's hostility. A smile touched his lips. The soft, susceptible woman mending clothes from his maw's laundry basket was a far cry from the fierce mother bear he'd seen protecting her cubs against a wild beastie.

His humor faded. What if Dobbs *was* involved with Rhymer in some way? The confrontation yesterday could have held a more sinister meaning. Had the union man thrown blame for the over-pressurized tank on the lassies to scare them off . . . or was he setting the stage for something bigger?

Alex wanted to believe the latter, yet he still had doubts. An experienced saboteur wouldna draw attention the way Dobbs did yesterday . . . unless he was just Rhymer's pawn.

Frowning, he rubbed the back of his neck. Just twelve days remained until the month of August. According to Kahverengi's scheme, Moorside would then become fair game for Rhymer's destruction.

Alex needed a miracle.

❖❖❖

"'Tis good yer home, son, and not a moment to lose! Did the package arrive?"

Surprised when his maw met him on the front porch, Alex handed over the brown paper sack from the haberdasher. Then he lifted his nose, sniffing the air. "Is that haggis?"

"Aye." She opened the sack, inspecting its contents. "Yer sister's birthday request." She gazed up at him then, her eyes twinkling. "I seem to remember 'tis yer favorite too, so tonight ye'll both enjoy a Burns supper."

He bent to kiss her. "After being away for so long, I've missed your fine meals more than you know."

"Och, go on with ye." Yet as he leaned toward her, she reached to touch the side of his face. "I'm just so grateful to God that ye're here with us now to enjoy them."

The pressure against his chest eased. "Me too, Maw."

Her touch lingered another moment before she turned to go inside. "I must finish making our supper before your sister and Miss Lockhart return from practice," she called back. "Yer da's in bed having a wee kip, so I need ye to check on Fergus and James and help them to hang Hannah's birthday banner over the front door. They've been out back painting on it for the past thirty minutes, and well . . ." She turned to him again, laughter in her voice. "I'm sure 'tis the thought that counts."

He chuckled as he imagined the lads set loose with brushes and a can of paint. "Aye, and they've likely colored half the yard by now. I'll go and find them."

Moving through the parlor, Alex determined to clear his mind of his troubling thoughts, at least for tonight. It was Hannah's birthday after all, and he wanted it to be special for her. How often did a lass turn sixteen?

He found Fergus and James on the back porch, kneeling over their masterpiece. As he watched them put on the finishing touch, he angled his head to try to make sense of the smeared letters, **Hapy birdday Hana.**

"A fine job, laddies." He smiled as he gazed over their shoulders. "I'm sure our sister will be surprised."

"Alex!"

Both looked up at him then, and Alex stared in shock at the wide swaths of blue paint along the sides of their faces. "Och, what were you thinking to mark yourselves like that?"

"Me and James are warriors. Da says the auld Celts painted their faces blue before they went into battle." Fergus held up his small pot of paint. "See? Maw gave us blue, so we tried it." He squinted up at Alex. "What do ye think?"

Alex tried to look serious while he appraised his brother's efforts. Then he looked at James, whose wide grin showed off his two missing front teeth. "Well now, I'd be shaking in my boots if I came face-to-face with such fierce-looking laddies on the battlefield."

At their gleeful chortles, Alex dropped the boom. "But that's nothing compared to what Maw will do to you both when she finds out."

The two pairs of dark eyes widened, their blue faces puckering in alarm. Then they both glanced toward the dog, lying in the grass off the steps. Sensing their attention, the wee beastie rose to his feet, tail wagging as he turned to them.

"I canna believe . . ." Alex stared at Winston, the blue stripe vivid across one side of his snout. "You painted the dog for battle? What will you tell Miss Lockhart when she sees what you've done?"

"Da says Winston is Scottish, so I made him a Celt just like us." James held up his brush, still soggy with blue paint.

"Da said he's a Scottish *terrier*," Fergus corrected his brother.

Alex turned on his heel, his sides aching. "Bring your sign around to the front and let's get it hung." He barked the order, then went back inside through the house before he lost his battle with laughter.

It was terrible, aye, painting the dog like that. But considering his own mischief with Ian at their ages, he had to grin at his brothers' outrageousness.

He exited through the front and went to the shed to retrieve a few tacks and a hammer, and when he returned, the lads had carried the sign up the front steps. Each held an end of the sticky wet paper, blue faces looking as though they were about to face a firing squad.

Alex took an end of the sign and tacked it high over the door, then the other. When he finished, he eyed each brother sternly.

"Go in now and show Maw what you've done. And dinna forget to tell her about Winston. I willna have your stunt ruining our sister's party tonight."

As he watched them drag their feet into the house, he allowed himself another grin. Best to stay clear of the coming blast.

Exchanging his hammer for the ax, he returned to the back to chop wood. The afternoon was warm, and he started peeling out of his shirt when he remembered Miss Lockhart's reaction the last time he did. He kept it on, leaving it unbuttoned and rolling up the sleeves. It occurred to him then that no one in his family made mention of the scars. Had she kept his secret?

He dropped the first blow with the ax while his thoughts circled around their mysterious boarder. All he really knew about her past were the high points—she'd been orphaned when she was about his sister's age and grew up in Glasgow.

Would Miss Lockhart be leaving at month's end? His already heated skin ignited, remembering their dance. The scent of lavender and her warm hand in his, the delicate outline of her softness as he'd pressed at her back, leading them through the steps.

Of course she should stay. His family had taken to having her here, and she'd been a bonny help to his maw and to Hannah.

She could even keep his room. God willing, he'd succeed in discovering Rhymer before next month and finish his mission. Once Weatherford had him reinstated to active duty in the RAF, Alex would leave Gretna.

And what of your family? Can you just walk out on them? He swung the ax hard at the next chunk of wood. After Ian's death, he'd started sending home half his pay, and he could do a bit more. But with Da unable to work, would it be enough?

At least while he was here his factory wages added to the family's income. And he could chop enough wood for the winter and perhaps re-shingle the auld roof. But what about once he returned to France?

Consumed with working out solutions for his family, he almost missed the sounds of female laughter approaching. He paused, inclining his head. Hannah's girlish humor he recognized, but the other . . .

He turned to see Miss Lockhart standing with his sister on the dirt drive still several yards from the cottage. Smiling, she wove a pretty green ribbon into Hannah's hair, and the sight filled him with warmth. Then his sister launched at her and they embraced, before Hannah laughed and pulled the pin from Miss Lockhart's straw hat and snatched both away.

Again the soft peals of laughter reached his ears, and his pulse quickened as he watched their dark-haired boarder. She was quite bonny when she wasn't trying to be so serious.

"Alex!"

The silence of the ax must have drawn his sister's attention. She hailed him just as Miss Lockhart turned.

Surprised when Hannah giggled and ran off, Alex swiveled his attention to Miss Lockhart. She remained staring at him, her pale face bright as Christmas. It was a moment before he understood and he grinned, dropping the ax to reach for the edges of his open shirt.

❧ ❧ ❧

Rose saw his humor, and the heat in her face intensified before he finally covered his chest. What was she doing, gawking at him like that?

Then she thought of the puckered flesh that stretched across his upper back and shoulders. Even with the afternoon sun, he'd kept his shirt on. Perhaps he didn't want anyone else to see what she'd seen?

How *had* he received the injury? Clearly, the scars were burns. Had his plane crashed?

As if he'd caught her prying into his thoughts, he finished buttoning the shirt and looked up at her, all amusement gone. Then, sinking the ax deep into the stump, he headed toward the cottage.

"Open it!"

Kneeling at their sister's feet, Fergus and James bobbed up and down, eager for Hannah to tear away the paper wrapping and reveal the contents of her birthday package.

Mr. Baird looked on with amused curiosity from his favorite chair in the parlor while Mrs. Baird sat on the couch beside her daughter.

"What is it? A new football!" James poked a finger at the wrapping, his cheek still flecked with blue paint. As Rose watched from the cushioned chair beside Mr. Baird's, she smiled thinking back to the boys' forced confession at supper. Their "face painting" incident had included her poor dog! Winston must love the boys very much to have stood still for that. Hopefully a good scrubbing tomorrow would remove most of the blue from his snout.

Relaxing for the first time in days, Rose was glad to be a part of the family's birthday celebration. She'd been grateful for the fine meal, and even more relieved when Julien failed to make an appearance. Dare she hope he would never return to Gretna?

"Hurry!"

Fergus nudged his sister's knee, and Hannah eyed him sharply. "'Tis my birthday gift, Brother, so you'll wait until I'm ready." She smiled, handing him the scissors. "I'll let you cut the string."

Elated at the prospect, he quickly made the cut before Mrs. Baird snatched the sharp instrument from his possession.

When James thrust out his lower lip, Hannah let him unravel the brown paper, and once it was opened she gasped in delight. "A new costume!" Her eyes glowed as she looked at everyone in the parlor. "'Tis so modern and beautiful!"

She held up the rich green skirt and matching jacket, and Rose again admired Mrs. Baird's workmanship. With the arrival of the pearl buttons today, she had helped Hannah's mother with the finishing touches before supper and then wrapped the gift.

"There's no football?" James sifted through the wrapping for anything his sister might have missed. He sat back, clearly bemused. "Who wants a dress?"

"I do, silly." Hannah grinned at him before reaching to hug her mother. "Thank you, Maw!"

"'Twas my pleasure, lamb. But I couldna have finished those pretty clothes in time if not for Miss Lockhart's help."

"Oh, thank you, Miss Lockhart!" Setting aside her gift, Hannah clambered over her brothers and launched herself at Rose.

Beneath the young girl's smothering embrace, a floodgate of emotion opened in Rose and she hesitated only a second before raising her arms to encircle the slim young girl. "Your mother did most of the work," she said in a hoarse whisper. "I just helped a little."

Hannah leaned back, eyes shining. "Maw tells us that even a wee bit of help makes the grander things possible."

Rose could only manage to smile. Heavens, but she was growing to love this family more and more each day. Too much. How would she tell them good-bye next week?

Her gaze drifted to the captain, standing near the hearth. As he watched them, he didn't smile, but his rough features had softened and his tender look made Rose tingle all the way down to her toes. Had she been imagining his hostility earlier? Because at this moment, he hardly seemed suspicious or watchful. Instead, he clearly enjoyed the company, hers included.

"And now for some Cranachan." Mrs. Baird rose and headed toward the kitchen while Hannah returned to the couch to admire her new clothes. Rose went to assist her mother, looking forward to the delectable whipped cream and berry treat she hadn't sampled since childhood.

She helped to bring the servings out, and while Fergus and James were restricted to the dining room table, Hannah and the adults enjoyed their treats in the parlor—an allowance only on special days, Mrs. Baird informed her.

Rose breathed in the sweet smell of honeyed cream and raspberries as she held the bowl in her lap. "This looks delicious, Mrs. Baird, but after that wondrous meal tonight I am not certain I can eat another bite."

"I dinna doubt it, Miss Lockhart, after watching you tuck into the haggis."

The captain had made the remark and she tensed, until she caught the gleam in his eyes.

Was he jesting with her?

Buoyed by his change in mood, she lifted a brow and smiled. She could give as good she got. "I dinna ken why you'd be surprised, Captain, when I'm a Scots lassie after all."

Laughter filled the room, and to Rose's ears it was a wonderful sound of home. At last the captain said, "I'm glad you can still talk like a Scots and not a Sassenach when it suits you."

Though he was teasing her again, the remark—especially after her revelation earlier today—struck her heart. In six years' time, she had become a different person.

"So where did you learn to speak so properly, Miss Lockhart?"

At his curious gaze, Rose's humor faded. *More lies.* "I . . . was schooled at the orphanage, but I picked up my Sassenach as a paid companion to an English lady from Perth, before I ended up in Nottingham."

"Nottingham?"

His green eyes pierced hers, and Rose gripped her spoon. It was the first time she'd told the Bairds exactly where in England she'd come from. "Yes, my . . . my mistress passed away in Nottingham a while ago, and I stayed on for a time, but I wanted to return to my homeland."

"But not Glasgow?"

Rose pressed her lips against any more lies, stirring the whipped cream in her bowl until it began to liquefy. "I did return to Glasgow for a short while." She shoved away the memory of the horrid clockmaker and added, "On the train north, however, I'd heard a few women mention HM Factory Gretna and the decent wages they offered. I decided to apply, and once I was hired, your sister kindly brought me home to meet your parents and here I am."

"And glad we are."

Mr. Baird beamed at her over the top of his dessert bowl, and again she warmed at the memory of the Baird couple's kindness to her when she first arrived. They'd made every effort not only to welcome her but to include her as part of their family.

Rose smiled at them both, sadness squeezing her heart. As she would soon be leaving, she must make her last memories with them unforgettable.

"So, dear brother, what did you get me for my birthday gift?"

At Hannah's mischievous smile, Rose turned her attention to the captain. He straightened from the mantel, still holding his bowl of dessert. "What's your fancy, lass?"

"Well . . ." The girl's gaze swept over her new clothes. "Maw and Miss Lockhart have gifted me with this lovely costume, and I'd dearly love to wear it out somewhere besides church." She glanced at her parents. "And since I canna go anywhere by myself, I'd like you to take me to Edinburgh."

"Edinburgh?"

"Aye! Please, Alex, you can take me tomorrow." Hannah leaned forward, her eyes lit with hope, the forgotten bowl still in her lap. "We have the day off and I can wear my new dress and . . . if I could invite Gladys Dunham to join us to see the sights, it would be braw!"

Hannah's gaze darted back to her parents, who frowned at their daughter. Mrs. Baird said, "I think after what happened with Miss Lockhart, the lass wouldna be suitable company."

Noting the girl's flagging enthusiasm, Rose asked gently, "Hannah, aside from football practices, have you and Gladys truly made amends?"

"Aye! She came to me this morning and apologized for getting me into trouble at Carlisle." Her eyes pleaded. "Can you forgive her as well, Miss Lockhart?"

Rose considered the live worms in her pockets, the sand in her lunch bucket, the oily boots, the powdered whistle, and discovering salt in her tea. Yet her lasting memory of Gladys Dunham would always be the two lovely posies of heather now hanging in her room. "Mrs. Baird, I believe Miss Dunham has had a change of heart. She's already given me proof of her regret for the foolish incident at Carlisle."

"So ye'd be willing to accompany them?"

"Oh no . . . this is Hannah's birthday outing." Tempting as it was to visit her childhood city, Rose doubted Gladys would want to spend her only day off with her supervisor.

Up until now, the captain had remained silent. He turned to his sister, his look apologetic. "I'm sorry to put a tear in your plan, lass, but I must go into the factory tomorrow after church, at least for a bit. Edinburgh is a full three hours by train. We'd arrive at the city in time to turn back around and come home again."

Again the light dimmed in his sister's mood, and Rose longed to help. "Are there any places closer to home you might consider for a birthday outing?"

The girl shook her head. "Edinburgh has the castle and so much history."

"All right." The captain set his bowl on the mantel. "If castles and history are what you want, lass, then be ready to leave here tomorrow at noon."

"But . . . where will we go, Alex?"

"I'll tell you tomorrow." He smiled and winked at her. "Just bring your maps and a picnic lunch."

"We're to have an adventure?" Again the clouds parted to reveal Hannah's radiance. "I canna wait!" She glanced at her mother. "And Gladys? Can she come along?"

"If Miss Lockhart is willing to give her a second chance and agrees to go with ye, then aye, ye may include the lass."

The captain eyed Rose. "Would you care to accompany us?"

"Please, Miss Lockhart!" Hannah pinned her with a look of desperation. "Surely you must love history?"

Rose did enjoy history, and the idea of spending a Sunday out of doors with a picnic lunch held grand appeal. Besides, if she declined, then Gladys wouldn't have her chance at redemption, and it *was* Hannah's special outing after all.

She smiled at him. "I gladly accept your invitation, thank you."

"You are most welcome."

His warm gaze made her heart beat a little faster. He really was quite charming when he didn't scowl. "What should we wear?" Rose asked.

"Whatever you like." He turned to his parents. "Maw, Da, will you come with us?"

Mr. and Mrs. Baird exchanged a look before his father said, "You children go and enjoy yourselves. Your maw will appreciate a few hours of rest here at the house, and I'll oversee the lads outside, giving the wee dog a bath."

"I must go and find my maps!" Hannah vaulted from the couch, forgetting her bowl so that her mother made a quick grab for it. Undaunted, the girl scooped up her new clothes and headed toward her room. "I'll go and tell Gladys after church tomorrow," she called back. "We'll have such fun!"

Shaking his head, the captain grinned, and Rose's pulse leapt at the rare show of white teeth against his tanned skin. Surely it was just her relief; after all, he hadn't acted suspiciously toward her. He'd even teased her earlier and was quite pleasant all evening.

Her instincts told her he wasn't playacting either, a trait she reserved for Julien alone, who presented his best in public but then abandoned the charade once he was behind closed doors.

"A penny for your thoughts, Miss Lockhart."

Pulled from her musings, Rose realized they were alone. Mrs. Baird had collected the other dessert bowls and returned to the kitchen while Mr. Baird disappeared into the dining room, likely to check on his mischievous sons.

She looked toward the broad-shouldered man at the hearth. "I think that wherever you take us tomorrow, you have made your sister very happy on her birthday."

He offered a slow smile that made her senses tingle, and as she studied his face she saw no guile. Perhaps her secret *was* safe. She wanted to hope, anyway.

"I'll borrow a truck from the factory. We'll need it for where we're going."

Rose nodded, seeds of excitement beginning to sprout in her at their upcoming adventure. It was years since she'd last enjoyed a simple holiday, and this one would be spent in good company. She prayed the day would go well with Gladys too, giving them all plenty of sunshine, sight-seeing, and her an opportunity to learn more about Captain Alex Baird.

She stood and went to him, taking his empty bowl from the mantel to return it with hers to the kitchen.

"Will you be sitting out back again tonight?" he asked her.

"I will." Already she'd determined to make herself useful to Mrs. Baird with the mending before she left Gretna. "Will you be chopping wood?"

Instead of answering, he drew a deep breath, and Rose couldn't help but notice the way his chest expanded. She stood close enough that the familiar smells of leather and spice and a musk that was uniquely his filled her senses. "Aye," he said at last. "I must make sure they have enough fuel for the winter."

His words gave her pause. It was July, and while the split wood must certainly dry out before winter, he'd said "they" and not "we," as if he didn't intend to remain at the cottage.

Did the captain have his own secrets? She hoped for the opportunity during their outing tomorrow to learn more about him. Perhaps inquire about his scars, or the braver question, his relationship with Julien.

And reason enough, Rose Graham, to be on your guard lest he asks you the same question.

23

*B*rother, you've found us a truck!"

Alex had killed the engine and set the brake on the borrowed Leyland when his sister rushed out the front door of the cottage. This morning at church she'd worn her new green frock and still looked as bonny as Miss Lockhart did in her pink as she followed along, carrying the large wicker picnic basket.

He'd gone into the factory earlier to check the employee roster. With Rhymer as yet unknown, Alex wanted to see who was scheduled for the Sunday shift. In truth, he would have preferred to remain at the facility all day, but it was his scheduled day off, and unless he could justify his sudden presence, he ran the risk of raising suspicion. *"Everything by the book,"* Weatherford had said.

Hannah's birthday outing had given him the idea to seek out Mr. Timbrell and request the use of the truck. Then tonight when he returned it, he could review the security log to see who had come and gone during the day.

"Where is your friend, lass?" Alex approached the pair and relieved Miss Lockhart of the large basket. He stowed their lunch into the back of the Leyland's open bed. "Is she not coming?"

"Aye, Gladys will meet us at Gretna's train platform."

"We can all squeeze into the front for now, but you and your friend must sit in back once we get on the road."

Nodding eagerly, his sister rushed with her maps to the Leyland

and climbed into the truck's cab. Miss Lockhart didn't move. "Tell me, Captain. Where exactly *are* we going?"

He noted her uncertainty in the tiny creases at her forehead. Would she change her mind if his answer didna suit her? "I thought you liked surprises, Miss Lockhart."

"Not particularly."

"Well, you needna fash, I thought we'd tour a few countryside castles."

Her relief was almost comical. Did she suspect he'd take them mountain climbing?

"I just wanted to be certain I had dressed properly."

He grinned as she followed his sister into the cab.

Once he'd gone inside to inform his parents, Alex returned and gave the engine a hearty crank before climbing behind the wheel. "Find Lochmaben on the map, Hannah."

"Truly? The castle?" She squeaked her excitement and quickly unraveled the first map. "See, Miss Lockhart? Lochmaben is right here!"

She traced her finger to a point twenty miles northwest of Gretna. "About a half-hour drive," he said.

Her shining eyes met his. "Is that where we'll spend the day?"

"'Tis but a start, lass." He smiled. "If time permits, we'll visit Caerlaverock as well."

"Alex, you're the best brother!"

She turned in the seat to embrace him, and he chuckled, heat tinging his face as he leaned to drop a kiss against the top of her hat. Sweet heaven, how he'd missed this. If Ian were here, it would truly be fine . . .

His mood wavered as he gently set Hannah back against the seat. Alex looked up then and caught Miss Lockhart's gaze, and her eyes held such sadness and longing it made his chest hurt. He'd forgotten she had no family and he tried to muster a smile for her, but she quickly turned her attention to the open window.

With a sigh, he reached to adjust the throttle. Releasing the brake, the Leyland began moving down the long dirt drive. "Let's collect your friend before the day leaves us."

They soon arrived at the platform, and while his sister and her friend climbed into the back of the truck, a very quiet Miss Lockhart remained with Alex in the closed cab.

He'd removed his coat and rolled up his sleeves, but as he drove, the sun continued to roast his exposed skin through the open window. He leaned to peer up at the sky through the windscreen, noting the clear blue color. Then he glanced toward Miss Lockhart as she was blotting her brow with a handkerchief.

She turned to him, and he realized her eyes were the same hue as the sky. "Is July always this hot in the north, Captain?"

Her ivory skin had become a mottled shade of pink, and he began to doubt his judgment in choosing their particular outing. "Our weather's usually dreich. Overcast skies, rain, and the air is brisk even in July. But we've been gifted with a true summer day, so you're welcome to remove your jacket if you wish."

When she appeared to waver, he craned to glance back through the cab's rear glass window at his sister and her friend, now jacket-less. "Guess the lassies had the same idea."

As he turned, Miss Lockhart gave him a shy smile and removed her coat, carefully folding the cloth onto her lap. "Was it warm in Nottingham before you left?" he asked her.

"Yes, it was extremely hot, even more so than today."

"How did you manage once your mistress passed away?"

She seemed to hesitate as she wet her lips, and he imagined their softness. "I found work in a factory for a time, but all the while I was homesick for Scotland."

Alex nodded. She'd said the same last night. He knew he should probably let things lie, but the memory of her longing and sadness prodded him. "You were still fairly young when your parents died, and with your brother already gone, you had no one else?"

"No one." Her skin turned a bright shade, and she reached to fuss with the purple brooch at her collar. "As I told your family, being alone has not been so difficult."

He didna believe her. Miss Lockhart's slender back had gone ramrod-straight, and he'd witnessed the yearning she tried to hide.

He sought a different angle to draw her out. "What did your father do for work?"

She was quiet a long moment, staring at the jacket in her lap. "My dad was in trade. A weaver," she said finally, looking up at him. "He and my mum had a shop—haberdashers, selling lace, ribbons, buttons, scissors, that sort of thing. My mum made dresses to order in the back. They worked the shop together, and we lived in the rooms above."

Alex listened, glancing between her and the road, and saw her expression soften, her eyes wistful and dreamy as though she'd forgotten he was there.

He forced his attention back to driving. "You had a happy childhood, then."

"Yes, while it lasted." She tipped her head toward him. "Would you . . . tell me about the scars, Captain?"

Alex gripped the wheel. He'd wondered when she would ask. "Burns. I received them after my brother's plane went down."

❧ ⚬ ❧

Seeing him tense, Rose leaned forward and waited, but he said no more.

Likely the enemy had shot down Ian's plane. But how was the captain burned in the process? Had they been flying together?

Seconds passed before she sighed and sat back against the seat. She shouldn't have asked him; in fact, last night she'd weighed the decision and decided it was none of her affair.

But just now he'd probed *her* emotions with questions about her mum and dad. Memories still raw and painful, especially after the last six unhappy years. So she'd turned the tables on him and tossed out the first safe question that came to her mind.

Leave him be, Rose. Clearly he didn't wish to speak of his scars, so she shouldn't press him. Not when she kept so many secrets of her own.

"Ian's plane went down over northern France about a year ago."

191

Rose jerked her head toward him. "Hannah told me he died over there. I'm very sorry."

"Not as sorry as I am, lass."

A lump rose in her throat at the agony in his expression.

"I had to be quick in pulling him from the burning wreckage to get him to safety. There was an enemy squadron of planes approaching." He spoke in clipped tones as he shifted his attention to the road. "I tore off my jacket, used it to reach for him. I was out of time, so I hauled his body over my shoulder. His clothes were still burning."

She drew in a sharp breath. *His brother . . . Dear Lord, he'd been on fire!*

He glanced at her then with the same look she'd seen the afternoon he bared his back to her while chopping wood. Grief haunted his face, and she ached for him. "I . . . please, accept my sincerest condolences, Captain. I . . . I cannot imagine how it must pain you and your family."

He nodded, his knuckles white against the steering wheel. "I've not told them what I just told you. I'd like to keep it that way."

"Of course!" Impulsively she reached for him, but then the heat of his skin met her palm and she quickly pulled back. "I promise, I shall say nothing. It is your secret to keep or share as you wish."

Again he offered a brusque nod while keeping his eyes on the road. Rose turned to her open window, the rush of warm air assuaging her sorrow and cleansing her of the awful memories of her own friend's death.

Already they'd driven north several miles beyond Gretna into hillier, forested country and passing small villages with odd names like Kirtlebridge, Ecclefechan, and now a sign for Castlemilk. She glanced at him. "Why the name Castlemilk? Is there a castle?"

"Aye, a small one that sits beside the river known as Water of Milk." He turned to point out her window toward the west. "'Tis now used as a hospital for our wounded returning home. If you look closely, you can see the estate between the trees."

Gripping her hat against the wind, Rose leaned her head out

of the window. "I see it!" When her glimpse of the distant gray stone turret vanished, she turned to him. "Is Lochmaben Castle equally grand?"

Her question seemed to amuse him. "Castlemilk is nothing more than a large manse built about fifty years ago. Lochmaben, on the other hand, is a castle proper. 'Tis centuries auld and filled with history, though now only remnants remain."

She continued to gaze at the sweeping expanse of gentle hills beyond the mansion, appreciating the patchwork golds and greens of farms hemmed in by thick copses of oak, birch, and ash. Rose couldn't recall when she'd been so at ease, with no Luther or Uncle Ridley watching her every move. A smile touched her lips as the wind caught her hair. Despite her reservations about the captain's acquaintance with Julien, she reveled in this newfound freedom.

She looked back at him. "How much farther?"

"About twenty minutes. I hope you find Lochmaben up to your standards, Miss Lockhart."

Rose caught his smile. He was teasing her again. She grinned, grateful he no longer brooded over the past. "I am certain that I will. Your sister was right. I do love history, and your castle tour today was a fine idea."

"Glad you think so. Edinburgh was too far to travel in an afternoon." He kept his focus on the road. "I once lived there as a lad, when my real maw was alive."

"Did you? I too lived . . ." Rose bit her tongue before she could say more.

She was too late. He gave her a sharp look. "You lived in Edinburgh?"

Fool! She looked down at her lap. "What I meant to say is that I have *stayed* in Edinburgh for extended periods of time." She swallowed past the lie to tell another. "With my former mistress."

"Ah, I see. And did you find Auld Reekie to your liking?"

She drew a deep breath to steady her pulse. "The city is quite busy, though I found it interesting with all there was to see. Especially Princes Street with its shops and markets."

"Busier than Glasgow, then?"

Rose pursed her lips. It would be the one and *only* time she ever appreciated her visit to the clockmaker. "I'd say they are both quite grand."

He glanced at her and grunted before turning back to the road. "There's the town of Lockerbie." He pointed ahead. "Lochmaben and the castle are only a few miles to the west."

She was relieved to end their conversation when ten minutes later they entered the small, quaint town of Lochmaben. Passing by a neo-Gothic church that served the local parish, the captain slowed the lorry when they reached a cobbled square, the town hall made of lovely red stonework. Rose also noted a public house and various small shops with flats above.

At the heart of the square stood the statue of a medieval king.

He'd followed her gaze. "Robert the Bruce."

"The king of Scotland was here?"

"Aye, at one time all of this area belonged to his family. See the mound up there?" He pointed west toward an abrupt rise in the land. "The original site of the Bruce castle before the English took it."

He circled the lorry around the statue, and they again left the town of Lochmaben, this time following a road south alongside a rather large body of water. "That's Castle Loch, and the site we'll visit is at the far end."

Before long they took another turn down a graveled road shrouded by trees of pine and birch and, moments later, emerged into a clearing. Rose glimpsed the stone ruins of a fortress surrounded by more trees with wild grasses growing in and around the site.

Ivy had overtaken much of what remained of the taller crumbling walls. "It looks more like a stone skeleton than a castle."

"True, but there's plenty of history." The captain parked the lorry and killed the engine. "And I'm sure my sister will be eager to give us a lesson over lunch down by the loch. Then we can stretch our legs and do a bit of exploring."

Before they could exit the cab, however, Hannah and Gladys bounded from the back to run toward the castle.

"Maybe we'll eat after." He shot her a grin and then climbed out of the cab to shrug into his jacket. Rose remained in her seat and did the same, watching him from the corner of her eye.

She'd noticed earlier how fine he looked dressed in his Sunday best; the white linen shirt fitted snugly across his shoulders, and the brown waistcoat with gold buttons complemented his lean frame. He'd left off with a tie and removed his collar, doubtless due to the heat, and she observed the way the white linen contrasted sharply against his bronzed skin. Certainly he must have spent much time in the sun over in France.

He glanced at her then, a knowing smile on his lips, and quickly she averted her attention. Soon he came around the lorry and opened her door, and after helping her to alight, he offered his arm. "Shall we, Miss Lockhart?"

She stared up at his face, then at his proffered arm.

"No need to fear me, lass. I've been known to be a gentleman on occasion."

Goaded by his amused badgering, she tucked her hand into the crook of his arm, letting him lead her along the grassy trail toward Lochmaben's stone ruins. She could feel the muscles in his arm flex as they walked. "Did this castle also once belong to Robert the Bruce, Captain?"

"You can call me Alex, if you like. By now I'd say you've become well acquainted with my family, and we do live under the same roof."

She gazed at him. Was this the same man who once thought her naïve? The same man who claimed a friendship with the monster she'd almost married?

He's also the man who danced the waltz with you. And he let you win at football. "Alex." She smiled, her cheeks warm. "So was Lochmaben once home to Scotland's king?"

He glanced toward the castle's crumbling walls, where the two girls already tromped about in the grass. "Hannah's the one you should ask. She's read much about the castle's history, the dates, births, deaths, and battles fought here. She told me she intends to become a teacher after the war. Or was it a librarian?" He shrugged. "I canna remember."

He looked down at her, and his boyish grin made her heart do a flip. "I imagine your sister might like to draw maps. She would make a fine cartographer, don't you think?"

"Aye. From the time she was a wee lass, she loved tracing maps of different countries from the books at the library. Maw told me that during the past year, Hannah's been especially impatient to see new places outside of Gretna."

"Indeed." Rose smiled. "Your sister said as much during our first meeting. She is young still but wishes to be grown up. I think in part it has to do with her work at the munitions factory and her association with older girls." She weighed her next words. "Your sister is still learning good judgment in that regard."

His features sobered. "Especially those lassies who like to torment her chaperone?"

Rose nodded and sighed. "The ipecac, of course."

"And more, aye?"

She raised her head sharply, meeting his gaze. Did he know of her troubles at work?

His expression softened. "My sister may have mentioned a few of the . . . surprises you've had to deal with at the factory."

"Hannah? She knew?" Disappointment pierced her. Had the girl been involved with the others in their cruel pranks?

"'Tis not what you think." He halted them on the path. "She confessed to me just this morning before church. She swears she didna take part, and I believe her. But she overheard conversations between those who did, including the lass who's here with her today." He paused. "Hannah's been afraid to speak, but I told her she must tell you."

Rose turned away and nodded. "Thank you. I'm relieved to know she wouldn't stoop to such tricks."

"Yet you never said anything."

Why would she tell anyone her shame? It was bad enough Hannah's admission had revealed to him her weakness as a supervisor. She raised her chin. "It was a matter I needed to handle myself."

Humor lit his gaze. "Aye, I've seen how you handle yourself, Miss Lockhart."

She started to pull away, but he gripped her hand against his body. "Dobbs?"

Rose stopped fighting and relaxed. He hadn't been mocking her.

"I'll admit, I was impressed with the way you stood up to him."

A shaky laugh escaped her. "You have no idea how frightened I was. The man is a troll."

His smile faded. "He willna harm you. You have my word."

Rose saw the way his nostrils flared slightly, the green eyes now dark as the lake. Oddly his fierce look gave her comfort, but it was more than that. "I appreciate your promise, Alex, though I doubt Mr. Dobbs will be bothering us again. And I believe my situation at work is much changed for the better."

She glanced toward Gladys and Hannah, both laughing as they struck silly poses beside the castle's remaining walls. "I think Miss Dunham will become a good friend to your sister."

"I find that hard to believe, when she and the other lass nearly poisoned you and then landed with my sister in jail."

"You may have your opinion, of course. But Gladys has redeemed herself in my eyes." Rose angled her gaze up at him. "Believe me, it makes a world of difference when you know someone cares."

"Alex, Miss Lockhart, hurry up! We want a picture!"

Hannah and Gladys stood together beside one castle wall, each pretending to hold a shield and wield a sword and giggling at each other.

The birthday girl looked lovely in her green ensemble, and Rose was pleased to see Gladys wore a simple yet attractive beige skirt with white shirtwaist and tan jacket. The small straw hat perched atop her dark hair held sprigs of the same purple heather she'd gifted to Rose yesterday.

"Alex, did you bring your Kodak camera?"

This time Rose halted. "Camera?"

Reaching beneath his jacket, he retrieved a small camera from his waistcoat pocket. "I picked this up while I was in France."

"Miss Lockhart, come and join us!"

"Oh, no." Once again she started to pull away from Alex. "You girls should have your own picture so you can show your friends."

Alex turned to her. "What harm could it do?"

"Quite a lot." She searched her mind for an excuse. "My . . . being in the picture with the girls would be construed as favoring them over the others."

Rose hoped her reason would satisfy him. She flinched to imagine her photograph being passed about and possibly discovered by Julien, or Luther, or her uncle.

"I can take a few snapshots of the lassies, and then one with all of you that you can keep for yourself, if you like."

Did he want to take a picture of her to share with her fiancé? "No, thank you." She freed her hand from his grasp and stepped back. "I would be most happy to take a picture of *you* with the girls, however."

"So you're shy of the camera, then?"

"Absolutely."

His lips broadened in a quick smile before he walked over to the girls and began taking pictures. Rose exhaled, grateful he hadn't pressed her. She'd keep a sharp eye on his camera for the rest of their outing, as she could ill afford to have his lens catch her in any unexpected shots.

When they finished their photographs, she joined them on the other side of the wall and surveyed the brick and rock-hewn carcass of what was once a sizable fortress. A marshy slough ran inside along its width, cutting through parallel stone arches. "Hannah, will you tell us about the castle? Your brother says you've studied its history quite extensively."

"Lochmaben is one of my favorite castles." Hannah smiled, her face pink with pleasure. "And actually, this is the second. The first motte castle stood over beside the town."

She pointed across the lake, and Rose nodded. "Alex showed me the rise of land on our way here."

"Aye, well the de Brus family built that fortress in the twelfth century. They received all of this land from Scotland's King David when he appointed them Lords of Annandale. But a century later, during the first battle for Scottish independence, King Edward the first of England defeated the castle and had this one built to house his army."

Hannah took a seat on a boulder of standing rock. "Over the years and lots of battles, the castle changed hands back and forth, but in 1306, Robert the Bruce declared himself King of Scotland and retook this castle from the English and held it for several years."

"Must 'ave been dangerous, livin' back then," Gladys remarked as she took a seat on the edge of an eroding section of wall.

"Aye, but how exciting to live when the Bruce and William Wallace both fought for Scotland's freedom." Hannah's face glowed, clearly impassioned about her subject. "Just think—this castle has been held and destroyed and rebuilt by both English and Scottish kings, and in 1565, Mary, Queen of Scots, and her husband, Lord Darnley, attended a banquet here while her troops chased down rebels who supported her half brother, James Stuart!"

She surveyed the ruins. "After more years of war and a very bloody religious battle, our King James the sixth became James the first of England, Ireland, and Scotland, and this garrison castle was no longer necessary. Lochmaben was abandoned, and now much is gone." She turned to Rose. "So that's what I know, Miss Lockhart. If only these walls could speak."

"Thank you, Hannah." Rose smiled. "And I am certain the walls would tell us many stories about kings and queens and battles . . . and too much death."

She turned to Alex, who leaned with arms crossed against one of the taller walls. "Why is it that men have such a penchant for fighting?"

"And why did I ken you'd ask me that?" He grinned at her and shrugged. "I suppose our nature demands it. Men do fight to defend themselves, but also for power and territory. We fight to settle grievances between us or to establish boundaries. Some men also enjoy fighting for the sport."

"Some sport!" Hannah snorted.

"Aye." Gladys bobbed her head. "In London, I've seen enough clobberin' in the streets and behind closed doors to know they like it."

"I was speaking more about boxing," Alex said. "The pugilist fights in the ring for money and glory, not because he's angry. And in America, they use boxing techniques to train their men for war."

Rose shook her head. "For sport or not, fisticuffs still makes no sense to me."

"That's because you're a woman, and as a rule you are nurturers and not fighters. And I'll readily admit, the world couldna survive a man's hard edges without a lassie's soft hand to smooth them out."

She smiled. "That is quite poetic for a man of war."

He chuckled. "Aye, I suppose it is." He pushed off the wall and approached. "All this talk of fighting has given me an appetite." He winked at the girls. "Shall we go and have a bite to eat down by the loch?"

"Aye!" Hannah and Gladys shouted, and Rose watched them race toward the lorry for the picnic basket.

"How about you, Miss Lockhart?" His eyes gleamed. "Has our bloodthirsty history of kings and queens made you hungry?"

Rose laughed, and he chuckled as he again offered his arm. Tucking her hand against him, she said, "'Tis made me positively famished, Sir Knight. Lead on."

24

"Thanks for lettin' me come along today, Miss Lockhart. I'm 'avin' a grand time."

Gladys spoke in a hushed tone beside Rose as the two sat at the lake's edge, watching a pair of swans glide through the water while dragonflies danced above its dark-green surface.

Alex and Hannah sat across from them as they all shared the plaid blanket laden with Mrs. Baird's delicious oatcakes, raspberry jam, carrots, boiled eggs, and Dunlap cheese.

"I'm pleased that you joined us, Gladys." She leaned toward the girl and smiled. "The purple heather you gave me was lovely, and a very nice gesture. Thank you."

Gladys dropped her gaze. "I owed it, ma'am. With all o' the trouble I made for ye."

"Let's not speak of the past." Rose reached to lift Gladys's chin. "Everyone deserves a second chance to become the person God meant them to be." She pressed a hand to her heart. "In here."

Gladys offered a crooked-tooth smile, her dark eyes aglow. "Never 'ad anyone take up for me like ye did with Mr. Dobbs. Ye weren't afraid of 'im atall!"

Rose laughed, drawing the attention of the others. "That seems to be the consensus, but in truth my dislike of bullies outweighed my fear."

"You mean Mr. Dobbs?" Hannah had paused with a wedge of cheese to her lips. "Miss Lockhart, you were brave defending us against that awful man on Friday." She gave Gladys a smile. "It reminded me of David and Goliath."

"Who are they?" Gladys reached for a hard-boiled egg.

"From the Bible! You've not read it?"

When Gladys shook her head, Hannah set down her cheese. "'Tis the story of how a wee lad named David killed a giant named Goliath, hitting him between the eyes with a stone from his sling." Her amber eyes sparkled. "But instead of a stone, our wee Miss Lockhart hit big auld Mr. Dobbs in the head with a piece of her mind!"

"If only it 'ad stuck!" Gladys crowed, and the two girls doubled over in a fit of giggles.

Rose looked from one to the other, then glanced helplessly at Alex. He only grinned and shook his head.

The girls were still merry when they climbed back into the open bed of the lorry an hour later, and once Alex had checked Hannah's map for directions to the next castle, he drove them south toward the town of Dumfries.

"I'm so glad Hannah is enjoying her day," Rose said after a few minutes, thinking of the two girls laughing over their own jest.

"Aye, she's had to go to work at a young age, and you ken the hours are long at the factory." He added gruffly, "She deserves to be just a lass for a day, without cares or responsibilities."

"Mm." Rose nodded. "And she is very fortunate to have you as her brother."

"You think so?" His eyes crinkled at the edges with humor.

"I do." Her heart thrummed to see his soft smile. What was happening? She should be on her guard with him yet found herself drawn, not only by his obvious physical appeal but more importantly by his love and care for his family. She didn't doubt he would sacrifice all to help them through their troubles; he'd proven that when he almost died to save his brother.

She continued gazing at his profile. It was because of that love he hid his scars and the burden of truth about the horrible way Ian Baird had perished. Like Rose, concealing the heartache of losing someone so dear to her.

"You've grown quiet, Miss Lockhart."

She cleared her throat. "Just woolgathering." She glanced ahead as they seemed to be approaching another village. "Is Caerlaverock Castle on this road?"

"Aye, but we'll stop in Dumfries first to get petrol. The castle's to the south, and once we've finished we'll drive back along the Solway Coast into Gretna."

"Is Caerlaverock also situated beside a lake?"

"Just a wee body of water and marshland. Hopefully the foot-bridge is still in place, otherwise we'll need a boat to row across." He glanced at her. "Have you ever been afloat, Miss Lockhart?"

Rose nodded. "Dad had a friend who sometimes loaned him the use of his boat, and he and I would go fish one of the small lakes." Smiling at the memory, she recalled the worms in her smock pockets. "I was not squeamish about baiting the hook, and it was a wonderful way to spend time with him."

"You loved him much, then."

His deep voice had gentled, and her heart swelled with emotion. "Yes." She turned to him. "Aye. Very much."

"When I was a wee lad, Da would sometimes hop the train over to Leith and tell me later that he'd gone out with the men of Newhaven to help bring in the catch. He'd take away some fine cod and haddock for his trouble. Here in Gretna we've angled for trout and salmon off the waters of Border Esk, but one time he took us out on the Solway and we brought back sea bass and one pollock that Da fought like the devil to get into the boat."

Rose saw how his features softened as he reminisced. "Your father is a good man, Alex. In fact, he reminds me much of my own." She clung to the memory of Mr. Baird's fatherly gaze and his kindness toward her when she'd told him about life with her mum and dad.

"Da's always been a hard worker," Alex said, turning his eyes toward the road. "For the past thirty years he's been in charge of rail and equipment maintenance for the Caledonian Railway. When the big Quintinshill crash happened three years ago just north of Gretna, he and his crew worked night and day to repair the damage. I know it must grieve him now, being unable to work. Though he does a fine job helping Fergus and James after school with their lessons."

Rose wondered if Alex mourned his own medical discharge from the RAF. He was an officer and had doubtless seen much action overseas. Was he satisfied working in the munitions factory? "Your father is wise, and I'm sure your mother appreciates his help with your brothers." She smiled recalling the peas in James's nose during her first dinner at the Baird home. "Those boys certainly do stay busy."

Alex chuckled, and she was glad to be able to lighten his spirits. "Aye, especially when it comes to their imagination with paint."

He turned and flashed a wink at her, and Rose's pulse gave a start. Absently her fingers went to the thistle brooch at her collar. "I wonder if Winston's bath proved successful."

"If not, he'll be branded a Celt for life."

She laughed and dropped her hand to her lap. Wouldn't dear Tilly be proud of that? "If he is to be a Celt, then we must get him his own plaid."

She and Alex shared another amused look before Rose ventured to ask more about his family. "Hannah told me Mrs. Baird is your stepmother. When did you first meet her?"

"I was nearly five when my own maw died. Da met Mairi Hamilton a few weeks later when he interviewed for someone to care for me while he was at work. They married a year later, and we eventually moved here when Da transferred to the station at Gretna." He glanced at her. "Mairi's a good woman, and I know she loves me like her own."

"She dotes on you."

Her remark seemed to please him. "Aye. She is my maw in all the ways that count."

"She spoke to me about you and Ian with much love." Realizing too late she'd brought up the tender subject of his brother again, Rose still plunged ahead. "You two were once 'thick as thieves' as she put it, and always full of mischief."

He was silent for a long moment, his posture stiff while his hands clenched the steering wheel. Regret filled her. Why had she pressed him with more unhappy memories? It seemed any mention of Ian Baird pained him.

His next remark surprised her. "Ian was . . . a bit wild, but he had a good heart and a fine sense of humor. He loved teasing Hannah when she was a bairn, but he always made up with her, giving her a piece of sugared fruit or a ride on his bicycle."

Rose eased back in the seat. "And the story about the mischief?"

He laughed, a low rumble from deep in his chest that made her shiver with pleasure. "'Twas more like Ian getting us *into* trouble and me trying to get us *out*." He turned to her, his eyes gleaming. "We were six years apart and so it was my responsibility . . ."

His voice trailed off, along with the light in his eyes as he turned toward the road. "I was to take care of him, always. I failed in that as well."

Again, Rose ached for his loss. "I am sure you did your best."

"How could you possibly know that, Miss Lockhart?"

She flinched at his tone yet held her ground. "I've seen the way you care about your family, Alex. Even your scars are a testament to the love you hold for them. You tried to rescue your brother, but daily this war kills so many young men—"

"The war didna kill him." He bit out the words. "I'm the one who pressed him too hard, too far."

Rose stared at him. What could she say? He was correct—she hadn't witnessed the plane crash or what led to his brother's death. She had no right to make assumptions. Hadn't she accused him of the very same sin that morning after their first encounter?

Yet in her heart she couldn't believe he'd intentionally harmed his brother. Though guilt did terrible things to the mind, as she well knew.

She frowned as he raised a hand to rub at his forehead. "Have you had more trouble with your headaches since you arrived back in Gretna?"

He turned to her sharply, his look much like an angry bear. She hesitated. "You mentioned to your parents last week that you suffered headaches from the battle fatigue?"

"Aye, sometimes."

His shoulders relaxed, and he shifted his attention back to the road. Relieved to have soothed his mood once more, Rose wondered if she dared use the moment of calm to ask him about Julien.

How should she go about it without raising his suspicions? She folded her hands in her lap and said, "I imagine you enjoyed flying very much. I hope you'll get the opportunity to do so again. Does this battle fatigue eventually go away?"

"In most cases," he said. "The condition's called aeroneurosis, a common enough symptom of war pilots who spend too many hours in the cockpit. Many suffer headaches and nervousness as a result, but it can be cured with time and rest"—he turned to her—"though for some, like me, it can take longer to recover. 'Tis similar to shell shock in soldiers, if you've heard of it."

Rose vaguely recalled an article in the newspaper about the condition. "Do any of the other pilots in your squadron suffer from it?" She paused, deliberating her next words. "Does . . . Lieutenant Dexter have aeroneurosis?"

"Why the deuce would you ask me that?"

At his thunderous look, she pressed herself up against the truck door. *Oh, Lord, I've gone and done it!* Pulse racing, Rose combed her mind for an excuse. "Because . . . I understand that you know the lieutenant. Hannah mentioned that the two of you have flown together."

"Aye." Jaw working, he stared at the road. "Aeroneurosis has never been his problem." He flashed another heated look at her. "Does that satisfy your curiosity, Miss Lockhart?"

Far from it. Still, she nodded briskly. Were Alex and her fiancé less than friends after all?

Silence ensued as he continued to drive, though his muscled arms and shoulders flexed while his knuckles whitened against the steering wheel. When he didn't look at her, Rose exhaled and turned back toward the open window. Strands of her hair beneath the hat blew wildly about as she stared at the pastoral scenery.

Unwanted thoughts of Julien resurfaced, like him standing beside Alex and the newspapermen while he worked his charm on Hannah and the other girls. And Rose had watched all from the safety of her hiding place. What if her return to the vats had been just a few minutes earlier?

A shiver ran through her as she reached to pull away a wisp of hair the wind had caught. The possibility didn't bear imagining.

Her gaze darted back toward the man seated beside her. Was he friend or foe? Their time together at Lochmaben Castle and a lovely picnic beside the lake hardly seemed the subterfuge of a man intending to turn her over to her fiancé.

There is more than yourself at stake if you are wrong. Rose squeezed her eyes closed, fear warring against her desire. If only she could be certain!

She hated pulling up her tender roots in Gretna. Leaving her job, even her girls now that Gladys had made amends. And especially leaving the Bairds, including Alex. But the only way to safeguard Duggie and Samuel was to remain dead to the world. Rose had called the school again on Thursday, still pretending to be her aunt, and was glad to learn the boys were still there.

They soon arrived in Dumfries, and Alex pulled up beside a petrol pump. Longing to ease her restlessness, Rose exited the cab and stretched her legs. Hannah and Gladys were quick to clamber out the back of the lorry and rush across the street to a department store, where they stood at its large plate-glass window and admired the items on display.

Alex had already started adding fuel for the rest of their journey. Rose studied his capable movements while her disquiet continued unabated. She wanted to trust that he and Julien were more rivals than friends—a situation she could believe knowing her fiancé's arrogance, his cruelty *and* his corruption.

What would happen if she simply asked Alex?

Do you really want to take that chance? She turned away and sighed. Let it be enough that she was leaving Gretna in a few days. Until then, she and Alex were enjoying a lovely afternoon, and she hoped the earlier friction between them was at an end.

Resigned to her decision, she looked across the street at the two girls. A smile touched her lips, observing their animated conversation as both pointed to something in the window.

She glanced toward Alex, and his tender expression as he watched his sister made Rose again doubt her suspicions.

Hannah looked up then, and her face filled with joy as she waved at him. Once more a deep hunger seized Rose as she witnessed their silent exchange. How she longed for her own little family!

"Are you ready to continue, Miss Lockhart?"

She turned to see Alex had completed his task and stood with his back against the lorry. "Or shall we see what trinket has those two girls jabbering like magpies?"

His smile lifted her spirits and she nodded her assent, strolling with him across the street to the store.

"D'ye think them comely, Miss Lockhart?"

Gladys pointed in the window, her dark eyes shining. "I once seen the like in a display window at Selfridges in London."

Rose eyed the pair of stylish green gloves the girls had been ogling in the display. Then her gaze drifted to the other items offered in the store—woolen tams and ready-made dresses, an array of buttons, spools of silk thread, ribbons, and knitting needles. So many of the same wares her mum and dad once sold in their Edinburgh shop.

"Miss Lockhart?"

Swallowing, she turned to meet the pair of expectant faces. "The gloves are quite lovely. And the color matches your jacket and skirt perfectly, Hannah."

Pleasure lit the girl's face. "And to think, the very same gloves in Selfridges are being sold here in Dumfries!" She glanced at her brother. "What do you think, Alex? Would they not be perfect to wear to church in Gretna?"

Alex merely shrugged and continued perusing an array of hand-carved pipes and various brands of smoking tobacco in the window.

Hannah turned to Gladys, her bubble of pleasure deflated. "I should have expected my brother's reaction when it comes to fashion . . . Oh, look, Gladys! Aren't those lavender ribbons fine?" And like quicksilver, their attention was averted.

"If you lassies want to see the next castle, we'd better go."

Alex made the announcement, and Hannah heaved a dramatic sigh, no doubt meant for her brother as she turned away from the window with Gladys and the two trudged back to the lorry.

He remained in front of the display. "Go on ahead to the truck, Miss Lockhart. I need to make a purchase and I'll be out in a minute."

"Of course." She too glanced toward the tobacco and pipes in the window. How thoughtful to buy a gift for his father! Mr. Baird enjoyed having a smoke on the back porch, and no doubt tobacco was a luxury in the Baird home.

She returned to explain his purchase for Hannah's father, then climbed into the cab. Alex soon arrived, having again shed his coat. He handed Rose the folded bundle, and once they were back on the road, he steered them south toward Caerlaverock Castle.

"I'm sure your father will enjoy his gift." She held the coat, noting the thickness of a package hidden within its folds.

"That would be a sight." He looked amused. "And I can assure you he willna be caught dead in those."

"But . . . I thought you purchased tobacco?"

"Aye, that too." He patted his waistcoat pocket. "Open the package, but take care the lassies dinna see you from the back."

Rose craned her head toward the rear window to see the girls safely occupied. She opened the folds of the coat, already guessing

Alex had purchased the pretty green gloves for his sister. She cast another glance before peeling back the paper and running a finger over the soft leather. "Hannah will be delighted."

"My sister's hints are like a brick to the head when she wants something." His crooked grin made her pulse leap. "'Tis her birthday, though, and I've got several to make up for."

Of course, he'd been away during his years at war. Rose smiled and tucked the gift back into the folds of his coat.

"I imagined that shop in Dumfries was much like the one your parents had in Glasgow?"

Glasgow . . . Jerked from her pleasant moorings, Rose focused on trying to keep her story straight. "Yes, though our shop was not nearly the size of the department store. Still, we had many of the same items, including a few pairs of ladies' gloves like these." She patted his coat.

"Do you plan to open your own shop one day?"

She eyed him sharply. Surely it was a harmless question. "I have been thinking about it. It has been years since I assisted my mum with dressmaking and my dad with the accounts and purchases, but I believe I would be capable of running a shop, if I set my mind to it." She decided to give him equal treatment. "What about you? Do you have any plans beyond the munitions factory?"

"Flying." His response was immediate, before he glanced at her, a slight coloring in his features. "That is, if I'm able to get back in the air."

"How did you get started flying planes?"

He smiled. "I've always loved being around planes and the idea of flight. Before the war, I worked as a mechanic at the Larkhill Aerodrome in Wiltshire, and I met my best friend, Simon Forrester, who was a pilot-in-training." Alex turned to her. "He had a gift for flight and soon moved up the ranks in the Royal Flying Corps. Once the war started, he and I shipped off to Dover, and he got his orders to fly to France. A few months later, I decided to begin pilot training myself, and before I was recently discharged, I was flight commander for our squadron at Saint-Omer in France."

So his best friend was not Julien? Rose wet her lips. "Is your best friend . . . still flying?"

"Aye, he's training RAF pilots now at Stonehenge. Though he's stuck in an office job until his wife has the bairn in a couple of weeks." He grinned. "He hates being grounded."

Rose eased back against the seat. Thank goodness she hadn't broached another awkward topic. "So, will you return to the RAF?"

"No. I've been doing some reading, and a few years ago the first British pilot transported mail by air between Hendon and Windsor. And during the past two years, the RAF has flown some supplies to our troops in the east. I believe long-distance mail delivery by plane will become a standard for the future." He smiled at her. "And I want to be a part of that."

"Will you remain in Scotland?"

"Aye, I want to be based near my family." He paused. "Will you return to Glasgow?"

Rose hesitated, debating what to say. She had to maintain some secrecy, but she cringed with each lie she told, even to Alex. Especially to Alex. "Not Glasgow. I want to see more of the world first. Perhaps sail across the Atlantic and visit Canada." She decided to hedge. "Or America."

His brows lifted. "That would surely be more of the world."

"I've seen brochures. The lands across the ocean look beautiful. The advertisements encourage people to come and make a new start. Fitting for after the war, don't you think?"

"Aye." He focused on the road ahead. "A new start can be a good thing."

"Yes." Rose stared at her lap as she imagined Duggie and Samuel's faces. "A time to forgive . . . and to be forgiven." Then recalling the preacher's words, she added, "To let go of the past and look ahead to a new future."

When Alex made no comment, she looked up. Had she managed to anger him again, reminding him of his own wounds?

He met her gaze then, and Rose took heart to see a new light dawn in his eyes. "I hope you're right, Miss Lockhart." He turned back toward the road. "I pray that you are right."

The sun hung low against the horizon by the time Alex finally pulled up near Timber Town in Gretna to allow Hannah's friend a short walk to the factory huts.

With the truck's motor still running, he climbed from the cab and glanced back inside, a smile on his lips. Miss Lockhart slumped at an angle against the opposite door, sound asleep, her small straw hat askew as the side of her face pressed into the cushioned seat. *Och, that I would be able to sleep again like the angels.*

He headed to the back to see to the lassie's departure, and once she and Hannah said their good-byes, his sister asked to stay in the back of the open truck. With the night air still balmy, he agreed.

"Thank you for a perfect day, Alex." She leaned back against the cab's rear window, her expression tired but happy. "Having you home is the best gift of all, but now I have these gloves." She held up her hands encased in the soft green leather he'd gifted her once they reached Caerlaverock. "And I got to spend the entire day with my big brother and Gladys and Miss Lockhart." She sighed her contentment. "'Tis a birthday I shall never forget."

He tipped his head. "You're not tired of castles, then?"

"After today, I want to see more!" She reached to prod him in the chest with a gloved finger. "And once this war is over, you'll have time to take me."

She grinned at him, and Alex managed a smile, the vise on his chest tightening. He'd soon be gone. After he completed his assignment, he would return to the war and his duty.

The plans he shared with Miss Lockhart earlier were just dreams. Only God knew if or when he'd ever come home again, and until then he would be lost to his family. "Aye, lass," he said, his voice thick. "We'll go and visit them all."

Walking back to the truck's cab, he turned his mind from the future to the present. There was the mission to think about. Would he find Rhymer tomorrow?

He opened the cab door and paused. Miss Lockhart slept on, but she'd left her place at the opposite door to sprawl on her side, her head resting on the seat under the steering wheel.

Grinning, he reached in and gently nudged her back to an upright position, almost laughing when she failed to stir at all. Once he maneuvered his way behind the wheel, he tilted her head with its crooked hat back against the top of the seat. "Sleep well," he murmured.

Releasing the brake, he set out toward home. He still wanted to check the log sheets when he returned the truck to the factory later. Would he find anything? Someone in the factory outside their scheduled shift or in an unassigned area?

An unexpected weight landed against his shoulder; at the same time Miss Lockhart's straw hat smacked the side of his face. Reaching up, Alex pulled the decorative pin from the hat and tossed both across the seat so that only her dark head bobbed gently against him.

As she continued to sleep, he slowed the truck so he could study her. In such a tranquil state, she made a bonny sight. Her milky skin seemed as soft as lamb's wool, its smoothness broken only by her rosy lips, now relaxed and faintly parted. Tiny spots of pink revealed where the afternoon sun had kissed her cheeks and a slightly pointed chin.

With her eyes closed, he allowed himself to peruse the fine brows arched high above thick lashes, while the hair she'd worn pinned up all day unraveled at her temples.

Not so different from their very first meeting. Alex smiled recalling her attempt to brandish him with his nine-iron, her long braid of hair the color of rich earth coming completely undone. He remembered a few nights later when she'd waltzed with him in her bare feet, surrounding him in the scent of lavender, her soft hand in his . . .

"'Tis a wasted flight your thoughts have taken, lad," he muttered as he turned his full attention to the road ahead. Once he returned to France, his future was uncertain. And Miss Lockhart made it clear she planned to cross an ocean once the war was over.

The weight against him grew heavier as the sleeping woman turned into him. Then she reached to rest that same soft hand across his shoulder.

His smile returned as he imagined her shock when she awakened to find herself in such a state. Yet he hesitated to nudge her away. Aye, she *was* soft and vulnerable, yet she'd shown her courage against a man like Dobbs. She was smart and determined and bonny and—

"No more." Pushing out a sigh, he wheeled the truck onto the long dirt drive that led toward home. As he parked in front of the house and killed the engine, Alex found his angel still sound asleep. Gazing at her upturned face and the dark lashes fanned against her fine cheekbones, he was reluctant to wake her. He'd give himself just a wee bit longer—

"Maw! Da! We're home!"

His sister's noisy clambering from the truck managed to awaken Miss Lockhart. The lashes fluttered open, and for an infinite second her languid gaze met his, soft and warm and inviting. His heart thudded heavily as he watched her, pierced with a sudden need that the moment should go on forever.

But as she slowly raised her head, he kenned the spell was broken. Her fair complexion surged with color as she yanked her arm from his shoulder and straightened to sit rigid against the seat.

"Alex? Miss Lockhart? Aren't you coming in?"

Alex glanced out the window in time to see his sister approach. "Go on inside, Hannah. We'll be there in a moment."

She spun around to head back to the front door. Alex turned to his sleeping angel. "Are you all right?" he asked gently.

She looked away. "I . . . yes, I . . . I need to find my hat and the pin."

He reached around her, fetching them from the other side of

the cab as she pressed herself against the seat. Handing her the hat and pin, she quickly began fixing her hair.

Exiting the truck, he went around to the other side to help her down. She clung to him after her feet had touched the ground, and he held her fast for another few seconds until she got her footing. Not once did she look at him, her face still a rosy hue.

"I need to return the truck to the factory tonight, so I'll be off and return in a couple of hours. Will you let my family know?"

Her eyes darted to the cottage entrance, and she nodded.

"All right then. I'll see you later."

Once he let go of her, she strode to the front porch where she paused and turned, her head down so he couldna see her face. "Thank you, Alex."

Without waiting for his response, she opened the door. Alex watched her, his pulse still racing as she raised her head and disappeared inside.

25

OFFICE OF THE ADMIRALTY
WHITEHALL, LONDON
MONDAY, JULY 22

Once again the game was on.

"They've found her." Elation shot through Marcus as he replaced the telephone receiver on its hook and turned to his friend.

"Found who?" Simon had taken up the leather wing-back chair across from him.

"Miss Tilda Lockhart." He waved toward the telephone. "That was the desk chief at MI5. Last month they installed a man at Moorside to pose as a clerk in the payroll office, hoping to flag any new hires with the name Thomas Brown or Rhymer. However, this morning it was Miss Lockhart's name that surfaced on the payroll list."

Simon looked bemused. "And how is finding this Miss Lockhart significant?"

"This." Marcus reached into his file and retrieved the frayed paper tag from St. Ezekiel's orphanage in Glasgow. He handed it across the desk.

Simon took up the tag and read it. "What is this, Marcus?"

He glanced up, his brow creased. "I canna make sense of your sudden revelation."

"That tag was discovered months ago in Kahverengi's abandoned flat."

"You mean when they found the list of targeted munition factories?"

"Righto." He nodded. "From the information you hold in your hand, we were able to track down Miss Lockhart at Aylesbury Prison. Detective Quinn of Scotland Yard's Special Branch accompanied me to Buckinghamshire to broker the deal."

The gray eyes across the desk narrowed on him as Simon tossed the tag back onto the desk. "I assume that you'll tell me before the sun sets what all of this means?"

"Miss Tilda Lockhart is Rhymer's sister."

His friend straightened in the chair. "Why is she at Moorside . . . ?" He paused, frowning. "Rhymer's getting ready to make his move."

"Exactly."

"But . . . if you knew all of this when we met with Alex, why did you not tell us?"

"At the time, Miss Lockhart had disappeared without a trace. We believed that she fled the country after the Chilwell explosion."

"Marcus." Simon eased back in his seat, propping an ankle across his knee. "Back up just a wee bit with this story and explain."

Marcus relayed the details of his meeting at the prison with Miss Lockhart. "In exchange for a pardon, she agreed to let us place her at Chilwell. She was only required to find her brother and make a positive identification." He paused. "We needed to make an arrest and get Rhymer's testimony in order to catch his boss, Kahverengi."

Simon angled his head. "But . . ."

"Two days before the explosion, she received a small package from him. Her brother must have seen her at the factory or discovered her on the employee roster, and he decided to test her loyalty by recruiting her. The package contained explosives with instructions to get the bombs inside Chilwell and then meet with him."

"And did she do it?"

"Not directly," Marcus hedged. "Scotland Yard had a man acting as her contact, and they arranged to switch the real bombs for dummy charges. Two detectives were already inside the factory and instructed to follow Miss Lockhart to the meeting place where they would arrest Rhymer. But then suddenly the factory exploded, and she disappeared . . . until today."

"If she carried only dummy charges, then how did the factory explode?"

"We have no solid answer to that." He sighed. "And because the two detectives died in the blast, we cannot even confirm if she met with Rhymer. At the time, we surmised that either Rhymer did not trust his sister and planted the explosives himself or she'd tipped him off about Scotland Yard's plan, and he set the explosives while she made her escape. But now that she's resurfaced at the next munitions target—"

"Clearly, Miss Lockhart *was* his accomplice and she's connected with him to the arms dealer." Simon eyed him gravely. "That about sum it up?"

Marcus hesitated. "There's more."

"More?" Simon frowned.

"MI5 reported a blunder in the payroll office with Miss Lockhart's employment paperwork. She's actually been working at the factory for over two weeks."

Simon leaned forward in the chair. "Alex needs to know, Marcus. *Now.*"

"Trust me, he will before the day is out."

"So Rhymer is there?"

"We haven't confirmed it. Scotland Yard interviewed every employee at Moorside named Thomas Brown—a total of seventeen. All have been cleared as suspects."

"Did you ever make a connection between Thomas Brown and Rhymer? You said both names were written on the target list."

Marcus shook his head. "Miss Lockhart told us she once had a brother, Thomas, but she did not recognize the name Brown. We only made the connection between her brother and Rhymer when she mentioned some Scots legend from their childhood, a story about 'Thomas the Rhymer.' Seems her brother was quite taken with using the moniker."

"I remember the tale. Thomas the Rhymer was a real bard from the Middle Ages who wrote about his visits to the fairies—"

"Enough, please." Marcus held up his hand. "I've been briefed on the story." He rose and came around the desk. "Honestly, Simon? If I think too long about these *scraps* of evidence we've collected, it seems an impossible task to catch this saboteur." He scowled. "In fact, I suspect the name Thomas Brown on that list is fictional, and Kahverengi's plan is to waste our time. He's got Scotland Yard expending most of their resources, interviewing every man with a name so common there must be hundreds working inside our munitions industry. And while we waste manpower, *he* takes his time orchestrating the next explosion."

"So, what will you do now? Have Miss Lockhart arrested?"

"Of course not." He dismissed his friend's surprised look. "We must wait until she makes contact with her brother. Once Rhymer is known to us, we can catch him in the act." He began to pace. "It is maddening to know she has been at Moorside all this time without our knowledge. I can only hope we haven't missed something already."

"That means everyone living in Gretna is in danger."

Marcus paused and turned to him. "We still have ten days, if Kahverengi keeps to his August schedule. That is why I want you to tell Alex."

Simon rose from the chair. "Me?"

"Make it clear he is to locate her, but under *no circumstances* is he to confront her. Then report back to me, understood?"

"I'll send a telegram right away."

Marcus nodded. "Keep me apprised."

Once Simon left his office, Marcus resumed his pacing. He clung to one last hope—that if they didn't know until today Miss Lockhart was at Moorside, perhaps her brother didn't know yet either.

He returned to his desk and reached for the telephone. "Get me Quinn."

Marcus could only pray they were not too late.

26

*T*ime was running out.

Alex frowned as he stared at the clipboard and the names of his new suspects. He'd stayed late at the factory last night after returning the truck, checking log sheets and running them against last week's work roster to see if anyone not scheduled was inside the factory yesterday.

Three names had popped up, and Dobbs was one of them.

Two nights ago he'd sent in the union steward's name with his cronies. How long would it take Scotland Yard to investigate and get back to him?

As for the other names, two machinists in the boiler area, he'd spent the morning observing them and planned to send his inquiry to Stuart during lunch.

Tucking the clipboard under his arm, he headed toward Dobbs's work area. Alex intended to ask the union steward if he'd resolved the leaky tank issue after his skirmish with Miss Lockhart on Friday. Any excuse was good if it meant he could keep an eye on the man.

Passing through the nitroglycerine section, he paused to glimpse Miss Lockhart near the vat tables, speaking earnestly with one of her charges.

Warmth seeped into his chest. His sleeping angel in pink was back to being the factory lioness minding her cubs. Hopefully, after sharing their afternoon yesterday with Gladys Dunham, the pranks against her were at an end, too.

She looked up then and smiled, and his pulse picked up its pace. Giving her young lassie a pat on the shoulder, she walked in his direction.

"'Tis a good day?" he asked as she approached, relieved she'd finally recovered from her embarrassment of last night.

"What do you think?" She wore a satisfied look. "I finally received my wages."

He raised a brow. "Now, that's cause for a celebration."

"I think so." She bounced up on her toes. "I can afford now to splurge on a cup of tea at the canteen."

He smiled. "I'm just happy to see you in better spirits, lass."

Her face turned pink. "I was not trying to avoid you, Alex."

"Aye, you were," he said, amused. This morning at breakfast was the first he'd seen of her since she awoke in his arms last night and went inside the house. And all the way into work, she barely gave him a glance.

"Well, I may have been just . . ."

"A wee bit self-conscious?"

She nodded and sighed. "A wee bit." Then her large blue eyes met his, and Alex thought he might drown in their depths. "I have not properly thanked you for yesterday. You know, for . . . for . . ."

He reached to brush his hand along the side of her face. "No need, lass," he said. Then he winked. "I enjoyed every minute."

She straightened, her fine forehead creased. "Are we speaking of the same thing?"

"I thought we were." He tipped his head, grinning. "What do you think?"

Her color brightened. "I think I must get on with my paperwork." Yet as she headed toward her office, she turned to him and smiled.

Alex followed her with his gaze, heart thrumming as he looked forward to the evening when they would converse at supper, and knowing she would be near while he chopped wood as she sat on the back porch with his maw's basket of mending.

It still surprised him how much he'd shared with her yesterday about Ian's death and the scars he'd received on his back. Except for Captain Weatherford last year, Alex had not spoken of the accident with anyone else, not even Simon. Yet Miss Lockhart was practically a stranger.

No, not a stranger. Again he envisioned her face as she'd first opened sleepy eyes to him, her smile soft and dreamy, just before she roused to full consciousness. An intimate revelation that had pierced his soul. And he found he could talk with her and he needna fash about her passing judgment, at least not as harshly as he judged himself.

What *had* her life been like? She'd been younger than his own sister when death took her maw and da and forced her into an orphanage. A place that likely meant strict rules and not enough love to go around, especially to the aulder bairns.

Yet she wasna hardened by the experience; he'd seen her kindness, the way she responded to his family, and they had come to love her. *And you, man, you're not a bit smitten too?*

Alex shook off his musings. The constant thought of her was becoming a habit he couldna risk while he was here. Just ten days remained until Rhymer initiated his plan to try to detonate Moorside. And if the madman succeeded, the shock waves alone from an explosion would wreak havoc on thousands living in the area.

He continued on toward Dobbs's work area when sounds of laughter caught his attention. Alex turned, gazing back at his sister, who was showing off her warrior "poses" of yesterday to the other lassies at the vats.

A smile touched his lips. Once he accomplished his mission, he'd ask to extend his stay for a couple of weeks. Weatherford still owed him furlough.

His heart thumped at the prospect. He would take his sister

to see a few more castles. And, against his better judgment—he could spend more time getting to know Miss Lockhart.

❖⟩ ─ ⟨❖

She was still on his mind at lunch when Alex left the factory for Gretna's post office.

The bell over the door rang as he entered the establishment. "Mr. Wylie?"

"Captain, good to see you." The auld postmaster appeared from the back office. "Another telegram?"

"Aye."

Alex offered him the message for Stuart, but instead of taking it, Mr. Wylie turned to remove a yellow envelope from the maze of cubbyholes along the back wall. "Got one for you as well."

"Thanks." Alex took the telegram and straightened his stance. *London.*

While Mr. Wylie went to the back to send Stuart's message, Alex looked around the small office. Assured he was alone, he tore into the envelope. Quickly deciphering the code, his mouth went lax as he stared at Simon's words: *Locate new bird at Moorside. Tilda Lockhart. Discretion critical. Advise.*

Blinking, he reread the statement, his pulse thudding like a death knell in his throat. An image of Ian flashed in his mind—the wounded dark eyes and scorched flesh. The papers he'd carried on his person along with *her* photograph, the final betrayal.

Alex swallowed hard, glancing up from the missive. "Wylie!" he barked at the man in the back office. "When you've finished sending that telegram, I've got another for you."

He then coded Simon a swift response: *New bird found. Nesting with me.*

27

*I*ncredible."

Seated in his friend's London study that afternoon, Marcus reread Captain Baird's telegram. "What are the odds she would be living with the Bairds while plotting treason with her brother at Moorside?"

"Wait until you hear the rest," Simon said from behind the desk. "I spoke with Alex before you arrived—"

"He telephoned you?" Marcus gripped the arms of the chair. "Blast it all, Simon! We cannot afford any more mistakes. That *means* absolute security!"

"Relax, friend." He raised a hand. "*I* called Timbrell's office from the Admiralty. Alex and I spoke only briefly, using the code, and no names were mentioned. According to him, when Miss Lockhart arrived in Gretna and got the job, there was a factory housing shortage. Hannah Baird, who incidentally works *for* Miss Lockhart at Moorside, suggested she board with the family. *And* our co-conspirator happens to work in the same site building with Alex." He smiled. "Seems you and Timbrell called it right."

Marcus worked his jaw, hardly appeased. His concern in sending Captain Baird for this mission had much to do with their closed-door meeting last year. He'd bent the rules for him with regard to his reckless brother, giving the captain his promise of silence in exchange for receiving compromised, albeit dated Allied intelligence, and the real prize—a photograph of a woman who turned out to be a prominent German spy.

He'd sensed there was more to the story, but the captain wasn't talking. In the end, Marcus honored his promise, putting him on the hook for a future assignment.

This assignment. He frowned. The captain had the highest stakes in this mission, but those stakes could also be his weakness. And if he failed . . . "What did you tell *him*, Simon?"

"Not nearly enough." His friend flashed a sullen look. "He's expecting you to give him more information about Miss Lockhart."

Easing back in his seat, Marcus glanced again at the cryptic telegram. He'd waited months for a break in this murderous chain, and now Alex Baird could monitor every move Rhymer's sister made, both at the factory and at home.

But the chase was still in its early stages, and Marcus debated how much to tell him for the present. Alex would be in close contact with Miss Lockhart at work, at home, and in between. Would he overreact at some point and arouse her suspicions? The odds were good any man in those circumstances might let something slip and scare her off.

"Hand me something to write on." He fished a pen from inside his breast pocket as Simon slid a sheet of paper toward him. Marcus scribbled the note, folded the paper in half, and handed it back to him. "Send him this." He eyed him sharply. "And no more calls."

Simon held his gaze while he opened the note. Scanning the words, his mouth whitened. "I dinna like this secret keeping, Marcus. Especially from Alex."

Marcus stood and leaned against the desk. "Duly noted, Captain."

He left the study to return to his office at Whitehall. He'd make no compromises, not this time. Their failure at Chilwell would haunt him for the rest of his days.

Marcus wasn't about to add the weight of thousands more to his conscience.

28

L possible key. Surveil only. Report daily Bonny Prince.

A prickle of unease crept down his spine as Alex stood beneath the large oak across from the post office after work that evening and read Simon's second coded message. He was to spy on Miss Lockhart. Why? And what did his friend mean, "possible key"? Did she know what was being planned at Moorside?

Frustration gnawed at him. Simon had been a clam on the telephone earlier. Alex frowned as he tried to recall all she'd told him about her past. Orphaned in Glasgow. No family. Worked for a wealthy English lady out of Perth before the auld woman died in Nottingham . . .

"I found work in a factory for a time, but all the while I was homesick for Scotland."

"Sweet heaven, Chilwell," he groaned, gripping the telegram. Had she been involved with that factory explosion? He nearly choked on the possibility, and then thought of another woman, Olivia Charles, who had been bent on destroying a brother he'd held dear.

Would Miss Lockhart be the one to bring his whole family to harm?

It was the memory of her peaceful beauty resting against his side that made him ache. Her expression, so free of guile or cunning. Could that be the face of treason?

His pulse thundered as he imagined confronting her and demanding her guilt, then having her arrested. A firing squad . . .

He took a deep breath, forcing calm. Again he glanced at the telegram. *Possible key.* What if she wasna culpable? Simon and Weatherford could just be fishing for answers, and they expected her to reveal . . . something. Though they didna want to scare her off before she did.

His hope flared. Miss Lockhart could be an innocent party to Rhymer's plan.

And your brother likely deluded himself in the same way with Miss Charles.

Alex's mouth hardened. Either way, this change in duty was going to make it difficult to remain unaffected around her and keep from arousing her suspicions.

Once more he reflected back on their time together yesterday, the conversations they'd shared and her reactions. He found more proof in her compassion and kindness than any artfulness on her part, like with his struggle and grief over Ian's death, and her defense of the troublesome Miss Dunham, even giving the lass in her charge a second chance.

He did recall she objected to having her picture taken. *Was* Miss Lockhart shy in front of a camera . . . or was she seeking to remain hidden?

Alex tucked the telegram into his pocket and prayed the suspicions about her were wrong, for his family's sake if nothing else. *And not for your own, man?*

His shoulders hunched as he trekked along the dirt track toward home. It didna seem possible she could be involved with a killer. Though as much as he dreaded his orders, if spying on her meant the eventual arrest of Rhymer, then Alex was more than willing to do it.

29

"Dear Tilly, what should I do now?"

Seated on the bed, Rose rested her arms on her make-shift desk—Mrs. Baird's cutting board—and stared at the inscription written on the back of the photograph she'd brought with her from Attenborough. *"R and T—Rose and Me—Sisters of the heart we shall always be."*

Flipping the picture to gaze at the pair of them, her mind drifted back to that May Day picnic. The spring air redolent with the fragrance of sweet peas and honeysuckle, while the factory band played "It's a Long Way to Tipperary" and the popular "Good-bye-ee!" The canteens feeding their munitionettes with army-sized portions of meat stews, bread puddings, chicken casseroles, and a special serving of fruitcakes and jam scones.

She'd come far since that day, leaving Nottingham to find a place for herself in Gretna, responsible for the work and welfare of several young girls. Her home with the Bairds and a new sense of belonging she hadn't felt in years.

Rose turned her attention back to the handwritten letter still lying unsigned against the cutting board. Her resignation from all of this, once she'd penned Tilly's name.

Earlier today she'd been thrilled to finally receive her wages, but then it struck her how naïve she was, thinking to find another job that paid as well. And leaving on such short notice without good cause would hardly recommend her for any kind of referral letter. And what about the football elimination games on Thursday? Mrs. Nash was counting on her. The Gretna Glycerin Girls needed to make the play-offs in order to compete against the Carlisle Munitionettes for the Challenge Cup on Saturday. If Rose left now, she'd receive no recommendation from her supervisor.

She *had* been fortunate the day Mrs. Nash hired her on the spot without a single reference from Chilwell. Rose could hardly be so lucky a second time. Likely she'd have to settle for domestic work or another lesser-paying job. She might grow old before she ever earned enough to afford three ships' passages! And what would happen to her little brothers?

A sense of urgency filled her. She hadn't yet found another opportunity to call the school from her supervisor's office and check on them. Rose knew that the higher her earnings, the sooner she and the boys could leave and start their new lives abroad.

Winston's soft whine roused her from her gloom just before the dog jumped up onto the bed and tried crawling across the cutting board into her lap.

She replaced her precious photograph inside the half-packed valise beside her and removed the board to scoop her little dog into her arms. Indulging in his affections, she buried her face in his soft fur. He was still so white and smelling of lavender after his bath yesterday. And not a blue streak to be seen.

She still anguished at the thought of leaving him behind, but logic must prevail if she was to succeed. And with Fergus and James as his new companions, Winston would have a good home.

Saying good-bye to her Gretna family was going to be equally painful. From the very first, the Bairds had treated her like a daughter, accepting her without reservation. She'd selfishly enjoyed their affection these past few weeks, discovering for the first time in years a real sense of the home she remembered as a girl in Edinburgh. And if she was brutally honest, at times keeping her secret had less to do with hiding from Julien and more to do with being able to stay in this wonderful family. And Alex . . .

Lately in his company she'd been both surprised and disquieted as each smile from him, or warm gaze, or the way his voice gentled as he spoke to her deepened the stirrings in her heart, causing her to doubt her uncertainty toward him. She found herself more than pleased by their friendship, a miracle considering how badly they'd started off with each other.

Since their return from yesterday's outing, she'd relived in her mind several times those moments with him, their conversations and laughter and the way Alex had trusted her with his secrets. Something had changed between them, though she couldn't be certain what it was. A new softness perhaps, a new depth of caring . . .

Her face tinged with heat as she remembered her rude awakening in the lorry last evening. She'd been more at ease than she had in weeks and simply fell asleep. Cozy and comfortable and secure, her worries over the past had vanished as she rested beside him.

But then she awoke, so serene at seeing his face, his green eyes dark with emotion—until she realized she'd practically lain on top of him all the way home!

A chuckle escaped her. She could not even look at him, poor man.

Yet as she'd neared the front door, it had occurred to her that Alex took great care in preserving her dignity. Keeping others away while he gently helped her out of the cab. Then making his excuses to return to the factory so she could walk inside on her own and recover from her embarrassment. Rose smiled. Her own Sir Knight.

Rubbing her cheek against Winston's soft fur, she let her eyes drift back to the cutting board and the as-yet-unsigned letter. Her dreamy mood gave way to a pang in her chest, as the desire to stay warred with her fear at being discovered. If only she knew the truth about Alex and his relationship with Julien!

Surely he couldn't know the fiend he'd chosen for a friend. He was such a different kind of man: thoughtful, unbridled in his affections. A stark contrast to Julien's cold indifference. She yearned for what Alex offered to others, the kind of love she'd lost and might never have again.

Don't forget you saw them posing together for the camera. Were pilots thick as thieves?

Carefully, she set Winston aside and returned the board with the letter to her lap. She couldn't afford to be wrong about Alex, not with her brothers' lives at stake. And accepting a lesser-paying job might take her longer to save, but it could mean their protection.

Lifting the pen, she signed Tilly's name, then folded and tucked the sheaf into an envelope. She would deliver the notice to Mrs. Nash first thing in the morning.

"Miss Lockhart? Supper's ready."

Rose startled at Hannah's voice. How would the family react to her leaving so suddenly? They hadn't been happy the last time she broached the subject when Alex decided to stay.

And what about her agreement to board for the full month? While Rose intended to pay them the additional week owing, she couldn't cover the rest of July *and* still have sufficient funds for . . . wherever she was going.

Climbing off the bed, she placed the letter on the nightstand and grabbed up her new rations book she planned to give to Mrs. Baird. Then, smoothing her skirts, she went to open the door. Whatever their reaction, it was best to let them know now. "Come in, Hannah."

The girl glanced at Rose's traveling bag on the bed and drew a sharp breath. "Miss Lockhart, you're not leaving?" Tears brought a sudden sheen to her eyes.

"I think it is time that I did." Rose looked away with a sudden rush of guilt.

"'Tis my fault!" the girl cried. "I should have told you about the tricks the other lassies were up to at work, but I was scared . . ."

"Hannah, no." Rose reached to give her a hug. "I do not blame you."

She patted the distraught girl on the back and offered the fresh handkerchief tucked in her sleeve. While Hannah blew her nose,

Rose agonized over how the rest of the family would take the news. "There are . . . reasons for my leaving that have nothing to do with you. I shall explain at supper."

Hannah nodded and tried to return the handkerchief. "You keep it." Rose smiled. "I will be out in a few minutes."

Once she left, Rose began pacing the floor. What would she tell them? She'd cited "personal reasons" in her resignation letter to Mrs. Nash, but the Bairds would ask too many questions she wasn't prepared to answer.

She'd first thought to claim her charges were simply too much to handle, forcing her to seek employment elsewhere. But after giving Gladys a second chance and their happy outing yesterday, the family would know it for a falsehood.

Besides that, after confronting Mr. Dobbs on Friday, Rose had noticed a change in attitude among the girls. Colleen and Betty hadn't quite warmed to her yet, but Rose was no longer the object of their vengeance. Overall, the girls treated her with new respect.

What if she complained that Mr. Dobbs continued to harass her? Alex had witnessed her altercation with the odious man, so he could hardly doubt it.

Leaving her room armed with an excuse, Rose arrived in the dining room and noticed at once the absence of any usual chatter. The food was set out on the table, but only the small boys had been served, while the mournful, frustrated, and distressed faces gazing up at her told her that Hannah had already broken the news.

Taking her place beside James, she felt all eyes upon her as they seemed anxious for her to explain. Especially Alex.

In fact, she'd barely placed her napkin on her lap when he turned on her. "Exactly why do you feel the need to leave?"

Glancing up at him, she was jarred by his thunderous look. "I . . . have been dealing with some difficulty at work." She swung her gaze to Mrs. Baird, who sat blinking back tears, her rounded face edged in sorrow.

Mr. Baird's weary expression tore at her heart. Rose quickly returned her attention to Alex. "Some of the men have been harassing the girls, and me in particular . . ."

"Dobbs again? Was this today?"

"Yes, he and a few of his co-workers." She moistened her lips. "I have decided to seek employment elsewhere. Perhaps to the north."

"Miss Lockhart." Alex leaned against the table. "I made you a promise that he wouldna harm you. Have you forgotten?"

When she locked eyes with him, the memory of that promise conjured other images: the warm sun beating down on their shoulders, and her hand tucked securely within the strength of his arm; the sweet smell of tall grass as they stood beside the castle ruins of a Scottish king.

His words had held for her such protection, with her senses attuned to his being so near. "I seem to recall you did say that to me, but—"

"I also saw you stand up to that scunner. You didna blink an eye when you told him off." He inclined his head. "You showed the courage of a lioness that day. So why are you now letting him run you off like a scared rabbit?"

"Alex." Mr. Baird frowned at his son. "Miss Lockhart has her reasons for leaving, and we must respect that." To Rose he said, "Though I confess, lass, it breaks my heart to see you go. You've become our own in this short time, and your help to Mairi has been a godsend."

Rose couldn't form any words around the lump in her throat. This was more difficult than she'd imagined. Beside her at the table, James gave her a nudge. When she looked down at him, he grinned and held up a green pea between his fingers. As he reached toward his nose, her sudden urge to laugh collided with an ache the size of Scotland and she gently pried the pea from his grasp.

"I am truly sorry." She looked around the table at all of them, horrified when her voice began to break. "I . . . I really should go."

"I'll talk with Dobbs tomorrow. Set him straight. That goes for his followers too." Alex's voice was like granite. "I made you a promise, lass. I plan to keep it."

Rose offered him a weak smile. Despite her worry over his friendship with Julien, she would miss him terribly. "I am certain you would wish to have your own room back, Alex." *And your bed.*

Faint color singed his cheeks as though he'd read her last thought. When he looked away, Rose withdrew the rations book and handed it across the table to Mrs. Baird. "I want to go with you to the shops in the morning before I leave, and you are welcome to my rations."

"Och, ye must keep the book for yerself!" Mrs. Baird tried giving it back.

"Please, it is the least I can do since I will not be staying the full month. And my thanks to you for the wonderful food." She pressed her lips, then added, "I would also appreciate it if you kept my dog—"

"Aye, we want Winston!" Fergus and James shouted together.

"Hush now!" their mother scolded before she turned her teary eyes back to Rose. In the barest of whispers she said, "I feel as though I'm losing a bairn all over again . . ."

"She's not leaving!" Alex slammed a fist on the table, making everyone jump, including Rose. "Miss Lockhart." He hesitated. "May I call you Tilda?"

Rose gaped at him before she managed to squeak, "Tilly."

"Tilly, then." He smiled, though it seemed somewhat stiff. "I dinna want my room back, if that's why you're leaving." His Adam's apple bobbed up and down as he swallowed. "The bed in Fergus and James's room will suit me fine."

Ian's bed. Compassion filled her, knowing what it cost him to say the words.

He reached for her hand. "There's no need to fash about Dobbs or his thugs either, not while I'm around." His touch was warm against her skin. "Stay with us, Tilly." He scanned the other faces at the table. "None of us wants you to go."

Rose stared at his roughened hand covering hers and then looked up at him, searching his face for any sign of deception. Could she trust him?

She looked to the others, her chest aching as the need to remain with them warred with her fear. Each nodded at her, faces hopeful, some eyes wet, all of them smiling with affection.

Rose drew a shaky breath. "If you're certain . . ."

A cheer went up around the table—first Hannah, then Fergus, then James who looked confused but cheered, and finally Mr. and Mrs. Baird, who reached for her, the woman's face awash in happiness.

When their joy was spent, Rose turned to Alex. Leaning back in his chair, arms crossed, he watched her with an unreadable expression. Had she made a mistake?

She offered him a hesitant smile, more a plea than a gesture of friendship. And then she waited, hardly daring to breathe.

Seconds passed—an eternity—before he tipped his head and returned her smile.

Drawing breath, Rose eased back in her seat, her world all at once brighter. *"For I know the plans I have for you . . . plans to prosper you and not to harm you, plans to give you hope and a future."* Jeremiah's blessing. The Bible verse Mum and Dad had prayed over her and her brothers each night. Rose silently added her own prayer—that being here *was* God's plan, allowing her this time to savor the love the Baird family wanted to give her. That she need not fear Alex, despite his association with Julien, but could trust him to protect her and help her safeguard her dream.

Seeing her relief, Alex hid his own beneath a tight smile. Simon and Weatherford wanted her watched and that couldna happen if he let her slip away.

But why had Tilly really wanted to leave Gretna? He doubted Dobbs was still causing her grief. Alex had sought out the union steward and his cronies earlier today, and though they still grumbled, the men seemed resigned to the situation of the leaky tank and had moved past their grudge with Tilly Lockhart and her crew.

If he just had more information to go on! But Simon hadna offered him even a hint where Tilly was concerned, and Alex resented being left in the dark.

Did he and Weatherford not trust him with all the facts?

Maw seemed happy with Tilly's decision to stay as she smiled broadly and passed him a steaming plate of rumbledethumps. He tucked into the mashed tatties and cheese while the same question kept revolving in his mind. *Was* Dobbs harassing her? Despite his own observations today, had he been mistaken?

Tilly also fashed about having taken his room. Maybe she'd caught him sleeping on the couch? He chewed his food slowly. Either way, she'd drawn him out, and now he had no choice but to sleep in Ian's auld bed and like it. Proving to her that she was welcome to stay.

Alex just prayed she wasna playacting to secure a hiding place or an alibi for some unscrupulous reason. His family meant everything to him.

He would not fail them again.

30

DOVER CLIFFS
KENT, BRITAIN
TUESDAY, JULY 23 — NEXT DAY

*W*as your flight from Paris satisfactory, Effendi?"
Emin Tabak called over the wind.

Nodding, Didymos Kahverengi stared in
amusement at his older, dark-haired manservant. The chill gusts
sweeping in off Dover's coast billowed their clothing as the two
paused along the trail above the chalky cliffs some distance from
the lighthouse. He'd given up wearing his hat and held it in his
grip, while Emin stubbornly clamped his fedora onto his head
with both hands.

The comical sight of his distress served to lighten Kahverengi's
mood, especially after his pointless meeting at dawn with Dexter
at *Cimetière du Calvaire*. It was bad enough the earl's son arrived
empty-handed, but knowing he'd been selling the same secrets to
the British munitions magnate, Sir Ridley Cutler, further enraged
him.

Kahverengi ground his teeth. He should have left the wastrel
to bleed out behind the Paris gambling hall and found another
muhbir to take his place.

Emin suddenly lost his grip on the fedora, sending the hat tumbling along the short grass farther inland. As he raced to catch it, Kahverengi laughed and struck out toward the lighthouse.

Minutes later, on the lee side of the structure, Emin joined him, breathing heavily as he replaced the runaway hat on his head. "This is . . . far better here, Effendi. Thank you."

Kahverengi gazed fondly at the man who had saved his life. He'd been just fifteen when Emin found him half dead in the Australian outback after making his escape from that plantation for homeless boys. "Hell," he'd called it, his years of suffering abuse in silence.

Since that day, his manservant had been faithful, including bringing him the good news in a telegram he'd received this morning before his flight out of Paris. "So it is true, Emin? She is at Moorside?"

"Indeed, Effendi. And a happy day." Emin smiled. "She is working at Site Three. My source tells me she has been there just over two weeks."

"I thought she was lost to us." Kahverengi breathed deeply as new energy coursed through him. "I am glad I was mistaken. Where is she staying? The hostels for factory workers?"

"She lives at the home of Captain Alex Baird and his family in Gretna Green."

"Ah, I see. Then it is time to start making plans for Rhymer." He arched a brow. "Have you seen her?"

Emin shook his head. "I just learned of the news. Shall I make contact?"

"*Hayir*, not yet. We both know there are many eyes on her." He frowned. "It still disturbs me that she's made no contact since our last event."

"But she *is* loyal, Effendi." Emin's dark gaze searched his. "She proved it."

"She did," he agreed, nodding. "Still, you must watch and wait to see what your sources reveal."

He lifted his gaze to the powerful lamp mounted high above the lighthouse. A beacon overlooking the coast, illuminating for miles a path to those lost in the mist and wishing to come home. Perhaps *he* would find home once this last deed was finished, though it pleased him to continue tormenting Scotland Yard, making them pay for what they had done to him.

He glanced back at Emin. "You are confident your sources will continue to provide you with information about her?"

"Yes, Effendi. I will keep you advised."

"*Çok iyi.*" He nodded again, pleased. "I must get back, but keep me informed. When the time is right, I will have Rhymer contact her." He reached to lay a hand on his friend's shoulder. "And soon the two of them can finish what we have started."

31

I appreciate the offer of help, Alex, but you needn't take up your time."

Rose glanced at Alex as he walked beside her toward the train. "Your mother and I can see to the food shopping well enough on our own."

She'd rushed out of work once the shift ended and planned to meet Mrs. Baird at Malcolm's Grocers in Gretna. They tried going yesterday, but with the new rationing system, hundreds of munitions workers and other families had already queued up at the shops in town to claim their quotas of food.

"But I have a scheme that should work today." He held up his own rations book. "We'll lay siege to the food shops in true clan fashion."

"But I am not in your clan."

"Of course you are."

"Is that so?" She smiled at him, warmed by his words. "Then I suppose you may come along. Your mother and I will let you carry the groceries."

"Your Majesty." He bowed. "I am ever your Sir Knight."

Rose grinned. "I think it is time you had a promotion." She reached to touch each of his shoulders with her rations book. "I now dub thee Chancellor of the Pack Mule."

His hearty laughter made her whole being shimmer with plea-sure, and then she jumped as the train's whistle blew the one-minute warning before departure. "We must hurry! I intend to get a seat in the first car before the others start spilling out of the factory with the same idea."

"Let's go!"

They took off at a half run to catch the train before it ran the circuit back into town.

Rose settled into her seat, acutely aware when Alex took the place directly beside her. Not for the first time, she noticed his marked attention toward her, especially after her decision on Mon-day to remain at the cottage. And last night she'd crept out into the parlor, relieved to see the couch empty of his sleeping form.

She imagined him lying in his brother's old bed. How it must disquiet him when he bore the weight of Ian's death on his shoul-ders. "How are you sleeping these days?" she asked.

Their eyes met, and she caught an almost imperceptible flare in the green depths. "Well enough. Da was right. With your wee dog around to tire them out, Fergus and James nod off as soon as their heads hit the pillow."

"I'm glad you are getting some rest, Alex." She held his look another moment before turning to the open window, staring out at the extensive munitions complex as the train chugged toward Gretna's platform. The breeze was still balmy this late in the af-ternoon and pungent with the brackish waters of the Solway.

"Tell me, do you ever miss working in Nottingham?"

She turned to him with a guarded look. "Why do you ask?"

"Curiosity." He shrugged, though his gaze seemed intent. "I thought maybe you left friends behind when you came here? You now have several lassies at work hanging on your every word, including my sister." He smiled. "Hannah is devoted to you."

"Why, thank you, Alex." His kind words touched her—and added to the burden of her own regret at having to prevaricate once more. "I . . . did supervise several workers with my last job, though I was not as close to them as I am with your sister and the others." Her need for honesty made her add, "I did have one very close friend, but she died."

Rose looked away, haunted by the image of the scorched patch of earth where Tilly had been working. "It was shortly after that I decided to come home to Scotland."

"I'm sorry." He reached for her hand, and her pulse leapt. "How did she die?"

"We had . . . an explosion. She did not survive."

His grip tightened, and Rose looked up in alarm. Again his gaze pierced her, his face taut. "Was it Chilwell?"

She blinked. "You know?"

"It was in the papers. I'm truly sorry, lass." He squeezed her hand more gently this time. "I am glad you found us here in Gretna." He swiveled his attention back toward the approaching platform. "Looks like our stop."

Rose knitted her brows, eyeing him. How had he guessed which factory in Nottingham she worked for? The newspapers had been vague about the explosion and its location, and Rose hadn't told a soul in Gretna—except Mrs. Nash, for it was on her employment application.

Had Alex spoken with her supervisor?

"I hope I didna make you uneasy, bringing up the past," he said as he turned back to her.

"Of course not." She offered a smile. Though it *had* disturbed her, she would say nothing. After all, she'd done the same to him with regard to his brother.

❧ ❧

At least she didna lie.

Alex allowed her to exit the train first, relieved Tilly had been truthful with him. He suspected Chilwell was the factory after reading Simon's telegram, and it now reinforced his earlier impression, that perhaps she'd seen or knew something Weatherford chose to glean from her without her knowledge. Would it

243

lead them closer to the same saboteur who had destroyed that factory?

Last night before he left work, he tried contacting Simon, first at the Admiralty and then at home—only to learn from the bemused housekeeper, Mrs. Kerr, that "Mrs. Forrester went into hospital to have her bairn, and Captain Baird should contact 'the bonny prince,' if necessary, as Captain Weatherford is unavailable."

Though he was delighted his friends were about to become parents, Alex made the decision to borrow another truck and drive to East Fortune in the morning to see the "bonny prince" in person. Since the football teams had elimination games at Baxter's Farm most of the day, Tilly would be away from the factory while he was gone.

Alex hoped Stuart could shed more light as to why the War Office was so interested in her.

They arrived at Malcolm's Grocers and spotted his maw waiting in line to get food.

"I've an idea to save us time," he said as the three met up. "Maw, you stay here at Malcolm's while I go and sign up for rations at Croser's, the new market across from the community center. Tilly can start at Jenner Meats across the street from Croser's and then we'll all switch until we've got our rations and registered with each of the stores."

"Divide and conquer. Is that what clans do?" Tilly gave him an arched look, her eyes shining.

He grinned. "Aye. The Bairds have been known to be a fierce lot."

His maw chuckled behind them as he and Tilly struck out farther into town. As they reached their destination, each stepped into lines across the street from each other.

Alex scanned the queues, noting they had thinned from yesterday. Once the food controller issued the ration books to a nation already short on food, the line had stretched clear back to the train depot.

Line or no line, he was still grateful to be here and to help contribute to his family. Fergus was starting to get a real appetite, and his own could be considerable after a day of work and chopping wood. During the past two nights, he'd also started repairing the damaged roof shingles, determined to help his da as much as possible before returning to France.

He glanced at Tilly across the street as she slowly moved forward in the queue for the butcher. Such a crowd of bodies made the afternoon heat oppressive. Seeing her wipe her face with a handkerchief, Alex twitched at the sweat rolling down his back beneath his clothes. He looked forward to sitting out on the porch later tonight and enjoying the cool breeze once the sun had set.

He was only three customers away from being served when he glanced behind him at a crowd of men and women coming from the train. As the second wave of hungry workers converged upon the city to take their places in line, a loud voice caught his attention.

Taller than most, Dobbs was easy to pick out as he shoved his way through a group of women, heading toward the butcher's shop. Alex tensed as he watched the union man pace up and down the line at Jenner Meats like a cat ready to pounce.

Dobbs slowed as he drew nearer to Tilly. Alex growled and cursed under his breath.

Her eyes widened, and she stepped back as he towered over her.

Alex started to leave his line, intending to go and help her. Then he glanced back to see that just one person remained ahead of him. He stared at the rations book in his hand, then glanced back at Tilly.

She'd straightened, shoulders back, looking ready to face down Dobbs.

He would wait a few more seconds . . .

Rose recovered her composure and craned her neck to stare at the ogre in front of her. "Mr. Dobbs, good day."

"Let me in line."

He dipped forward then, and Rose caught a whiff of alcohol. The man was drinking so soon after his shift? She squared her shoulders. "That would not be fair to the others, Mr. Dobbs. You must wait your turn at the end of the line."

"That so? And would ye like me to tell this hardworkin' lot behind ye that yer leavin' work early so's to get here first?" He turned to the shift workers queued up behind her. "What d'ye think, lads? Management can cut out o' work whenever they like, while us poor blokes carry the load and then pay for it when the food's gone by the time it's our turn."

Rose followed his gaze and saw the mass of grumbling faces, many of them women, nodding and frowning to one another. "I left when our shift was over," she called to them. "The same as you. I just caught the first train, that is all."

"But yer not the same as us, are ye?" Dobbs announced to the crowd. "Yer pretty speech an' yer shoddy workers."

"Now, you just wait one minute, sir." Fuming, Rose didn't care one whit about herself, but she refused to let him speak badly about her girls. She glared at the man, again seeing Julien's dark eyes and cold gaze. "You have obviously been drinking, Mr. Dobbs, and so I'll assume the alcohol has made you slip. But you will not speak to me in that fashion or talk disparagingly about my workers. They are fine girls who do a good job at the factory."

From the corner of her eye, Rose spied several of the women in line nodding again to each another but without the frowns. She turned back to the ogre. "Furthermore, you will go to the back of the line just like anyone else. Why should you get ahead of these good people?"

Rose did turn to the line then, and the many faces had changed from angry to righteous. "Hear, hear, Dobbs! Get to the back o' the line. Yer only the union steward, not the Almighty!" one of them shouted.

Several guffaws erupted from the crowd, and Dobbs stepped closer to her.

"You must be thick, man, to keep tangling with the lass."

Suddenly Alex was there, as tall as Dobbs and standing a few feet away, his arms laden with packages. "You heard her and these good folks. Get to the back of the line."

"Looks like yer reinforcements arrived," Dobbs sneered at her. "Saving ye once again."

"Maybe the drink's gone to your head, Dobbs." Alex tipped his gaze toward the crowd. "Because I could swear Miss Lockhart did her own saving."

"That she did!" An older woman in a mobcap cried from the line, looking at the others, who nodded.

"Aye, she's fit tae take on all comers!" cried another, a young woman. Rose was startled to see her Dublin girl, Colleen Shire, standing alongside Betty Pierce. "She's our gaffer and ye'd better not cross 'er if ye know what's good for ye."

Rose met the two pairs of shining eyes while both girls touched their caps to her.

"Move along, Dobbs!" came another shout from the crowd, and the union man snarled as he pushed past Alex. Instead of getting in line, he stalked down the street toward a local canteen.

"Would you like help with those packages?" she asked Alex once he'd left.

He merely shook his head, a proud gleam in his eyes. All at once her heart soared, and she realized that for the first time since leaving her childhood behind in Edinburgh, she *had* reclaimed a sense of herself, who she had been, who she *was* . . . and the sudden urge to cry mingled with her joy. *You have your courage back, Rose.*

She could keep on fighting and following her dream, not only because she'd face down her Goliath a second time but also because she'd gained the respect and acceptance of her girls.

A few of the other workers in line cheered her. Misty-eyed, Rose smiled back at them.

And best of all . . . She turned to the tall, handsome man beside her.

Alex Baird had helped her find her wings.

32

EAST FORTUNE
THURSDAY, JULY 25

Sweet heaven, how he missed this freedom.

Alex parked the truck in front of RAF East Fortune's headquarters the following day and sat in the cab watching a new prototype of the Sopwith buzz overhead. The whine of the plane's engines and the smell of petrol combined with the sweet grass of the airfield to tantalize his senses.

He'd climbed out of the truck and headed toward the door when Colonel Landon came outside. "Captain Baird, this is a surprise."

"Colonel." Alex checked himself before offering a salute. He was a civilian now. "Thought I'd stop in to see my auld pal if he's around. Lieutenant Stuart?"

"You might try the officers' mess. Thursdays they serve a brunch." A smile rose beneath the salt-and-pepper mustache. "You timed that well, Captain, if you'd care to join them."

"I can always eat." Alex grinned and then looked up at the Sopwith overhead. "That's a fine machine."

"We do testing here now as well as training." The colonel squinted up at the gray sky. "Strictly need-to-know basis, of course."

"Understood, sir."

Alex gave a brisk nod and headed for the dining mess. Lured by the delicious smells of kippers and eggs, he made his way toward the Nissen hut when a familiar Irish brogue sounded behind him.

"That be ye, Captain Baird?"

Alex turned and smiled. "Cadet Donovan, good to see you, lad."

"And ye as well, sir." The young cadet grinned. "Are ye here tae see the colonel?"

"No, I stopped in to say hello to Lieutenant Stuart and catch up with him."

"Ye know the lieutenant's been my flight instructor since ye left?"

"Has he? And how is flight training coming along, Cadet?"

Donovan's freckles reddened. "Mostly ground training in the simulators where we practice maneuvering and shooting." His eyes lit up. "But a week ago, I flew up for the first time with Lieutenant Stuart! Before ye know it, I'll go solo and have my wings and fly tae France for the real fight."

Alex smiled at Donovan's eagerness, even as he prayed the lad would make it through the war in one piece. "Godspeed, Cadet."

"Thank ye, Captain." Beaming, Donovan gestured toward the airfield and the array of tents. "I saw Lieutenant Stuart going into his tent a few minutes ago. Second from the right, and once yer inside, all the way back."

"I'm obliged." Alex would forfeit his meal to get answers about Tilly Lockhart. "If I dinna see you before I go, take care of yourself."

"Aye, sir." The cadet slipped him a quick salute, then winked before he rushed off toward the mess.

Alex strode across the field, occasionally glancing up to watch the plane perform in the skies. If he could just be up there right now taking her through her paces!

He remembered sharing with Tilly his plans for the future, the coming age of airmail service and his decision to keep flying. As he gazed up at the Sopwith, like a bird soaring overhead, he imagined Tilly with him as they crossed the skies over Britain and beyond.

Dream on, lad. Alex shook his head. Duty came first, and right now his job was to find out why Weatherford and the War Office were so keen to have her watched.

He found Stuart at the back of the tent, scraping a razor across his face.

"Captain Baird, good to see you!" The lieutenant had seen his approach through the small mirror over the washstand and turned to greet Alex. "Anything wrong?"

"I took a few hours off and thought I'd take a drive this way." He eyed Stuart. "You dinna think it late in the day for a shave?"

"Aye." Stuart turned back to the mirror. "But I hopped another supply train during the wee hours and just got back from London."

London? Alex stared at Stuart's reflection. "What about my updates?"

"Relax, Captain. I was gone only a few days. I received orders to check in at the War Office and so I had the airfield forward your telegrams to Captain Weatherford's detective at Scotland Yard. I'm sorry to tell you they didna come up with anything on the names you sent last week. Though that union steward Dobbs is a hooligan, stirring up the munitions workers at Moorside."

He dipped the razor into the washbasin. "Have a seat while I finish and tell me what really brings you here. Have you another suspect?"

Alex took a seat on one of the empty bunks behind him and scanned the tent to be sure they were alone. "I want to know more about Tilda Lockhart."

"Aye, Miss Lockhart." Stuart worked the blade up from the right side of his jawline. "I was told she's living with you." His foamy face grinned in the mirror. "Is she bonny?"

Alex stood. "'Tis not what you think, Stuart."

"Ah, so she is bonny." The lieutenant arched a blond brow in the mirror. "You're a jammy man to have that duty." He took a pass at his chin with the razor. "What does she look like?"

When Alex hesitated, Stuart straightened and turned. "Och, man, I'm stuck here in this hole all week with nothing to look at but scores of pocked-faced laddies fresh from home. Show me a wee bit of mercy, will you?"

Alex scowled. "She's got dark hair and blue eyes. Slim and not too tall."

"That's all I get?"

"Aye." Alex bristled. "Now your turn. Why have I been assigned to keep an eye on her?"

"What have you been told?"

"Only that she's a possible key, whatever that means. It doesna tell me a thing."

"No, you're right. Did you know that she was at Chilwell?"

He nodded. "I figured that out from what she'd told us and then she admitted it to me yesterday."

"Us?"

"Me and my family."

"What else did she say?"

Alex sneered. "So like you sly devils, asking more than you're telling."

Stuart finished the last pass with his razor, then wiped his face with a towel. "All right." Tossing the towel onto the washstand, he faced Alex. "Because she was at Chilwell, the War Office believes she might recognize Rhymer if he's at Moorside."

Alex sat down again, his relief mingled with a guarded sense of hope. "So they dinna believe she's involved in the actual explosion?"

"Well, I wouldna rule anything out." He shrugged. "But they seem to think otherwise. What are your thoughts?"

But Alex was envisioning Tilly in Gretna yesterday, giving Dobbs a good tongue-lashing and winning over the crowd with her cry against injustice. A smile touched his lips. He'd never been more proud.

"What has you amused?"

He glanced at Stuart. "I'm just glad to get answers." Leaning forward, he rested his arms against his thighs. "But why do they want to keep it from her? Why not just ask Tilly to watch for anyone who looks familiar instead of having me play the spy?"

Stuart leaned against the framework of the opposite bunk. "I think they're fashing over the possibility she'll let the cat out of the bag. Better to have her stop and say hello to an auld face so we can go in and nab him rather than have her running the other way and scaring him off. Rhymer's been canny so far, and I believe he'd sniff out a trap in a minute."

Alex sighed. Stuart was right, though it seemed a much slower process. Especially when the urgency to find Kahverengi's man was increasing daily.

And after the way she handled herself in town yesterday, he knew Tilly could be brought in on the assignment without giving herself away. But he had his orders, and until he could speak with Simon or Weatherford about it directly, he must stay the course.

His spirits lifted as he rose to his feet. Stuart's explanation only served to further convince him she was innocent. "Think I'll head over to the mess and grab some food before I take off."

"I'll come along." Stuart grinned as he reached for his shirt and tie. "You ken that the real benefit of being here is that there's always enough to eat."

"Aye." Alex flashed a rueful smile. "The new ration laws have all of us 'civilians' counting our beans and our bacon."

They strode from the tent toward the mess. "How's Donovan doing?"

"The laddie's got potential. Like most of the cadets, he's impatient to fly and dislikes all the ground practice. I took him up last week, and he's eager to stay in the air."

"I remember those days." Alex gave a wistful smile. "But I'm grateful for the new Gosport style of training. 'Tis saving the lives of many young pilots."

"And that many more for the Huns to get their hands on."

Alex sobered thinking about his brother's meaningless death. "Aye, but 'tis better to die for a good reason than not."

Stuart met his gaze. "True enough, Captain."

They soon arrived at the mess, and after an hour and a half spent talking with the instructors and cadets and savoring oat porridge, beans, sausages, black pudding, bacon, eggs, and tattie scones—a feast Alex hadn't enjoyed in weeks—he and Stuart departed for Alex's truck.

"So how about I drive over to Gretna next week, Captain? That way I can see your bonny lassie for myself."

"She's not mine." Alex climbed into the cab and, after setting the throttle, frowned at Stuart. "And 'tis a bad idea. If you're in Gretna, who will I make my reports to?"

"We can both keep an eye on her. Just a day or two." Stuart's eyes gleamed. "You can see her at work, and since I'm an auld friend, invite me over to supper so I might meet her at home." He glanced back toward the Nissen huts. "I'm desperate for wee bit of softer scenery, man."

"What about London?"

Stuart made a face. "I dinna consider my meetings with a bunch of auld men in uniform scintillating." His eyes pleaded. "Come on, pal, what do you say? Share a bit of the wealth?"

Alex glowered at him. The mere thought of this Casanova ogling Tilly set his teeth on edge. "Like I said, bad idea. With two of us watching her, she'll get suspicious."

He knew his words for a lie, as more likely Tilly's head would be turned by Stuart's brash good looks. Still, he wasna letting the scunner anywhere near her.

He started to climb back out of the truck to crank over the engine when Stuart halted his progress, his blue eyes full of devilment. "Like it or not, Captain, when Rhymer does show his face, you'll have to get used to seeing me in Gretna. My orders are to move in once we have a confirmation."

"Then I'll let you know when that happens. Until then, stay here and I'll send you my updates."

Stuart grinned knowingly before he went to the front and cranked over the truck's engine. Then he raised a hand in parting, and while Alex turned the truck around, he yelled, "See you next week!"

"Over my dead body," Alex muttered to himself before he increased the throttle. As the truck leapt forward, he gripped the wheel and drove in the direction of home.

Aye, Tilly Lockhart didna belong to him. *Yet.*

33

*D*id you need something, Captain?"

Rose looked up from her desk where she'd been re-cording on index cards the work hours and any incident reports for her young charges.

Alex Baird's tall frame leaned against the doorjamb. "Just keeping my promise, lass," he said, smiling, and her pulse gave a pleasurable start. In the few days since she'd agreed to stay on with his family in Gretna, he seemed to be everywhere she turned. Whether she was speaking with Mrs. Nash in her office or supervising her girls in the nitroglycerine section, her silent watchman was always close by. Except for yesterday when she'd coached her football team through the factory's elimination games at Baxter's Farm. And because her Glycerin Girls had played fabulously, they'd been selected to go up against Carlisle at Saturday's Summer Sports Day.

"So, are you ready for the Challenge Cup tomorrow?" he asked.

Had he read her thoughts? Rose certainly hoped they were ready. It was all Hannah could talk about at supper last night. "I think my girls are in fine form, and despite a constant cough, Jane has done well as our team goalie. Your sister's turned out to be an impressive halfback, too." Pride filled her voice, but Rose didn't care. Her charges had come far in the past few weeks, and in more ways than one. She still warmed at the memory of Colleen and Betty touching their brims during her second confrontation with the odious Mr. Dobbs in town the other evening.

And while she understood Alex didn't doubt her ability to take care of herself, Rose admittedly had no idea if or how the offensive union man might claim his revenge for humiliating him in front of his fellow workers.

Collecting her index cards, she tucked them back inside the small filing box and rested her hands on the desk. "I am grateful for your efforts, Alex, but I think I'm safe enough. Mr. Dobbs works at the opposite end of the building."

"'Tis lunchtime, and the men's canteen is less than twenty yards past this office." He eyed her, his strong features determined. "I just wanted to make sure he and his union lads didna stop in here along the way."

She pressed her lips together to keep from smiling. He really was being gallant. "What about you? Should you not go and eat as well? I imagine following me around all morning has made you hungry."

"Aye." He pushed away from the doorjamb. "Chasing after you can surely work up a man's appetite."

Rose flushed with heat at the glint in his eyes. Primly, she said, "Perhaps, Captain, you should consider keeping an eye on the wolves rather than the sheep? It would be less exhausting."

"Aye, but not nearly as pleasant."

Again he gave her the look that sent her pulse racing. Self-preservation made her glance at the wall clock. "Since it is lunchtime, I really must go."

His heavy sigh echoed across the office, and she stifled another grin.

He grabbed for the doorknob. "I'll see you later, then. Watch yourself."

She nodded, and once he'd closed the door behind him, her relief mingled with a sense of loss. In truth, she quite enjoyed his company and she also trusted Alex. Even her fears about his spying for Julien now seemed absurd.

Rose wasn't certain when her feelings for him had changed, only that her awareness of him had become stronger, the stirrings in her heart more widespread until the mere thought of him seemed to encompass her entire being.

Was that love?

Abruptly she rose from her chair. Indeed, she'd come to care about him, and more than she should. One thing was certain—Alex spent far too much time watching her during the day, and she wondered when he had time to work at his post. What if her invented excuse for wanting to leave Gretna ended up getting him the sack?

I must put a stop to this. She would catch him after work and make him listen to reason. He and his family could ill afford his loss of wages, and it would be *her* fault.

Rose left the office and headed toward the ladies' canteen. Since she'd made the decision to stay on at the factory, she had money coming in and could occasionally afford to charge lunches against her pay and save on the Baird family's foodstuffs.

And no more worries about tricks with her food.

She chuckled. Not that she was too concerned these days when most of the "rough girls" in her charge seemed to *want* to work for her. Rose was still amazed at her own audacity in town on Wednesday. Had she really managed to turn the tables on Mr. Dobbs and accuse *him* of taking advantage of his fellow workers?

Her dad had always told her that she was "a canny lass," but until recently that confidence had been undermined, through years of her uncle's silent contempt and then Julien's cold disdain.

Until now.

Rose smiled as she relived the moment in her mind, standing up to Dobbs and the crowd cheering what she had to say. And Alex, gazing at her as though he believed she could conquer the world.

The pleasurable memory continued as she arrived at the canteen and made her way into the food line. *Oh, Tilly, if you could be here and see me now, would you believe it?*

"Miss Lockhart! Can we ask you a question?"

Still smiling, Rose received her lunch order and walked over to Hannah's table. The girl sat with Gladys, Jane, Colleen, Betty, Dorothy, and Sarah—most of their team. "Are you all excited about the game tomorrow?" They nodded, and Rose added proudly, "I have no doubt the Carlisle Munitionettes will rue the day they took on the Gretna Glycerin Girls."

"Thanks, Miss Lockhart!" they chorused, their sallow faces turning rosy with pleasure.

It was Gladys who spoke up. "Me an' Colleen moved outta Timber Town last week t'share rent at Betty's flat in town." The girl glanced at the others. "We want t'know, Miss Lockhart, would ye consider joinin' us for afternoon tea on Sunday? Hannah and Dorothy and Sarah and Jane, too."

Jane coughed then, while Hannah and the others beamed.

Gladys turned to Rose. "That is, if ye'd think it proper. An' I figure we could talk about the win." She winked at the other girls.

For an instant, Rose eyed them slack-jawed. "Why . . . thank you for the invitation, Gladys. It is most kind of you." She scanned the faces of the other girls, making certain her instincts hadn't been wrong. Yet as she met each shy look and nervous smile, her heart melted. "I would be pleased to come along with Hannah on Sunday for tea. At four?"

Gladys released a happy sigh and smiled at her coworkers. "Thank ye, Miss Lockhart. Four would be jus' grand."

"We'd be 'onored tae 'ave ye," Colleen said with uncharacteristic softness as she lifted dark eyes to Rose. "An' if yer fine with it, we'll ask two others lasses from the nitrocotton section to come over as well." She bowed her head. "They were with us in line at the butcher's on Wednesday, and now they're keen tae make yer acquaintance."

Rose blinked in startled pleasure. "Of course, you may invite whomever you like."

It was the first time she'd ever seen Colleen smile, the receding gums and missing teeth likely from the acid fumes. The girl touched the edge of her bonnet. "Thank ye kindly."

Betty spoke up. "I'll drop off the address at yer office, Miss Lockhart."

Rose nodded, her heart full to bursting as she continued toward the supervisors' table. To know she'd somehow made a positive impact on these girls after all filled her with such gratitude and joy. *Lord, thank you for showing me another sign that I should be here. Helping other lost girls make a difference in their lives.*

Her mood still hummed later that afternoon when she returned to her office. Taking a seat in the chair, she reached for the small filing box on the desk and saw beneath it a parchment envelope with the name MISS TILDA LOCKHART typed across its front.

How lovely! Reaching for her letter opener, she smiled over the tea invitation as she opened the missive. Then, scanning the note, her high spirits of moments ago plummeted.

> Peekaboo, Miss Lockhart, I see you
> My net is wide, so you cannot hide
> There is a post due at Gretna for you
> So do not wait to meet thy fate

Rose stared at the somewhat ominous lines. Who had left this message for her? Whoever it was knew her and where she worked.

Surely not her charges in the canteen. She frowned. Millie Parson hadn't been at lunch with the others; in fact, except for the play-offs yesterday, the girl had been absent for a few days. And today at work, Rose noticed her brooding most of the morning.

Did Millie have cause to be angry with her? Enough that the girl would compose this poem in order to play some kind of prank as the others had once done?

Rose's shoulders slumped as she folded the note and slipped it back inside the envelope. Here she'd thought to finally succeed in guiding these girls and changing their lives for the better. But it seemed she'd failed to break through the glass wall surrounding Millie's heart.

So much for your pride, Rose Graham. Frustrated, she tucked the missive into her smock pocket. Perhaps she should meet with Millie later today, before the problem festered further. Once they had talked things over, the girl might soften.

Rose could hope anyway.

34

*B*ird laid no eggs.

Alex bit back an impatient sigh as he handed Mr. Wylie his message for Stuart. Upon receiving his receipt, he left the post office and returned on the train to Moorside. Lunch was almost over, and he'd made sure before leaving that Tilly was surrounded in the canteen by her co-workers.

Once again he'd sent in the same report—*nothing*. And with Dobbs cleared along with the other names on the lists he'd been sending, Alex was out of patience—and suspects.

Tilly had yet to acknowledge anyone from Chilwell, and at this rate it was like looking for a toothpick in a woodpile. Rhymer could slip in and slip out again, leaving Moorside in ashes and the town destroyed before anyone realized what had happened.

He ground his teeth. She could aid in their quest and speed things along if Weatherford would let him reveal to her his mission here. Alex resented the decision to keep her unaware, and if he wasna bound by his duty, he'd enlist her help. Tilly had the ability to think clearly and that's what was needed if they were to find and apprehend Rhymer.

Five days. All that remained until Moorside's month of demise, and Weatherford was cutting his strategy way too close. Tilly had a stake in her own safety too, and the possibility she might walk innocently into a trap with their saboteur made him furious.

Arriving back at the factory, he paused at her office, and seeing the empty space he made his way toward her work section.

She stood at the vat tables, examining Hannah's hands, his sister's face pinched in pain.

He quickly approached. "What's the matter with her? Is she all right?"

Removing a handkerchief from her pocket, Tilly wrapped it around his sister's right hand. "The acids in the cordite paste have made her hands raw to the point of blisters. I'm worried about infection, so I'll take her to the clinic."

She turned to his sister, Hannah's eyes wet with tears. "There now, you'll be fine, dear," she said, brushing a hand along her cheek. "The nurse will give you salve and then we'll find you different work until your hands heal."

"B-but what about our football match tomorrow?"

"Well now, it's your hands that are blistered, not your feet." Tilly smiled. "You can still play in the tournament if you feel up to it."

While Hannah's head bobbled up and down, Alex moved aside to let them pass on their way to the clinic. Contentment settled over him seeing them together. Tilly *had* become a part of his family, living in his home where they all spent time together, and there was her obvious love for his sister and brothers and parents.

Perhaps for him, too?

He realized he'd been on edge after Stuart promised to show up and charm his way into Alex's home and Tilly's heart. Even now, Alex rejected the thought of sharing her with the lieutenant, or anyone else for that matter. He'd admitted his defeat—that despite his efforts to distance himself, thoughts of Tilly Lockhart filled his every waking moment. Not only because of his duty to watch over her but also his desire to *be* with her.

In his dreams, he saw her tranquil face and the dreamy-eyed look when she'd first awakened, her arms clinging to him in sleep.

And then they danced, sweeping across the room, her warm hand lightly against his shoulder, the softness of her as he held her.

He smiled, reflecting on their pleasant evenings spent out on the porch, with him finding excuses not to chop wood so he could sit with her while she helped his maw with the mending.

They had discussed much—the past with its sorrows, the present with his family, and their dreams for the future. And he'd begun to see a future with Tilly, regardless of her wish to sail across an ocean or his duty to the war.

Would she wait for him? 'Twas a question that crept into his mind more often of late. And each time he tried to push it away, merely weakened his resolve to part with her after his mission. He'd begun to imagine her staying in Gretna with him when peace finally came. Taking her up in his plane. Maybe opening her own dress shop . . .

His smile faded. Had Ian been this love-sick? Yet it might be easier to stop his heart from beating and his lungs from taking in air than to end his desire for more time with her.

In truth, that meant when Lieutenant Stuart did arrive in Gretna, he must deal with it, because it would mean Rhymer had been found. And above all, Alex intended to protect what was his—Hannah, Tilly, and the rest of his family.

With that in mind, he determined to leave work a few minutes early and return to the post office. It was time to contact Simon and change the way this game was being played.

35

*W*hat do you mean he wants 'a change of strategy,' Simon?"

Marcus stood beside the tall bookcase in his office and gazed toward the two men seated near his desk. For an early Saturday morning, his friend already looked a bit done-in as he stretched out in one of the leather chairs.

"Alex believes it would be more expedient to include Tilly Lockhart in the search for Rhymer."

Marcus scoffed. "A bit like inviting the fox into the henhouse, don't you think?"

"That's because we havna told him the full story." Simon's coppery brows drew together. "He went to see Stuart on Thursday while you were away and I was with my wife."

"Congratulations, by the way." Marcus smiled. "Boy or girl?"

"A lass." He eased out a grin. "Zoe Louise, after Eve's sister and mother."

Marcus nodded. "How are they?"

"Eve's doing well, despite an exhausting few days. She's home now with the bairn. Zoe made a bit of an early appearance, but she's got a good weight and she's healthy, thank God."

"Good to hear. Please give them my best." He sobered. "So Alex went to see Lieutenant Stuart . . . ?"

"Aye. He wanted to learn more about Miss Lockhart and his new orders. Stuart told him she'd worked at Chilwell and could likely identify the saboteur if he's at Moorside."

"Clever."

"To a point." Simon tipped his head. "When Alex asked him why Miss Lockhart couldna be brought in on the hunt to speed up things, Stuart told him you were concerned that she'd panic and alert Rhymer to a trap. He said it was better to have her recognize him on her own, and with Alex surveilling her, he could report it."

Marcus grunted. "Not the best logic considering our time frame, but Stuart was caught off guard."

"I told Alex I'd contact him later today with your answer."

Marcus drew a breath and glanced at the silent detective next to Simon. "Quinn, any results from the information I sent you on Wednesday?"

The swarthy detective withdrew a notepad from his inside jacket pocket. "When you said Orly Airfield reported the unsanctioned flight of a Nieuport 11 out of Paris heading across the Channel, we tracked down all British airfields within the plane's fuel range. She didn't land at any of the coastal RAF bases here on the mainland.

"However, we discovered a report at the constabulary in Dover that five days ago a small craft landed in a pasture on Kent Downs. I went to Dover to follow up, and the man who made the complaint takes care of the property while his neighbor is fighting overseas." He scanned his notes. "He reported seeing the plane land and then a truck approach. The pilot and driver both left to walk toward the cliffs near the lighthouse. An hour later they returned, and once the pilot had refueled, both truck and plane took off."

"I've been told Kahverengi's a bit of an aviation enthusiast, and he's got a particular fondness for Nieuports," Marcus said. "How about the driver of the truck?"

Quinn frowned. "The neighbor was some distance away and

didn't get a good look. He reported both men as tall and about average weight, but that's all he could say."

Marcus grimaced. "If we go on faith that it *was* Kahverengi this neighbor saw, and the man with him was Rhymer, then in all likelihood they are about to make their move." He glanced sharply at Simon. "How do you think Alex would react knowing he's got our saboteur's sister living in the same house with his family?"

Simon shifted. "I know where this is going, Marcus. You want to continue stalling."

"We're too close now to risk him scaring her off so she can inform her brother."

"What should I tell him then?"

"He's to be patient and keep a sharp eye on who she talks to, especially in the next few days. Tell him we hope to have an update on Monday."

"And what if this pilot landing a plane in Kent was just some joyriding hooligan?"

Marcus snarled. "Like I said, we go on faith, because right now that's all we've got." He glanced at Quinn. "I want you back in the Glasgow office standing by. If Rhymer's about to make contact, you need to be ready. I'll notify Stuart as well."

He glanced at both men. "Believe me, I sympathize with Captain Baird's frustration. He wants an end to the uncertainty, as do I. And I believe all of us can agree that the sooner Rhymer makes contact with Tilly Lockhart, the better our chances to catch him and save Moorside."

36

*J*ulien . . . ?

Heart pounding, Rose sat in her office the following day and reread the latest missive—another poem in a typewritten envelope, much like the one she'd received yesterday, only this time placed prominently on her desktop where she would be certain to find it.

> Do not dally, Miss Lockhart, we both know the truth
> Your reasons at Gretna and what you must do
> Heed my warning this time, and no more escapes
> Remember, your gift at the post office awaits.
> P. S.
> If you value the love and welfare of your clan
> You will not cross me or tell of my plan.

Her fingers gripped the note. She had thought the first missive from Millie, but after speaking with her at the end of her shift yesterday, Rose learned the girl had received a hand-delivered telegram earlier in the week with news all women fear. Millie's husband had died as a casualty of war.

The girl hadn't yet sought counsel for her loss, and so Rose spent time offering comfort and referred her to the matron at the hostelry.

So, if not Millie, then who? The menacing note seemed far beyond what even the brashest girl might conjure. And she couldn't imagine Mr. Dobbs creating such lyrical verse.

Heed my warning this time, and no more escapes. It was like Julien had spoken the words directly to her. She'd escaped him once, and then he'd recently shown up at the factory. If anyone, he was most capable of being a menace *and* literary. And the monster had no qualms about being underhanded or committing what amounted to criminal activity—she'd witnessed proof enough of that.

Had Alex told him?

No. Rose had come to admire his straightforwardness. If Alex had doubts, he would have confronted her with them by now. Besides, their time together of late had been idyllic and peaceful, and they'd enjoyed each other's company. He was gentle with her, his smiles warm, and she cherished his laughter and his tender looks. Surely a man couldn't keep up that kind of pretense for long.

But you have, Rose. She recoiled at the reminder of her own charade . . . and then relaxed. It was true she'd contrived to become Tilly's past, present, and future, yet her attachment to the Bairds, her affection for Alex—no, her *love* for him, making her light up inside when he was near—belonged to Rose Graham.

She glanced at the poem. Julien must have discovered her here by some other means. He could have seen her while she was taking Sarah to the infirmary. But why wait so long to confront her . . . unless he was back?

She shuddered at the possibility. Both poems instructed her to pick up this "gift" at the post office in Gretna. She'd much rather it be some foul prank by Dobbs to get even rather than find Julien lying in wait for her.

Regardless of the sender, the note threatened the welfare of the Bairds, *her clan*, if she didn't follow his instructions. And while she longed to find Alex and show him the messages, that warning weighed heavy on her heart.

Until she knew the sender and how they'd come to place the notes on her desk, she wouldn't jeopardize Alex or his family.

⤐ ⟞ ⟊ ⟍ ⤏

Standing back from Tilly's office out of view, Alex observed her at the desk. She seemed upset by a letter, and when she reached for her throat, he disregarded their conversation of last night and strode toward her office.

"What's wrong, lass?" Her head shot up as he entered, and Alex frowned to see her face pale, the blue eyes dark with anxiety. "'Tis bad news?"

"No . . . I mean, yes, it is bad news, but it does not affect me." She wet her lips, glancing back toward the note. "One of my charges, Millie Parson, she . . . she recently learned that her husband was killed in the war. It is quite distressing."

Alex relaxed his stance. He'd been sure it was some personal loss to her, or a threat, perhaps involving Rhymer and his own assignment to keep her under observation. "I'm sorry to hear it. Is the lass going to be all right?"

"I think so. She's at the hostelry this morning, and she plans to meet our team on the field after lunch when the factory lets out for the championship game." She looked up at the clock. "Which gives me two hours to finish up my work." She turned to him. "Where are *you* supposed to be right now?"

He straightened. She was about to give him another lecture. "I was passing by the office and saw you in here—"

"Alex." Her eyes narrowed. "I thought we resolved this issue after supper last evening. If you continue in this way, you are going to lose your post. Surely you must have work to do?"

Aye, and the best job there is. He smiled, pleased when the color returned to her face. She fashed about his job at Gretna, and last night she'd actually *instructed* him to pay more attention to his duties at the factory and to stop following her around.

He'd wanted to laugh at her giving him orders, but then he'd seen her careworn expression, eyes troubled just as they were now—and in the end he'd agreed to keep his distance. "I ken what you said to me, lass, and I appreciate your concern, but I have things under control."

"I care about you, Alex. I . . . I don't want anything to happen to you or your family."

Her breathing had quickened, her gaze searching his, and the hair rose along his nape. Was she still speaking of his job . . . or something else? He took in the taut lines against her smooth face. "Are you certain there's nothing more that's fashing you, lass?"

"No . . . though perhaps just the game this afternoon." She looked away, then rose from her chair and came around the desk. "I must check on my girls." Slipping the envelope with the note into her pocket, she looked up at him. "I trust you have things to check on?"

Alex ignored the question, his eyes fixed on her pocket. Was there something else in that letter bothering her? Why did she not tell him? Inspiration struck as he said, "I'm planning to borrow a truck for tomorrow. How about a drive up toward Canonbie? 'Tis only a few miles, and there's a bonny place by the Esk where we can stop and picnic. We'll celebrate today's win against Carlisle, just you and me."

She smiled, though the tension in her expression tore at his heart. "Thank you, Alex, but shouldn't we first wait to see if we win? And besides, Hannah and I have plans tomorrow."

"Win or not, we'll still go to the river. And I'll have you back in plenty of time for your tea with the lassies." He reached to lay a hand on her shoulder, so soft beneath his touch. "I'll wager a quiet hour or two by the water is just what you need," he said gently.

A flicker of hope lit her face, and when she finally nodded, he exulted inside. "It sounds wonderful. Shall we leave after church?"

"Right after." He grinned. "I'll ask Maw to pack us a basket. And I'll bring fishing poles."

Her eyes teared up suddenly, and he felt her tremble beneath his hand. "I look forward to it, thank you," she whispered. Too soon she broke contact with him. "I'm sorry, Alex, but I must be on my way. I'll meet you at Baxter's Farm for the game later, all right?" She offered a weak smile before rushing past him out of her office.

His chest tightened as he watched her leave. Was it the letter about the poor lass losing her husband that caused her such anguish? Or his work, or even the coming game? None of which satisfied his peace of mind. Tilly had been more than just fashing, she'd been . . . afraid.

Whatever the reason for that fear, he intended to find out.

❖~❃~❖

Pulse racing, Rose stood beside her locker and peeled out of her smock and boots. With the factory's early shutdown for Summer Sports Day, the changing room was already bustling as dozens of factory girls and older female staff washed and dressed into their street clothes, chattering excitedly about the coming ladies' football match against the Carlisle Munitionettes. There was also talk of a band and refreshments afterward, with vendor exhibits and Highland dances and singing at the Gretna Community Center.

No doubt the first few trains would be full, taking factory spectators out to Baxter's Farm, where the match would start in an hour. Which meant she'd have to wait until after the game to visit the Gretna post office.

What kind of "surprise gift" awaited her? All morning, Rose had fretted about it, and even Alex knew something was wrong. Obviously she was being watched. Would she find Dobbs and his laughing cronies waiting for her later when she arrived . . . or Julien, ready to pounce? At this point, the worry had exhausted her, and she longed to end it and uncover the culprit so she could lose this fear.

Entering the ladies' washroom, she began the ritual of removing the factory toxins while forcing her mind to pleasanter things—

like the picnic with Alex tomorrow, perhaps giving her a chance to ease the strain of the past two days over these bizarre poems dogging her every waking moment.

Rose examined her skin as she scrubbed, noting for the first time a slightly sallow hue. Hannah's complexion now wore a dandelion shade from the sulfurs in the cordite paste. Alex's sister had become a true canary girl, which seemed to please her immensely. Rose suspected it was the girl's badge of honor for her important work at HM Factory Gretna.

She was proud of all her young charges. Not only did they excel at football, their courage and hard work were helping to save the lives of thousands of Tommies overseas.

Rose was also anxious for her girls, as the hazardous chemicals they worked with affected them daily. Not only with their skin, gums, hair, and teeth but also the noxious fumes they were constantly forced to inhale. She'd already had to send Dorothy and Gladys to the infirmary to sleep off the drugging effects, and surely no bodily good came from such exposure!

How they could still play football several times a week was a testament to their youth and energy. Though with Jane's cough worsening, would she manage today as their goalie? Twice she'd sent the girl to the clinic, and both times Jane had been returned to the job after receiving a bottle of cough syrup.

Rose toweled herself dry and sighed. Peace couldn't arrive soon enough, and she prayed the girls would be able to find safer jobs and still earn a good wage. It was widely viewed now that women's prospects in the workplace had much improved because of the war, and she hoped someday that improvement would extend into Parliament.

Once she'd donned her jersey and cap, she grabbed the whistle and exited the factory, making her way toward the train platform.

She found Alex already there. His green eyes searched hers. "You all right?"

His tender expression made her yearn to share with him her trouble about the notes. Then she remembered the threat and instead compressed her lips and glanced toward the coming train. She wouldn't put him or his family at risk. "Just nerves."

"Dinna fash, Miss Lockhart, those Carlisle lassies dinna stand a chance against us!"

Rose turned to find Hannah, clad in her uniform, stepping onto the platform beside them. The girl had played well, despite her blisters, and the green leather gloves Alex had bought for her now protected her hands, while her agile feet were an asset to the team.

"I have no doubt you will all do your best." Rose smiled, and for a moment her worry was replaced by another surge of pride.

"I wanted to meet here to tell you I'm going after the truck," Alex said. "I'll give you and Hannah a ride to the field."

"Thank you, Alex." It would speed up their arrival, giving her girls more time to warm up before the game started.

Twenty minutes later, he pulled in at the farm. "We'll meet up with you later," Rose said.

"I'll be in the stands cheering you lassies to victory." He smiled, and Rose's heart gave a thump as she led Hannah to join their team members.

Rose was surprised when Mrs. Nash and Colleen, the team captain, rushed toward her. "We've a situation, Miss Lockhart." Her supervisor's brows knitted above her hawkish face.

Rose quickly glanced about the crowded stands. Was this about the note? Had Julien arrived and revealed to Mrs. Nash her secret?

"'Tis Jane, Miss Lockhart," Colleen said, her features concerned. She held a uniform in her hands. "She's 'ere and brought this uniform, but coughin' so badly, she can't stand on 'er feet. We need a new goalie."

Oh dear! Rose's relief that it wasn't about Julien tangled with her new panic to find a goalie replacement. Why hadn't she considered adding a couple of substitutes for the team? So much for her brilliant coaching. Perhaps one of the other Gretna team's players?

"There's no time, Miss Lockhart." Colleen read her thoughts and held out Jane's uniform. "Ye must be our goalie this afternoon. Ye know our team plays best, and ye've coached us well."

Rose started to rear back from the girl's offering. She couldn't possibly play football in a tournament! Her only experience had been a backyard practice with Alex and the children.

She opened and closed her mouth, unsure of what to say.

"Ye can do this, Miss Lockhart." Colleen's eyes implored her. "Just like ye stood up tae that blighter, Dobbs. Ye just protect the goal and we'll do the rest, all right?"

Still dazed, she found herself nodding and accepting the uniform.

"Come with me," Mrs. Nash said to her. "There's a concession booth where you can have privacy to change."

Minutes later, Rose peeked around the door of the concession at the thousands of noisy spectators in the stands. Then she glanced at her bare knees, and the urge to giggle at defying her uncle's edicts about a 'lady's comportment' mingled with the terror that Julien—if he'd sent the notes—might be watching her from somewhere in the crowd. Would he recognize her in the Glycerin Girls' red jersey, khaki shorts, and khaki cap?

"Courage, Rose," she murmured. Then taking a deep breath, she hurried off to go meet her team on the field. After some quick instruction from Colleen, the coin was tossed, and Rose took her place between the goal posts. Her pulse pounded as the referee's loud whistle blared for the kick-off, and Colleen shouted to her players, "This is for the win, Glycerin Girls!"

37

"Congratulations, Team Gretna!"

Alex stood beaming at the foot of the dais two hours later while an exhausted Rose and her players descended the steps. They'd just accepted the Challenge Cup from the football Master of Ceremonies. "That was a braw match against Carlisle, and you lassies deserved the win!"

Rose chuckled as her feet returned to the grassy field, her mood still aglow after their victory. "It would be fairer to say these girls of mine deserve the Cup, though it is sweet of you to include me, Alex."

It was true; Rose had asked for a miracle, and in her view, God had seen fit to give her girls superhuman ability, as she'd never before seen them play so well or so defensively. And they'd done it in order to keep the other team from scoring inside her goal as much as possible.

"Miss Lockhart, ye did block three balls on yer own, and that made the difference in the final score," Colleen said, grinning to expose her missing teeth as she held the Cup in her arms.

Mrs. Nash, who had represented the factory's day shift for the award, followed them down from the dais. "I knew all along I'd made the right choice in you for coaching the team, Miss Lockhart," she said, smiling.

"Aye, she saved the day!" Gladys cried, and the rest of the girls cheered her words.

Still euphoric, Rose laughed. Admittedly, she'd held her own in the game considering her inexperience, though to her credit she'd coached enough and observed enough in the past few weeks to understand her duties as goalie. She'd also secretly accomplished her dream of actually being in the game, like the girls she'd watched play long ago at Chilwell's field.

"Are any of you coming over to the Community Center later?" Mrs. Nash asked.

The girls eyed each other, most of them looking done-in after playing football for nearly two hours. "For my part, I plan to go and change and then get a good night's sleep," Rose said, and she was surprised when Hannah nodded her agreement. The girl must be near collapse to refuse the chance to be social with her friends.

It turned out, however, that almost all her charges made the same decision, except for the girls from the niter stores. After saying her good-byes, Mrs. Nash struck out across the field toward the center and the rest of the festivities.

"I'll just go change." Rose turned toward the concession where she'd left her clothes.

"We'll wait for you in the truck," Alex said.

Her ebullient mood suddenly crashed remembering what she still must do. "No need . . . I'll take the train back to Gretna." She forced a smile. "I have an errand first." Instinctively she looked to the emptying stands, scanning the faces there. Was she being watched?

"I can make a stop if you like," Alex said.

He was frowning at her now. Rose hesitated. "I . . . I must go to Timber Town to look in on Jane."

"Shall I come with you?" Hannah's amber eyes lit with compassion.

"That is sweet of you, dear, but I will not be long, and Jane needs her rest. Hopefully she'll feel well enough to join us for the tea tomorrow."

Alex eyed her another moment. "We'll see you at the cottage then."

"Hannah!"

The rest of the Glycerin Girls were walking toward the train platform. "Come on!" Betty and Gladys shouted, and Hannah turned, giving her brother a pleading look.

"Alex, I'll ride back on the train with my teammates, if that's all right. I'll see you at home?"

He nodded and then took off toward the truck. Rose released her pent-up breath. Being with him tempted her to reveal her predicament, but she must take care of this herself.

Quickly she made her way to the concession. Once more clad in her blouse and skirt, she carried her bundle of uniforms and went to the train platform.

She was relieved to discover Hannah and the other girls had already departed, and she waited with some of the spectators for the next train, keeping her eyes on the faces of those who joined the throng. When, minutes later, Rose had boarded along with the others, she sat alone toward the back, hands fisted in her lap as she imagined what might await her at the post office.

At the Gretna station, she disembarked with the crowd and started for Timber Town, glancing behind her for any signs of Hannah or the other girls.

When she was assured they'd all gone home, she changed direction from the huts and headed instead toward town. Staying close to the shoulder with the other workers while lorries, motorcars, and horse-drawn carts milled back and forth in the streets, Rose continually scanned the masses for a glimpse of anyone who might be watching *her*.

At the post office, several people were already inside. She surveyed every corner of the lobby as she entered, seeking assurance that the enemy—either Julien or Dobbs—was nowhere to be found.

The older man behind the counter had kind eyes above his white mustache. "I believe you have a . . . package for Tilly Lockhart?"

He shuffled toward a maze of cubbyholes at the back and returned with a rather small box wrapped in brown paper. "Here you go, Miss Lockhart."

"Thank you—" she looked up to see the postmaster's nameplate on the wall—"Mr. Wylie."

"You're most welcome, lass. And I hear Gretna won the match against Carlisle." He eyed the bundled uniforms under her arm. "Congratulations!"

She smiled, and then after leaving the building, she paused to carefully wrap the package inside her cloth bundle before heading toward home. As the workers thinned the farther she walked, Rose glanced behind her every so often, her skin tingling with a sense she wasn't alone.

Jittery nerves! She took a deep breath and tried to force calm, grateful she hadn't run into either one of her nemeses. The package seemed ordinary enough too, though she'd wait until later to open it in her room. Perhaps she'd find a note inside with the sender's name.

The package had piqued her curiosity by the time she reached the long drive to the Baird home. The lorry sat in front of the cottage, but she was still far enough away that she stopped and cast a furtive look around her before peeling back the uniform cloth to get to the box.

"Miss Lockhart!" Hannah hailed her from the house and began running in her direction. "Supper's almost ready," she said breathlessly when she arrived. "Maw sent me to look for Alex. Have you seen him?"

Rose shook her head, her grip once again tight on the bundle as she darted another look around her. "His lorry is there."

"Aye, but I canna find him."

❧ ⚙ ❧

Alex stood behind a pair of leafy birches only yards away and mouthed a silent oath. Leave it to his sister's timing.

Once the two started back down the drive, he retraced his steps, taking the path toward Blood Pond and the neighbor's pasture, then cutting back toward the small wooded area just behind the house. He ran the distance, determined to get there ahead of Tilly and keep his surveillance a secret.

He'd driven by the Gretna platform in time to see her leave the second train with several other workers. Carrying a bundle of red cloth, likely her team uniform, she moved in the direction of Timber Town, he assumed, to go see the lass who had taken ill just before the match. Alex thought to simply head the truck toward home.

Then he'd almost missed it—Tilly, giving a backward glance toward the platform before she surprised him by avoiding the hostels altogether and taking the other direction into town.

He'd slowed the truck, following at a distance, hoping to blend in with the other road traffic as her gaze darted everywhere. She was definitely nervous about something.

She'd gone into the post office and come out again with a small parcel, hiding the box inside the cloth bundle, much the way he'd done with Hannah's gloves inside his coat.

Who had sent her the package? And was this the reason she'd been upset? Tilly was an orphan without family, and those dearest to her had died in Nottingham. Was it just a catalog order? If so, then why hide it?

As soon as she'd started back toward the crossroads, he turned the truck around and beat her to the cottage. Taking the path behind the woods, he'd worked his way to the main road on foot to keep an eye on her—a difficult task since she had turned around at least a dozen times.

Was she afraid . . . or was she hiding something? How could that package be so personal that she didna open it and worried someone else might take notice?

The fact she'd lied to them about where she was going disturbed him most of all. Tilly had lied *to him*. And she was as jittery as a sheep before shearing. Why?

Alex burst into the backyard, breathless and relieved to see he'd left the ax embedded in the stump. Quickly he unbuttoned his shirt and rolled up his sleeves before grabbing up the blade to start hacking.

❖⬦ ❧ ⬦❖

Rose had reached the front door with Hannah when the sounds of chopping wood reached her ears. The tightness in her shoulders eased. "He's in back."

"Och, I thought I checked, but I didna see him."

"Perhaps he was in the shed?"

The girl shrugged, but Rose felt relieved that her constant fear of being followed home was unfounded.

As they entered the house, the delicious smells coming from the kitchen made her stomach rumble. "I'll just put this uniform away and help you and your mother lay out the food."

Tucking the package beneath her pillow, Rose returned to see that Hannah was already setting the table. Mrs. Baird appeared from the kitchen. "Hannah, lass, go and fetch Fergus and James. They're in their room with the dog and that smelly stocking ball, so be sure they wash their hands." She smiled at Rose. "Congratulations on winning against Carlisle, lass! Mr. Baird and I are so proud of the team and yer fine coaching!"

Warmed by the praise, Rose ducked her head. "Thank you, I'm delighted for the girls."

"Not just them," Mrs. Baird corrected. "I ken that ye were a key to helping the lassies win today." When her face suffused with more heat, Mrs. Baird took pity on her. "Och, ye'll turn into a beet if I go on. Please go call Alex in from the back, and I'll get Mr. Baird so we can all sit down to eat."

Relieved, Rose stepped out onto to the back porch just as Alex collided with her. Sweat beaded along his throat where he'd left a shirt button undone, and she caught the faint spice of his cologne. "Supper is ready."

"Aye," he said, clearly out of breath as he tunneled his fingers through the damp, chestnut locks. "How was your visit to see the young lass? Jane?"

Rose's voice faltered beneath his piercing gaze. "She . . . was asleep when I arrived. I had no wish to disturb her, so I'll go back and check on her tomorrow before the tea."

"I see." His lower lip curled. "At least you *made the effort.*"

Was it his look or the way he'd emphasized the words that made her cringe with guilt? "Shall we go inside?" Quickly she turned to reenter the house, eager to escape his scrutiny.

Supper was no better, however, as he continued staring at her, his expression brooding. Rose was relieved when the meal finally ended, and she stood as Mrs. Baird began clearing dishes. "I'll help you with that."

"The lads and I can take care of cleaning up." Mrs. Baird appraised her and then glanced at her eldest son. "Ye both look a bit haggard tonight, poor lambs. Go have a seat in the parlor and I'll bring tea."

"I am a bit tired," Rose admitted, seeing her escape. "I think I'll retire early tonight. I will see you all in the morning." She glanced around the table, her eyes darting past Alex. "Good night."

Upon reaching her room, Rose found Winston had nudged the door open and now lay inside on the rug, stocking ball in his mouth as he whipped his head back and forth, killing the wild beast.

She closed the door behind her and went to sit on the bed. Removing the package from beneath her pillow, she laid it on her lap and stared at the brown paper. Her pulse leapt to notice the postal stamp from London. Julien . . . ?

She tugged at the string, loosened the paper, and immediately the faint scent of roses reached her nose. Tearing off the wrapping, she let it fall to the floor and drew a sharp breath. The red box with French gold lettering—exactly like the one in Tilly's locker.

Rose spied the note then, tied to the box with string. She removed it and began to read:

> Carry these two scented gems if you dare
> On the first day into the factory with care
> And just as before, wear your thistle for me,
> The cotton stores at noon and I'll take them from thee.
> P. S.
> This mission is everything to us, sister. I'm counting on
> you.
>
> —Rhymer

Sister. Rose gripped the missive. Who was Rhymer? And why had he sent her this package? Dropping the note, she opened the red box to find two small perfume canisters. Again the powerful fragrance assailed her—the very same scent in Tilly's red box. Rose had thought the perfume a surprise for her party, a showing of the gifts.

She observed the brand. Dralle's *Illusion* perfume. Aunt Delia wore Dralle's in lilac scent. The perfume was quite costly. How could Tilly afford such an extravagance? Or had it been a gift from this Rhymer?

Her hands shook as she opened the first tiny canister. No vial of perfume but instead a small, oblong-shaped device similar in looks to the shortened stub of a pencil.

The second canister held the same.

She picked up the note and again considered the poem. *Just as before . . . into the factory with care.* Had Tilly received similar devices in the red box in her locker? Had she planned to carry them inside the factory to this Rhymer person?

Her friend would have been searched for any contraband each time she entered the factory. Rose couldn't imagine why Tilly would risk her job, unless . . .

Had she been threatened in this same way at Chilwell?

Wear your thistle. Rose eyed the jeweled pin on her nightstand.

Tilly wore the thistle brooch on Rose's last day of work. *On their last day.* She'd said it was her mother's, having hidden the pin in her hair to get it inside the factory.

This mission is everything to us, sister. A shiver rippled through her as the word *sister* took on new clarity. Rhymer was claiming to be Tilly's brother? Her friend spoke of a brother only once and rather abruptly, just to say that he'd died somewhere overseas. Rose imagined the memory too painful to discuss, so she'd not pursued it.

But what if he *was* alive? Had he met with Tilly? Had he sent her this same perfume box and convinced her to take these devices into the factory?

She gazed at the tiny canisters. What had her dear friend been about that night? And why would Tilly's brother need these odd devices brought to him? Though his not-so-subtle threats gave Rose a sense of foreboding.

Tilly had seemed unusually pale that last day, and Rose assumed it was because she weakened from the TNT poisoning. And her friend's melancholy had been due to the fact they would soon be parted from each other . . . or was it something else? *I've just a final task to finish . . .*

Rose hugged herself. What should she do? Rhymer had threatened her with the Baird family's welfare if she didn't cooperate; yet if she did manage to slip the devices into the factory *without* getting caught, what was their purpose?

She should take these canisters to the authorities. But Rhymer seemed to know her every move. Would he then harm Alex and his family before anyone discovered him? And if she involved the police, it would certainly bring to light her own secret.

How was she to resolve this *and* protect herself and the family she'd come to love?

Closing her eyes, Rose rubbed at her temples. Her physical exhaustion had combined with tension and mental fatigue. If she could only crawl into bed, she would be able to sort this all in the morning.

Replacing the canisters with the devices inside the red box, she leaned to retrieve the paper from the floor—and found Winston chewing on it. "No, Winston! Bad dog!"

Rose managed to salvage the soggy paper from his mouth and rewrapped the box, tucking the note beneath the tied string. Setting the package on the bed, she changed into her nightgown, and after completing her ablutions at the washstand she slipped beneath the covers. When Winston hopped up to lie against her, she took the parcel and slid it under the bed.

Tomorrow. *Lord, please help me to figure a way out of this.*

Yet despite her prayer and her weariness, she tossed and turned into the small hours, finally drifting off into a fitful sleep near dawn, stirring only once at Winston's low growl.

38

*I*t seemed she'd been asleep just minutes when Winston's barking awakened her.

"Hush," Rose grumbled. But his yipping continued, and she opened her eyes to stare at the plaid coverlet. He was gone.

Sitting up, she squinted against the light from the window and listened.

His barking persisted somewhere in the house.

"Daft dog." Throwing off the covers, she swung her feet onto the floor. She donned her robe and slippers and stumbled from her room toward the excited barking. "Hush, Winston!" she called in a loud whisper, moving through the hall.

Rose finally entered the parlor—and went perfectly still.

Alex sat on the couch with the perfume canisters in his hand. His other held the now damp, tattered note from Rhymer.

The red box and brown paper wrapping lay at his feet, soggy and chewed to pieces, while Winston kept lunging back and forth, barking and jumping up to nip the paper Alex held beyond his reach.

"Winston, hush!" Rose ran to grab him. "You'll wake everyone!"

"They've already gone to church."

What? She glanced at the mantel clock. Nine o'clock. She'd overslept . . .

Her breath caught as Alex began opening one of the canisters and removed the small pencil device. "What were you planning to do with this, Tilly?"

He lifted his face to her, and Rose quailed at his fierce look. "I . . . I don't know, Alex."

He rose from the couch and swiftly closed the distance between them. Looming over her, his eyes blazed like some wild Celt warrior as he held up the tattered note. "How do you know Rhymer?"

His deep voice vibrated with fury. Rose had never seen him like this before. "I . . . I've never met him . . ."

"I'll ask one more time." He thrust both canisters toward her. "What were you planning to do with these explosives?"

"Explosives?" Staring wide-eyed, she began to tremble. *Chilwell*. Fragments of memories flashed in her mind: the acrid black smoke, bloody debris raining from the sky . . .

"Answer me!" His angry voice jarred her. "Did you plan to sabotage the factory and kill innocent workers, *including my sister*? Do you wish to harm my family when they've been so good to you?"

How could he believe such a terrible thing? Her eyes welled with tears. "That is absurd! Of course I would never hurt them!" She wavered on her feet, struck by the full gravity of her situation. Rhymer wanted *her* to help him blow up the factory.

Had Tilly done the same at Chilwell that terrible night?

She tried to imagine an explosion of the same magnitude in a facility the size of HM Factory Gretna. The destruction would kill or injure hundreds, maybe thousands of workers, with the damage extending to the townships of Gretna, Eastriggs—even this cottage!

She had to tell him the truth about everything, no matter the consequences. "Please, wait here. I want to show you something."

Rushing back to her room, she returned moments later and offered him the two other notes from Rhymer. "He sent me these on Friday and Saturday," she explained as he scanned the poems. "I thought the first was a prank from one of the girls, but when he sent the second one yesterday, I had to go to the post office to pick up the package. He . . . he threatened your family, and I couldn't let him harm you."

❧ ⚭ ☙

Alex read the words through his rage—*Rhymer's words*—and only half listened to her blethering. The devil had referred to her as his "sister" in the note the dog was chewing this morning beside her bed.

Restless last night, he'd lain in bed wondering why she'd lied to him and hidden the package that seemed to have her so on edge. As sleep continued to elude him, his family awoke shortly after dawn and he made his excuses to miss church. After they left, he rose and slipped into Tilly's room, where he found Winston sprawled on the rug.

The dog had stood and let out a low growl, and Alex halted— then spied the package on the rug beneath him, the paper wet and torn. He made to grab for it just as Winston snatched up the box and shot out the open door into the hall.

Tilly barely stirred, and Alex had been grateful she was such a sound sleeper. He'd left the room and entered the parlor to find Winston in Da's chair, chewing on the paper—and then barking his head off when Alex took away his prize.

Now his "sleeping angel" stood telling him more lies, while in her possession were letters from the saboteur he'd been sent to find—*her brother*—along with what appeared to be some kind of explosives Rhymer intended to use to blow up Moorside.

Of course she would deny knowing anything and try to save her own hide.

"Go and get dressed," he barked, and when she jumped, an ache pierced through his anger.

"Wait! Alex, I haven't been entirely truthful with you." Her voice shook. "I am not who you think I am—"

"And you must think me a dunderhead not to ken that fact?" Hurt filled him as he glared at her. "You come into *my* home and gain the trust of *my* family, when all the while you've planned sabotage against those I love?"

"B-but I'm trying to tell you, I am not Tilly Lockhart. My name is Rose Gr—"

"What, some alias you think will satisfy me into letting you go?" His mind filled with an image of his brother and the photo of the woman who destroyed him. "I already ken that you're a spy, so you can save your lies for Scotland Yard. Now get dressed."

"You're taking me to the police?" Her large blue eyes widened like moons, the ivory skin paler than he'd ever seen.

"Aye, now go!" He gave her his most intimidating look. "Or do you want some help?"

"No! I'll . . . be just a few minutes." She turned and darted back to her room.

He stared after her, then at the notes and perfume canisters in his hands. Fury and self-reproach threatened to suffocate him while his heart felt rent in two.

Love had done this to him, made him a fool for believing Tilly, or Rose, or whatever name she wished to offer—it didna matter, as she'd used him as a means to an end.

What an actress! Calculating this scheme from the moment she arrived in Gretna. When Simon first sent him the telegram to watch her, Alex had considered and then discarded the notion that she took advantage of his family in order to hide here and maintain her privacy outside of work, even as an alibi should she need it.

It sickened him now to realize he'd been right.

Had his best friend and Weatherford known all along she was Rhymer's sister?

The betrayal stung. They'd blinded him to the truth, allowing him to believe her innocent, merely an eyewitness they hoped would recognize Rhymer from Chilwell. Not evil, like the woman who had cast her spell on Ian, weaving seduction and vice around his heart until he'd brought dishonor upon his family and nation. Alex was beginning to ken what it felt like . . .

"I-I'm ready."

Tilly had reappeared, dressed in her pink frock and eyeing him anxiously.

"Let's go." He'd take her to East Fortune and meet with Stuart, and since it was Sunday, Rhymer wouldna be the wiser if he *was* watching them. Alex had already intended to take Tilly on a picnic.

Fool. He gritted his teeth at the reminder while his pain and anger continued to do battle. Leaving his family a brief note, he ushered her out to the truck.

❧ ⚬⚬ ❧

Rose sat stiffly on the cab's bench seat as Alex drove them east. While she had no idea as to which constabulary he intended to take her, she wasn't eager to engage him in conversation.

Never had she seen him so angry, and certainly not at her. Even when he first arrived in the small hours and she attacked him with his golf club thinking he was a thief, he'd been more exasperated with her than incensed.

"What did your brother mean when he wrote 'Just as before, into the factory with care . . .'?" He glanced at her, his rough features taut. "Did you take the same devices into Chilwell when you worked there?"

Rose crossed her arms, ignoring him as she looked straight ahead. She'd actually tried to tell him the truth, knowing his relationship with Julien and putting Duggie and Samuel at risk.

Yet Alex didn't believe her.

Let him stew! Perhaps once they arrived at the authorities, she could tell *them* the truth about her quandary, including the illicit transaction she'd witnessed between her uncle and Julien—provided they promised to safeguard her little brothers.

Alex's question nonetheless disturbed her, resurrecting her doubts about Tilly. Had her friend played a part in Chilwell's destruction and the explosion causing her death?

No. Rose stared out her window. Tilly was not capable of committing cold-blooded murder. Yes, the scent of the perfume and the box had been in her locker, but it didn't prove she'd actually taken the devices inside the factory. *Unless her brother had threatened her with something terrible.*

"Do you wish to go to prison, Miss Lockhart?"

Rose jerked her head toward Alex, his cutting tone making her chest ache. His cold manner reminded her of Julien. But Alex wasn't anything like him! She yearned again for his gentle words and his tender looks. The hearty laughter and lopsided grins that made her melt inside.

Those were gone, however, and Rose again felt trapped. How could she extricate herself from this nightmare without doing someone harm—her brothers, the Bairds, or the innocent workers at the factory? "I will not go to prison, Alex," she said stubbornly. "I've done nothing wrong. I am not who you think I am, nor did I ask to receive that package. I have never seen those devices before."

"But you know Rhymer." He glanced at her, his gaze intense. "He's your brother."

"He is not my brother." Rose turned back to the window. It seemed pointless arguing with him. She could only hope for help from the police.

39

*B*y the time they arrived at RAF East Fortune, Alex had grown weary of questioning her. When he'd asked about the details to sabotage Gretna, either she refused to answer him, or when she did, her response was always the same. She wasna Tilly Lockhart, she was innocent, Rhymer was a stranger to her, and she had no idea what he intended.

Pulling up in front of the airfield headquarters, he exited the truck and came around to collect her, taking her inside the green cinder-block building.

Donovan sat in the first office, manning the communications. "Captain Baird!" The cadet launched from his seat to stand at attention.

"Cadet, have you seen Lieutenant Stuart?" he demanded.

Donovan darted a sidelong glance. "I . . . no, sir. Colonel gave him a few days of furlough. I think he went back tae London."

Did the lieutenant ever do his job here? Blowing air through his nostrils, Alex considered his next course of action. Time was short. He told Tilly the devices were explosives, but having never seen their like before, he'd only been guessing.

Still, he wasna about to take chances. He'd contact either Simon or Weatherford at the Admiralty. "I need to send a telegram immediately."

"Aye, Captain!" Donovan thrust his shoulders back another inch.

Alex turned to size up his prisoner. "Have you got a secure room?"

"Uh . . ." Donovan gave him a bemused look. "The supply room, sir?"

"That'll work."

Donovan grabbed a key from the desk and led the way beyond Colonel Landon's office to a door across the hall. "Here, sir." He handed Alex the key.

"Thanks, Cadet. I'll be with you shortly."

"Aye, sir!" Again the young pilot-in-training straightened before beating feet back to the communications room.

As he opened the door, Tilly's eyes widened. "Why do you need . . . ?"

He quickly nudged her inside. "Stay put."

Before she could turn around and argue with him, Alex closed and secured the door.

Now to contact Weatherford, and this time no more games.

Alex had their "possible key" locked up tight.

❧—⊰⊱—❧

"Let me out!" Rose banged on the door inside the supply room. A slice of daylight from the tiny window cast shadows on a variety of mops, brooms, buckets, rags, and beeswax.

She couldn't believe he'd locked her in here. It happened so fast, she didn't realize his intent until it was too late. "Alex, don't treat me like a prisoner!"

"You are a prisoner."

She jumped to hear his muffled voice on the other side of the door. "Please, Alex. I'm telling you the truth."

"You'll stay there until the authorities arrive."

"I won't!" she cried. "You have no right. I am innocent."

"We'll leave that for Scotland Yard to decide."

Panic gripped her as she pressed her fists against the door. Earlier, she'd decided to tell the authorities everything if they would agree to protect Douglas and Samuel. Now, however, the reality that she'd soon reveal her secret to the police unraveled her. Uncle Ridley was powerful, while Julien was the son of an earl. What if Scotland Yard refused to help her brothers?

She picked her way through the brooms, dustbins, and boxes to take a seat on an overturned mop bucket. Angry despair overwhelmed her. Alex hadn't believed the truth when she'd told him, and he still thought she'd planned to conspire with Rhymer.

You can hardly blame him. Her gaze dropped to the floor. She'd thought this was her chance; God's rescue after what she'd witnessed in the library, and the threats against her brothers if she didn't go through with a horrible marriage. Her means to freedom and having the choice to make a better life for her and the boys.

Rose also agonized to think that soon Mr. and Mrs. Baird would know her for a fraud, while Alex triumphed in his vindication. And Hannah . . . what kind of role model could she possibly be to the girl and the rest of her charges at the factory once they knew she'd been living a lie?

Oh, Tilly, what really happened? She and Rose had only known each other a few months, but in that time they'd become like sisters. And that sister made sure Rose left the factory before she did, shooing her out of the building, offering her own chain necklace . . .

Rose sighed and scrubbed her face with her hands. There was so much she didn't understand about any of this—except that her determination to avoid an arranged marriage had placed her in the middle of some deadly intrigue!

"Fetch Captain Baird from the hangar. I've got a telegram."

Rose stood and picked her way back toward the door. That voice—Donovan, the cadet whom they'd met on their arrival. Her pulse pounded at her throat. Had Alex received word from the authorities already?

The key turned in the lock minutes later, and Rose stepped

back as her jailor opened the door. "A detective from Scotland Yard is en route from Glasgow. He'll arrive in two hours to take you into custody."

Alex spoke in a rough voice, his bronzed features stony as he gazed at her.

Rose reached for the wall beside the door. This bad dream was becoming all too real . . . Her knees gave out then and she started to collapse toward the floor. Alex reached for her, holding her waist, and for a precious moment concern replaced his animosity.

She remembered other, similar intimacies with him, his gentleness as he'd held her and danced with her across the floor, careful to avoid her bare feet. And in the cab after their castle holiday, his tenderness as he'd held her, waiting while she tried to stand after waking to find herself wrapped around him.

His concern now faded toward bitterness, and pride made her gather her strength to stand on her own. She pulled away from him. "So I am to be your prisoner then, locked in this room for the next two hours?" She raised her chin, pursing her lips to keep them from trembling.

"You're a traitor to Britain." He leaned in, his face inches from hers, the words cutting her like the ax he so expertly wielded. "And I can only pray that you get a prison sentence instead of a firing squad."

Dizziness assailed her. "I . . . I've done nothing wrong." She struggled against full-blown panic. "Alex, you must believe me!"

But he turned on his heel and left her, closing the door behind him. She stood in stunned silence, until the click of the lock signaled her continued incarceration. At his receding footsteps, she slumped back onto the mop bucket and buried her face in her hands. *Lord, what should I have done? Remain in Leicester trapped in misery and suffering? Or here now to either face death for someone else's treachery or risk the truth with the authorities and endanger my brothers' lives?*

Rose wasn't aware of how long she sat there when again the

click of the lock drew her attention. Her mouth went dry. Would her executioner appear in the doorway?

She was surprised to see a policewoman standing on the threshold. "You're to come with me, miss." The older woman's brusqueness held no animosity as she indicated Rose should follow her.

"Where are we going?" she asked hoarsely.

"To the ladies'." The officer eyed her a moment before her tone softened. "The captain sent for me from Edinburgh. To see to your . . . comforts, miss."

Rose's fear eased somewhat as she allowed the policewoman to lead her to the washroom. Afterward, she was directed to an office along the opposite wall near her prison. The plate on the door read, *Lt. Colonel N. Landon, Commandant.*

Alarmed, she glanced at the policewoman as she opened the door. "You may go inside, miss."

Rose drew a deep breath as she entered . . . and paused at the array of food laid out on the colonel's desk.

Alex rose from behind the desk. "Have a seat."

He waved her toward the empty chair across from him and retook his own. As she'd had no breakfast, Rose eagerly moved toward the food, but her appetite died when he called to the policewoman, "Constable Edwards, please remain at the door."

She was still a prisoner then. Taking her seat, she observed Alex had already filled his plate. Rose eyed the tray, her stomach churning. How could she possibly eat now?

"At least have a wee bite. You havna eaten since last night."

She glanced up at him, then selected a few breakfast foods and put them on a plate.

Abruptly he pushed back from the makeshift table and crossed his arms. "All right, I'm ready to hear what you've got to say for yourself."

With her comforts now seen to, and being able to sit in the commandant's office instead of the supply closet, Rose's stubbornness returned. After all, she'd done nothing worthy of prison, though it would be "Tilly" they wished to incarcerate. But her friend was dead, and even if she wasn't, Rose refused to believe her capable of such a heinous crime.

What's more, Alex hadn't given her a clue about what was going on. He seemed familiar with Rhymer but said nothing other than to threaten her with prison and a firing squad.

Her pain rekindled at this last. Once again he'd judged her, making assumptions and accusations when she'd tried to be truthful with him—albeit having done so only this morning and not weeks ago.

And if she repeated what she'd already told him, would he believe her? At the moment, Alex seemed bent on convicting her and passing sentence. "I've decided to take your advice, *Captain*." She tilted her chin to meet his gaze. "And save my explanations for Scotland Yard."

❧⟶ ❦ ⟵❧

Alex stared at her across the desk, his simmering ire now at odds with the realization she hadna pretended to further sway him to her cause or to be coy.

Her anger at him was genuine.

Grudgingly, he admired her courage in standing up to him, much the way she had with Dobbs. Though since being fed and seated in a comfortable chair instead of her temporary jail, her prickly nature had returned.

If their circumstances were not so dire, he might have been amused. But the pain of her deception, and now the uncertainty of what to believe from her, cut him deeply. He might not have been led to treason as his brother was, but unknowingly he'd come dangerously close to being taken in.

Yet even as his mind set its course, he couldna let go of the memory of her vulnerability the night of their first meeting, or the trust he'd seen in those sleepy eyes as she'd awakened that Sunday night in his truck. Not the look of a murderess spy.

He thought of their talks together, the pining in her voice when she spoke of her family. Her fond memories of life in Glasgow and her yearning expression as she watched his own family share their affections. She'd seemed terribly lonely at times, as if she were the only person on earth and could rely on no one else. And Alex had found himself wanting to be that one person she could count on.

He expelled a sigh. His heart would get him into trouble if he wasna careful. He could easier empathize now with his brother. And it had cost Ian his life.

Weatherford's reply to his telegram was adamant. *Do not let her out of your sight.* Anticipating every possibility of her escape, the captain had also arranged to have Scotland Yard send over the policewoman from Edinburgh.

Alex couldna let emotion outweigh the facts. Tilly was in possession of potential explosives, and she had communications from Rhymer. She'd also denied the devil was her brother. Was that another lie?

And how would his family take the news? If *he* was miserable, his maw and da would be devastated, as would Hannah, who believed the sun rose and set on Miss Lockhart, *if* that was her real name.

Alex eyed her angrily. "Tell me this—how can you live with yourself and your actions? Your lies to my parents, to Hannah, and the lassies at work?"

She looked up from sipping her cup of tea, weariness in her expression. "I never did it to hurt them, Alex. All I ever wanted was the freedom to choose my own life."

What did she mean by that? "Has Rhymer made any other threats against you?"

She shook her head, the large blue eyes sad. "No, *he* hasn't."

❧ ⚬ ☙

Listless, Rose sat back in her chair. Alex looked as though he could barely stand the sight of her. "How much longer until this detective arrives?" she asked quietly.

"Anytime now."

She sighed. Soon enough her veneer as Tilly Lockhart *would* be stripped away and her innocence with regard to Rhymer vindicated. Yet Rose would pay the bigger price—hauled back to Leicester by Luther or someone else, with the wedding to Julien rescheduled.

Treason or marriage, her prison sentence would be the same, though perhaps not the firing squad. Still, Julien was capable of providing worse torments.

"Captain Baird, Detective Quinn of Scotland Yard has arrived. He is waiting in the communications office."

Rose turned to see a tall, lean older man in uniform standing on the open threshold.

"Thank you, Colonel." Alex rose from his seat at the desk while the colonel looked at her with kindly curiosity before disappearing back down the hall.

Her insides did somersaults as Alex stood over her, sadness in his eyes. His tone softened. "Is there anything else you want to tell me, lass? Before I bring him in?"

Shaking her head, she held back a sob. Her truth to the detective would come out soon enough. Though Rose intended to fight to save her brothers.

He strode from the office, and she heard him give orders to the policewoman as he closed the door.

Minutes passed as she sat with hands clenched in her lap, staring at the door. How would she begin to explain the sequence of events that took place the fateful night after Chilwell exploded? And would the detective believe her story? The only way to prove who she *really* was meant contacting her uncle . . .

The door cracked open, and she jerked in the seat, her heart pounding furiously.

Alex walked in first and strode across the room to stand beside her. The man who followed wore a black bowler hat and was tall and solidly built. He moved to close the door behind him, and Rose shot to her feet, her whole body trembling. She bent her head, unable to look at her executioner directly and instead let her gaze travel up his length—taking in the sable trousers and matching jacket, the dark hair slicked to a shine beneath the hat . . .

He turned and went completely still, staring at her. "Miss . . . Graham?"

The room seemed to shift. Rose grabbed for the back of her chair. "Luther?"

40

What was her uncle's chauffeur doing here?

Luther quickly regained his composure. "When did you come back from the dead?" He glanced at Alex, then frowned at her. "And what game are you playing?"

From the corner of her eye, Rose saw Alex stiffen in shock, yet she was too afraid now to crow over the fact. "How did you find me?" Her voice trembled. "Did Uncle Ridley send you?"

A sudden light came into his dark eyes, and his mouth curved upward. It was the first time Rose had ever seen him smile. "I think I know." He tipped his head. "Did you by chance acquaint yourself with a clockmaker in Glasgow a few weeks ago?"

His question made her pause. She nodded. "We . . . we did not get on well at all."

"The Glasgow police recently arrested Clive Liddle, who was charged with several counts of forgery. When I interrogated him at the station about Tilly Lockhart, he confessed to knowing her but said a woman similar in looks had come to see him weeks ago, pretending to be Tilly, and to get new identity papers." He paused. "That was you."

Interrogation? Glasgow police? "Are you no longer working for my uncle?"

Again, he looked toward Alex, then shook his head. "I'm Detective Quinn with a division of Scotland Yard."

Rose struggled to grasp his words. "How . . . do you know Tilly?"

"I was about to ask the same question." Alex spoke up beside her. "What's going on here, Quinn?"

"I was Tilly Lockhart's contact at Chilwell. She was working for us."

"So you knew she was Rhymer's sister? And Captain Weatherford . . ."

Quinn nodded. "The captain brokered the deal with her to help us catch Rhymer."

Rose heard Alex snarl under his breath. Detective Quinn narrowed his gaze on her. "Tell me, Miss Graham, where is she?"

Tilly . . . working for Scotland Yard? And who was Captain Weatherford? Still dazed, she waved a shaky hand toward one of the chairs against the wall, then turned to Alex. "You had both better sit down."

Once the men took their seats, Rose angled her chair to face them. She was conscious of Alex's eyes on her as she haltingly began to explain, starting with the note and how Tilly had urged her to write to Luth—Detective Quinn, so that she could have her bridal party.

She finished with the explosion, and discovering the brooch, and realizing Tilly's death was her only chance to escape an awful marriage and seek a new life. "But now I seem to find myself in some terrible trouble," she said, glancing at Alex.

Detective Quinn's leathery features were a mix of shock, grief, and wonder. "Tilly sent me her own note that evening, along with your message. I received both only minutes before the blast. Her note said she would soon have her freedom."

His smile wavered, the dark eyes filled with pain. "She'd received instructions from Rhymer several days before, much like the notes you received and which Captain Baird has turned over to me. That last day, she was to wear the brooch and meet her brother at the Mixing House with the explosives at the end of the shift."

"Those stubby-looking devices that were inside the perfume canisters?"

He nodded. "They're called pencil bombs—they're timed explosives."

"Timed explosives?" Her pulse jumped as she turned to Alex. He'd been correct. "Where are they now?" She edged forward in the seat, her eyes back on Detective Quinn. "Will they go off?"

"Not to worry, our bomb division will soon have them in their possession. They're designed to detonate anywhere from a few days to a week, based on the copper wall thickness inside. They also require a small top piece to be broken off before they can be detonated."

She sighed, leaning back in her chair. At least now no one would get hurt. "Did the pencil bombs Tilly carried inside go off then?"

He shook his head. "When she received the perfume box from Rhymer, we exchanged the real bombs for dummy charges. Scotland Yard had placed two plainclothes detectives inside the factory to make an arrest once she met with her brother and handed over the bombs."

"Then why the explosion?" Alex asked from behind the desk.

"It is believed that Rhymer didn't trust her to meet with him and had a contingency plan."

"That means my friend is innocent!" Rose cried.

"I agree with you, Miss Graham," he said softly. "Though when Tilly failed to check in with me afterward, some were convinced she'd tipped off Rhymer about Scotland Yard's plan and so he provided the timed devices. After making her escape just before the explosion, she vanished." His expression held sadness. "Now I know that's not what happened. Though Rhymer still must have activated his bombs and hidden them in a highly flammable area before making his exit, leaving the incendiaries to go off after he was gone."

"But you could find no record of him leaving?" Alex asked.

"Unfortunately, Captain, there was such a high death toll at Chilwell with so many missing and unidentified, we were not able to track his escape."

Rose shivered at her memories of that black night. "And you are certain Rhymer *is* her brother? Tilly told me that he died overseas many years ago."

"Thomas Lockhart was twelve when he was arrested in Glasgow for setting fire to a chemist's shop. The authorities shipped him off to a work farm in Australia. Tilly was still a small child, so she was taken off the streets and put into a local orphanage. We believe Rhymer is her brother from what she told us when we enlisted her for this assignment, but I don't think she realized then that he was still alive."

"Well, brother or not, I don't believe she helped him." Rose thrust out her chin. "My guess is, she wasn't certain what Rhymer would do."

She gazed at her clasped hands while her mind relived those last moments with Tilly. "Her eyes were so sad before we parted that last day. Tilly insisted I come to the party, even ordered me to take her bicycle to the cottage and wait for her. She promised she wouldn't be long." Rose looked up at Detective Quinn. "And then finding the gifts—she'd left me a five-pound note and a brochure to Nova Scotia. Her dream." Rose glanced at Alex, and something in his eyes warmed her. "I think . . ."

Her voice halted. The cottage door had been *unlocked*. Making Tilly's chain with the key and ID unnecessary. Then she recalled the words on the trade card Tilly had written: *"Become a new person, Rose. If you have the courage."*

She swallowed hard and looked up at the two men. "Tilly must have known she might not make it out of the factory in time," she whispered. "I think she was saving me."

The detective's eyes glistened. "I believe you're right, Miss Graham."

"You miss her too, don't you, Detective?"

He cleared his throat, his face tinged with color. "Tilly and I worked closely together for months. In that time, I grew fond of her. She was a rough gem, but she loved life and her proud spirit touched me. If our lives had been different . . ." He stared at his hat, his fingers working around the brim. "I will never forget her."

"Nor will I." Rose smiled as tears welled in her eyes. "Tilly was my best friend. My only friend."

Detective Quinn shot her a knowing look. "Your uncle could be very unpleasant. Many times I wanted to offer you encouragement, but I could not risk my cover."

"Why *did* you take the job as his chauffeur?" Alex asked.

"Tilly told me about Miss Graham." He turned to Rose. "She said your uncle kept you under close watch, having his chauffeur drive you back and forth daily from the factory. So we arranged to pension the old driver, and I applied for the job. A bit of luck involved, I'll grant you, but the visits to the factory twice daily allowed me to contact her without arousing suspicion."

Rose's mouth slackened. So "Miles Luther" hadn't been watching her after all.

She noted then the angry red patch near his temple—and recalled the head bandage the day he'd stepped from the Rolls. "When you stopped at Tilly's cottage after the explosion, you were looking for her, weren't you?"

"I wanted to make certain she was all right." He paused, brow arched. "You were there?"

Rose flashed a rueful smile. "I hid with her dog under a brass tub in the shed. I feared you would drag me back to my uncle."

"I'm sorry you had to worry about that with me. When we recruited Tilly—"

"How *did* you and Weatherford recruit her, Quinn?"

He gazed at Alex. "Weeks before she and I met, Scotland Yard discovered Rhymer was in some way connected to her. We tracked her down and found Tilly serving time at Aylesbury Prison in Buckinghamshire. The captain offered her freedom in exchange for confirming the identity of her brother, who was believed to be sabotaging munitions plants. Chilwell was next on his list of targets, and we wanted to catch Rhymer red-handed."

"Tilly was in prison?" Rose stared. "But . . . she told me that after the orphanage, she'd worked as a maid for Lady McAllister of Perth and hired on at Chilwell after her mistress died in Nottingham."

"As I said, she went into an orphanage when her brother was arrested," he said quietly. "The rest of her story had to be fabricated so she could obtain employment at the factory."

So Tilly had lied about her past. What about their friendship? Rose didn't want to believe it was a lie too, not when it seemed Tilly had spared her life.

"What crime did she—?" Rose stopped, recalling his remark about the clockmaker in Glasgow. "Forgery?"

Detective Quinn nodded.

"I don't understand why she couldn't trust me with the truth . . ." Her words trailed off and she glanced at her lap. Alex could ask her that same question.

"It was necessary, Miss Graham," he said. "The assignment was of the highest priority. Tilly was sworn to secrecy or she risked the penalty of death for treason."

How little she'd known Tilly Lockhart . . . or Luther, for that matter. Rose shifted her eyes toward Alex. He knew just as little about her, didn't he? *Trust him, Rose.*

Taking a deep breath, she turned back to the man who had worked for her uncle. "Have you seen Douglas and Samuel? Are they well?"

"Your brothers are back at school." His look held mild censure. "While I understand your reasons for leaving, they took your death very hard." He hesitated. "Lady Cutler as well."

Rose could feel Alex's eyes boring into her. She was relieved to know the boys were still safe, though the accusation in Detective Quinn's tone made her agonize even more at having abandoned them.

It was on the tip of her tongue then to confess to the incident she'd witnessed in the library; the drawer where Uncle kept his secret files and the shares he'd placed in Julien's hands. Her true reasons for leaving Leicester and the urgent need to protect Duggie and Samuel. "Detective Quinn—"

"I have a plan."

Rose sat back as he stood and began pacing the room. Finally, he turned to her. "Tilly's brother must already be inside the factory since he was able to get two letters to you." He glanced between her and Alex. "Likely he learned at the same time we did, that his sister—or at least you posing as her—had arrived once your paperwork was officially logged into the payroll."

She glanced at Alex, who grumbled, "Aye, about the same time I was notified to surveil Tilly Lockhart."

Her jaw dropped. "You . . . were surveilling me?"

"The captain's mission in Gretna has been to help us uncover the saboteur," Detective Quinn clarified.

She continued staring at Alex. He was here on a mission? Her anger stirred, along with her amazement. No wonder he'd been watching her every move over the past few weeks. He thought *she* was working with the saboteur!

"Rhymer is ready to make his move." Detective Quinn's words drew her attention, his dark features intent. "He is about to initiate the next target."

Rose shivered. "How . . . will you stop him?"

"No, Quinn," Alex growled as he, too, rose from his chair.

"I won't stop him, Miss Graham." Quinn looked at Alex before his eyes pierced hers. "You will."

41

*M*e?" Rose stared at him. "How can I stop a murderer?"

"By keeping your secret." His leathery face became animated. "Continue to be Tilly Lockhart and meet with Rhymer. Deliver the pencil bombs. We'll provide you with dummy charges just as we did for Tilly." To Alex, he said, "Everything will stay as it is now. She will accompany you and your sister into work as always, and once inside with the brooch and dummy charges, we'll get her cleared through to the factory floor. Several plainclothes detectives will be on hand at Site Three to make the arrest once Miss Lockhart meets with Rhymer."

"What if he realizes she's not Tilly?" Arms crossed against his chest, Alex scowled. "What then, Quinn?"

Detective Quinn's brow creased. "I don't believe Tilly and her brother met prior to Chilwell. She wasn't able to confirm his identity for us before the explosion." He paused, then added, "I suspect it's the reason he wanted her to wear the brooch—so he would recognize her."

Rose began to shiver. This was ludicrous! "Is it possible she did meet him and simply neglected to tell you?" She knew by living with the Bairds that family ties ran deep.

"I suppose it is." Detective Quinn's expression sobered. "I won't lie to you, Miss Graham. This is a dangerous undertaking. Rhymer has already proven to be clever. He may even have spies working inside the factory watching you. Which is why you cannot tell anyone your secret."

"What if she *is* found out?" Alex glared at him. "She could die, and my entire family and all the people who work at Moorside along with her."

"Whether or not we go ahead with this scheme, Captain, I fear Rhymer's plan to sabotage the factory will continue. This enterprise *is* risky, but if Tilly Lockhart's words were true, that she hadn't seen her brother in years, and with Miss Graham's similar looks, Rhymer will believe she *is* his sister. At least until the exchange is made. At that point our men will apprehend him."

"Aye?" Alex scoffed. "And how did that work for you at Chilwell?"

"As I've said, Rhymer must have set his own timed explosives, and he could have done so days before the meeting. I also suspect his bombs detonated sooner than expected, so while he obviously made his escape, Tilly . . ." Again he cleared his throat. "It leads me to believe the two never actually had a chance to meet. For all Rhymer knows, she delivered the explosives, and now that she's at Gretna, his next target, it's apparent she's earned his trust."

Alex sneered, "Or 'tis another trap."

Was it a trap? Overwhelmed by the detective's revelations, Rose sat in her chair, only half listening while they argued. *She* was to be bait for the saboteur!

During the past few weeks, she'd managed to re-claim the strength and confidence she'd lost so long ago, standing up to bullies like Dobbs and speaking out for her girls, for all women. She'd even helped to win a football championship. But did she have the daring to accept this task?

She couldn't forget that Rhymer had threatened her with the welfare of her clan, the Bairds. And she maintained the belief that Tilly had refused to go along with her brother's plan, yet he still blew up the factory at Chilwell. Had he willingly sacrificed his own sister to accomplish his ends?

It shouldn't surprise her, given her own uncle's treachery. Yet beyond getting the bombs inside, and wearing the brooch to meet with Tilly's brother—would she fool him?

If Tilly *had* met him while working at Chilwell, it could mean her own life.

And if I refuse? But Rose knew what would happen. Rhymer would still harm Alex and his family and then sabotage the factory.

Haunting memories of the explosion flooded her, and she imagined thousands dying, the surrounding towns damaged or destroyed. She couldn't let anything happen to the people she'd come to love because of her own fear—and it seemed she was the only one who could get close enough to Rhymer to put the evidence into his hands and have him arrested.

Her heart pounded. What if she and Tilly had never traded chains? If she'd simply gone to Tilly's flat and waited for her? Her friend would be the one pronounced dead, while she . . . she would be married to Julien, a different kind of death.

Was she any better off now? *Lord, was this your plan for me all along?*

Rose gazed up at both men, now facing off with each other.

Most of all, she didn't want anyone else to die. "I'll do it."

42

*H*is world had suddenly gone off its head.

Seated in the truck's cab, Alex gripped the steering wheel as he drove them back toward Gretna. He was still amazed to learn that Tilly wasna Tilly at all, and the real Tilly had worked with Scotland Yard at Chilwell to stop Rhymer, and paid for it with her life.

Earlier he'd listened, only half believing as Miss Rose Graham began her tale—a best friend's death in the Chilwell explosion, which she'd mentioned to him before, and her own desire to escape an overbearing guardian and a marriage she didna want. She'd assumed Tilly's name and, with her paperwork, fled Nottingham for Scotland, having no idea of the dangers associated with her friend. She wasna alone in the world after all, but had two brothers, as well as an aunt and an uncle.

His anger at Simon and Weatherford's secrecy continued to fester. Alex tried to imagine a reason why they would have hidden the facts from him, especially when they believed Rhymer's sister had been staying in his home and jeopardizing his family!

He considered the quiet woman seated beside him, his bitter disappointment conflicting with apprehension, knowing she would soon be taking her friend's place to catch their saboteur.

She stared out her window at the passing miles, likely because every time she'd looked at him, he scowled. Alex still resented her deception; all the while he'd thought her shy when she was actually harboring a lifetime of secrets, including information that might have proved helpful in his investigation.

Miss Graham had lied about her past to his family, her co-workers, *and* to him. He gritted his teeth remembering how he'd shared his grief with her, his burden of shame at Ian's death—while she'd remained a clam about herself, unwilling to offer him the same trust.

And that's the real thorn, man. She didna trust you. His shoulders hunched as he focused on the road ahead.

"Alex."

He turned to find her large blue eyes gazing at him. The same eyes he'd seen yesterday, and the day before, and the day before that. "Miss Graham?"

"I haven't grown horns, you know. I want you to trust me."

"Like you did me?" He growled the words.

"I couldn't tell you. I couldn't tell anyone. If I did—"

"If you did *what* exactly?"

"There is so much at stake." The soft touch of her hand as she placed it against his bare arm seared him. "Please, call me Rose. At least when we are alone. I cannot do this without you, Alex. I need your help."

He frowned. "And I told Quinn I would give it. Is that not enough?"

She pursed her lips, drawing his attention to their softness and shade. His eyes grazed over the familiar face, her smooth skin a slightly sallow hue but still fine like her dark brows, and the rich brown hair tucked beneath her straw hat.

At least her features didna change with her name. They could belong to no one else.

"I did tell you the truth about a lot of things."

He snorted, staring at the road. "Like what?"

"My mum and dad. She *was* a dressmaker, and he was a weaver, and they did have a shop—Graham's Drapers and Haberdashery on Princes Street in Edinburgh, not Glasgow."

Auld Reekie? He remembered then her near slip when he'd told her about his childhood there. The reminder of how much he'd shared with her angered him. "And what about your two brothers? You neglected to mention them."

"I . . . was trying to protect them. My uncle would have been furious if he'd known that I had escaped before the marriage. I worried that he would take it out on Douglas and Samuel."

How was she protecting them when they believed her dead? Alex shook his head in disgust. "When did you go and live with this uncle of yours?"

"As I told you and your family, I *was* fourteen when my parents died. The shop had debts, and I suppose we were fortunate that my mother's sister took pity on us. I attended English boarding schools until two years ago when I returned to Leicester and served as my aunt's companion. About four months ago I begged my uncle to let me go to work at the munitions factory in Nottingham, and that's where I met Tilly."

As he listened, the name *Graham* and *Leicester* seemed familiar. It dawned on him—the article in the *Times*. "Your uncle is Sir Ridley Cutler, the munitions magnate?"

"He is my guardian."

Stunned, Alex was only vaguely aware of the tremor in her quiet response. Cutler Industries was a leading manufacturer of munitions and armaments. Miss Graham—Rose—had lived a life of luxury, yet she fled to take on the life of a woman who by all accounts had been a poor domestic. He turned to her. "Why did you do it?" When her expression clouded, he added, "You staged your own death merely because you didna wish to marry?" He grimaced, turning back at the road. "The man must have been a real scunner."

"Trust me, he is the worst of men." Her voice vibrated with emotion.

"Who is he?" When she didna answer him, he darted a glance and saw the color had drained from her face. Was she frightened . . . or thinking to come up with more lies?

"May I ask you a question first?"

"Aye."

"How well do you know Julien Dexter?"

He slowed the truck, then turned to her. "Dexter?"

"You two are friends." Her blue eyes darkened, and he noted the tremble in her chin.

He sighed. "Dexter is a preening dunderhead, and 'tis my hope I've seen the last of him in this lifetime." He lifted a brow. "Does that answer your question?"

A slow smile spread across her face, and his traitorous pulse leapt. "It does."

"And?"

"I was supposed to marry him." She arched a fine brow right back. "Does that answer yours?"

So he was right, though it still jarred him. Alex leaned back against the seat. "The only thing it doesna tell me is why you only ran as far as Gretna."

She giggled then, and he couldna help but smile. Her reasons for secrecy were beginning to make sense. "And you saw me with Dexter at the factory," he said.

"Yes, and I heard him tell Hannah and the girls that you two once flew together. The newspaperman also claimed you were pals."

"How did you hear what was said?"

"I was hiding behind the concrete support."

"So you ran." He angled his head. "You were never sick, were you?"

Her smile fell. "I can say truthfully that seeing him made me ill. I was terrified he would notice me and drag me back to Leicester."

"When was the wedding to happen?"

"My first day at the factory."

Alex absorbed the information. She'd mentioned Dexter during their ride to visit the castles. No doubt trying to figure out which camp he was in. "You couldna speak with your aunt or uncle about Dexter?"

"Uncle Ridley arranged the match." Her tone held bitterness. "He wanted a connection with the Earl of Stanton."

Alex grunted. It surely fit the mold of any opportunist who had made his fortune in new money. Cutler was knighted and wealthy as Midas, but the chance to tie his bloodline to the auld nobility, like the Earl of Stanton, must have been too good to resist, offering up his attractive ward as sacrifice. "What about your aunt?"

Again she fell silent, and he turned to see her blue eyes flare. "Aunt Delia was conditioned long ago to be seen and not heard."

Disquiet settled over him, and he tried to imagine Rose's life with an uncle she'd described as overbearing and who had used her to barter his way into Stanton's realm.

And an aunt who could not save her. "So tell me more about your brothers."

"Douglas and Samuel are close in age to Fergus and James."

He glanced at her. "Where are they now? Quinn mentioned something about school?"

"Caldicott School in Hertfordshire. I've telephoned a couple of times to check on them, pretending to be my aunt. We remained at school year-round, except at Christmas."

All year? His mind flashed with the memory of her face when he'd kissed the top of his sister's head in the truck. The sadness in her expression tore at him.

He also remembered her glow when she spoke of her maw and da and their shop. "What about your plans to go abroad? You said earlier it was Tilly's dream. Is it yours as well?"

"Not at first, but I decided it would be mine after she died. I shall take Douglas and Samuel out of school, and we'll sail for Nova Scotia, 'New Scotland,' where we can start a new life together. A real family."

Seeing her smile and the hope in her eyes was a sharp reminder of their coming plan and his growing fear she wouldna live long enough to see her dream fulfilled.

Regardless of his struggle to reconcile the woman he'd known with the woman beside him, Rose Graham was about to risk her life for his family, his home, and all those at Moorside.

He wasna going to stand by and watch her die.

43

*T*illy Lockhart is dead?"

Perched on the edge of his desk, Marcus observed Simon's shock. Then he glanced toward Quinn, seated in the leather chair beside his friend. "Care to enlighten the captain?"

The detective took several minutes to explain his working as Sir Ridley Cutler's chauffeur and driving Cutler's ward back and forth to the Chilwell factory each day. Allowing him to make contact with Miss Lockhart without arousing Rhymer's suspicions.

He also relayed yesterday's surprise confrontation at East Fortune, when he'd come face-to-face not with Tilly Lockhart but with Cutler's ward, Rose Graham, posing as her friend and giving him the sad news it was Tilly who had died in the Chilwell explosion.

"That's a tangle if I ever heard one," Simon said when Quinn had finished. "And now the plan is to have Miss Graham meet with Rhymer pretending to be his sister?"

"Correct," Marcus said. "It is our only choice if we still want to catch him."

"And if he realizes he's been given a substitute sister?"

"A chance we have to take, Captain," Quinn said. "I want to believe that Miss Lockhart and her brother did *not* meet prior to the explosion at Chilwell, but there is no guarantee. Miss Graham is still willing to participate, as is Captain Baird, though he's not pleased with the idea."

"I dinna doubt it." Simon looked at Marcus. "And I'm certain Alex has branded us both traitors for not telling him the whole story. He believes we put his family at great risk."

Marcus met his friend's angry gaze, a barb of guilt piercing his conscience. Then he considered the hundreds who had already perished in the past three explosions and pushed off the heavy yoke. "It needed to be done, Simon. If we had exposed Tilly Lockhart, Rhymer would have discovered something was up weeks ago *and* detonated Moorside in revenge. As it is now, we still have secrecy on our side and some control over the situation, thanks to Miss Graham's willingness to help. Rhymer believes she is his sister and he's sent her the timed explosives. All we need to do is to get her and the bombs inside to meet with him." *And pray the blighter hasn't outfoxed us again with his own arsenal.*

He turned to Quinn. "When will your department have the dummy charges ready?"

"Wednesday morning. I've arranged to meet Captain Baird in Carlisle rather than Gretna to hand them off, and he'll see that Miss Graham gets them." Quinn eyed them both. "We don't know if Rhymer's been surveilling them, and if he saw me before at Chilwell . . ."

"Righto," Marcus agreed. "I want absolutely no one else privy to this new information on Miss Graham. We are too close now to take chances." He tipped his head at Quinn. "When will Scotland Yard have their men in place?"

"We've had two plainclothes detectives working at Moorside in Gretna for the past month. They relocated to Miss Graham's section this morning. Transfers are common, and because the men have been employed awhile, they shouldn't raise suspicions. Our own officers have replaced factory police stationed at all gates and we've added extra policewomen. They'll stay focused on Miss Graham, while the two detectives are put in charge of off-loading bales in the cotton stores where Rhymer's meeting is to take place."

"Miss Graham has this brooch Rhymer speaks about?"

"Yes, and she'll have it with her on Thursday when she takes the dummy charges inside. A policewoman will ensure she gets through the inspection and onto the factory floor. From there she'll make her way toward the cotton stores at noon to meet with Rhymer."

"So, tell me truthfully," Marcus said, giving voice to his most urgent concern, "can Miss Graham pull this off?"

Quinn's dark brows veed. "A month ago, I would have said no."

Marcus moved around to sit at his desk. "Explain."

"I'll begin by saying that Sir Cutler is not an easy man to live with or to work for. As his driver, I discovered he takes a dim view of children and in particular his wife's Scots relations. For the six years Miss Graham and her young brothers have been in his care, he's kept them isolated in boarding schools almost year-round, while Lady Cutler . . ." Quinn shook his head. "He's bullied her to the point that she's little more than an ornament at his social gatherings, and no support to the children.

"Once Miss Graham finished school, she served as her aunt's companion. During my employment at the Leicester estate, there were many times she endured the brunt of her uncle's displeasure. She became more reserved and often tense, especially in his company, and with her fiancé."

At this last, Marcus realized Miss Graham had been at Moorside for weeks. "Is there any chance Lieutenant Dexter saw her at the factory when he was there?" Though they hadn't yet made the connection between the lieutenant and Kahverengi, Marcus recoiled at the possibility Dexter reported her presence to the arms dealer and Rhymer was advised.

"I doubt the lieutenant saw her, otherwise he would have arranged for Sir Cutler to bring her home." Quinn paused. "And

Rhymer would not have sent her explosives if he believed she was other than his sister."

Marcus leaned back against the seat, his rapid pulse ebbing. "So what changed your mind about her?"

"The Rose Graham I met yesterday has a strength I hadn't seen before. Courage in her stance and in her actions, and she holds great affection for Captain Baird's family and the young women she supervises." He shrugged. "I cannot be more specific, just to say the look in her eyes and the tone of her voice tell me she's committed to protecting her own."

"That's reassuring." Marcus drew a deep breath. "I regret the death of Miss Lockhart, but I believe Miss Graham's presence and her willingness to help at Moorside is Providence." He gazed at both men. "Our last hope of putting Rhymer and Kahverengi out of business permanently."

44

*W*as he watching her even now?

Again, Rose tried tucking the question into the back of her mind without success. Since returning to work yesterday, her thoughts had been preoccupied with Rhymer and the events to come. Each task she performed in her job now seemed like a mountain to climb, and it was an effort to appear calm and assured in front of her girls, especially when she had to explain why she missed their tea on Sunday—a question Hannah confronted her and Alex with late Sunday night when they arrived back at the cottage.

Alex's ability to prevaricate had rivaled her own. He offered his sister a concocted story about the lorry having engine trouble, and his needing to walk to the nearest town to get a part before they could return home. Rose relayed that same story to Gladys, Colleen, and Betty yesterday in the canteen.

Seated at her desk, she continued the tedious work of filling out reports for her section, and soon her thoughts wandered back to the airfield and her shock at seeing Luther—Detective Quinn. He'd assured both her and Alex that Scotland Yard would prepare the dummy charges she was to bring into the factory, and he would meet Alex in Carlisle tomorrow, on the eve of her encounter with the devil himself—and hand them over.

A shaky sigh escaped her. At least Alex was on her side *and* he knew the truth about her. She'd also been relieved to discover he held Julien in the same contempt. A smile edged her lips, recalling his remark about her escaping only as far as Gretna. He knew Lord Julien Dexter's stripes well!

Rose had even braved telling him about her brothers, and it was true she worried for their safety if Uncle ever discovered she'd fled the marriage. Though the secret transaction she'd witnessed in the library would remain with her until she could guarantee the boys wouldn't be harmed.

Alex too had harbored his share of secrets—like returning to Gretna *not* because of a medical discharge, but instead receiving orders to come here and find Rhymer.

It seemed they'd each worn a mask of sorts, yet she hoped the secrecy was at an end, at least between the two of them. As the coming meeting with Rhymer drew closer, Rose would need his help and friendship more than ever.

Did they still have a friendship?

Last night at the cottage, it felt strange hearing the rest of the Baird family call her "Miss Lockhart" or "Tilly" while Alex looked on knowingly. His silent censure of her made the ruse all the more difficult to maintain.

If she could only regain his trust . . . yet it so much was more than that. She longed for his soft looks, and those tender smiles. Their shared laughter. He'd shown her a glimmer on the way home Sunday, and she ached all the more to return to the way they had been before.

"How are you holding up, lass?"

As if summoned by her thoughts, Alex appeared at the door into her office. She gripped the pencil in her hand. "Much the same as yesterday—on pins and needles. I keep expecting to see *him* around every corner, though I have no idea what he looks like." Her eyes beseeched him. "I just want this to be over, Alex."

"You and me both." He angled his head, gazing at her. "I am here for you, lass, so dinna fash too much, all right?"

His voice had gentled, and Rose fought an impulse to leave the desk and rush into his arms. The courage she'd mustered over the past two days was beginning to crumble, and she desperately needed his strength.

Instead, she rose from the chair and drew her shoulders back. "I'll do my best." But then tears misted her eyes as she added, "Alex, I am glad that you're here."

He started to take a step closer, then halted, giving her the barest of smiles. He checked his watch. "I'd better get back. Quinn asked me to check in with the two detectives who transferred to the cotton stores yesterday. I'll see you after work."

"'After' cannot get here soon enough." She longed to escape the factory and Rhymer's watchful eye, and return to the warm security of the Baird home.

"I'll meet you at the platform when the shift is over," he said.

Then he turned and was gone, taking with him a piece of her heart.

⋘ ⧑ ⧒ ⋙

"Alex, Miss Lockhart, truly?" His sister eyed them both at the supper table later that evening, and Alex caught her nervous excitement in the pink suffusing her cheeks.

"As long as your mother and father approve."

Tilly . . . Rose glanced again at his maw and da, who smiled and nodded their consent. "So long as ye mind yerself with yer brother and Tilly," Maw warned her.

"Aye!" Hannah turned her grin on him and Rose before leaping up from her chair at the table. "Thank you both so much! I'll be dressed in just a tick."

As she rushed from the dining room, Alex swiveled his attention to Rose. "Are you certain you're up to a dance?" He'd noted her lines of exhaustion as she'd agreed to chaperone his sister tonight

320

for the Mixed Club dance at Gretna's Border Hall. He had decided to go along as well, to make certain she didna run into any trouble with Dobbs, in case the union man was skulking about town.

"Of course I'm up to it." Rose turned to him and smiled. "Hannah deserves a night of dancing, so she can practice on you what she's learned." Despite her weariness, a teasing light entered her eyes and sped up his pulse. She sobered, adding, "I want her to have fun tonight, Alex. These days, there seems precious little time for enjoyment."

He kenned her meaning only too well. In less than forty-eight hours Rose would face and try to fool a madman. God forbid, but if she failed there would be nothing left for any of them to enjoy.

Hours ago at work, he had seen her fear and heard the waver in her voice while her eyes welled with unshed tears. He'd wanted to go to her but checked himself. Likely he would have done her more harm than good, making her soft when she needed to be strong for what was to come.

Alex still disliked Quinn's plan, though there were few other options. The detective was right—if they didna go through with it, the sabotage would still happen. Better she—they—had a chance to stop Rhymer, or die trying.

He tossed his napkin onto the table. Just the thought of losing her pierced his soul. While he resented her not trusting him with the truth, and deceiving his family, he also applauded her desire to escape a marriage to Dexter. And Rose hadna been entirely untruthful with her story, but just enough to keep herself safe, especially when she believed Alex was pals with that scunner.

She'd been a great help to his maw over the past few weeks, and she paid her rent on time. Rose had even added her rations to his family's stores so they would all have enough to eat.

In fact, if he was honest, his parents and siblings were no worse off for Rose keeping her secret. *And neither are you, man.* It was his pride that fueled his resentment, and *had* he known the truth about her any earlier, Tilly Lockhart would have ceased to exist and this plan about to unfold with Rose couldna take place.

Alex pushed out a sigh as he rose from his chair. *Aye, your ways are not our ways, Lord, but I pray she succeeds.*

"I'm ready to go!" His sister had reappeared, wearing her new green frock. Her joy dimmed as she looked first at Rose, then at him. "Well now? If you two dinna hurry and get changed, we'll miss the dance altogether!"

❧ ❦ ☙

Illuminated by the evening sun shining through an array of windows, Border Hall seemed festive, as balcony walls strung in blue-and-white bunting surrounded the spacious, polished wood floor. Lining the perimeter were covered tables holding glass jars filled with summer heather and pink begonias, set amidst punch bowls of lemonade and plates of jam biscuits, tea sandwiches, and fruit tarts.

The factory band had set up on a dais at one end of the hall, playing continuously as dozens of couples, most of them young girls from the factory, cavorted across the room showing off dance steps like the Grizzly Bear, the Lame Duck, and a fast waltz to the energetic tempo of Scott Joplin's music.

Rose had taken a seat among an assembly of chairs lining the wall. In her mauve jacket and skirt, she watched while Alex danced with his sister. It was a fast tune, and she smiled while observing several of the young girls eyeing Hannah with envy as her brother effortlessly swept her across the floor in a ragtime waltz. Though the past few weeks of dance practice had improved Hannah's steps, Alex was such a fine partner it left little for the girl to worry about as his sure, strong movements kept her light on her feet.

Rose had wanted this night for Hannah, and for herself too; in two days neither of them might ever again have the chance.

The song slowly faded, and once Hannah flew off to meet Betty, Colleen, and Gladys, who had recently arrived, Alex grabbed up two glasses of lemonade from the refreshment table and walked in Rose's direction.

"Where did you learn to dance so well?" she asked him, taking the glass he offered her.

"There's more to college than just football," he said with a devilish smile. "I remember asking you that question once, but we were interrupted." He glanced toward his sister, then back at her. "Well?"

She made a face. "Six weeks of finishing school, I'm afraid. Once my fate was sealed as a prospective Lady Stanton, Uncle Ridley sent me off to try to turn a 'sow's ear into a silk purse.'"

His expression darkened. Rose looked away as heat stole into her cheeks. Perhaps she'd offered a bit too much truth. She raised her eyes to him again and lifted a shoulder. "Anyway, that's how I learned the waltz, along with a few other dances."

He turned and surveyed the room. "Well, I noticed you havna danced with anyone, and already we've been here an hour."

She followed his gaze, scanning the few males in attendance. Most were elderly staff or boys who worked in the factory. "It would seem we women are in short supply of dance partners, Captain," she said in amusement. "Though I've been keeping an eye on the girls keeping an eye on you, and you're the most eligible. So be careful about wearing out your shoes."

He laughed, and it was like manna to the hunger gnawing at her heart. How she'd missed that sound! She schooled her features, however, and stood, intending to fetch a biscuit from a nearby table when the lilting notes of the next song began.

He set down his glass and held out his hand. "You ken that I've one spot still open on my dance card, so are you willing?"

Her heart sped, seeing his expectant gaze. "I have shoes on this time, so I suppose I'm safe enough."

"Always with me, lass." He grinned, and as she set down her glass and gave him her hand, he led her out onto the dance floor. Recognizing the tune as he took her in his arms—a new American song titled "Will You Remember?"—Rose was suddenly whirled into a waltz across the floor.

His gaze held hers as he swept her aloft, like the fluff off a dandelion swirling in the breeze. Soon Rose became immersed in the enchanting music, aware only of her pounding pulse and his strong hand pressed gently at her back while his other kept her warm in his grip.

Words seemed unnecessary as they stared into each other's eyes; hers pleading forgiveness for the lies and not trusting him, and his glowing with affection, and the sudden pressure of his hand offering sorrow for the harsh words that had passed between them.

Her smile turned bittersweet as she recalled the words to the music. Would they remember? This time together *was* precious, as their future and the future of all here at Border Hall, the factory, and its surrounding area could change in the span of a heartbeat or a breath. She gazed at his generous mouth. Even a kiss . . .

Or an explosion that could destroy everything they both held dear.

45

*H*e'd almost kissed her last night.

Alex stood on the train platform at the end of shift the following day, his thoughts veering between the memory of Rose in his arms and their intimate, silent exchange . . . and the harsh reality of today's rendezvous with Quinn to pick up the dummy charges she'd take into the factory tomorrow to meet with Rhymer. If anything happened to her . . .

"Dear God, please help us," he muttered softly.

"Are you blethering to yourself now, Brother?" Hannah strode up to him, grinning.

"I was thinking how you nearly wore me out dancing," he teased. "I'm not a young lad anymore."

She laughed. "Some auld man you are. At least two dozen lassies came up to me last night to find out who I was dancing with." Her eyes glinted against her yellow complexion. "If I charged a bob for each time I answered, I could have bought two new hats to go with my gloves."

He chuckled, and his sister turned to glance behind her. "Miss Lockhart's here!"

Alex looked up at her approach, his heart thudding in his chest. Again his mind filled with the memory of holding her, light as a fall leaf, as they'd danced and entered into a world all their own. For those few minutes he'd realized that she was the same woman, with the same dark hair, the same blue eyes, the same intelligence and humor and kindness. She was Tilly, aye, and she was Rose.

"Hurry! We can catch the first train!" Hannah cried as she rushed forward.

Alex and Rose followed behind, and when her hand reached for his, he gave her fingers a squeeze before they separated to board the train.

His sister thankfully filled the silence between them as she blethered on about her day, and Alex sat beside Rose, hoping his presence would ease some of her nervousness. Later he'd go over tomorrow morning's details with her and make sure she was still ready.

Twenty minutes later, they arrived home, and he was surprised to see a truck parked next to the cottage. Entering into the parlor, he paused and his mood darkened. "Stuart."

"Good afternoon, Captain Baird." The blond lieutenant set his teacup on the table, then rose from the chair beside Da's.

"Alex, I was just visiting with your friend from the airfield." His da came to his feet, leaning on his cane. "He arrived no more than ten minutes ago."

"This is a surprise, Lieutenant." Alex offered a tight smile. "If I'd known you were coming, I would have made an effort to leave work earlier."

"Och, dinna fash, Captain." Stuart grinned, displaying his straight white teeth. "I had to come to the village on factory business and I've taken a room at the hotel."

Alex nodded. With Rose about to meet Rhymer, Weatherford had ordered Stuart to Gretna.

"And who is this?" When Stuart looked beyond him, Alex turned to see Rose and his sister enter the parlor.

"Lieutenant Charles Stuart, this is my sister Hannah and Miss Lockhart."

Stuart inclined his head. "I'm pleased to meet you both."

Mrs. Baird appeared from the kitchen. "Hannah, would ye be a lamb and set the table, and add a plate for our guest." She turned to Alex. "Fetch the lads, will ye, son? They're in back with the dog."

"I'll join you," Stuart offered, and before Alex could object, the lieutenant followed him through the parlor toward the back porch.

"A wee bit of warning would have been appreciated," Alex muttered as they reached the back door.

"Aye, but I only got my orders last night. My 'transfer' out of East Fortune processed this morning so no questions would be asked, and there was not time to give you notice."

Alex opened the door to call his brothers inside, and Winston suddenly darted past him into the cottage.

"Och, what a bonny wee dog you've got."

As Stuart knelt, the dog went right to him, licking his hands and wagging his tail.

"Winston likes you."

Alex and Stuart turned to see Rose gazing down at the dog. "I've never seen him do that. He usually growls first, until you give him your hand and he catches your scent."

Stuart rose to his feet. "No doubt he smells my mascot."

"Mascot?" She took a step closer to Stuart while Alex looked on, clenching his smile.

"Aye, my fox, Queenie. She actually belongs to the instructors, but she often rides with us in the cockpit when we go up."

"Truly?" She glanced at Alex. "Did you know about these mascots?"

His smile eased. "Many pilots fly with a mascot. Pigeons, small dogs, snakes."

"Eek!" She made a face. "I should not wish to have a snake for a pet."

"You're a Sassenach?" Stuart asked her suddenly.

Her eyes widened at Alex before she turned to Stuart. "I was born in Glasgow, but I became a lady's companion to an English-woman for several years, and she influenced me."

Alex admired her calm, relieved when Stuart seemed satisfied with her answer. "Fergus, James, supper!" he bellowed, and once the lads scurried inside, he instructed them to go and wash.

"I'll just take Winston outside." She smiled at Alex, then at Stuart before grabbing up the wee beastie in her arms and taking him out beyond the porch.

"Och, what a jammy dog to be cuddled by such a bonny lass," Stuart breathed once she'd gone outside.

"Keep your focus, Lieutenant."

"Believe me, Captain. I'm very focused." Stuart's dark eyes gleamed.

Alex glared at him. The sooner their meal was done and this wolf could be on his way, the better.

Once Rose rejoined them, they went into the dining room. Alex saw that his da had already settled the lads, and his maw and Hannah were seated at the table.

"Allow me, Miss Lockhart." Stuart rushed forward to pull out Rose's chair.

"Why, thank you, Lieutenant." She smiled, and as she took her seat, Stuart leaned in and said, "My pleasure, lass."

Alex worked his jaw watching the exchange. He waited until Stuart was seated on the other side of the table next to Hannah before he finally took his own chair.

They said grace, and his maw began serving the meal. "Lieutenant, please tell us how ye know Alex," she said as she passed out the first plate of collops and tatties.

"He didna tell you, ma'am?" Stuart shot him a wounded look Alex easily dismissed. "He and my brother Donald went to primary school together in Edinburgh."

"Och, is that so? Stuart . . ." Maw turned to his da. "I seem to recall a Donald Stuart when I was caring for wee Alex." She beamed at the lieutenant. "Where is he now?"

Stuart's smile faded. "I'm sorry to say Donald was killed in action. The Battle of Jutland."

His maw's face paled, piercing Alex with a fresh blade of guilt.

"We lost our Ian last year," she said.

"I am aware, ma'am, and you have my sympathy."

Maw reached out to touch Stuart's hand. "'Tis sad, this war takes so many of our lads."

She glanced at Alex, and he warmed at her loving gaze. "I'm happy that our auldest is here with us."

"Aye, 'tis a blessing," Stuart offered. "Though the lads at the airfield miss him."

"Do they?" His da's brows arched.

"Indeed, sir." He smiled at Alex. "A distinguished captain, your son. The cadets think very highly of him."

"Well now, that's a fine thing to hear, thank you, Lieutenant." The pride in Da's voice worked to thaw Alex's temperament. Stuart had a bit of the devil in him, but he could be decent when it suited.

Maw too seemed pleased as she finished passing around the filled plates. As Alex tucked into his bacon and potatoes, he only half listened while Stuart reiterated for his family the work he'd done with the oil company before the war, and his traveling throughout Europe.

Occasionally Alex glanced up from his meal, disheartened to see Rose completely taken in by Stuart. He was relieved when supper was finally over. Now the Bonny Prince could go back to his hotel.

Then Maw stood and announced, "Since we've a special guest tonight, we'll take our dessert out to the back porch and enjoy this lovely evening."

"A fine idea, Mrs. Baird, thank you." Stuart rose to his feet, then helped Da from his chair before the two headed back toward the porch.

Alex's sister and brothers were quick to follow.

"What a thoughtful lad." Maw watched the pair as she began clearing dishes.

"The lieutenant does seem quite likable," Rose said as she helped his maw. "Did you know his brother for very long, Alex?"

He shrugged. "A year or two, before we moved to Gretna, but the lieutenant still remembers Donald and me playing football with the aulder lads from school."

"Och, I remember, too!" Maw smiled at Rose. "They had a fine time after school most evenings, playing their game in the street. I seem to recall aging a few years, watching them wait until the grocer's truck was about to drive past before they kicked that ball."

Alex chuckled. "We were young, Maw, and had no sense. We lived for the thrill."

"Aye, ye did, and ye gave me the gray hairs to prove it." She glanced at them both. "Go on now. I'll be out with a tray soon."

Rose walked with him toward the back door. "Do you like Lieutenant Stuart?"

Alex shrugged. "He's all right. A bit full of himself."

She gave him a knowing smile, and heat crept along his neck. "I think he is quite charming."

Alex snorted. "I dinna find him so."

"I should think not."

Her smile broadened, and he stilled an urge to rub his thumb across her lips and test their softness. "Stuart was the man we were to meet at East Fortune on Sunday." Instantly her humor fled, and he regretted his words. "'Tis all right, he's just here to observe."

Her blue eyes searched his. "Does he know . . . about me?"

Alex took her hands and placed them between his. "Quinn said again today it has to remain our secret. As far as anyone's concerned, you *are* Tilly Lockhart." He gently pressed his palms against her skin. "Even with Stuart."

❧ ─ ⊰ ⊱ ─ ☙

Rose nodded, comforted by his warm touch. She hadn't forgotten their dance, the way he'd looked at her, as if to say they were once again as they'd been before.

He released her and opened the back door, ushering her out

onto the porch. The summer evening was redolent with the scent of pine and heather.

"Miss Lockhart, will you come and join me?" Lieutenant Stuart had taken the wicker chair beside hers. He smiled. "I blethered on all through supper about my life, and now I'd very much like to hear about yours."

She glanced at Alex and, noting his frown, lifted her shoulders before moving to sit beside the lieutenant. Rose had to admit, with his curly blond hair and eyes the color of twilight, Lieutenant Stuart was quite dashing. Even Winston had taken to him surprisingly well.

His sunny, lighthearted nature also appealed to her, as lately she'd lived hourly under a cloud of nervous apprehension. Tonight she had determined to forget what lay ahead, and she enjoyed listening to Lieutenant Stuart's adventures in Argentina, Russia, Turkey, and so many other places the Shell Oil Company had sent him. How many languages he must have heard spoken in those different countries! And no doubt strange customs, making her even more curious about the people she would one day meet when she and her brothers arrived in Nova Scotia.

"So tell me, Miss Lockhart. You said you were born in Glasgow. Did you live there most of your childhood?

"I did."

He nodded. "Glasgow's industry has been mostly shipbuilding. Is your father in the trade?"

"He and my mum had a shop—a draper and haberdashery. I was fourteen when they died and I was sent to an orphanage."

"Och, I'm sorry, lass." His brow furrowed. "Do you have siblings?"

Rose glanced over at Alex, seated in his usual chair across the porch. He seemed intent on their conversation. "A brother." She turned back to the lieutenant. "But he died very young."

She gazed at her lap, forcing herself to concentrate. "When I finally left the orphanage, I took the post as lady's companion, as I told you, and my English mistress had a holding in Nottingham.

She passed away there several months ago, so I stayed on and took a job at the local munitions factory."

"What finally brought you to Gretna?"

She lifted her face, noting the intensity in his gaze. "I wanted to return to my homeland, and after . . . after my dearest friend died in a factory explosion, I chose to leave and come north."

"Poor lass." He reached to cover her hand with his own. "You've had a rough time then?"

Conscious of his touch, Rose didn't dare glance at Alex. Likely he was glowering at them both. She gently extricated her hand. "Life never turns out the way we expect," she said, seeing the truth in her own words. "Anyway, I was fortunate to get work at the Gretna factory and take a room here with the Bairds."

As she spoke, Rose gazed fondly across the porch at Mr. Baird, cleaning his pipe and smiling at his two youngest sons playing in the yard. Hannah had taken up her place on the stump, laughing over her brothers' antics.

She turned to him. "They treat me like one of the family."

"I can see that," he said quietly. "You're a jammy lass to have such a home."

Suddenly Winston's excited barking drew their attention. All eyes turned to see the dog dancing on hind legs as little James held the stocking ball in the air. When he finally threw it out into the yard, the dog raced like a rabbit toward his prize.

Stuart chuckled. "They seem to love that wee dog. Winston, is it? Is he yours?"

"Yes, I've only had him about a month." She grinned, watching the boys chase hopelessly after her much faster dog, the smelly wool ball in his mouth. "And he's quite lovable, though I'm glad he gets his exercise with the Baird children."

She turned and found the lieutenant staring at her. As heat climbed up her neck he grinned. "Aye, would that a man had that kind of energy."

Rose didn't have time to register his innuendo. "Dessert everyone!" Mrs. Baird appeared with a tray of Cranachan, much to the boys' delight. They stopped chasing Winston and ran to the porch.

The lieutenant leaned forward. "Cranachan! I canna recall when I had it last."

"I hadn't tasted it in years, until we recently celebrated Hannah's birthday." Rose lifted a brow. "Consider yourself an honored guest."

He laughed, and she turned to take her bowl of raspberries and cream from Mrs. Baird and caught Alex brooding across the porch.

Why was he determined to be so sour? Tomorrow was soon enough to fret about the danger they were about to undertake. Lieutenant Stuart had been the perfect gentleman and very attentive. Rose made a point to hand him her bowl of Cranachan. "Take this, and I'll get another."

"Why, thank you, Miss Lockhart." Accepting the bowl, he balanced it on the arm of his chair. "Excuse me, but I noticed Mr. Baird also enjoys a pipe. I've a pouch of choice Turkish tobacco in the truck I think he might like to try. I'll be right back."

"How kind of you! I'm certain he will be pleased." Rose watched him go, then gave Alex a look of censure before taking another bowl of the Cranachan for herself.

Minutes later, the lieutenant returned and went directly to Mr. Baird with his offering. Delighted in accepting the pouch, Alex's father quickly filled his pipe and struck a match. Soon the exotic fragrance filled the air, and Rose again tried to imagine the strange, wonderful places Lieutenant Stuart had visited.

He returned to sit beside her, and while they enjoyed their desserts, Mrs. Baird brought out her basket of mending.

"May I help?" Rose called to her, setting her bowl aside.

"There's plenty of time for that, lass. Enjoy your evening." Mrs. Baird gave her a loving smile, and unexpectedly Rose's eyes burned.

She remembered when she'd intended to leave, worried Alex would tell Julien she was here. Mrs. Baird had said it felt as though she were about to lose another bairn; and in the weeks since Rose had come to live with this family, she realized she'd found a second mother. And a father, she thought, looking at Mr. Baird puffing on his pipe.

Hannah was the sister she'd never had, and Rose shifted her attention to the reddish-haired blonde seated on the stump. The girl applauded each time Winston got the best of her brothers.

And Alex . . . Rose gazed at him next, seeing his broad shoulders tense, the strong features set as he eyed her from across the porch.

"I fear 'tis time I took my leave."

Beside her, the lieutenant rose from his chair. "I had a long drive and a long day and I'm ready to enjoy a comfortable bed at the hotel."

Alex also stood. "I'll see you out."

The lieutenant nodded. "Miss Lockhart, meeting you tonight was like shining a light into my dark world. I look forward to our next encounter."

Her mouth opened as he reached for her hand and bent to kiss it lightly.

Hannah giggled from the yard.

Once he'd thanked Mrs. Baird for her fine meal and said his good-byes, he and Alex left the porch. "Miss Lockhart, he kissed your hand!" Hannah said with a good-natured pout after they'd gone.

Again Rose blushed and said primly "It only means that he's a gentleman, Hannah. Nothing more."

"So you say, but I noticed he didna kiss my hand or Maw's."

At that, everyone laughed, including Rose.

⟡

Standing out on the front porch, Alex heard their laughter in back, though it failed to lighten his mood. "I trust you enjoyed yourself tonight, Lieutenant," he said tersely. Despite Stuart's pleasant overtures to his family, he resented his playacting the love-sick swain to Rose. Surely she'd seen through his manure!

"My evening with Miss Lockhart was very enlightening." Stuart smiled while his eyes held challenge. "You're fashing over my attention to her?"

"My concern at the moment is how this Rhymer business will play out tomorrow." He eyed Stuart. "You've been briefed by Weatherford?"

"Aye. Miss Lockhart's to meet her brother at the cotton stores with the bombs at noon tomorrow. I've been issued a constable's uniform and will stand by at the section entrance."

"Good enough." He walked with Stuart to the truck. The lieutenant climbed in and set the throttle while Alex went to the front and cranked over the engine. He stopped back at the cab window.

"I'm grateful you didna boot me out once you found me here, Captain. My parents died long ago, and with Donald gone, 'tis nice spending time with one of his auld friends."

Nodding, Alex averted his gaze. He hadna considered that Stuart might now be alone in the world. "Take care driving back to town," he said, his tone gruff. "Wouldna want you running over a football."

Stuart grinned. "Thanks for the warning, pal. See you tomorrow."

Alex watched the lieutenant drive away, his thoughts lingering over fond memories of his childhood when he and the lads played in the streets after school. Days and years of innocence blurring together, but always filled with love and friendship and his hope for the future. A time before the war and his brother's death, before the scars on his back and those in his head that would haunt him forever. *"A time to forgive and be forgiven, Alex. To forget the past and look ahead to a new future."*

Rose's words to him. He tipped his face to the sky remembering back to that Sunday evening, her smooth skin and soft pink lips, the dark lashes fanned against her cheeks while she slept like an angel. Harboring a peace that always seemed to elude him.

He suddenly yearned to turn back the clock—past the death and destruction, when he still took joy in each morning viewing the world through a child's eyes.

When men like Rhymer and the death merchant didna pose a threat to Rose or his family.

✦⌇✦

The summer sun had already begun its slow descent below the trees. Rose hugged herself as she stood out on the porch, gazing up at the myriad pink and purple tufts hovering against the sky. Everyone else had gone inside, but she remained, wanting to make the moment last while her hope for the future tangled with what was about to take place in just hours.

In the morning, Alex would give her the dummy charges that she was to carry into the factory. And at noon, she planned to meet Tilly's brother—a murderer by all accounts—and she hoped for his arrest and an end to the danger threatening those she'd come to care about so deeply.

"Tilly, are you listening?" she whispered to the heavens. "You once said that if I had courage, I could be free to make my dreams come true. But now that courage is being put to the test. *Your* test, dear friend, and you failed. And now I'm afraid I will fail, too . . ."

A creak of the door sounded behind her, and she turned to find Alex. Barefoot, the front of his shirt opened, he wedged his hands into his front pockets and approached. In the orange dusk, his tanned skin seemed to glow.

"What are you still doing out here, lass? I thought you'd gone to bed."

He came to stand beside her, and despite the cool evening, his heat radiated through the thin fabric of her sleeve. "I don't think I could sleep right now," she said.

"I'm the same." He breathed deeply as his gaze lifted toward the sky.

There was so much they still hadn't talked about. "Detective Quinn said that you were here in Gretna because of Rhymer and the mission. Does that mean you'll return to France when this is over?"

"Aye."

"I thought so."

He looked down at her. "How would you know, lass?"

"A couple of weeks ago, you'd mentioned needing to chop more wood and you worried 'they' and not 'we' would have enough for the winter."

"Well, I'm glad you pay attention to what I say." He smiled, and she thrilled at the way his expression softened, his eyes creasing at the edges.

"Of course I pay attention. Why would you doubt it?"

"I noticed you were hanging on to the lieutenant's every word at supper."

"Ah." She nodded. "Lieutenant Stuart is rather handsome *and* chivalrous, and he's been to so many exotic places around the world. I should think anyone would listen to him." She turned back to admire the sky.

"Aye, especially since *you* want to travel across the world as well. Maybe the two of you should see it together once this is all over."

Rose looked at him in surprise. She'd only been teasing. Yet he was glaring at her, his sullen features set. "Alex." She reached for his arm.

"He kisses your hand and makes love to you with his words, and right away your head's turned. I'd thought you more canny than that, especially after Dexter."

His brutal remark stung. "Do not even compare Lieutenant Stuart with him! Julien was a bully, telling me how to behave and when to speak and what to say and do." She glared back at him. "I've grown a lot stronger, Alex Baird, enough to know that I'll not let any man tell me how to live. Obedience is not a substitute for love." She swallowed past the ache in her throat. "I want this. I want . . ." She looked away from him, toward the trees now shadowed in twilight.

"What do you want, Rose?"

The warmth of his hand touched her chin as he turned her back to face him. "Tell me, lass," he said softly, his gaze searching. "Tell me and 'tis yours."

She looked up at him, her heart pumping. Each breath of air quivering in her chest. She wanted *him*, the man whose rare smiles tantalized her, whose tenderness and laughter illuminated the darkest and loneliest parts of her soul.

Even now his gentle gaze called her home, to a sense of peace and happiness she'd not known in so many years. "I want . . ." she breathed, tilting her chin so that their faces were close. "I need . . ."

"This?" he whispered, and cupping the sides of her face with his roughened hands, he pressed his lips gently against hers. "And this . . ." He leaned in then, capturing her mouth in a kiss that was warm, tender, insistent, and Rose closed her eyes, his touch sweeping her off to dizzying heights even as she remained standing with him. His hands slowly drifted from her face to graze along her neck and shoulders, and finally surround her in his embrace, his skin searing her through the cotton blouse.

She kissed him back, shyly at first, then more ardently, seeking, tasting, discovering, and a low groan sounded in his throat as she ran her hands up along his chest. The smooth heat rippled with muscle as she threaded her fingers around his neck and met his desire with her own. No longer thinking of the past or to the future but just this moment in his arms, safe and sheltered for the first time in a long, long while.

Finally he ended the kiss, his breathing heavy while she leaned her cheek against his chest, the rapid beating of his heart in her ear. They remained that way for some time until she lifted her face to him, a smile hovering at her lips. "Does this mean you like the way I dance?"

He chuckled and bent his head to kiss her again. "And more," he said when they parted.

This time Rose struggled to catch her breath. "Does it matter to you that I'm not Tilly?"

He raised a brow. "Is it just Rose?"

"Rosalind," she said. "My mum loved Shakespeare."

It was a moment before he grinned. "*As You Like It?*"

She nodded, and he sighed, pulling her close. "As I recall," he said softly against her ear, making her shiver with pleasure. "Rosalind disguised herself as a shepherd boy who escaped to the woods with her cousin and found her true love." He drew back then, kissing the tip of her nose. "Not exactly *your* story, but I'll wager closer than your mum ever could have imagined."

Dazed with happiness, she persisted in teasing him. "You haven't answered my question, Alex. Does it matter?"

His green eyes held hers. "I've fallen in love with *you*. Tilly or Rose, it matters not. You're the same lass to me, either way."

Love. She leaned against him once more, her arms encircling his waist. His heat penetrated her skin, while the faint smell of musk and leather and spice filled her senses, her whole being.

She realized she'd been dreaming to hear those words from him, to be held in his arms, surrounded in his warmth. Feeling cherished. "Thank you," she whispered thickly, and tightened her hold on him.

They stood beneath the twilight sky for several minutes, the silence broken only by the gentle hush of the breeze and the sounds of frogs from a nearby marsh.

"Well, lass," he said finally, his tone gruff. "We should try to get some sleep."

"Aye." She looked up at him then and their eyes met, each knowing what the morning would bring. Then she rose up on tiptoe and pressed another kiss to his lips before stepping back. "Good night, Alex."

⇦⟩⟩ ❧❦ ⟨⟨⇦

She *did* love him . . . so why hadn't she said the words?

Rose crawled into bed a half hour later and closed her eyes, exhausted. Yet sleep evaded her, as the real world had returned and along with it, her precarious future.

In a matter of hours, she must meet with a killer, and if by God's grace she—all of them—survived tomorrow, then Alex would leave Gretna to return to France. And Rose would still be left to deal with her uncle and Julien and keeping Douglas and Samuel safe.

She couldn't forsake her dream or abandon the boys to Uncle's mercy. Nor could she remain here and expect to keep her secret, not now.

Rose still held the hope that once she'd told Detective Quinn everything, he would arrest Uncle Ridley and Julien and finally set her free. But she couldn't forget her uncle's powerful influence or that of Julien's father, the earl. And if despite the detective's efforts, her cause came to naught, she might be forced to go back to where she'd started. And Rose had vowed never to tolerate that kind of existence again.

And Alex? She touched a finger to her trembling lips, remembering his kiss and his tender declaration, *"I've fallen in love with you . . ."*

How could he help her, when he would soon be going back to the war?

Turning into her pillow, Rose let her silent tears flow unchecked. She longed to be in his arms once more, to feel the steady beating of his heart that could somehow banish the ache in her own, and with it, the dread in knowing she might have no choice at all.

And if that happened, then after tomorrow she and her brothers must find a way to leave as soon as possible.

Even if it cost her own happiness.

46

*H*e lay on the bed in his hotel room, still wearing his uniform. The orange sky had deepened to dusk through the open window, making him stir from a near catatonic state.

Slowly, he stood up, his heart resuming a steady beat. He turned on the bedside lamp and then withdrew from his tunic pocket the photograph.

He'd been glad to have the Turkish tobacco on his person once he saw that Captain Baird's father smoked a pipe. Giving him time to leave the porch on the pretense of retrieving the pouch from his truck when instead he'd walked through the house to find *her* room.

Right away he noticed his mother's brooch on her nightstand, and it took him less than a minute to discover the valise tucked beneath her bed.

"R and T—Rose and Me—Sisters of the heart we shall always be." He read the scrawled words on the back of the photograph, and then turning it over, he stared at the two women smiling into the camera lens. A summer's day, it seemed, and both looking so happy and carefree.

He grazed his thumb across the face of the woman he'd just met and considered how pleasant their evening had been. Not only was she attractive and charming but she'd been quite receptive to his attention. They all had, especially after he told them the story about watching Captain Baird and the lads play football in Edinburgh's streets.

He'd learned in his trade that most people rarely recall every detail of early childhood, and added to the fact the captain's family moved shortly afterward, had made his fabrications all the more believable.

He sneered recalling Mrs. Baird's claim that she remembered his fictional brother, Donald Stuart—a common enough name. Nearly as common as Thomas Brown.

Captain Baird had resisted his pleasantries all evening, but that was due to his jealousy, which Thomas had fostered in order to distract him from his real purpose in being there—to see Tilly for the first time in twenty years.

He'd listened patiently while she told her story; how her parents, once drapers in Glasgow, had died when she was fourteen—along with a nameless brother who died earlier.

Thomas recalled how, at six years old, he'd watched his mother die in childbirth; four years after that his father was killed in a shipyard accident.

She'd said she had the dog only about a month, and he remembered back in early spring, having arranged with Emin to deliver Winston as a gift to his sister, once she'd been released from prison and set up with a cottage in Attenborough. The dog had been his for a time, and so Winston nearly gave him away tonight with his affections. Thomas smiled. It was fortunate the Bairds and their pretty boarder were so easily swayed by his story of the fox.

Despite her lies, Thomas appreciated her wit and sense of humor. And of course, that lovely smile. He recalled the end of her tale—about the death of her dearest friend and deciding to leave Chilwell for Gretna . . .

His throat worked as he moved his thumb to caress the face of the other young woman in the photograph. Recognizing the single dimple in her right cheek, and his own mother's look about her.

Glasgow's harsh city streets and living by their wits after their father died . . . his little sister hot with fever. Thomas the "Rhymer" coming to her rescue and robbing a chemist's shop for medicine . . .

It was the accidental fire that led to his arrest. And Thomas had wondered how Tilly would survive without him, especially after Scotland Yard put him on that ship bound for hell.

Emin had found him near death and had taken him to the home of his master, Bay Kahverengi. Thomas was sixteen when the arms dealer adopted him, surrounding him with tutors, educating him, including teaching him several languages. And once his adoptive father contracted cancer, he taught Thomas the business of selling arms and how to manage his great fortune. While traveling the world together, the son learned the father's skills in business and in making new contacts.

After his father's quiet death in Paris, Thomas rose to take his place, dealing weapons to the highest bidder and increasing his profits, the ever-faithful manservant at his side.

With Emin's help, he'd found his sister after two long decades, serving time in a British prison. And what good fortune when Captain Marcus Weatherford wanted to set her free, thanks to his own carelessness.

He'd intentionally left the munitions list in his Paris apartment, along with the names Rhymer and Thomas Brown. Knowing that eventually Scotland Yard would waste precious resources interrogating hundreds of workers while *he* arranged to sabotage the next target. But Thomas had not meant to leave the numbered tag; he'd scoured every orphanage around Glasgow before finally tracing her back to Ezekiel House.

When Tilly went to work at Chilwell, his next target, he'd been both glad and dismayed. Women *did* make the best explosives runners, adept at getting them into the factory. But his sister had made a deal with Scotland Yard to trap him, forcing him to test her loyalties first.

He stared at her smiling face in the photograph. After the explosion and her unexpected death, he'd grieved. Tilly *had* been faithful to him and yet he'd refused to see her, refused to reunite with her, and then it was too late.

And then tonight, he'd thought to have his chance.

But Emin had betrayed him.

He crushed the photograph in his fist. Scotland Yard, those curs, had thought to trap him using this stranger, *Rose*, to take his sister's place.

Heat flooded his face, while gasps of rage whistled through his clenched teeth. His temples throbbed. He . . . must . . . make a trap of his own . . .

It was minutes before he leaned back onto the bed, exhausted. Looking down at the crumpled picture in his hand, he smoothed it out and then tore it in half, pocketing the face of his beloved Tilly, while he stared at the image of her impostor.

Whatever I decide, dear Rose, there is no choice but that you must die.

47

GRETNA
THURSDAY, AUGUST 1

*R*ose drew in shallow breaths as she stared at the large factory clock mounted high on the wall—11:35 . . .

Only minutes remained. All morning long, going about her tasks at work, she'd sensed Rhymer's eyes upon her.

And not only his—Alex was also in the shadows observing her, along with several undercover policewomen and Detective Quinn, who had assured Alex that his plainclothes detectives were in place and keeping Rose in their sights.

She hadn't yet noticed the detective or the extra policewomen, except the one who passed her through the factory inspection this morning. Constable Edwards was the same policewoman who had arrived at East Fortune on Sunday to guard her.

Before leaving the cottage for work, Rose had tucked the brooch and two phony pencil devices into her thick braid and then pinned it up tight. Now that she had the devices transferred into her pocket and the brooch pinned beneath the collar of her smock, she endured the minutes of growing terror as she awaited the noon hour.

Oh, how she wanted this to be over!

Returning her attention to her girls at the vat tables, her heart bled each time they glanced up at her and smiled, so unaware of what was to come. Would they live to see tomorrow?

Hannah's hands had healed, and as she grinned across at Betty, she dug into the cordite paste, her strong arms kneading the "devil's porridge." The girls had set a new date for their tea next Sunday and planned for a football match next week and another dance . . .

She closed her eyes against her own anguish and fear. *Lord, please help us!*

"For I know the plans I have for you . . ."

Her eyes opened. The book of Jeremiah. As she glanced back at her girls, a sudden calm settled over her. For whatever reason Tilly had died in that explosion, for whatever reason the clockmaker rejected her request for a new name and drew her back to Gretna, she understood now that she *was* supposed to be here. *For them.* Acting as their welfare supervisor, even the wayward girls, standing up for their honor against Mr. Dobbs and his cronies. And now defending them against a force more devilish and determined than any union man.

Hannah and others, their very survival—everyone's survival—depended on her.

Bending her head toward the clipboard, she prayed. Prayed for courage—not Tilly's bravery, though it had helped, but now Rose prayed for grace from the only heavenly power able to defeat the kind of evil she was about to face. *Lord, please, I cannot do this alone.*

When she'd finished, she looked up again at their young faces. Their smiles, and the laughter they shared while laboring together to help their countrymen, renewed her strength. She *would* meet with Rhymer, glad to see him arrested and locked away for good.

She checked the factory clock again—fifteen minutes before noon. Taking her leave of the girls, Rose headed toward Gladys and her group in the Acids Room before stopping back by her office.

The typed envelope lay on her desk.

She went still, blood pounding in her ears. Had Rhymer changed his mind about their meeting time or the place?

With shaking hands, she picked up the envelope and opened it. She removed the letter—another poem.

> A rose in bloom, so lovely to behold,
> But for the nasty thorn that took its hold
> Upon this heart to make it bleed,
> As women do when they deceive.
>
> So now 'tis time that thee must pay
> And find the bombs I've stowed away;
> One clue I'll give, to where you seek,
> It heals, it cleans, it kills, and is sweet.
>
> Hurry, dear Rose, 'tis almost noon . . .
>
> —Rhymer

"Miss Lockhart?"

Rose jerked around to find Hannah at the open door. "Goodness, you scared me!"

"Och, you're looking peely-wally, I can tell." The girl eyed the note in her hand. "Is something in that letter troubling you?"

Rose breathed deeply, struggling for her calm of moments ago. "Hannah, I want you and the other girls to leave the factory building at once."

Hannah's eyes widened. "What's wrong, Miss Lockhart?"

"Don't question me, just do as I say!"

The girl jumped and, teary-eyed, fled the office.

Rose reread the poem, panic gripping her. *He knew the truth!*

How had he discovered her? Rhymer spoke of *her love* making his heart bleed. Who . . . ?

"Lass, what's happened?"

Hannah had returned with Alex. He entered her office, and she rushed to him, handing him the poem.

Scanning the lines, he muttered an oath. "What the devil does this mean?"

"I don't know, but it sounds as if I broke his heart. He knows the truth about me, Alex. And this place that he's hidden the real bombs, I cannot fathom where it might be. We've less than fifteen minutes! How can we get everyone out?"

Once again, Hannah fled and then returned in less than a minute, breathless. With her were all the girls in Rose's charge. "I told you all to leave!"

Instead of flinching, Hannah set her jaw. Seeing the note in her brother's hand, she snatched it from him.

"Hannah!"

"Wait!" She turned to the girls and recited the poem, repeating the last line: "'It heals, it cleans, it kills, and is sweet.'"

"The chemists' room!" Gladys shouted, and Jane, Sarah, and Dorothy all bobbed their heads. "The bloke's talking about glycerin. It heals—they use it in burn salves. An' it cleans—it's in our soaps and face creams. It kills when we use it to make cordite, an' glycerin has a sweet taste." She looked at Rose. "An' it's kept with the chemists. They cook it in with the acids to make nitroglycerin."

"Blimey!" Betty cried. "This Rhymer's plannin' to blow up our factory?"

Alex was already running toward the chemists' room.

"You girls leave now!" Rose ordered before she rushed after Alex.

She'd passed beneath the overhead sign NITROGLYCERIN SECTION when she turned to look behind her and saw all her girls in fast pursuit, along with Detective Quinn.

"We want tae 'elp ye search," Colleen called out when they caught up with Rose.

"Where's Alex?" Detective Quinn looked pale as his gaze searched the area.

"In the chemists' room by now," Rose answered. "Hurry and follow me!"

They were about to enter the room when she glanced up to see Lieutenant Stuart. Clad in a constable's uniform, he was about to turn the corner into the area of the cordite vats when he paused to stare back at her, a strange light in his eyes.

"Effendi, no!" Detective Quinn rushed after him while Rose and the girls burst into the chemists' room.

"Over here!"

Alex lay on the floor, his leg pinned beneath a large lead canister. Quickly the girls worked together to free him, and he struggled to his feet. "I saw him doing something over there."

He led them to a stack of glycerin stores, and with all of them searching it took under two minutes before Alex had produced two pencil bombs. "These look as if they've been detonated." He glanced behind Rose and the girls toward the door. "Have you seen Quinn?"

"He's following Lieutenant Stuart toward the cordite vats," Rose said.

"I'll go after them." He handed her the pencil bombs. "Take these outside and throw them into the cooling pond beyond the track." He clasped her arms, his features anxious. "Run, lass! I dinna ken when those will go off."

For an instant, Rose thought he might kiss her. Instead, he let her go and stepped back. She turned to Hannah and the others. "Come, girls! There's no time to lose!"

Leaving the chemists' room, Rose soon found herself carried on a wave by her eight charges as they held her aloft, her feet barely touching the floor while they rushed her toward the double doors of the factory entrance.

When a policeman stepped forward and tried to barricade their progress, she called to him, "Please, we've got the bombs—let us through!"

Immediately he cleared a path, and the girls didn't pause as they ran with her, passing the train platform and dozens of curious onlookers, then across the railroad tracks to the cooling pond, where they promptly tossed her in along with the bombs.

"Saints above, not Miss Lockhart!" Colleen cried breathlessly, running up after them. "Just the bombs!"

Quickly she and the others waded in to fetch Rose out of the water.

"We're sorry, Miss Lockhart," Colleen called from behind while the girls quickly retraced their steps toward the factory. As they half carried a wet and bedraggled Rose along, they passed by the train platform once more. "Ye'll surely be wantin' that bath now."

She turned to Colleen, the girl's sallow face all earnestness and concern. Suddenly Rose couldn't help herself. Relieved after days of tension and fear, worry and excitement, she began to laugh. Soon all her girls were laughing with her, their sides aching by the time they got back inside, then headed toward the changing room to clean up.

Alex followed in Quinn's direction, running as fast as his legs would take him. They couldna lose Rhymer, not this time! And sweet heaven, not in the area of the cordite vats!

Please, God, let Stuart and Quinn have caught him! There had been no time to alert the detectives still waiting in the cotton stores.

Rhymer obviously planned this diversion. How had he discovered the truth about Rose? Or had he known all along and played Scotland Yard the whole time?

His mind raced as fast as his feet. He didna want to think of what would happen if Rhymer intended to set off another explosion . . .

Turning the corner, Alex glimpsed the vats—and saw only Quinn and Stuart.

Confused, he paused and scanned the area. There was no one else.

"Effendi, please! Do not do this!"

Quinn's voice, but he sounded different. Then Alex stared in horror as Stuart, guised as a constable, held an open lighter over a full vat of devil's porridge. If he struck the flint . . .

No! Alex tried to rush past Quinn, but the detective grabbed his arm to hold him back.

"Effendi. Thomas, listen, you do not want to do this," Quinn pleaded with Stuart.

Stunned to realize he was facing their saboteur, Alex watched

Stuart's handsome features contort with rage. "Emin, you betrayed me!" He spat the words. "Those hounds at Scotland Yard, they have poisoned your mind against me. I trusted you!"

"I can explain if you give me the lighter." Quinn's calm voice rose above the factory noise. "It was all a mistake. You are not a killer."

"You lied about my sister. She is dead, and you put that pretender in her place to try to trap me!"

"I did not know Tilly was dead until Sunday, Effendi. She died because of the explosion at Chilwell. Your timed bombs . . . they killed her."

"My bombs?" His lips pulled back in a savage snarl. "Again you lie! I cannot forgive you, Emin."

As he spoke, Stuart struck the flint, and Quinn rushed him just as the lighter dropped into the vat, before the detective wrestled him to the floor.

Realizing what was about to happen, Alex ran in the opposite direction, falling hard against the concrete as the blast reverberated past him through the factory. Acrid smoke blew through the air, filling his lungs as he struggled to sit up. He glanced back to see flaming globs of cordite flying in every direction, including over the screaming men still tussling on the factory floor.

Dear God, no! Alex struggled to his feet and donned his gloves as he ran back toward the two burning men. His last haunting memory of Ian flooded him as he reached in to grab hold of a man's pant leg—not certain which man—and pulled with all his strength.

Detective Quinn soon emerged from the inferno, unconscious and severely burned. Alex smothered the remaining fire on him, then rushed back after Stuart—but he was far too late.

By now, several male workers had rushed into the area, carrying sacks of sand to extinguish the flames. Alarms blared, while others shouted orders to evacuate the remaining workers from the section. As orderlies arrived with stretchers, Alex took off at a run, his thoughts only on Rose. Had she succeeded? *Please, God, let her be safe!*

❖➤⸎ ❧⸎ ❖

Dear Lord, is Alex safe?

Rose huddled with her girls, still wet, shivering, and smelling of the cooling pond as they stood with hundreds of other workers a half mile from the factory building. Their escorts, several of the uniformed Women's Police Force, had corralled them a safe distance away, where they awaited the all-clear signal from those inside.

She and her charges had been about to enter the changing room when the explosion sounded. Moments later, an alarm had blared as male workers and police began running toward the nitroglycerin section of the factory.

Rose stood tense, her humor of minutes ago vanished. She gazed at her girls, all of them looking frightened, some holding hands as they waited for news.

A weepy-eyed Hannah stood trembling beside her, and Rose pulled her close. "All will be well, lass," she said softly, though she wasn't certain at all. If anything happened to Alex . . .

Half an hour passed before a lone figure approached.

"'Tis my brother!"

Hannah turned, her face suddenly radiant, while Rose blinked back tears. She managed to squeeze the girl's hand. *Lord, thank you.*

"The fire's been contained," Alex called out to them. "You should be able to return inside in a few minutes."

As he cut through the crowd to reach her and the girls, Rose noticed he looked the worse for wear. With his face red and his clothing singed, he was covered in the acrid dust. *And he is alive!*

Once he was beside them, his eyes searched hers. "What happened to you?"

Rose shivered in response, and he removed his singed coat, placing it around her shoulders. "My g-girls did a fine job getting the b-bombs into the pond."

"And you as well, it looks like."

She hoped he might hold her, but then his sister launched at him, wrapping her arms around his neck. "Alex, I'm so glad you're still with us!"

Grinning, he gave her a bear hug, then he reached out a hand to Rose, and she clasped it tightly, meeting his eyes.

Once Hannah had released him, Rose asked, "Where are Detective Quinn and Lieutenant Stuart?"

"Quinn's in the factory infirmary. He's unconscious and suffered severe burns."

Rose drew in a breath. Would the detective die? "And . . . the lieutenant?"

"He didna survive the flames." He leaned in to add in a low voice, "I'm not certain, but I believe he was our man."

Her eyes widened. "You mean . . . Rhymer?"

"Aye." He grimaced. "His visit last night would explain how he realized you were not his sister, especially if he'd already seen her at Chilwell. So instead, he made fools of us all."

A whistle blew in the distance, and the policewomen began shepherding everyone back toward the factory. As Rose walked beside Alex, her skin grew chill, though not from the dampness but in remembering how Lieutenant Stuart had charmed her and laughed with her last evening. She cringed recalling the way he'd kissed her hand—a sensation now reptilian to her, considering he'd been plotting her murder and everyone else's while he wooed her.

And poor Detective Quinn! While she'd feared him as her uncle's "sheepdog" Luther, in truth he'd been helping her friend and was compassionate toward Rose in her day-to-day struggles at Leicester. In her mind, since their meeting on Sunday he'd become her champion, a man she knew she could trust.

Now, as he struggled for his life, she grieved for him and for herself. Because if he died . . .

Any hope that she might be able to remain in Britain, and any possibility of a future with Alex—would be lost.

48

Quinn's dead?" Alex said.

Weatherford nodded from behind the desk in Colonel Landon's East Fortune office. Yesterday after the explosion, Alex had contacted the captain in London, and he'd taken the first train north, spending the night in Gretna's infirmary with the dying detective.

"I stayed with him until the last," he added, his gaze somber.

Alex glanced at Rose, seated in the chair beside his own across from the desk. Her blue eyes welled with grief. "I'm sorry, lass," he said gently and reached to squeeze her hand. "I ken that you two had some history together."

She nodded and gave him a watery smile.

"Before he died, he told me quite a story," Weatherford continued, drawing their attention. "In fact, I still find it hard to believe."

Alex leaned forward. "What did he say?"

"I should start by telling you that Quinn had many faces." He glanced at Rose. "You know that he was Miles Luther, your uncle's chauffeur, and acting as Tilly's contact at Chilwell. He was also Quinn, the plainclothes detective with Scotland Yard's Special Branch whom I took with me to the prison to meet Miss Lockhart." He paused, eyeing them both. "And he was Emin Tabak, manservant to the arms dealer, Didymos Kahverengi."

"Ah, Thomas Brown."

Weatherford rose to his feet as all eyes turned to Colonel Landon, who had suddenly reappeared and stepped into his office.

"As you were, Captain. Excuse the intrusion." The colonel reached for a file on a table beside the door and was about to leave when Weatherford stopped him. "Colonel, why did you say 'Thomas Brown'?"

Colonel Landon's salt-and-pepper brows drew together. "Early on in the war, Captain, before I trained as a pilot and received this post, I served in the BEF. We fought that bloody battle at Gallipoli against the Ottoman Empire, and while I was there, I picked up a bit of Turk. *Kahverengi* is their word for the color brown."

"And Didymos . . ." Weatherford paused, a smile in his voice. "The Bible, of course. Our doubting Thomas."

"Righto." The colonel nodded toward Alex and Rose, then slipped from the room.

"That would fit with what Quinn . . . Emin Tabak told me," Weatherford said once the colonel had left.

Alex and Rose listened as he then explained how the manservant found Thomas Lockhart half dead in the Australian bush and took him to his master, Bay Kahverengi, who adopted the boy and taught him the arms-dealing business. Thomas took over after Kahverengi's death and continued to amass his fortune.

"It also explains why the name Thomas Brown was on the munitions list the French found in the Paris apartment," Weatherford said. "I began to suspect Kahverengi was wasting Scotland Yard's time and resources by offering up the common name as a decoy. Emin told me Thomas never forgave the bobbies for sending him off to that hellish boys' farm.

"He also confirmed that Kahverengi contracted with the Germans to destroy several British munition factories. The Huns' last desperate attempt to gain the upper hand in the war."

"Excuse me, Captain," Rose said, edging forward in her seat, "but I'm a bit confused. We already know that Tilly's brother, Thomas Lockhart, was Rhymer . . . but you're saying he's also Thomas Brown *and* this Kahverengi fellow?"

"That's correct, Miss Graham. Like his adopted father, Thomas Brown became a master of disguise, making it impossible for us to pin him down."

"What about Lieutenant Stuart?" She glanced at Alex. "He tried to blow up the factory."

"Again, Thomas Brown." Weatherford opened a file on the desk. "I received a telegram this morning from Scotland Yard. The body of one Lieutenant Charles Stuart was recently found floating in the Thames." He looked up, his expression grim. "Brown eliminated the lieutenant so that he could pose in his place as our MI5 liaison to Captain Baird."

Alex fell back against his seat. "Because he found out through Quinn—Emin—that I'd be working at Moorside to find Rhymer."

"Indeed." Weatherford's tanned face tinged with color. "I'm afraid that he fooled even me, Alex. With all my efforts at secrecy, even to the point of withholding information from you, Quinn was privy to all."

"Did he tell Rhymer . . . Stuart . . . the truth about me?" Rose asked softly.

"No, lass," Alex said, gazing at her. "Just before the explosion I heard Stuart accuse him of betrayal because he'd kept your identity secret."

"When Quinn met you, Miss Graham, and you agreed to take Tilly's place, he made the decision to hide your identity from his master," Weatherford said. "He, too, hoped to put an end to the killings."

Rose frowned. "But then Lieutenant Stuart . . . Rhymer . . . met me at the Bairds the night before and must have realized I wasn't his sister."

"We found a torn piece of a photograph in his room at the Gretna Hotel." Weatherford slid a wrinkled snapshot toward Rose.

"It's a picture of me at Chilwell." She turned to Alex. "He must have taken this from my room while we were out on the back porch! Tilly was in the other half of the photo. He obviously recognized her and knew he'd been betrayed."

"I'm just thankful Quinn . . . Emin had a change of heart," Weatherford said. "Miss Lockhart's death at Chilwell shook him."

"He was certainly shocked when he came into this office and saw me instead of her," Rose said. "No doubt he'd held the hope she somehow escaped."

Weatherford nodded. "He told me that he felt responsible for her death."

"Why?" she asked. "I know he cared for her very much. I think he loved her."

Alex noticed that as she spoke, Rose avoided his gaze. When he'd declared his love to her the other night, she hadna responded in kind. Yet her passion when they'd kissed had revealed to him how much she cared. But did she love him?

"You are right, Miss Graham, he was in love with her," Weatherford said. "When Tilly received the package with the bombs, she hadn't yet identified Rhymer. Because Quinn wanted to ensure she received her pardon, he urged her to go through with the meeting in the Mixing House that night. His hope was that once she'd fulfilled her part of our deal, she would then be free to leave and go to Canada, far away from Thomas."

"But instead of being free, she died," Rose whispered.

"Yes." Weatherford sighed. "Quinn told me last night that he hadn't expected Rhymer's bombs to go off so soon. He thought she'd be safe."

"Are you saying he knew for certain Rhymer set his own explosives at Chilwell? When Alex and I spoke with him, he only suggested the possibility."

"Wait." Alex sat forward as her words triggered a memory—an exchange between Stuart and Quinn just before the cordite vat exploded. "I heard Quinn accuse Stuart of placing the bombs, but Stuart seemed surprised and called him a liar."

Rose turned to him. "You mean the explosion could simply have been an accident?"

"It's possible." Weatherford spoke up. "Scotland Yard investigated the Chilwell site for weeks and found no solid evidence to prove the blast was caused by sabotage. And the lead coating on the pencil bomb leaves no trace, so we may never know the truth."

"How was it that Quinn . . . Emin went with you to the prison to see Tilly in the first place, Captain?" Alex asked. "Did he know she was there?"

Weatherford nodded. "The French had also found in Kahverengi's Paris flat a numbered tag from an orphanage in Glasgow. They sent it to London, and I had Scotland Yard track it down. That's how we found Tilly Lockhart." He sighed. "But Kahverengi had already located her and installed Emin in Scotland Yard—who knows how he did it—and because as Quinn he was already assigned to the case, I kept him on."

"And likely the deal you made with Tilly saved Quinn the trouble of breaking her out of prison."

"It would seem so," Weatherford said. "Just like his employer, Quinn was highly skilled in deception—he managed to fool Scotland Yard, and that is quite a feat."

"Did Kahverengi have other women helping him with the earlier factory explosions?"

Weatherford's dark eyes studied him. "I asked Emin that question. He told me the female plant they'd used at Barstow and Linworth died in the last explosion." He paused. "Apparently, Olivia Charles is no longer a problem."

Alex launched from his seat, ignoring Rose's gasp. "That witch is dead?"

"From Emin Tabak's own lips."

Alex heaved a sigh. "Well, I canna say I'm sorry."

"Alex?" Rose eyed him with concern.

"'Tis all right, lass. The woman was an enemy agent who tried to lead my brother down the wrong path. I would have rather she faced a trial and a firing squad, but it seems justice has been served."

She looked as if to question him further, then changed her mind, much to his relief.

"In any case," Weatherford continued briskly, closing the file on the desk, "Thomas Brown and all his aliases are no more. And while Emin's confession would have provided the proof needed to convict our saboteur, Rhymer died by his own brand of poison."

❧ ❧

Rose had listened throughout as Captain Weatherford and Alex worked to unravel the enigma surrounding Thomas Brown *and* Emin . . . her friend, Detective Quinn. Both men whose lives had been rampant with secrets and bad deeds.

Her heart also grieved for Tilly and the memory of her horrible death. Yet Rose was proud, too. Her friend had been truly brave, especially that last day at Chilwell.

"I'm glad Tilly Lockhart has been exonerated in all of this." She gazed at both men. "She sought only peace and an end to the killing, and she died trying to accomplish that." Her lower lip began to quiver. "She's the true hero of this tale."

Alex laid a hand on her shoulder, and his warm touch brought her comfort. She no longer knew what the future held for her, but with God's grace and Tilly's example she would face whatever was to come. Even Julien.

"You, too, are heroic, Miss Graham," Captain Weatherford said. "Despite great personal risk, you chose to help us in our effort to catch Rhymer. That took no little amount of courage."

Reaching into his breast pocket, he withdrew an envelope and handed it over to her. "I know about your difficult circumstances in Leicester, and you'll find a cheque inside from the War Office for any expenses you might accrue in the future."

Rose stared at him in surprise, before she peered inside at the amount and drew a sharp breath. It was more than enough to purchase passage for herself and her brothers on a ship to Nova

Scotia, along with ample seed money for her dress shop. "Thank you, Captain."

Somewhat dazed, she turned to Alex. His features were like stone. Again the thought of leaving him and his family, leaving her girls at the factory, made her ache. But what else could she do? Detective Quinn was dead, and even if he wasn't, he could never have helped her.

"I suppose now you'll be sailing off on your ship to 'New Scotland.' Your fresh start?"

The edge in his voice pained her. "Alex—"

"'New Scotland,' Miss Graham?"

Captain Weatherford eyed her curiously.

"Nova Scotia, in Canada," she explained.

His dark brows veed together as he glanced at Alex then back at her. "If I may ask, why so far away?"

She moistened her lips, turning her eyes back toward Alex. "Because I have no choice," she said in low voice. "My brothers . . . will be in danger . . ."

"What kind of danger, Miss Graham?" Captain Weatherford had leaned forward.

"I must get them away from my uncle. And Julien Dexter."

"That scunner." Alex snarled. "What's he got to do with your brothers?"

Captain Weatherford looked keen. "Yes, please explain, Miss Graham."

She raised her chin, her pulse pounding. "I'll first need your promise, Captain, that you'll protect Douglas and Samuel."

The captain frowned while Alex spoke gently beside her. "Tell us why, Rose."

She turned to him. "I told you before that if Julien discovered I was alive, he would have taken me back to Leicester. I also told you my uncle arranged the marriage." She paused. "But what I didn't say was that Uncle threatened to ship my brothers to an overseas orphanage if I didn't marry Julien and keep silent about what I'd seen."

"What did you see?" Captain Weatherford demanded.

Rose compressed her lips and he softened his tone. "Pardon me, Miss Graham. The answer is yes, I will see that your brothers are protected."

The tightness in her chest suddenly eased. "I happened upon Uncle Ridley and Julien in my uncle's library two months ago, where I witnessed . . . an exchange." She looked down at her lap, her mind replaying the scene. "Julien had given him documents. I don't know what they contained, but my uncle thought them important enough to unlock the hidden compartment in his desk."

She glanced up. "It attaches behind the center drawer. You must pull out the drawer almost entirely in order to reach the hidden lock. He put Julien's documents inside, then went to his safe and withdrew a packet of company stock and banknotes and gave both to him. I tried retracing my steps, but Uncle saw me. Suddenly the wedding was moved up, and he threatened me with Douglas and Samuel's lives."

"If the documents in that compartment are what I think they are, Miss Graham, I believe we can make an arrest." The captain's eyes gleamed. "I'll wager Dexter sold your uncle secret munitions information he'd obtained from his father's files.

"We've suspected a government leak for some time, and it was the reason I sent Dexter to Gretna. French reports revealed the lieutenant had an alleged connection to Kahverengi. We hoped Dexter's presence in Gretna would draw out his agent, Rhymer." He snorted. "And Quinn was in on that too, playing both sides. He confessed last night that Kahverengi went in as the photographer, giving our saboteur a firsthand look at the factory."

"Holden!" Alex fell back against his seat once more. "The man spoke maybe half a dozen words during the tour, and he kept himself busy behind the camera."

"The art of disguise," the captain agreed.

"So much intrigue." Rose shook her head. "It's a miracle we survived through all of Rhymer's scheming and double-crossing."

"Indeed, Miss Graham." The captain smiled. "And you were

the most unexpected twist of all. To his detriment and to our benefit."

She ducked her head at his praise before turning to Alex. "I never wanted to keep secrets from you," she said. "But I've already caused Douglas and Samuel enough grief and I couldn't risk telling anyone about this until I knew that I could protect them from my uncle." She reached for his hand. "And I never planned to take Tilly's place, but I hope now you understand why I did. It seemed as though God had intervened to help me."

He enfolded her hand into his larger one. "I think He did, lass." He glanced toward the desk. "And so does Captain Weatherford. The man's as good as his word, so you can trust him."

"We just need a way to get into that hidden compartment." Captain Weatherford rose to his feet, his fingers combing his mustache. "We need to get our hands on the proof before we can prosecute."

"I would imagine my aunt knows where he keeps the key." When he paused and turned to her, Rose smiled and said, "And I'm certain she would probably unlock it *for* you."

His mouth broadened. "From what I've heard, Miss Graham, I think you're right."

❖⟶ ❧ ⟵❖

Weatherford looked as if he might crow.

Alex gazed at the remarkable woman beside him and then at their joined hands. Rose had taken a chance opportunity to escape her circumstances and had sacrificed much in the process.

He'd seen the hunger in her face many times as he and his family expressed their love for one another, especially when Fergus and James laughed and chased her wee dog around the yard. He understood now how much it must have hurt denying herself the remaining fragment of a loving family.

He was glad his own clan loved her and had embraced her presence at the house, though again he wondered what was in her heart and her future. Maybe she'd been too afraid to declare her feelings for him, believing she had no other choice than to flee once more.

Which now left Alex longing to know . . . if after the arrests were made and her future was secure, would she still choose to leave?

49

*I*n a few hours, she would finally see Douglas and Samuel. Fear and excitement rippled through Rose as she strolled with Alex beneath a canopy of trees heading toward McCrory's Tea Shop in London's Highbury District.

When Alex had asked to accompany her on Saturday's train into the city, she welcomed his support and his offer to help collect her brothers from Caldicott School.

The tea shop was just a short walking distance from the Forresters' house, where Alex's friends, Simon and Eve, had offered them a place to stay the past two nights.

The midmorning breeze ruffled the leaves on the trees overhead and carried the faint scent of roses. The Forresters would follow them along to the tea shop once baby Zoe had been fed and put down for her nap under the watchful eye of Mrs. Kerr, their housekeeper.

"Are you nervous, lass?"

She glanced at Alex and realized she was clutching his arm as they walked. She tried to loosen her grip, but he held her fast and smiled. "Dinna fash, all will be well."

"I wish I could share your confidence." She sighed. "I've been trying to imagine the reunion with my brothers, certain my sudden appearance from the dead will come as a shock. Do you think they'll understand the reasons for my actions?"

"I canna say." He bowed his head. "Not when you consider my own poor reaction to the truth." He paused. "Though Eve and Simon had a difficult reunion when they were in Belgium, and she told me after that it was God's love that bound their wounds and brought her hope back to life. I believe it will do the same for you and the lads."

She smiled. "You have wonderful friends, Alex. I'm grateful they've made a place for us, and with having a newborn in the house as well."

He chuckled. "I enjoy watching Simon with his wee bairn. The way he looks done-in when morning comes, and he's been up and down with her all night. My goddaughter is exacting my revenge on her da for his keeping secrets from me."

Rose gave him an arched look. "I kept secrets."

"Aye, but you're a bonny lass and he's not." Gazing at her, he placed his hand over hers in the crook of his elbow. "I ken the reasons now why you had to hide from Dexter and your uncle." He shrugged. "And I dinna hold a grudge with my friend. 'Twas probably best at the time he and Weatherford withheld the fact Tilly Lockhart was Rhymer's sister."

"Yes, I imagine you would have kicked me out the door."

His bronzed face held the hint of color. "And I never would have discovered Rhymer or the truth about lovely Rose Graham."

It was her turn to blush, and she averted her eyes and spied the tea shop. "Shall we sit outside while we wait for the Forresters?"

He led her to an outdoor table on the patio, and taking their seats, they ordered tea and scones. Rose checked her watch. "Do you think Captain Weatherford has arrived in Leicester by now?"

"Aye. He'll move in on the estate once your uncle's left the house."

His words quickened her pulse. She'd told them her uncle

attended his afternoon board meetings in Sheffield, the first Monday of each month.

"Hopefully, your aunt will still help?" he asked.

"I believe she will. He's made her life a purgatory." Her worried gaze eyed him across the table. "But what about Julien? When will he be apprehended?"

"It canna happen soon enough to suit me."

Alex had opened up to her on the train about Olivia Charles and his reasons for bitterness toward the woman and Julien. Her former fiancé had corrupted Alex's brother and put him into the path of that "viper."

While he didn't elaborate, Rose sensed there was more to the story, but she didn't press him. It was enough that he'd trusted her with the truth, and after their meeting with Captain Weatherford last Thursday, Alex had warmed to her again, leaving her more torn about her decision to say good-bye and sail across an ocean to New Scotland.

He reached across the table to take her hand. "To answer your question, once Weatherford has the proof, Scotland Yard will arrest your uncle and get his confession to prosecute Dexter."

"What if my uncle won't confess?"

"I doubt Sir Cutler will shoulder all of the responsibility." He made a wry face. "From what you've told me about your uncle, he'll use what he knows to barter a deal. The Earl of Stanton would not wish a public scandal."

A shaft of panic pierced her. "You mean Julien and my uncle could go free?"

He squeezed her hand. "Treason's a serious charge, and at best they'll be sent off to some obscure prison to wait out the war." His tone softened. "Once their secret's out, the threat to you and your brothers is gone. They canna harm you."

She offered a smile. "You make a very persuasive argument, Captain Baird."

He chuckled. "So long as I convince you to relax."

"Hello there, Alex and Rose!"

Rose turned to see the Forresters hailing them.

"They made fast time," Alex said, and moved to sit beside her as Simon and Eve joined them at the small table. A young woman appeared moments later with Alex's coffee and a pot of Earl Grey for Rose and the others.

Eve inhaled deeply the fragrant morning air. "The babe is napping, and I've an entire hour to enjoy elevenses." She reached to pour herself a cup of tea. "I'm famished."

"We've ordered a plate of ration scones and gingerbread cup puddings," Rose said.

"Ah yes, the war continues to intrude on daily life." Still, she smiled as she turned to her husband. "Remember how we enjoyed strawberry biscuits and Darjeeling tea in this very place?"

"And I worked up the courage to ask you for your hand?" Simon winked at her.

Rose smiled at Eve. "Simon proposed to you . . . here?"

"He did, though I made him wait a moment or two for an answer."

"More like she aged me a few years." Simon grinned. "But once she said yes, we never looked back."

⊷⊰ ⧢ ⊱⊶

Alex saw the love between his two friends, and his chest tightened. He thought of his own parents and their deep affection for each other, and he longed to have that same kind of happiness. He was ready to settle down and prayed for the day when he could start rebuilding his life, put the war and his painful past behind him, and embrace the future. *To forgive and be forgiven . . .*

He gazed at Rose, and a light pink color dusted her cheeks. Again he dared to hope that once the threat was over, she'd change her mind and stay.

"What time will you go to the school, Rose?" Eve asked.

Rose turned to her. "Captain Weatherford said that after they have my uncle in custody, he will telephone your home. Alex and I will leave for Caldicott once that happens."

She turned to him, apprehension in her eyes.

Yet there was nothing more he could say to comfort her. And so he reached for her hand on the table, pleased when she twined her fingers with his. "And so we wait, lass."

❖ ❖

"Stop here."

Spying the tea shop, Julien halted the cabby on Crossley Street.

He'd just fulfilled his duty delivering army dispatches from Paris to General Howard, who was supposed to be on furlough at his home in Highbury, and now he was hungry. It was near to noon, and lunch would be just the thing before stopping back at the War Office for dispatches bound for Paris.

Why hadn't he heard from Kahverengi? Two weeks had passed since they met at Cimetière du Calvaire in Paris, though thanks to Percy's intrusion Julien had had nothing to offer the arms dealer.

He was glad now he hadn't cut off his arrangement with Cutler. In the event Kahverengi had taken umbrage over their last meeting, Julien still had the means to accrue a fortune.

Perhaps his friend was in Monte Carlo where he enjoyed spending time, or simply at work on another arms deal in some other country. It was just as well. Julien had tried twice to get into his father's study for the files, but between Percy's unexpected forays downstairs and the servants crawling all over the house, his timing was off.

Aggravation began to gnaw at him. He'd telephoned Cutler after last Tuesday's failure, and the man was keen to get more information and pay handsomely in stocks and currency. Julien had to find a way to get back to London tomorrow afternoon to ensure he would be successful.

Stepping from the cab, he paid the driver and walked toward the tea shop, the hot sun making his skin itch beneath the uniform.

What would he do after the war? Munitions would certainly drop in production and so he'd already decided to sell all his shares at the first breath of peace being settled. He'd buy himself a fine town house in London, and when the old man kicked off, he'd be there to take care of Percy. Perhaps he'd find an heiress to marry, someone with as much money as Cutler . . .

He'd started around the corner to enter the tea shop when he halted.

A foursome sat outdoors in the shade, and while he wasn't familiar with the couple facing him—a uniformed RAF captain and a beautiful woman sitting beside him—he focused instead on the broad back of the tall man seated across from her.

"And so we wait, lass."

That voice with the familiar Scots burr belonged to Alex Baird. Startled, Julien stepped back and then smirked. How was it he kept running into Ian Baird's older brother? And why was he in London?

Perhaps I'll go and say hello. His grin widened as he imagined the shock on the captain's face to see him so soon after Moorside.

The slender woman in a small straw hat beside him abruptly turned to Baird, showing her full profile. Julien froze. *Cutler's niece?*

He shook off the ridiculous notion, until she spoke: "I hope Douglas and Samuel will forgive me." The soft traces of an English education mangled with Scots.

Julien slowly retreated until he'd entered the back of the tea shop and then demanded to use a telephone. He rang up the man who could change his fortune, and after his assurance to make the arrangements, Julien hailed another cab, this time to a new destination and the promise of riches.

50

*I*t was midafternoon when Rose and Alex arrived in front of the green lawns and adjacent woodlands shading the redbrick façade of Hertfordshire's Caldicott School.

Her nerves taut over the upcoming reunion with her brothers, Rose gripped Alex's arm once they exited the cab. "Trust in God's love, Rose," Alex whispered and squeezed her hand as they started toward the front steps of the building to arrive at the main office.

Reaching the porch, she breathed deeply and gazed up at him as they walked inside.

"Good afternoon, how may I help you?"

A middle-aged woman, her hair cinched into a high bun, smiled pleasantly as she left her chair behind the desk near the door. Rose surveyed the spacious front room, the pale walls and continuous oak wainscoting broken only by a door beside the polished banister leading upstairs.

"I'm here to see Douglas and Samuel Graham," she said quietly and wondered if this was the same person who had answered her previous calls.

The woman frowned. "The Graham boys?"

"Yes, I'm their sister, Rose Graham."

"Surely not." Her eyes narrowed. "That young woman passed away last month in the Midlands accident."

How could she explain? She squared her shoulders and lifted her chin. "I am indeed Rose Graham, and if you'll kindly send for my brothers, they can confirm my claim."

The woman's pinched mouth lasted several seconds. "I must speak with our interim headmaster, Mr. Valmont," she said at length. "Please wait here."

She indicated a hardwood bench in the foyer, then went to knock on the door near the stairs.

Rose took a seat while Alex stood. "I confess, I didn't take time to consider that the rest of the world still believes me dead," she whispered.

"The lads will settle the issue quick enough. And now that your uncle is in custody, 'tis only a matter of time before Dexter joins him." He reached out and cupped the side of her face, his eyes glowing with promise. "They canna hurt you now."

She leaned into his touch, reassured by his presence and his words. It was still hard to believe that she and the boys would soon be free . . .

"Miss Graham, is it?"

Rose and Alex turned to see a distinguished gentleman approach from the opened door, his reddish-gray brows veed in concern. "My secretary tells me you're here to see Douglas and Samuel Graham?"

"Yes, Headmaster. If you'll send for them, we can clear up this matter. I've come to take them home."

His aged expression looked dubious. "Regardless of who you are, the boys have already gone."

Rose gasped. "What do you mean 'gone'?"

"I received a telephone call at the noon hour from their guardian, Sir Ridley Cutler. He instructed us to allow the boys an escort home with Lieutenant Dexter."

"No!" Rose grabbed for Alex.

"When was the lieutenant here?" Alex demanded.

The headmaster seemed shaken. "He . . . left two hours ago."

"And he was taking them to Leicester?"

"I would assume so, sir."

Alex glanced at the headmaster's secretary. "May I use your telephone?"

The woman nodded, and soon Rose heard him put a call through to Simon in London. "Aye, I'll hold," he said once he'd apprised the captain of the situation.

He held the receiver to his ear as he eyed Rose. "Eve overheard Simon's side of the conversation and told him she saw someone. She's got sharp eyes."

Simon must have come back on the line. "Can she describe him?" Alex nodded at Rose, and her heart began hammering in her chest. Then seeing his fierce look, she knew it was Julien that Eve had seen. "That explains it. He's got a place in London? You have an address?"

Another moment of silence. "Thanks, pal. See you there."

"We're going back into the city," Alex said once he'd rung off. "Scotland Yard is still at your uncle's estate, going through his records. If Dexter went there first, he wouldna risk going near the place with so many police. Likely he's taken the lads to his family's town house at St. James."

They quickly left the stunned headmaster and his secretary and returned to the waiting cab. Alex gave the driver Stanton's address.

As the vehicle rumbled back toward the city, he put his arm around her. "We'll be there in less than an hour, lass. Hold tight."

Rose looked up at him. "How did he find us?"

"Eve saw a man in an RAF uniform walking toward the tea shop. She described him and said she remembered because he came to a sudden halt a few feet away, and his face turned white. He began a slow retreat, then disappeared around to the back of the shop." He pulled her close. "Obviously Dexter recognized you *and* me, and if he overheard any of our conversation, he made a telephone call to your uncle and was told to fetch the lads."

She leaned against him. "I pray you're right, Alex."

"Do they know Dexter?"

She nodded against his shoulder. "They met him last Christmas."

"Then they willna be afraid of him." His deep voice held a confidence that gave her hope. "And Dexter's a schemer, but he wouldna dare bring harm to them."

Over the next forty minutes, however, and despite Alex's reassurances, Rose trembled as her mind conjured the scenarios she'd feared for months.

What if Julien wasn't in London? Perhaps Uncle instructed him to take them to Liverpool and put them on a ship bound for the Americas, or Spain, or even Australia, where Tilly's brother suffered! *Lord, please let me find them!*

She found a reprieve from her frightening thoughts as the cab pulled up in front of a three-story brownstone near London's St. James Square. As she and Alex quickly exited the vehicle, she gazed across the street to see Simon standing beside a dark car, and she assumed he'd brought along detectives from Scotland Yard.

He nodded to her before she and Alex mounted the steps and rang the bell.

An ancient butler answered the door, his wizened face looking harried.

"Take me to Lieutenant Dexter," Alex ordered.

"Who's there, Ames? Tell them to go away."

"Tell his lordliness that we're not leaving."

The frightened butler tried closing the door, but Alex gave the heavy wood a swift push, nearly knocking the reedy man to the floor. "Come on," he said and turned to grab Rose by the hand as they barged inside.

Behind them, the butler shouted in a puny voice, "You will stop, sir!"

"Ames, what is going on?" Julien strode into the foyer and abruptly halted. "Captain Baird, what brings you to my father's house?"

"Bring out the Graham lads, Dexter."

Julien raised an arrogant brow. "They're safe enough for the moment. Besides, I have permission from their guardian."

He glanced at Rose next. "That was some trick, my dear. Imagine my surprise seeing you in Highbury, come back from the grave. I'd love to know how you managed it." His smile made her skin crawl. "Still, it's not too late for us. I can forgive you, and we can still marry. I'm sure that would please your uncle and bring about his change of heart."

Incensed by the memory of his cruelty and the audacity of his conceit, Rose stepped forward, no longer afraid. Alex had said they would find her brothers, and she trusted him implicitly. "Even if you were the very last man in Britain, I wouldn't marry you." Her voice shook with anger. "You are a worm, Julien, crawling in your own dirt and that of my uncle's, and I want Douglas and Samuel back *now*."

Anger seethed in his dark eyes, his face mottled with color. He reached to grab for her, but Alex stepped forward and gave a hard shove to his chest, knocking him backward.

Julien struggled to regain his balance while Alex took another step toward him. "I've waited a whole year to get my retribution, Dexter. Here and now is as good a time as any."

"You blighted Scots!" Snarling, Julien started forward, face heavy with rage.

"Don't do this, brother. Please."

The quiet voice drifted down from above the stairs. Rose gazed up, along with Alex and Julien, to see a pale young man seated in a wheelchair on the second landing.

On either side of him stood two young boys. The younger eyed her with astonishment. "Sissy!" he cried and scampered down the stairs straight into her arms.

"Samuel!" Tears choked her as she embraced him, while his sobs muffled against her blouse as he clutched her waist. Rose buried her face into his soft brown curls. *Thank you, Lord.*

When she looked up at Douglas, he stood at the polished railing watching them, suspicion etched into every line of his young face.

Heart drumming, Rose moved Samuel to one side, and with her free hand she reached up to him. "Duggie . . . ?"

Mistrust suddenly gave way to his silent tears, and he rubbed at the wetness before he hurried down the stairs at a more dignified pace than his brother.

When he came to pause in front of her, he tipped his head, his damp blue eyes searching her face. Rose knew the question he wanted to ask. "Be patient with me and I will explain everything, Duggie." Then she reached to touch his head, grateful he didn't pull away. "For now, though, I promise you I will never leave you again."

Then she pulled him into her arms, surprised at the intensity of his embrace.

❖⟶ ϭϭ ⟵❖

"You are a better man than you believe, Julien."

Julien continued staring up at his brother, who smiled on him with love. He'd never heard such words from him before or witnessed this kind of display, not since they were children. "How can you say that, Percy?" Bitterness edged his voice. "You don't know me."

"I know that what happened years ago wasn't intentional, little brother. An accident, and we were children. Father has made a terrible muck of it over the years, but I do not blame you."

"You never said—"

"You never asked me, Julien. For years, I hoped we might talk, but you always seemed to avoid me." He lowered his head. "Your visits...usually when you thought I was sleeping." Finally he looked up. "I came to believe you never wished to discuss what happened."

So Percy knew. Julien flinched. It was the guilt, always preying on his mind in the form of his father's voice that had kept him away. He couldn't even look his brother in the eye, not since he'd become bound to a wheelchair.

Darby arrived on the landing, and it was a minute before Percy was being carried down the stairs by his valet. For a moment, Julien forgot everyone else in the room, and the fact Cutler's niece and Captain Baird had departed with her brothers. Then he turned and glimpsed the RAF captain he'd seen at the tea shop, standing with two gentlemen he didn't recognize.

The valet, Darby, set Percy into the wheelchair at the base of the stairs and then nodded toward the men at the back. Julien overheard one of the men standing behind him. "Julien Dexter, you are under arrest for treason, exchanging confidential government secrets for profit. You will need to come with us."

"Please! Just another moment," he begged. His dream had crumbled, and the sadness in his brother's expression told him Percy also knew what he'd been doing in their father's study.

He walked to the wheelchair and knelt down beside his brother. "I'm so sorry, Percy," he whispered, finally meeting his brother's eyes. "I'm sorry for everything."

Percy's pale features softened, and he reached to lay a hand on Julien's shoulder. "I forgave you long ago, Brother. But you failed to forgive yourself." Percy looked away, his burden of pain certainly the worst of all.

"I . . . I only wanted to show Father that I was worth something, and I wanted to take care of you, Percy, always."

Percy turned back to him. "Do what is right, Julien, no matter the cost. I will always love you, and I will pray that one day we can be together again."

Julien broke down against his brother's knee, and it was moments before he finally coughed and wiped his eyes. "Yes, Percy." He rasped the words, gazing up at him. "I'll do it for you."

Then, rising, he turned and accompanied the detectives out of the brownstone.

51

That evening, Rose, Alex, and her brothers stayed at the home of the Forresters in London. Once she had promised to explain all to the boys in the morning, Rose settled them into Nikki Marche's bedroom, since Eve's young brother was away for the summer in Southwold, serving as a Sea Scout to aid the Coast Guard in monitoring Britain's coasts.

Walking out onto the small terrace, Rose found Alex sitting in the wicker porch swing. The night was warm and clear, with a display of winking stars across the sky.

"May I join you?"

He gestured a hand toward the empty space beside him. Taking that as an invitation, she sat down on the swing and listened to the leaves rustling in the plane trees lining the sidewalk. Eve's honeysuckle bush grew wild along the east fence, surrounding them in fragrance.

"Eve said that Captain Weatherford called while I was tucking the boys into bed. There was a Zeppelin bombing tonight on the Norfolk Coast? That's just an hour from Leicester. How is my aunt?"

"She's fine," Alex said. "And the enemy's attempt failed. There was little damage after the RAF home defense squadron took down the airship."

"Thank goodness. You know, I still cannot believe this nightmare is over," she whispered, staring at him in the shadows.

"Aye." He tipped his head to gaze at the stars. "Weatherford told me that just before Simon contacted Scotland Yard to come to the earl's town house, the office in Leicester called to say your uncle had confessed and implicated Dexter."

Alex turned to her then, his broad grin making her pulse leap. "You were right about Aunt Delia, too. Once she learned her husband would likely go to prison, she was eager to give Weatherford the key to the secret compartment in the desk. The papers he found were probably the same documents you witnessed, and there were more going back several months. 'Tis fairly certain Cutler and Dexter will face long prison sentences, if not a firing squad for their treason."

Rose nodded. While she was relieved to finally be free to make her own choices, she did regret her uncle's fate. He'd been a difficult man and often a tyrant, but he had taken Rose and her brothers into his home, making certain they were provided for. Not with love, but they'd had enough to eat, a good education, and a roof over their heads.

As for Julien, Rose was glad he no longer held any power over her, and she pitied him. Simon had relayed the confrontation between the brothers after she and Alex and the boys left, and it opened her eyes to Julien's misery and the guilt he'd shouldered all his life. "It is sad the way some parents damage their children, blaming them. And the ways we damage ourselves. Julien Dexter became reckless because he thought he had no worth, nothing to live for."

"Hmm, you've a more tender heart than me, Rose Graham."

"Maybe you would too, Alex, if you forgave yourself." Pausing, she added, "God has."

He glanced at her, and in the shadows it was difficult to see his reaction. He changed the subject. "Your aunt told Weatherford she wants you to return to Leicester. She assured him that your lives would be very different in the future. No doubt she'll have some manner of access to her husband's fortunes."

Rose considered her aunt's offer. In truth, she no longer had a fierce desire to go to Nova Scotia. That had been Tilly's dream after all, and now that she had no fear of her uncle or Julien Dexter, perhaps she could stay. She would need to speak with Douglas and Samuel, to learn if they were happy at their school or if they wished for a simpler, less structured life.

Most of all, she wanted Alex to give her a reason to stay. As if he read her thoughts, she felt his roughened hand rest against hers. When she turned to him, he said, "You know, lass. You remind me of Eve Forrester. In your courage and in your willingness to sacrifice everything for those you love."

Though the waning moon kept him in shadow, the stars reflected in his eyes. "I ken that you've got a better offer before you, but I hope you will consider staying in Gretna Green. Surely, Maw and Da miss you, and Hannah and the lads. And no doubt Winston whines all day when you're not there."

A smile touched her lips, and her heart thumped in her chest as she asked, "Will you miss me as well?"

He moved his face so close to hers that she smelled the coffee on his breath and heard the soft burr in his voice. "Woman, you've not yet left this house and already I ache inside. That's how much I'll be missing you."

While her heart secretly thrilled at his words, she pretended to consider her decision. "You understand, it would mean sacrificing my plans to go to Nova Scotia."

"Aye, New Scotland," he bit out. "When there's nothing wrong with the auld one."

Rose hid her smile. "I suppose you're right. And since I do love you, Alex Baird, I will stay."

He went still beside her for a long moment, before she took pity on him and laid a hand against his cheek. It was her time to choose. "And I'll keep loving you," she said again softly, caressing him. "For as long as we both shall live."

He swept her into his arms then, and she closed her eyes as his lips touched hers, warm and tender and filled with passion. And as she gave him her heart in that kiss, Alex began to gently move the swing back and forth, both of them blissfully unaware of the couple standing near the door, arm in arm, and gazing at them with knowing smiles.

52

From her place high above in the cathedral's loft, Rose Graham looked out over her world for the last time.

For soon she would become Rosalind Baird. Had she really proposed to Alex that night in London?

Humor mingled with her nervous anticipation as she stood back from the balcony and observed the church beginning to fill with familiar faces. There were many from the factory, including some of the lady footballers, and girls she recognized from the dance that night at Border Hall—likely here to again ogle her dashing husband-to-be.

She was delighted to see her supervisor, looking lovely in blue as she entered the church. After the explosion, Mrs. Nash had been understanding about Rose's subterfuge, especially in light of her "heroic action" to save the factory and its workers. Rose suspected Captain Weatherford had planted the seed that she was working undercover for the War Office. Believing she'd kept such a secret, her girls were thrilled and now closer to her than ever.

Several uniformed officers from East Fortune arrived next, and she recognized Colonel Landon, dear man. Rose had been delighted when he offered Alex the post of flight instructor at the airfield, and the colonel would always have her gratitude. While the war was still on, Rose would continue her work at Gretna's factory, though it meant being apart from Alex a few days a week. But at least he could remain in Scotland, safe and close to his family. And the absences would make their reunions all the sweeter.

After London, she'd asked Douglas and Samuel if they wanted to live with her here in Gretna, but then they told her about their friends at Caldicott and how much they missed them. When she took them back, she stayed for a few days and discovered the headmaster and school founder, Mr. Jenkins, was a kind man devoted to teaching and guiding young boys to become fine men.

She had allowed them to stay on the condition they come home every holiday and during the summers, so they could get to know Fergus and James. Aunt Delia had been saddened, of course, over their decision to remain in Hertfordshire, yet Rose encouraged her to get involved with the war effort, and already she'd opened the Leicester estate to the Red Cross as a rehabilitation home for the wounded. Her aunt seemed to be thriving.

Uncle Ridley and Julien remained in prison, having managed to avoid a firing squad. Still, it would be a long time before either of them saw freedom again.

She gazed toward the altar and was filled anew with thanksgiving for the way God had moved Alex's heart. In recent weeks, he'd begun to visit his brother's memorial with her and his family; and then last Sunday she'd joined him in the parlor as he sat down with his parents and for the first time told them about the scars on his back and why they were there, assuring them Ian Baird had died bravely. It was an emotional time, but Rose sensed Alex had finally found peace in forgiveness, not only for his brother but also for himself.

"Rose?" Hannah called out in a loud whisper from the top of the stairs. "The pastor's here, so you'd better hurry. Maw's having kittens."

Smiling, she followed her future sister-in-law back down to the bridal chamber. Hannah had been overjoyed when Rose asked if she would be her maid of honor, and her seven other girls at the factory were eager to be bridesmaids. Rose had worked steadily every night after work over the past several weeks making the simple yet lovely gowns that each would wear.

"Och, there ye are, lass," Mrs. Baird cried in relief. "I need to finish that hem."

"No need to worry, Mrs. Baird." Eve Forrester stood ready and helped Rose up onto the round dais. "On her wedding day the bride is queen, and the world simply awaits." She winked at Rose while Alex's mother hurried to finish stitching the bottom seam on her lovely white gown.

Eve then retrieved the blue, green, and purple plaid of Clan Baird and draped the tartan across Rose's right shoulder. A trial run before Alex would perform the ritual during the ceremony.

"Where is the pin?" she asked, and Rose offered her the thistle brooch. Her final legacy from Tilly Lockhart, and now she would honor her friend by wearing it this day.

"You look stunning," Eve said, having fastened the pin and stepped back. "Alex is a lucky man."

"Och no, I'm the jammy one," Rose quipped in her best Scots burr. "He gets a wife to love, and I get a whole clan."

Mrs. Baird chuckled and tied off her thread, then she looked up with love in her eyes. "And I'm jammy to get myself another daughter."

Rose blinked back happy tears. It was true. She had started out as an orphan, losing her parents and then isolated from her brothers, with only a timid shell of an aunt keeping herself hidden among the somber halls at Leicester. Not like a real family, with people unafraid to express their love or to laugh and tease and stay true to each other. And now she was about to have it all.

"May I come in?' Hannah called softly from the other side of the door. "I've got the flower bearer."

At her mother's assent, the girl entered with Winston, a swath of the Baird plaid tied around his neck. "Are ye certain the wee dog will carry that basket of flowers . . . or chew it up?" Mrs. Baird asked her daughter.

"Winston will do fine. I've been training him."

Rose grinned, recalling the past two weeks as Hannah ran the dog through his paces.

"I've seen Alex, Rose. He looks so braw in his uniform kilt, even if he is my brother."

Rose's pulse leapt as she imagined how handsome her future husband must be.

The future. After he'd shared with his parents about Ian, she and Alex had made a promise—to forgive themselves and each other, and always to love and look ahead with God's guidance.

A knock sounded. "The pastor is ready when you are."

Her heart fluttered. "Thank you, Douglas," Rose called out. "Are you and Samuel ready with the bridesmaids?"

"We're ready."

At the sufferance in his voice, she smiled. Obviously, Douglas wasn't yet old enough to appreciate the face of a pretty girl.

Once Eve removed the Baird plaid and pin to give to Alex downstairs, Mrs. Baird handed Rose the bridal bouquet—the same purple heather, green ivy, and yellow tansies she'd made for Eve's wedding years before. Her bridal crown consisted of tiny blue hydrangea blossoms, white burnet roses, and more of the heather.

"'Tis time, lovely Rose." Mrs. Baird stood back and surveyed her from head to toe while Eve left to go in search of baby Zoe, who was in the care of her father, Alex's best man.

Rose drew a deep breath and hugged her mother-to-be. Surprisingly, the Bairds had taken her secret in stride and now enjoyed calling her Rose instead of Miss Lockhart.

She left the bridal chamber to find Mr. Baird already waiting for her. He looked smart in his kilt and jacket, his cane in hand.

"What a bonny sight you are, Daughter," he said, smiling as he held out his arm to her.

The music began once Mrs. Baird found her seat, and butterflies invaded Rose's stomach.

"Dinna think to run away now, lass, or I willna be able to catch you," her father-to-be said knowingly beside her, and she grinned, grateful for the way he'd put her at ease.

As they walked down the aisle toward the altar, she made herself wait to look at Alex—eyeing first her brothers, along with Fergus and James, escorting her bridesmaids; then Winston, who actually carried the flower basket handle in his mouth without stopping to chew it to shreds.

She smiled at Aunt Delia, standing in the pew wiping happy tears from her eyes; and Eve and the baby and then Mrs. Nash and others who beamed as they watched her procession.

Simon looked handsome in his uniform, now standing beside the man who would become her husband.

Rose finally let her gaze settle on Alex, and she thought she'd never seen a man looking more fine. Garbed in his RAF captain's tunic with his many medals and ribbons, he'd chosen to wear a military kilt, complete with stockings and boots.

He stood tall, his broad shoulders drawn back, and his steady, loving eyes focused entirely on her.

Mr. Baird gently handed her over to his son, while Simon stepped back and the pastor began the ceremony. She and Alex repeated their vows, their eyes never leaving each other. As he settled the Baird tartan across her shoulder and leaned to pin the plaid at her waist, Rose suddenly realized she'd needed to become someone else in order to find herself. And as her new husband straightened, his green eyes still gazing into hers, she knew she had found her home.

Author's Note

Dear Friends,

Thank you for reading *As Dawn Breaks* and spending time with Rose, Alex, and the rest of the Baird clan.

For all of us, 2020 was a strange year, the COVID-19 pandemic ushering in a "new normal" of masks and social distancing, struggling economies, and the grief of losing loved ones. A time when we yearned to be with family and friends but for safety's sake kept ourselves in a state of self-quarantine.

I believe inspiration for the novel, in part, came from this longing; in creating my fictional family, I was allowed to relive some of my own fond memories and to some extent appease that deep yearning to see my loved ones living far away. My hope is that the story did the same for you.

I'd also like to add that while my novel takes place in 1918 and the birth of the Spanish Flu, I chose to set my story during midsummer, when the influenza pandemic had temporarily abated—staying true to the history while offering a respite to readers from our modern-day reality.

In starting my book research for any given time period, I love discovering those nuggets of interest that spark an idea, and the female munitions workers of the First World War certainly captured my imagination. In 1915, the "Shell Scandal" underscored Great Britain's lack of ammunition in a war that was taking far longer to win than anyone had initially foreseen. Construction of munitions factories began raging across the country, and with so many men fighting overseas, women were recruited into this branch of the workforce.

Known as munitionettes, these ladies worked in foundries manufacturing shell casings; they worked in the Pressing rooms to fill those shells with TNT Amatol and they operated overhead cranes and other heavy equipment to load the shells for shipment to the troops. In places like Gretna, Scotland they also made cordite, the propellant used in ammunition. Like the "Tommies" fighting overseas, munitionettes risked their lives daily with the ever-present threat of an accidental explosion, and enduring long hours of exposure to the harsh chemicals. Health problems like dizziness, jaundice, chronic lung congestion, rotting teeth, thinning hair, and internal organ damage were often the result, and many died. Those who worked closest with the disulfuric acids in TNT Amatol, nitroglycerin, and nitrocotton developed yellowed skin and bleached hair and were affectionately known as "Canary Girls."

Most were patriots, though some simply wanted to earn higher wages compared to those of domestics or shop help. Others did it for the adventure, or in the name of suffrage, or the chance to simply get out of the house and socialize in the workplace. Whatever their reasons, all were dedicated to their tasks, and if not for these women, the lives of countless more soldiers would have been lost, with the war ending badly for the Allies.

My research also led me to discover the real Merchant of Death—arms-dealing millionaire, Sir Basil Zaharoff. A Greek born in Turkey and living in Paris, Sir Basil was a true man of mystery and soon became the inspiration for my character, Didymos Kahverengi. Sir Basil enjoyed disguise and subterfuge, and allegedly sold weapons to both sides during the war. Though considered the most famous arms dealer of that time, he was never arrested for crimes linked to arms dealing, I suspect because his secret trysts were among many being clandestinely negotiated by armaments manufacturers across Europe. Sadly, war is and will always be a profitable business.

The pencil bombs Rhymer sent to both Tilly and Rose were in fact real timed explosives used by German agents against the U.S. prior to America's 1917 entry into WWI. As a neutral power, the U.S. sold and shipped desperately needed munitions to Britain, and it became the mission of a network of German spies living in America to sabotage those shipments and prevent their passing into Allied hands. Pencil bombs made it convenient for the enemy to detonate and place the three-inch timed device among a ship or a train's cargo, so that the blast would occur long after the culprit had fled. And the bomb's lead outer coating would leave no trace. One of the most devastating U.S. munitions explosions was the Black Tom Explosion of 1916. Two million tons of war materials packed into train cars had blown up in the Black Tom railroad yard on what is now a part of Liberty State Park. Thousands of windows shattered in lower Manhattan and Jersey City. Shrapnel pockmarked the Statue of Liberty. Three men and a baby were killed by the explosive energy that erupted from this act of sabotage.[1]

On that sober note, I'd like to finish with elucidating further some facts regarding the investigation into the real explosion at No. 6 Chilwell Shell Filling factory in Nottingham, on July 1, 1918. The British Home Office initiated their inquiry on July 8, and Scotland Yard investigated the premises for a mere two days. The official enquiry report was printed and presented on August 7, less than one month later, with no specific recommendations being made, although this report was marked SECRET.[2]

So, was it enemy sabotage? Or was it due to a range of possible reasons offered up by factory workers, like extreme temperatures

1. https://web.archive.org/web/20090715040912/http://www.fbi.gov/page2/july04/blacktom073004.htm.
2. Maureen Rushton, *Canary Girls of Chilwell* (Newton Books: Nottingham, UK, 2nd Edition, 2016), p. 65.

that day overheating the machinery, a spark, a hot bearing, spontaneous combustion, rebellious electricians? Even the IRA was mentioned.[3] I suppose we'll never know for sure.

If you'd like to read more in depth about the Gretna and Chilwell factories of WWI, I've included book titles and authors in my Acknowledgments.

Enjoy the history!

—K.B.

3. Ibid., p. 63.

Questions for Discussion

1. Rose Graham's life suddenly changes when she dares to fake her own death and take on the persona of her deceased best friend and co-worker, Tilly Lockhart. Rose's intent is to escape an unwanted marriage while saving her brothers from their guardian's threat. But her bold move proves more hazardous than she'd imagined, and she comes to realize she didn't know Tilly at all. Have you ever wished to be someone else—a school friend, co-worker, community member, or celebrity—only to learn their life wasn't what it seemed? What important lesson did you take away from the experience?

2. After her "death," Rose flees the unloving environment in Leicester to return to her Scottish homeland. Struggling with guilt, knowing her brothers grieve for her at their boarding school, Rose longs to one day make them a real family again, just as they were before their parents' deaths. Once employed at Gretna, Rose takes a room with the Baird family and receives more warmth and affection than she ever dreamt possible. In fact, she's loath to leave, even when she suspects Alex is spying for Julien. When you were growing up, did you ever enjoy spending time with another family

besides your own? If you'd care to share your reasons, why did you feel this way?

3. Living with the Bairds is a drastic change from Rose's restrictive boarding school life. She learns quickly the two youngest lads, Fergus and James, are a handful, while their sister, Hannah, is an emotional young woman who leans toward theatrics. As you read about these characters, were you reminded of any siblings or other family members in your own life? Do any funny anecdotes come to mind?

4. When she leaves for Gretna, Rose decides to take Tilly's small dog, Winston, whose antics prove to be cute but also detrimental when they reveal her secret to Rhymer. Do you have a pet? If so, what is their most memorable stunt or funny habit?

5. In the first two weeks at the factory, young Rose encounters difficulties with her workers. She becomes the victim of several innocent, yet annoying pranks and is at a loss of how to deal with the issue without revealing to her boss her lack of leadership skills. Have you ever experienced a similar situation at work or at school? Were you a prankster or the target? Any amusing anecdotes or lessons you'd like to share? How would you have handled Rose's dilemma?

6. After the Chilwell explosion, Rose returns to the cottage to discover Tilly's planned party gifts. Most important was a trade card for an alleged forger and the note on the back, *Become a new person, Rose, if you have the courage.* Rose recalls those words repeatedly as she imagines becoming just like her brave friend, through her work and football and standing up to bullies. What she discovers instead are her own strengths—the confidence that was once hers before her parents died. Discuss how you or someone you know had to overcome a personal challenge in order to accomplish a dream or a goal. What was that obstacle? Fear, shyness, or lack of confidence in learning something new? How did you

succeed, and were you surprised at what you learned from the experience?

7. Alex Baird carries the weight of guilt over his brother's death. While he tried to save Ian from deserting, his pursuit indirectly caused his brother's plane to crash. His faith helps him understand that God has forgiven him, but his conscience isn't convinced. This often happens with Christians, and the guilt we experience can end up ruining our lives. Discuss ways in which we can overcome this self-inflicted punishment through action and think of Scripture passages that may help us learn to trust in God's mercy.

8. After his brother's death in the crash, Alex Baird decides to keep secret from his family—and everyone else—Ian's attempted desertion and the treasonous papers found on his person. Do you think Alex was right to do so? What would you have done in his place?

9. Which character in the story surprised you the most? Which character did you find the most tragic and why?

10. The young women working at HM Factory Gretna, like those at Chilwell and other munitions factories, suffered side effects from the harsh chemicals and risked their lives by working with explosives. Deadly accidents were not uncommon, and over the course of the war, hundreds were killed. Still, a munitionette's wages were among the highest for women, and they enjoyed the freedom of wearing more comfortable clothes and doing important work for the war effort. Other jobs like policewomen, firewomen, tank builders, farmers, scientists, nurses, railroad engineers, and Lumber Jills, to name a few, were also available to women during the war. If you had lived then, what job would you have applied for and why?

11. If the story were continued, which characters would you want to know more about?

Acknowledgments

A lot goes into creating a story—researching an idea, then plotting, outlining, writing, revising, editing, and more revising. A seemingly endless process until the manuscript finally goes to print. Most importantly, though, it is a lot of prayer and hard work, and so above all I thank God for His gifts, for inspiring me to sit down each day and write the words. And to my husband, John, your love and support mean so much to me, not only in holding the fort during my long absences upstairs at the computer, but also being my wonderful first reader. Thank you!

As always, my deep affection and appreciation go to my critique partners, mentors, and friends, especially Anjali Banerjee, Lois Faye Dyer, Rose Marie Harris, Patty Jough-Haan, Debbie Macomber, Darlene Panzera, Sheila Roberts, Krysteen Seelen, and Susan Wiggs. Sharing your time, wisdom, and support for this novel has been a blessing to me!

My special thanks to Chris Brader for his 2001 PhD thesis, *TimberTown Girls: Gretna Female Munitions Workers in World War I*, an incredibly detailed history of Scotland's HM Factory Gretna and the young women who made up its workforce. And to British historian Maureen Rushton and her 2016 work, *Canary Girls of Chilwell*, depicting a day in the life of the munitionettes at No. 6 Chilwell factory and offering detailed, firsthand accounts from those who survived the horrific explosion of July 1, 1918. From both of you I gleaned much, and while mine is a fictional work, any literary license or errors in information are solely my responsibility.

To my dear agent, Linda S. Glaz, and my wonderful editors, Raela Schoenherr, Luke Hinrichs, Elizabeth Frazier, and the rest of the Bethany House family who helped to bring this project to fruition, I thank you for your guidance, encouragement, and support.

About the Author

Former bookseller-turned-author, **Kate Breslin** enjoys life in the Pacific Northwest with her husband and family. She is a Carol Award winner and a RITA and Christy Award finalist who loves reading, hiking, and traveling. New destinations make for fresh story ideas.

To learn more, visit her website at www.katebreslin.com.

Sign Up for Kate's Newsletter

Keep up to date with Kate's news on book releases and events by signing up for her email list at katebreslin.com.

More from Kate Breslin

In spring 1918, British Lieutenant Colin Mabry receives an urgent message from a woman he once loved but thought dead. Feeling the need to redeem himself, he travels to France—only to find the woman's half sister, Johanna, who believes her sister is alive and the prisoner of a German spy. As they seek answers across Europe, danger lies at every turn.

Far Side of the Sea

You May Also Like . . .

In 1917, British nurse and war widow Evelyn Marche is trapped in German-occupied Brussels. She works at the hospital by day and as a waitress by night. But she also has a secret: She's a spy for the resistance. When a British plane crashes in the park, Evelyn must act quickly to protect the injured soldier who has top-secret orders and a target on his back.

High as the Heavens by Kate Breslin
katebreslin.com

When suffragette Grace Mabry hands a white feather of cowardice to Jack Benningham—an English spy masquerading as a conscientious objector—she could not anticipate the danger and betrayal set in motion by her actions. Soon, she and Jack are forced to learn the true meaning of courage when the war raging overseas strike much closer to home.

Not by Sight by Kate Breslin
katebreslin.com

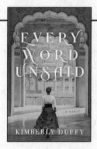

As the nation's most fearless travel columnist, Augusta Travers explores the country, spinning stories for women unable to leave hearth and home. Suddenly caught in a scandal, she escapes to India to visit old friends, promising great tales of boldness. But instead she encounters a plague, new affections, and the realization that she can't outrun her past.

Every Word Unsaid by Kimberly Duffy
kimberlyduffy.com

More from Bethany House

After Pearl Harbor, sweethearts Gordon Hooper and Dorie Armitage were broken up by their convictions. As a conscientious objector, he went west to fight fires as a smokejumper, while she joined the Army Corps. When a tragic accident raises suspicions, they're forced to work together, but the truth they uncover may lead to an impossible—and dangerous—choice.

The Lines Between Us by Amy Lynn Green
amygreenbooks.com

When lawyer Patrick O'Neill agrees to resurrect an old mystery and challenge the Blackstones' legacy of greed and corruption, he doesn't expect to be derailed by the kindhearted family heiress, Gwen Kellerman. She is tasked with getting him to drop the case, but when the mystery takes a shocking twist, he is the only ally she has.

Carved in Stone by Elizabeth Camden
THE BLACKSTONE LEGACY #1
elizabethcamden.com

After promising a town he'd find them water and then failing, Sullivan Harris is on the run; but he grows uneasy when one success makes folks ask him to find other things—like missing items or sons. When men are killed digging the Hawks Nest Tunnel, Sully is compelled to help, and it becomes the catalyst for finding what even he has forgotten—hope.

The Finder of Forgotten Things by Sarah Loudin Thomas
sarahloudinthomas.com

BETHANYHOUSE

Praise for

LATE MIGRATIONS

Winner of the 2020 Phillip D. Reed Environmental Writing Award
Finalist for the 2020 Southern Book Prize
Named a Best Book of the Year by the *New Statesman*, New York Public
Library, Chicago Public Library, *Foreword Reviews*, and *Washington
Independent Review of Books*

"A book that will be treasured." —*Minneapolis Star Tribune*

"What book would I want to see included on summer-reading tables everywhere? . . . A book of nonfiction by Margaret Renkl called *Late Migrations*
that examines a quiet life through the lens of family and the natural world. I
don't say this lightly, but [it] deserve[s] to be read for as long as kids have
been reading *Of Mice and Men*." —ANN PATCHETT, *Wall Street Journal*

"One of the best books I've read in a long time . . . [and] one of the most
beautiful essay collections that I have ever read. It will give you chills."
—SILAS HOUSE, author of *Southernmost*

"Reflective and gorgeous . . . I have recommended this book to everybody
that I know. It is a beautiful book about love, and [how] . . . to find the beauty
in the little things." —JENNA BUSH HAGER, the *TODAY* Show

"A lovely collection of essays about life, nature, and family. It will make you
laugh, cry, and breathe more deeply." —*Parade*

"This is the story of grief accelerated by beauty and beauty made richer by
grief. . . . Like Patti Smith in *Woolgathering*, Renkl aligns natural history with
personal history so completely that the one becomes the other. Like Annie
Dillard in *Pilgrim at Tinker Creek*, Renkl makes, of a ring of suburbia, an
alchemical exotica." —*The Rumpus*

"Like the spirituality of Krista Tippett's *On Being* meets the brevity of Joe
Brainard . . . The miniature essays in *Late Migrations* approach with mod-
esty, deliver bittersweet epiphanies, and feel like small doses of religion."
—*Literary Hub*

"Renkl holds my attention with essays about plants and caterpillars in a way
no other nature writer can."
—MARY LAURA PHILPOTT, author of *I Miss You When I Blink*

"In her poignant debut, a memoir, Renkl weaves together observations from her current home in Nashville and short vignettes of nature and growing up in the South." *—Garden & Gun*

"[A] stunning collection of essays merging the natural landscapes of Alabama and Tennessee with generations of family history, grief and renewal. Renkl's voice sounds very close to the reader's ear: intimate, confiding, candid and alert." *—Shelf Awareness*

"*Late Migrations* is a gift, and fortunate readers will steal away to a beloved nook or oasis to commune with its riches. Or they will simply dig into it, unprepared, like the mother with no gardening tools who determinedly pulls weeds until the ground blossoms. They might entrust it to fellow seekers they believe can handle its power. Consecrated, they'll leave initiated into an art of observation lived beautifully in richness, connection, worry, and love." *—The Christian Century*

"Renkl feels the lives and struggles of each creature that enters her yard as keenly as she feels the paths followed by her mother, grandmother, her people. Learning to accept the sometimes harsh, always lush natural world may crack open a window to acceptance of our own losses. In *Late Migrations*, we welcome new life, mourn its passing, and honor it along the way." —Indie Next List (July 2019), selected by Kat Baird, The Book Bin

"How can any brief description capture this entirely original and deeply satisfying book? . . . I can't help but compile a list of people I want to gift with *Late Migrations*. I want them to emerge from it, as I did, ready to apprehend the world freshly, better able to perceive its connections and absorb its lessons." *—Chapter 16*

"Renkl captures the spirit and contemporary culture of the American South better than anyone." *—BookPage*, a 2019 Most Anticipated Nonfiction Book

"[A] magnificent debut . . . Renkl instructs that even amid life's most devastating moments, there are reasons for hope and celebration. Readers will savor each page and the many gems of wisdom they contain." *—Publishers Weekly* (starred review)

"Compelling, rich, satisfying . . . The short, potent essays of *Late Migrations* are objects as worthy of marvel and study as the birds and other creatures they observe." *—Foreword Reviews* (starred review)

LATE
MIGRATIONS

LATE
MIGRATIONS

A Natural History of Love and Loss

Margaret Renkl

With art by

Billy Renkl

MILKWEED EDITIONS

First paperback edition, published 2021 by Milkweed Editions
Printed in Canada
Cover design by Mary Austin Speaker
Cover art by Billy Renkl
21 22 23 24 25 5 4 3 2
First Edition

978-1-57131-383-6

Milkweed Editions, an independent nonprofit publisher, gratefully acknowledges sustaining support from our Board of Directors; the Alan B. Slifka Foundation and its president, Riva Ariella Ritvo-Slifka; the Amazon Literary Partnership; the Ballard Spahr Foundation; *Copper Nickel*; the McKnight Foundation; the National Endowment for the Arts; the National Poetry Series; the Target Foundation; and other generous contributions from foundations, corporations, and individuals. Also, this activity is made possible by the voters of Minnesota through a Minnesota State Arts Board Operating Support grant, thanks to a legislative appropriation from the arts and cultural heritage fund. For a full listing of Milkweed Editions supporters, please visit milkweed.org.

The Library of Congress has cataloged the hardcover edition as follows:

Names: Renkl, Margaret, author. | Renkl, Billy, illustrator.
Title: Late migrations : a natural history of love and loss / Margaret Renkl ; with art by Billy Renkl.
Description: First edition. | Minneapolis : Milkweed Editions, 2019.
Identifiers: LCCN 2018044003 (print) | LCCN 2018057281 (ebook) | ISBN 9781571319876 (ebook) | ISBN 9781571313782 (hardcover : alk. paper)
Subjects: LCSH: Renkl, Margaret. | Renkl, Margaret—Family. | Journalists—United States—Biography. | Adult children of aging parents—United States—Biography.
Classification: LCC PN4874.R425 (ebook) | LCC PN4874.R425 A3 2019 (print) | DDC 818/.603 [B]—dc23
LC record available at https://lccn.loc.gov/2018044003

For my family

Margaret Renkl's Maternal Family Tree

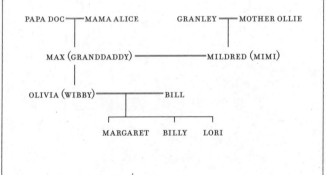

PAPA DOC — MAMA ALICE   GRANLEY — MOTHER OLLIE

MAX (GRANDDADDY) — MILDRED (MIMI)

OLIVIA (WIBBY) — BILL

MARGARET   BILLY   LORI

Well, dear, life is a casting off. It's always that way.

ARTHUR MILLER, *DEATH OF A SALESMAN*

Therefore all poems are elegies.

GEORGE BARKER

LATE
MIGRATIONS

PEACH

In Which My Grandmother Tells the Story

of My Mother's Birth

LOWER ALABAMA, 1931

We didn't expect her quite as early as she came. We were at Mother's peeling peaches to can. Daddy had several peach trees, and they had already canned some, and so we were canning for me and Max. And all along as I would peel I was eating, so that night around twelve o'clock I woke up and said, "Max, my stomach is hurting so much I just can't stand it hardly. I must have eaten too many of those peaches."

And so once in a while, you see, it would just get worse; then it would get better.

We didn't wake Mother, but as soon as Max heard her up, he went in to tell her. And she said, "Oh, Max, go get your daddy right now!" Max's daddy was the doctor for all the folks around here.

While he was gone she fixed the bed for me, put on clean sheets and fixed it for me. Mama Alice came back with him too—Mama Alice and Papa Doc. So they were both with me, my mother on one side and Max's on the other, and they were holding my hands. And Olivia was born around twelve o'clock that day. I don't know the time exactly.

Max was in and out, but they said Daddy was walking around the house, around and around the house. He'd stop every now and then and find out what was going on. And when she was born, it was real quick. Papa Doc jerked up, and he said, "It's a girl," and Max said, "Olivia."

1

Red in Beak and Claw

The first year, a day before the baby bluebirds were due to hatch, I checked the nest box just outside my office window and found a pinprick in one of the eggs. Believing it must be the pip that signals the beginnings of a hatch, I quietly closed the box and resolved not to check again right away, though the itch to peek was nearly unbearable: I'd been waiting years for a family of bluebirds to take up residence in that box, and finally an egg was about to shudder and pop open. Two days later, I realized I hadn't seen either parent in some time, so I checked again and found all five eggs missing. The nest was undisturbed.

The cycle of life might as well be called the cycle of death: everything that lives will die, and everything that dies will be eaten. Bluebirds eat insects; snakes eat bluebirds; hawks eat snakes; owls eat hawks. That's how wildness works, and I know it. I was heartbroken anyway.

I called the North American Bluebird Society for advice, just in case the pair returned for a second try. The guy who answered the help line thought perhaps my bluebirds—not "mine," of course, but the bluebirds I loved—had been attacked by both a house wren and a snake. House wrens are furiously territorial and will attempt to disrupt the nesting of any birds nearby. They fill unused nest holes with sticks to prevent competitors from settling there; they destroy unprotected nests and pierce all the eggs; they have been known to kill nestlings and even brooding females. Snakes simply swallow the eggs whole, slowly and gently, leaving behind an intact nest.

The bluebird expert recommended that I install a wider

snake baffle on the mounting pole and clear out some brush that might be harboring wrens. If the bluebirds returned, he said, I should install a wren guard over the hole as soon as the first egg appeared: the parents weren't likely to abandon an egg, and disguising the nest hole with a cover might keep wrens from noticing it. I bought a new baffle, but the bluebirds never came back.

The next year another pair took up residence. After the first egg appeared, I went to the local bird supply store and asked for help choosing a wren guard, but the store didn't stock them; house wrens don't nest in Middle Tennessee, the owner said. I know they aren't *supposed* to nest here, I said, but listen to what happened last year. He scoffed: possibly a migrating wren had noticed the nest and made a desultory effort to destroy it, but there are no house wrens nesting in Middle Tennessee. All four bluebird eggs hatched that year, and all four bluebird babies safely fledged, so I figured he must know this region better than the people at the bluebird society, and I gave no more thought to wren guards.

The year after that, there were no bluebirds. Very early in February, long before nesting season, a male spent a few minutes investigating the box, but he never returned with a female. Even the chickadees, who nest early and have always liked our bluebird box, settled for the box under the eaves near the back door. All spring, the bluebird box sat empty.

Then I started to hear the unmistakable sound of a house wren calling for a mate. Desperately the wren would call and call and then spend some time filling the box with sticks, building an elaborate scaffolding that formed a deep tunnel running across the top of the box and down to its very floor. Day after day: singing, sticks, singing, sticks. The side yard was his exclusive domain. No longer did the chickadees visit the mealworm feeder on that side of the house; the goldfinches abandoned the thistle feeder nearby; only the largest birds dared drink from the birdbath. I set another dish of water on the other side of the house because we'd had so little rain.

Meanwhile, the chickadees hatched out a magnificent brood of babies. Their voices were full and strong, and their parents worked continually from sunup till dark feeding them. After they fledged, right on schedule, I took the box down for cleaning. At the bottom was one fully feathered baby, probably only minutes from leaving the box. It was dead from a puncture wound to the head.

It's one thing to recognize the bloodbath that is the natural world and a different thing entirely to participate in it. There's nothing "natural" about offering wild birds food and water and housing, even in an area where human beings have systematically destroyed their original nesting sites and food sources. With that invitation comes an obligation to protect and defend the creatures who accept it. Even before I found the dead chick, I had made up my mind to take down my nest boxes after the house wrens fledged, both to discourage the wren from returning and to keep from attracting other native cavity dwellers—tufted titmice, Carolina wrens—to house wren territory.

Thing is, I love the little brown wrens too. Their courtship song is one of the most beautiful in the world, a high, thin river made of musical notes tumbling and rushing and cascading downstream. And it's hard to fault them for doing only what millions of years of evolution have taught them to do, in their impossibly tiny fierceness, to survive a world of high winds and pelting rains and predators. To see that small brown bird lifting his throat to the sky and releasing that glorious sound into the world, again and again and again, day after day—how could it be possible not to root for him, not to hope a mate would arrive, in this region where house wrens don't nest, to accept him and his offering of sticks? When a female joined him ten days later, I had to cheer.

Then a blackberry winter descended on Middle Tennessee, and that night it was twenty degrees colder than the temperature a house wren egg needs to remain viable. The next morning, the goldfinches returned to the thistle feeder.

Let Us Pause to Consider What a Happy

Ending Actually Looks Like

LOWER ALABAMA, 1936

In the story my grandmother told, there was an old woman of uncertain race who lived among them but did not belong. With no land and no way to grow anything, the old woman was poorer and more desolate than the others, and they looked the other way when she slipped into their barns after dark with her candle and her rucksack, intent on taking corn. Did a barn owl startle her that night? Did a mule jostle her arm? They never knew: she never admitted to being there. The howling fire took the barn whole and then roared to the house. Neighbors saved some of the furniture in a kind of bucket line, but an actual bucket line was impossible: the water tank had stood on a wooden scaffold already lost to the blaze. There was no time to save the clothes and quilts, the food my grandmother had stored for winter, the grain my grandfather had put up for his mules. Worst of all, there was no time to save the wild-eyed mules stamping in their stalls.

In my grandmother's story, they brought what the neighbors had salvaged to her in-laws' house half a mile down the road, and family came from every direction to resettle things, making room. The back porch became the room where Papa Doc and Mama Alice slept. The parlor became my grandparents' room. The nooks where my mother and her infant brother slept were upstairs, in what had been the attic.

Decades later, when my mother told stories of her girlhood,

she never seemed to recall how crowded the house must have been or how the tensions surely flared. Instead she remembered my great-grandparents' devotion. Every day Papa Doc would leave for calls with his black bag or, on slow mornings, head to the store to pick up the mail. When he came home again, he always called out, "Alice?" as soon as he reached their rose border. And she would always call back, formally, from the garden or the kitchen or the washtub on the porch, "I'm here, Dr. Weems."

My mother's grandparents went through the day in a kind of dance, preordained steps that took them away from each other—he to his rounds across the countryside, she to the closer world of clothesline and pea patch and barn—but brought them back together again and again, touching for just a moment before moving away once more.

But the shadow side of love is always loss, and grief is only love's own twin. My mother was twelve when Mama Alice died. Papa Doc sat down on the porch and settled there, staring at the rambling rosebushes growing beside the road. "He just made up his mind to die, I guess," my mother always said. "He lasted barely more than a month."

WATER LILY

Encroachers

The sun is setting on the lily pond, winking on the water between the floating circles of the lily pads, winking on the brown leaves caught on the green surface of the dense lilies. The wind is stirring the water, rippling the mirrored trees on the bank, and now the deep-red leaves of the sumac are falling too, and the yellow maples and the orange sassafras. Soon the pond will be covered over with lily pads and leaves. In only a little while—five years? ten? no more than a blink—the water will cease to echo these trees and this sky. Today the brown water is glowing in the autumn light, on fire with light and color and motion, but the pond is dying.

It is impossible to believe the pond is dying.

The lilies are choking it, starving it of light and oxygen. Soon there will be no room left for fish or frog or snake or turtle. There will be only lilies, lilies from edge to edge, a marsh of lilies where nothing else can live. In summer the lilies bloom—oh, how beautifully the lilies bloom, how fragrant their flowers!—and even now, at the very end of autumn at the very end of the day, the lovely pond is filled with light, encircled and embraced. Leaves resting on the lily pads, hawk floating overhead, rabbit crouching under the tree—all life piled on life—and still it is dying.

The pond is dying, and now I am thinking of starlings reeling through the sky at dusk, the glory of the starlings in motion, wheeling and dipping and rising as one black beast made of pulsing cells, as one creature born to live in air. But the starlings don't belong any more than the lilies belong; they are aliens here. This is not their sky. These are not their trees. They are robbing the dogwoods, leaving no berries for the mockingbirds. They have claimed every nest hole, leaving none for the titmice or the bluebirds or even the bossy chickadees.

The alien does not know it's an alien.

When a starling hangs itself at dawn on the wire holding up my peanut feeder, and I wake to find it dangling there, black and stiff and cold, I can only pity it, hungry and confused and now lost to the world. But a downy woodpecker, unconcerned by the specter hanging above its head, is finally getting its fill of peanuts.

In Which My Grandmother Tells the Story

of Her Favorite Dog

LOWER ALABAMA, 1940

I was still teaching when Max Junior and Olivia were in school. Our school was a very short distance from home, and we walked. Of course, I always walked by myself; they were always running and playing. And my dog, her name was Honey, always followed me, and she would get up under my desk and stay there as long as I was at my desk. If I went to the board, she went with me and laid down by my feet as long as I was writing on the board. One weekend she went missing, and we looked everywhere for her. We didn't find her until Monday morning. When we got to school, we smelled something, and it was this dog. She had crawled right up under the school building, right under where I sat. That's where she was when she died.

Howl

The old dog wakes when the door shuts fast. *Click* goes the back door, and *thump* goes the car door, and now the old dog believes he is alone in the house. When the whine of the car backing out of the drive gives way to the crunch of tires on the road, and then to silence, the old dog believes he is alone in the world. Standing next to the door, he folds himself up, lowering his hindquarters gradually, bit by bit, slowly, until his aching haunches have touched the floor. Now he slides his front feet forward, slowly, slowly, and he is down.

A moan begins in the back of his throat, lower pitched than a whine, higher than a groan, and grows. His head tips back. His eyes close. The moan escapes in a rush of vowels, louder and louder and louder, and now he is howling. It is the sound he made in his youth whenever an ambulance passed on the big road at the edge of the neighborhood, but he can't hear so far anymore. Now he is howling in despair. He is howling for his long life's lost companion, the dog who died last year and left him to sleep alone. He is howling for his crippled hips, so weak he can hardly squat to relieve himself. He is howling because it's his job to protect this house, but he is too old now to protect the house. He is howling because the world is empty, and he is howling because he is still here.

In Which My Grandmother Tells the Story

of the Day I Was Born

LOWER ALABAMA, 1961

*O*n *Mother's Day of 1961, Bill and Olivia came to our house, and Bill—this is the way he gave Olivia her gift—said, "This is to the sweetest little mother-to-be there is." That's the way he told us. And that was when she was going to have Margaret. And so we kept the road pretty hot between our house and yours after that. And when she was born, Bill called us and said he wanted me to go with him to Montgomery. They thought they would have to take Margaret up there. She was having the breathing trouble that that Kennedy child had later on, and he died. And so Max carried me down there, but when we got there, they had gotten it straightened out well enough that they thought it wouldn't be necessary to take her. So we stayed a few days, until Olivia could get up and was able to bathe the baby and look after her.*

To the Bluebirds

I know: there are too many dogs in the yard; and the giant house going up next door is too much hulking house lumbering too near the little nest box, never mind the beeping, growling trucks and the bellowing carpenters and the scrambling roofers with their machine-gun nails; and the miniature forest behind us still harbors agile-fingered raccoons and rat snakes as thick as my arm; and a Cooper's hawk still patrols the massive pine tree on the other side of the house.

But consider: the dogs are old and spend their time lying in the sun, their glad bird-chasing days long past. And the noisy builders, too close now in house-scouting season, will be gone by nesting time, replaced by neighbors who will drive straight into their garage, never lingering in what's left of their yard. Look at the predator baffle, much larger than last year's, and the now-bare ground where before the brush sheltered house wrens.

Look: see the sturdy birdbath I've moved to your side of the yard, and the special feeder designed to hold live mealworms? The greatest token of my love for you is that every day now I reach into a mesh bag full of live mealworms and pluck them out, one by one, and drop them into the ceramic cup in the feeder. The worms stay in my refrigerator, where the cool darkness is meant to keep them in a state of dormancy, but oh my God they are not dormant. No, they curl their segmented bodies around my finger, and they lift their nubby heads and rebuke me with their nonexistent eyes, but I harden my heart to their plight and plink them into that little white cup, and I walk away as they twist and curl around each other in search of purchase. They are my gift to you on these cold days when nary a cricket stirs in the dry grass.

The Way You Looked at Me

LOWER ALABAMA, 1961

Here are all my kin—my mother and my father, my grandmother and my grandfather, my great-grandmother in the placid wholeness of her white halo—arrayed around me. Born too early, tiny and frail, I am sleeping in every picture, and in every picture they are gathered around me, heads bent to watch me take each too-light breath, willing my lips not to turn blue again. I am too small and always cold, but my people are looking at me as if I were the sun. My parents and my grandparents and my great-grandmother, all of them, have gathered to watch over me. They are looking at me as if I were the sun, as if they had been cold every day of their lives until now.

I am the sun, but they are not the planets.

They are the universe.

Not Always in the Sky

Our neighborhood is home to a very large red-tailed hawk. The hawk's telltale color is muted in females, in certain lights almost brown, and the dead tree this hawk often uses as a hunting perch is distant enough from the street to make the bird's identity a matter for debate. My neighbors are convinced this bird is an eagle.

"Go home and get your camera!" one stops her car to say as I walk the dog. "There's an eagle in the dead tree!" I go home and get the camera, just to be safe, but the dog and I have just passed the dead tree, and perched in it was a large red-tailed hawk. When I go back with my camera, she is still there.

There's much talk here about the eagle who has taken up residence in our neighborhood, but no one seems to wonder what kind of eagle it might be. When I first heard the rumors, I thought perhaps my neighbors were seeing a young bald eagle. Everyone knows an adult bald eagle on sight, but juveniles always pose a challenge in birds. There was a remote possibility, too, of a visit by a golden eagle, a species generally found west of the Mississippi but reintroduced in Tennessee not long ago; several birds equipped with transmitters are known to spend winter on the Cumberland Plateau. But only by the most muscular effort of imagination could this bird be a golden eagle. We don't live on the Cumberland Plateau.

The bird is clearly a red-tailed hawk, but I don't say anything to my neighbors. People want to believe that something extraordinary has happened to them, that they have been singled out for grace, and who am I to rob them of one sheen of enchantment still available in the first-ring suburbs?

Working at my desk one day, I hear a great mob of blue jays sounding the alarm: a predator is in their midst. Minutes pass, and their rage shows no signs of dissipating, so I step outside. Perhaps the hawk that looks like an eagle has landed in my own yard.

But I see nothing in the sky, nothing in the trees, nothing on the utility pole at the corner of the yard, nothing on the power lines. And then I notice that the blue jays are looking down as they scream out their jeering cry of warning, and that all the smaller birds, even the ground foragers, have taken to the bushes and the honeysuckle tangles and are looking downward too. The little Cooper's hawk who hunts in this yard will often stand on his prey for a bit, working to get a better grip on his struggling victim before taking to the sky, but there is no hawk on the ground either.

Walking farther into the yard, I still don't see anything, even scanning the ground with a zoom lens. And then it dawns on me that the birds must be looking at a snake. This lot backs up to a city easement, only a few yards wide, that leads from the wooded area behind our neighbor's house out to the side street next to ours. We leave the easement untended, and the part of our yard that abuts it as well, because it serves as a kind of wildlife corridor. A very large rat snake, at least five feet long, hunts under our house and all over this yard, but I wouldn't be able to see it in the easement unless I was practically upon it. I walk a little closer but only a little. Though I am not especially afraid of snakes, I know they are afraid of me, and I like to give them their room.

Holding a useless camera, I suddenly realize that something extraordinary is happening right before me, a great serpent slowly on the move and all the songbirds aware of its presence and calling to each other and telling each other to beware. The miracle isn't happening in the sky at all. It's happening in the damp weeds of an ordinary backyard, among last year's moldering leaves and the fragrant soil turned up by moles.

Blood Kin

LOWER ALABAMA, 1963

In the picture I'm dressed entirely in white: white dress with puffed sleeves, white bonnet with white lace around the brim, white tights and white polished high-tops, the kind all babies wore. It must be an Easter picture, you think, because what parent would dress a toddler in white more than once a year? But it can't be Easter. My grandmother, who's holding me in her lap on the porch steps, and my great-grandmother beside her, each with a halo of white hair that matches my frothy bonnet, are wearing dark dresses. And no farm woman in Alabama would be caught dead wearing navy blue on the day of the Resurrection.

The picture's off-center; there's room for my mother beside my great-grandmother, but Mama is perched on the next step up, smiling behind us, a little out of focus from the shift in depth of field. She's hiding because my brother will be born in April, and she always hid from cameras when she was pregnant.

Never mind that birth and death were entirely unremarkable in the world of that photo. Every chicken she ate with dumplings was one whose neck her grandmother had wrung. Every Christmas ham was once a piglet in her yard. All the babies in that county were born in their parents' beds and too often died there as well. The cemetery is full of tiny graves whose headstones are carved with terrible phrases: "Many fond hopes lie buried here." "Another jewel for the Maker's crown."

My grandmother's third child was born too soon, so early he had no name. She never told anyone else about him, but she told me, years later, when I could not stop weeping after my own miscarriages: "I had him in the chamber pot on the floor next to the bed," she said. "Nights I cried for a long time after that. Days I went to work like always."

Nests

Oblivion would be easier—not to know when the rat snake noses aside the tangle of grasses the cottontail has carefully patted into place, not to see it lift the impossibly soft fur she has plucked from her own belly, not to fathom that it is slowly, almost mechanically, swallowing the blind babies she has borne for just this moment.

Better not to discover that a still brown cardinal is sitting on two speckled eggs in the hollow of the holly beside the fence, her orange beak the only hint of her presence in the brown nest in the crook of the brown branches. Better not to hear the crow flapping down to the fencerow or to see its black head driving her from the holly with a single plunging probe through the leaves, or to understand that it is eating her eggs, indifferent to the driving sweeps of her furious mate and her own piteous calls.

Oh, to unsee the Carolina wren waiting so patiently in the tunnel of fronds she has wrapped around herself deep in the potted fern, invisible, but not invisible to the side-eyed jay. Oh, to unwatch her disbelief as she hops around and around the edge of the flowerpot, searching in vain for a hungry mouth to open for the caterpillar she has brought.

Scolding will not save the little sac of mantis eggs the neighborhood boys are batting around like a ball, or the spider's web swept from the eaves by a homeowner's broom, or the cluster of frog eggs at the edge of the pond where the newt is hunting.

This life thrives on death.

But hold very, very still in the springtime sun, and a tufted titmouse will come to harvest your hair and spin it into a soft, warm place for her young. Keep an eye on the ivy climbing the side of the house, and one day you will see a pair of finches coaxing their babies from a tiny nest balanced among the leaves. Hear the bluebirds calling from the trees, and you might turn in time to see a fledgling peer from the hole in the dark nest box, gape at the bright wide world for the very first time, and then trust itself to the sky. Wait at the window on the proper day, and the cottontail nest hidden under the rosemary bush will open before you, spilling forth little rabbits who lift the leaves from last fall and push aside their mother's fur and raise their ears and wrinkle their noses and bend for their first taste of the bitter dandelion. And it will be exactly what they wanted.

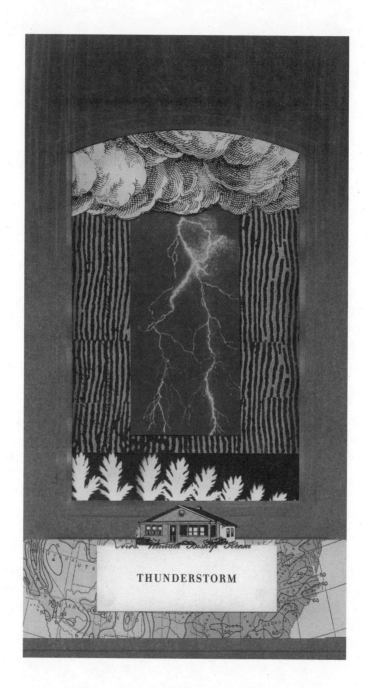

THUNDERSTORM

In the Storm, Safe from the Storm

LOWER ALABAMA, 1965

At my grandparents' house in the country, we live on the front porch, where the ceiling fan blows the bugs away and stirs the steaming air into something passing for a breeze. At home in town we are very modern and have no porch at all. There's a concrete stoop but only the barest overhang to cover it, hardly anything to keep away the rain or the blistering sun. When a storm comes, my father sets his chair right in the doorway, straddling the jamb. I love the storms. If I'm asleep, he lifts me up and carries me through the dark house to sit with him in the doorway and listen to the wind and the thunder.

The rain comes and I feel it with the tips of my toes, but they are the only parts of me that get wet, for I have drawn my knees up to my chest under my nightgown, and my father has unbuttoned his corduroy jacket and pulled it around me, and wrapped his arms around me too. I lean into him. I feel the heat from his body and the cool rain from the world, both at once.

Secret

Wild storms always come to Tennessee in the springtime. One year a wind shear hit a hackberry tree three doors down from us and snapped it off right at the middle. The crown of the tree came down hard in seventy-mile-an-hour winds, taking out a maple and several large cypresses and crashing through a length of cedar fencing, barely missing the next-door neighbors' car.

That night the local news was full of trees that had in fact smashed into cars, but the scene here was even more dramatic. The tragic hackberry, it turned out, was completely hollow. And in that hollow lived approximately forty-five thousand wild honeybees, who came pouring out of the broken trunk the way they do in that scene in *Little House in the Big Woods* where Pa chases a bear away from a bee tree so he can harvest their honey for himself.

Here in suburbia, the homeowners were keeping a wary distance. Who knows how long those bees had been living in our midst, three steps from the street? And yet we'd pushed our strollers and walked our dogs past it every day without a single sting. Even so, the sight of forty-five thousand distraught honeybees pouring into the sky at once can be deeply unnerving. Someone called the Nashville Area Beekeepers Association, and the next morning an expert arrived. He was the one who estimated the size of the hive and captured the queen bee from the fallen part of the tree.

The queen was not hard to find, actually: she was surrounded by an entire army of worker bees who really did not want to share her. But the beeman in his thin shirtsleeves was not alarmed. He just reached in, scooped her up, and installed her in a commercial beehive that he had set next to the fallen tree. Then he gathered several dripping honeycombs and smeared them in and around the hollow to give the bees something to eat while they were looking for their queen.

It was a good plan, a nature-friendly plan to preserve a surprisingly healthy population of a crucial pollinator that's long been in trouble. Every time I took our old dog for a walk, I noticed the bees still pouring out of the standing part of the hackberry trunk, but they were also buzzing around the honey and the hivebox next to it too. Everything seemed to be going according to the brave beeman's plan.

But the wild honeybees, hidden safely from human eyes for so long, had devised their own plan according to an ancient logic that did not involve that hivebox on the ground. Two days later they had gathered in one of the remaining cypress trees: clinging to each other and crawling on top of each other, they formed a giant, roiling, ice-cream-cone-shaped swarm. The whole cypress was humming.

Then one of the scout bees must have returned with word of an acceptable site for a new hive—when I checked again at lunchtime, they were gone. The wind-ruined tree, the hackberry that had kept those honeybees a secret for at least a generation, was silent again.

Confirmation

My mother attended Mass at the little clapboard church for years before she formally joined it. Until then, she wasn't a full member of the congregation and did not receive Communion—she didn't want to upset her own father, the lifelong Methodist. Tucked away in a remote corner of southeast Alabama, my grandfather had never laid eyes on a Catholic before he met his future son-in-law.

The day before the wedding, one of the retired farmers who gathered on the Holsum Bread bench outside the community store had some news for my grandfather: the priest who performed the wedding ceremony would also mount my mother that very night. Hadn't anyone mentioned it? It was a Catholic rule, the old farmer said. The bride must sleep with the priest the night before the wedding to confirm that everything was in working order, to be sure that other crossbacks would appear in due time.

In his wisdom, my grandfather said nothing. Only when my mother was confirmed into my father's church did my grandfather confess the terrible story he'd heard. He hadn't believed it, he said, and anyhow he was relieved she had finally seen her way to becoming Catholic: "I didn't want to say a word, daughter, but a woman belongs in her husband's church."

The Parable of the Fox and the Chicken

The plain yellow chicken stalks the green sward with the other plain yellow chickens and a few baroque brown ones with curling feathers and arching necks. Moving through the grass, they fan out across garden and pasture and compost pile, pausing to warm their reptile feet in its heat. They work tirelessly, clearing stubble and stalk of every small crawling thing too slow for their sharp black eyes and scratching pink toes.

Their eyes cast down, they do not see the fox step out of the trees at the edge of the wood, but the mares see. They push their velvet noses under the pasture fence to watch as the ragged fox pounces. The bird is fat, but perhaps the fox is young; the horses gaze, rapt, upon a struggle that should not be a struggle. The other chickens hasten on heavy wings away, away—up the hill, down the hill, into the low branches of the very trees that sheltered the fox—with no thought of their stricken sister or her shrieking cries or her fruitlessly beating wings.

The barn cat, hardly bigger than a yellow chicken, becomes the unlikely hero of this tale, entering the fray and driving the feckless fox back into the trees. But the cat does not exult in her triumph. The mares do not gaze at each other in amazement. The chicken is not grateful for her rescue. She is hurt but not mortally hurt. A day or two in the safety of the coop, and she will be fine.

Or she would be fine but for her sisters, who cannot, will not, leave her alone. On this hill there is a pecking order, and it is not a metaphor. The hens, not the fox, are now her enemies, the plain yellow chickens and the ornate brown ones alike. She cannot live safely alone, and she cannot live safely with her flock. The hands that fling the corn will dress her for supper, and the fox will go hungry tonight.

The Monster in the Window

The ceiling was sloped in my mother's childhood bedroom, all angles and lines in a sanctuary carved from half the attic. Even the attic itself was an afterthought, added willy-nilly to a peg-built dogtrot: two rooms connected by a breezeway, the only kind of house that makes sense in the oppressive heat of Lower Alabama. By the time my mother came to live there as a child, it had doors, four more rooms, and two attic nooks: one for her and one for her younger brother. Decades later, my own brother and I slept there when she was sick.

The stairs and the walls of that makeshift old house were covered with dark pine boards, and neither the staircase nor the landing was lighted. Climbing the steep steps to sleep alone in those close rooms felt like walking upstairs into a basement, ascending into an underworld. In summer the heat must have been suffocating, but I don't recall the sticky sheets or the hair clinging to the back of my neck or the restless turning all night long. What looms in memory is the fan at the top of the stairs. Built into the huge dormer window on the landing between the bedrooms, it faced out into a damp, bat-blasted night, a vast machine the size of an airplane propeller that pulled air from the screen doors through the still house and up the stairs. There was nothing, no screen or wire cage, between the spinning blades and a little girl's hand. My grandmother told me it would cut off my arm if I tried to touch it.

I never did, was never even tempted to, but at night I would lie in bed and listen to that fan, its roar drowning out the night-singing insects and the crunching tires as my father turned the family car from the dirt yard onto the blacktop, carrying my weeping mother into a blacker night than the one that enveloped our own house in town. I didn't hear them leave. I was listening to the terrible fan, afraid some larger force, something cold and inexplicable, might make me lean into those spinning blades and find myself sucked through and cast by bits into the black, fathomless sky.

When I could bear the darkness no longer, I would pull a string to light the single bulb in the closet. Thumbtacked to the narrow door were the curling tatters of my mother's old life, the life before me, the life before my father: 4-H ribbons and funeral-parlor fans and wedding announcements and corsages with petals turned to powder. I loved especially all the photos of my mother before she was my mother. In one she's posed on the grass, her waist surrounded by the full circle of a chiffon skirt: my mother the daisy, my mother the medallion. In another she's sitting on a low stone wall, the very center in a line of girls in pale dresses, all of them smiling and squinting into the sun.

When did she stop smiling? When did her dresses cease to sprawl so extravagantly across the jeweled grass? I always wondered. At home she would lie in her room with the curtains drawn on long, long Sunday afternoons, but I liked to imagine this other mother, this movie-star mother in the dancing dress with a flower tied to her wrist and a careless smile. That girl did not yet know there was a monster in the window, one that could chew her up and send her out into the night in pieces.

The Snow Moon

Here in this first-ring suburban neighborhood, we are far from the spongy paths of the forest peoples who gave this moon its name, but we are not far from the snow moon itself, which rises through the bare trees as it has done since long before we were here, since long before the forest peoples were here. The world is warming now, and this year the snow moon heralds no snow: the bluebirds are peeking into the sun-drenched nest box, the star magnolia is in full bloom weeks before its time, but still the snow moon rises between the black branches in our postage-stamp yards, as lovely as it has ever been, untouched by all our rancor, unmoved by our despair.

Let the earth cast a shadow across its golden glow. Let the green-headed comet streak past, unclasped, on its journey through the darkness. Still the snow moon rises and sets as it must. It has never burned, and it will never darken: all its light is borrowed light. Its steadfast path is tied to ours. The snow moon brought a time of hunger to the forest peoples, but we are fat in our snug houses, tethered to the shine of our screens. The snow moon is our hungry sister. The snow moon is our brighter twin.

Swept Away

For eighteen years, no one came to the front door of our house in Tennessee but local politicians and trick-or-treaters and teenagers selling magazines. The brick path was slick with moss and buckled by the roots of maple trees, and guests rarely chanced it. Better to follow the driveway around the house and take the stairs to the back door.

My husband's frail parents forced the issue, and we finally replaced the crumbling bricks with scored cement. I am in love with the jaunty stripes of monkey grass along the outside edge, and the solid place to squat as I weed the flower bed. I love to see it gleaming in the darkening light beneath the too-close trees, a welcoming path through the clover. As soon as the cement was safe to step on, I set to keeping it tidy. Left, left, left, I would swing the broom from the center out; then right, right, right, just the same. Left, left; right, right, and in a moment I'd cleared the windfall, put straight the gently curving track, brought to momentary order one bit of chaos.

And then one day: left, right, left, right, I'm swinging the broom like a metronome, like the pendulum of a grandfather clock. Left, right, and suddenly I am a tiny girl holding a broom too large for me, holding it halfway down the handle, dragging it too lightly across the footpath that leads from the road to my grandparents' house. My grandmother is saying, "Honey, swing it back and forth like this." Back and forth, left, right, she demonstrates, and I try, too, the bristles scraping the tops of my bare feet, the broomstick grazing the top of my head as

I bend to watch it whiff the air above the acorn crowns and the twigs and the brown petals from the blown roses and the crumbled bits of rock tracked in from the roadbed. Soon I am more or less copying my grandmother, making the motions my kin have made in this very place for four generations, back to when the path was hard-packed dirt.

Left, right, left, right, and now my grandmother is sitting on the swing in the dark, waiting for us on the porch as we drive down lonely county roads with never more than a single light shining in the towns—some not even towns, not even a crossroads where two blacktops come together in the middle of fields and fields and fields. Our grandmother rises and stands in the doorway while our weeping mother waits in the car, while our strong father lifts my brother and me from the back seat and carries us down the walk, across the porch, and up to the attic room where our mother slept as a girl, the room where my mother was happy as a girl. She is not always happy as a mother.

How long do I lie in the dark, listening? How long do I wait as that ancient house settles and sighs under immense trees that creak in the wind, to hear my father bringing my mother back to me from the long, dark highway? I wait and wait.

But when I turn over in bed, there are lights that glide like fairies across the wall between the shadows of leaves, and downstairs my grandmother is in the kitchen with Eola, who comes every day to help with the cooking and the housework and my ailing grandfather—Eola, who makes the lightest yeast rolls anywhere, and who once baked me a birthday cake like no other I had ever seen: a Barbie doll at the center of a hoop skirt made of frothy frosting. A Scarlett O'Hara cake made by the hands of a black woman who worked for a dollar a day.

And now, on my own front walk, I stand still with my broom and think of Eola, and I'm no longer sure it was my grandmother who taught me the proper way to sweep a sidewalk. Wouldn't it have been Eola? Not my grandmother at all but Eola, who walked down dusty roads in hand-me-down shoes to sweep my grandparents' walk every day of her working life? Wouldn't it have been Eola who offered me a turn when I asked? Eola, who let me string the beans; Eola, who traced my hand in the dough trimmings and baked me a piecrust turkey? Eola, who left behind no recipe for yeast rolls? Eola, forgotten until the seedcrowns brought her back to me on the wind?

Safe, Trapped

Inside the nest box, the baby birds are safe from hawks, sheltered from the wind, protected from the sharp eye of the crow and the terrible tongue of the red-bellied woodpecker.

Inside the nest box, the baby birds are powerless, vulnerable to the fury of the pitched summer sun, of the house sparrow's beak. Bounded on all sides by their sheltering home, they are a meal the rat snake eats at its leisure.

Things I Knew When I Was Six

LOWER ALABAMA, 1967

Flowers that bloom in the garden are called flowers, and flowers that bloom in the vacant lot are called weeds.

A grasshopper leaping away from your feet in the vacant lot sounds exactly like a rattlesnake coiled next to your feet in the vacant lot.

There is no worm hiding in the raised pink circle of skin that your grandmother calls ringworm.

From the top of a loblolly pine, your whole neighborhood looks simple and shabby and small.

When you dare your little brother to break a big rule, your brother is not the one who gets in trouble.

It's a mistake to play leapfrog with a kid who's bigger than you.

The roly-poly and the centipede both have lovely tickling feet, but the centipede will bite and the roly-poly will only roll away.

If your mother is crying and cannot stop, there's a little blue pill in the bathroom that will help her sleep.

Things I Didn't Know When I Was Six

LOWER ALABAMA, 1967

The God you believe in acts nothing like the God other people believe in.

The rhythm method is something secret for grown-ups, and it makes them very mad.

If you have a baby sister, it's because of two X chromosomes, not because you bribed your little brother to pray for the baby growing in your mother's belly to be a girl.

No black people live in your neighborhood even though black people work in every house in your neighborhood.

Just because birds eat the berries doesn't mean you can eat the berries.

Your father's new job in the city isn't better than his old job at home, but his old job went away, so the new job is lucky anyway.

Your mother wants to work too, but there are rules that don't let mothers work.

Sometimes Santa Claus has to wait till the hour before the store closes on Christmas Eve to get the markdown prices.

The hospital in Montgomery is better than the hospital at home because the hospital in Montgomery knows how to help a mother who can't stop crying.

Your mother's tears are not your fault.

Electroshock

LOWER ALABAMA, 1968

"If the baby is a boy, he'll sleep in Billy's room," our father says. "If it's a girl, she'll sleep with you."

I pray the baby is a girl. I tell my brother I'll give him my Jell-O if he'll pray for the baby to be a girl too. When our sister is born, I hold my finger up to her hand, and she holds on, gripping tight. I cannot believe it's possible for a person to have such tiny fingers. I cannot believe such tiny fingers can grip so tightly.

"What was I like when I was a baby?" I ask our mother. "Does Lori look like me when I was a baby?"

"I don't remember very much about when you were a baby," Mama says. "That was a long time ago."

Many, many years later, she clarifies: "I don't remember much about the time just before you were born or the time after that," she says. "The treatments took all those memories away."

And now I understand: before the "treatments" gave her back her life, they took her life away.

In Mist

It came in the night on a cold wind that rattled the windows, and it lingered after the cold rains moved out this morning. It seems to mean that we will have no autumn at all this year. The long, desultory summer has finally given way, but it has not given way to fall. Winter is here now, and to signal its arrival we got just a single night of wind and rain, a single morning of mist beading in the air above the pond and blowing off with the wind.

It won't last. In Tennessee we don't get much of a winter anymore, and highs below freezing are random and uncommon. I like the idea of mist as much as I enjoy the lovely mist itself. Aren't transitions always marked by tumult and confusion? How comforting it would be to say, as a matter of unremarkable fact, "I'm wandering in the mist just now. It will blow off in a bit."

The Wolf I Love

LOWER ALABAMA, 1968

The room is quiet in that humming, vibrating way of a dark house in the country with its windows open to summer. Tree limbs brush the metal roof of the porch with a thousand discrete scratches, each branch and twig a claw. Vast, uncountable orders of insects are just beyond the screen, and every winged creature has joined the whir in the restless leaves. There's a dog sleeping under the porch, his eyes closed and his ears pricked, but I don't know he's keeping watch. My parents are upstairs in the room where I sleep when I stay here without them, and I know they will never hear me over the roar of the attic fan. They will not hear me cry out when something tears this screen away. Neither they nor my grandparents, sleeping likewise beyond my reach on the other side of the shifting house, will hear my keening when great jaws close around me and carry me into the night alone.

I am awake in a house with too many holes in it, and all that lies between me and the dark world is a rusty screen—that, and an old woman in the bed beside mine. My great-grandmother has lived to an enormous age, and I console myself by thinking of how long she has slept safely in this room, all the years she has slept with her windows open to the creaking chain of the porch swing just beyond the screen, and no harm at all has come to her in the night. I hear her sigh and turn in her bed and settle again into stillness. But when the rattle at the window starts, she is silent, and when it grows louder, she is silent still.

"Mother Ollie," I whisper. I tiptoe to her side and put my hand on her shoulder. "Mother Ollie. There's a wolf outside our window. It's trying to come in."

She reaches up and sets her soft hand on top of mine. I feel her listen. There is no sound.

"Honey, that ain't nothing but that old bird dog," she says. "Ain't no call for you to be afraid of that old bird dog."

In seconds she's asleep again, but soon enough the wolf is back, louder than before. The wolf is panting, gasping, growling. The wolf will be through that screen in an instant!

"It's back," I croak, my throat too dry for screaming. "It's back," I try again, too frightened to get out of bed to shake her.

No sooner are the words out of my mouth than the wolf draws back. No longer scuffling and grunting, it is still breathing in the darkness. I hear it breathing as my great-grandmother stirs, and then it is growling again. This time I take the two steps between our beds in a leap, tear back the sheet that covers her, and climb in. The wolf retreats.

I feel my great-grandmother shaking, and I pull the sheet up tight around us both. Her shaking erupts into chuckles. "Honey, that's just me snoring," she says, scooting over to make room for me in her narrow bed and turning on her side to reach around me and pull me closer. "Ain't no wolf gone get my girl."

BLUE JAY

Jaybird, Home

LOWER ALABAMA, 1968

Two weeks before my seventh birthday, my family left the sandy red dirt of the wiregrass region of Lower Alabama and moved to Birmingham, a roiling city built in the shadow of Red Mountain in the southern Appalachians. The move should have been a shock—I was leaving a town untouched by open conflict for a city notorious for its racist convulsions of water cannons and police dogs and church bombings—but I was six. I knew nothing of that. I missed the pine trees.

We returned to Lower Alabama often because my grandparents still lived there, in the house where my grandfather was born, and our long family history and frequent visits might explain why I imprinted on that landscape so wholly. Or perhaps it was the open windows, a time when what happened outside the house was felt indoors, or the innocence that sent children outside to play after breakfast, not to return till hunger drove them home again. I am a creature of piney woods and folded terrain, of birdsong and running creeks and a thousand shades of green, of forgiving soil that yields with each footfall. That hot land is a part of me, as fundamental to my shaping as a family member, and I would have remembered its precise features with an ache of homesickness even if I had never seen it again.

It would take all the words in *Remembrance of Things Past* to catalog what I remember about the place where I was born, but there are three things that can bring it all back to me in startling detail: the sight of a red dirt road, the smell of pine needles, and the sound of a blue jay's call. And of those three, by far the most powerful is the call of the jaybird.

I love the blue jay's warning call, the *jeer-jeer, jeer-jeer* it makes when a hawk is near. I love the softer *wheedle wheedle wheedle* and *please please* song for its mate. Blue jays have an immense range of vocalizations—whirring and clicking and churring and whistling and whining and something you'd swear was a whisper—but the sound they make that takes me right back to 1968 is a call that mimics a squeaky screen-door hinge. I hear that sound coming from the top of a pine tree, and instantly I am in the wiregrass region of Lower Alabama, where the soil is red sand, and pine needles make a scented bower fit for all my imagined homes.

Barney Beagle Plays Baseball

It was already dark outside but not quite suppertime, late in the year we moved to Birmingham, and I don't know why I was alone with my mother in the grocery store. If my brother and sister weren't tagging along too, then my father must have been at home with them, but if Daddy was home, why did I come along with Mama to the Piggly Wiggly at the very worst time of day, when the store was swamped with husbands stopping on the way home from work to pick up the one missing item their wives needed for supper? I might never have been in the Piggly Wiggly at night before, but I knew that men did not understand the rules of the grocery store, did not understand which direction to push the cart to stay in the flow of traffic, did not recognize that standing perplexed in the middle of the aisle is bad grocery store citizenship, especially right at suppertime.

My mother was surely in a hurry. Maybe I was slowing her down as she tried to zip around the bewildered men standing despondent among the canned goods, and maybe she sent me off to pass the time in the corner of the store where books and toys were displayed. Or maybe I wandered off on my own, in those days of retail on a human scale and no thought at all that kidnappers could be lurking in the Piggly Wiggly.

The toys were a familiar, paltry offering—dusty cellophane packages of jacks and Silly Putty eggs and paddleballs and green army men—but the books were mostly new to me. The few children's books at our house belonged to an old-fashioned era of read-aloud classics, fairy tales and nursery rhymes and Bible stories and my own favorite, *Poems of Childhood*. The Piggly Wiggly display featured what seemed to be a vast array of Little Golden Books and early readers. I reached for a green book with a picture in the foreground of a dog wearing a cap turned sideways between its floppy ears. We didn't have a dog ourselves. I had not yet made friends in our new city, and I wanted a dog more than I wanted anything.

I scanned the rest of the book jacket, pausing at the picture of boys in baseball uniforms. I had heard of baseball, but I'd never seen a game, in person or on TV, and did not recognize the outfits the boys were wearing. Why were these boys wearing pajamas outside on the grass? I only glanced at the words at the top of the book jacket. I was learning in first grade the sounds that letters make, but I could not yet read, and words in a book meant nothing to me.

But then, as I stood in the bright light of the grocery store with darkness pooling outside, unable to reach me, the letters on the cover of that book suddenly untangled themselves into words: Barney. Beagle. Plays. Base. Ball. *Barney Beagle Plays Baseball. Oh,* I remember thinking. *Oh, it's about a dog who plays baseball,* and opening the book to see what happened. And only then did I realize I was actually reading the words. I was reading! I went racing to find Mama, dodging despairing fathers peering at can labels, to show her how I could sound out all the words on every page and understand each one. And she was so happy about my happiness that she told me we could bring the book home, even though we had no money at all, and it had not even crossed my mind that she might buy it for me.

Creek Walk

The rocks are gray slate, massive slabs cantilevered over the water as though the outstretched feathers of a great prehistoric bird had been caught in stone. My brother and I are barefoot, picking our way across the rock. We are always barefoot. The pads of our feet are thick, toughened by concrete and asphalt and gravel roads, and anyway shoes would be useless on this slick rock. Worse than useless.

We have not discussed a plan, and so we are making our way to the creek bed with no real intention. We have nowhere to be and nothing to do for hours on end, for days and days on end. It is summer, and autumn is inconceivable to us. School will be reinvented every year, an astonishment every year. Where were the nuns all hiding while we were walking barefoot on the hot concrete?

We are not thinking of school or of the nuns. We are thinking of nothing, or perhaps we are wondering if we will see another rattlesnake. Seeing any snake would be a cause for remark, but we have only once seen a rattlesnake. Mainly we will turn over rocks on the bank of the creek, looking for worms and roly-polies. We aren't fishing—no one has ever taken us fishing; we are not the kind of children who would enjoy fishing—but we know we can summon fish by tossing worms into the water, and we like to feel the fish mouthing the freckles on our legs.

Sometimes there are salamanders on the bank. Sometimes there are tadpoles in the foamy water at the edges of the backwash. Sometimes there are crawdads under the rocks that jut into the water. Always there are dragonflies—blue, and bottle green, and scarlet red—hovering over the flashing water. Always there are jays scolding from the dark pines. We see them and we don't see them, we hear them and we never register their sound. The mud and the moving water smell vaguely of decay, but the smell does not disturb us or inspire the first curiosity. We have never even noted it. These are our sights and our sounds and our smells, as casual to us as the smell of our own breath in our cupped hands, as the sound of our own blood in our ears when we lie down on the biggest rock and hang our heads over the edge to dangle tickletails in the water, tricking the fish into rising.

Farther down, closer to the highway, there are words scratched into the slate on the other bank. The letters are large and ghostly white: F U C K. My brother sounds it out, a perfect practice word for someone still learning phonics from the adventures of David and Ann, the Catholic school equivalent of Dick and Jane. "Fuck," he pronounces, correctly. Then: "What does it mean?"

"It's a word people say when they're mad," I tell him.

I don't know what it means.

We pick our way back toward the bank we will climb to start heading home. Clouds of minnows race from our feet. Clouds of grasshoppers rise from the timothy grass above the rocks. Clouds of gnats hover above the water, part for our small bodies, and coalesce again behind us. We climb out and sit together on the slanted rock to wait for our feet to dry in the hot sun. At home it is almost time for supper, but we can't tell time.

Bunker

All summer long the chipmunks dart in and out of the crawl space through the tunnels they've dug under every side of our house. Open either door and a chipmunk will flee, disappearing into a potted plant, up a tree trunk, or under the front stoop where they have fashioned their bunkers. Solitary creatures except during mating season, they ignore their own kind, each keeping to its personal private entryway into the dark. They are like neighbors who check the mailbox from the car and then drive straight into the garage, never a friendly word.

In and out, the chipmunks rarely stray more than a few feet from the safety of a tunnel. There must be yards and yards of tunnels under our house by now, yards and yards and yards of tunnels, with dens tucked off to the side where the chipmunks deliver their babies in springtime, where they store their acorns in autumn, where they will sleep all winter long.

But they have not yet gone to sleep—deep into October, the temperatures remain stubbornly stuck in summer—and my husband has become unnerved by their frantic bustle as they prepare for the cold. "Look at that," he says, watching them dive for cover when he steps outside. "I think we need to take them out to the park."

"It's too late," I say. "They won't have time to get ready for winter."

"It's ninety degrees out here," he says.

He sets a catch-and-release trap outside one of the tunnels, baits it with peanut butter and birdseed, and heads to the gym. Within two minutes, there's a chipmunk in the cage, digging at the wire with its powerful rodent teeth. "Come back," I text my husband. "You caught one."

But he doesn't come back. Ten minutes pass. Fifteen. Frantically trying to chew itself to safety, the chipmunk is rubbing its gray chipmunk lips raw.

An hour later my husband regards the empty trap. "Where's the chipmunk?" he says.

"I let it go," I say.

"Oh," he says. "OK." He is the kind of man who understands that a sunny and suddenly unencumbered Sunday afternoon is a gift.

I think of the nests the chipmunks have made under our house, the chewed bits of leaves cradling blind babies with translucent skin and only the lightest down for fur. I see them though I've never seen them. I want the hawks to stay in the trees. I want my neighbors to drive carefully in the road the chipmunks keep scooting across for reasons I can't guess. I want the rat snake that lives in the brush pile to be too fat for the tunnels they have made. I want my house to shelter them.

Operation Apache Snow

When the news comes on, my father sits in his chair, swirling just one jigger of Canadian Mist in a glass of ice water and piling up ashes in a silver-rimmed coaster meant to keep the sweating glass from leaving a ring on the end table. Walter Cronkite is on the screen, and I am learning that I say everything wrong. It's ce-*ment*, not *see*-ment. And "Vietnam" is a word that rhymes with "atom bomb," not with "Birmingham." I sit on the floor, my head against my father's knee, and breathe him in: Brylcreem and Aqua Velva and cigarettes and sweat. Smoke drifts around me as Walter Cronkite gives the week's casualty count.

I look up at my brother, who is drawing a picture at the table a few feet away, his tongue tucked into the corner of his mouth, his head tilted in concentration. He has not heard a word. *He would never come home from that place*, I think. *When he leaves for Vietnam, he will not be coming back.*

Of course he will go: this war has lasted my whole life. Every week for my entire life the news report has included a count of the dead. The war will never end.

Smoke settles on my head, on my shoulders, and I practice saying "Vietnam." Viet-*nahm*. I will need to know what to say when I figure out how to get to this foreign land in my brother's place.

BLUEBIRD

Territorial

In late summer, the season of plenty gives way to the season of competition as ruby-throated hummingbirds bulk up for the coming migration, and goldfinches stuff themselves with flower seeds against a lean winter. All day long the hummingbird who has claimed my feeder tries to drive away the goldfinches, and the goldfinches try to drive away the bumblebees, and the bees try to drive away the skippers. No one tries to drive away the red wasp.

Earlier this year the cardinals lost one set of nestlings to illness and another to predators, but now at summer's end they are at the safflower feeder with two healthy fledglings. The young ones follow them around the yard, hollering, and the parents work from dawn to full night feeding them and explaining to the house finch family, over and over again, that the safflower feeder is now off-limits to everyone but juvenile cardinals. When I put mealworms out for the bluebirds, I must sit nearby while they eat, or the male cardinal—in the middle of his August molt and comically bald—will dive at them from the branches like a tiny strategic bomber. This half-acre lot belongs to him, even if the bluebirds and the house finches refuse to defer.

There is still plenty to go around—plenty of flowers, plenty of seeds, plenty of bugs—but the creatures in my yard are not interested in sharing. For them, scarcity is no different from fear of scarcity. A real threat and an imagined threat provoke the same response. I stand at the window and watch them, cataloging all the human conflicts their ferocity calls to mind.

Tell Me a Story of Deep Delight

We are in the double bed. I am asleep, and my sister is scooched over next to me, awake. "Tell me a story," she says loudly. She is old enough to climb out of the crib but too young to know how to whisper. "Tell me a story!"

"I'll tell you a story in the morning," I mumble.

"Tell me *one* story."

"Once upon a time there was a little girl who wanted a story, but her sister was so tired the little girl said, 'OK,' and fell asleep."

I was born for sleep. My baby sister was born for waking. "Tell me a *long* story."

"It takes a while to think of a long story," I say. "You be real quiet and let me think."

Some time later, our mother stops to check on us. The room is dark and silent, but a wedge of light from the hall falls upon her toddler's open eyes. Mama tiptoes to the edge of the bed and squats to whisper in her baby's ear. "Lori, it's late," she says. "It's so late even big girls like Margaret are sound asleep."

"Her not asleep, Mama. Her just thinking of a story."

⸺

As a matter of unreliable narration, this story is hard to parse. I am quoting from memory a story my mother often told, a story that came from her own memory of a time long since past. Though I have no way of knowing how accurate my mother's memory was, I'm confident that I am quoting her word for word. "Her just thinking of a story."

I know these words by heart because my mother told this story many times. I am less confident of my own lines, but I remember well the miniature drama that played out night after night in the old double bed that had come to us from my grandparents, and my sister remembers it too. I would pretend to be thinking of a story—or, in a version my sister swears is true though I have no recollection of it, I would tell her I had to say my prayers—and promptly go back to sleep. She would wait in the darkness, restless, impatient, until she finally fell asleep as well.

I don't know why our mother loved this story so, but my husband and I used to spy on our own young sons at night, listening to them giggling through the baby monitor, listening to them keeping each other awake in the dark. I was amazed at the way their minds worked when they had no sense of being observed—amazed at the way their lives were already unfolding without me. Perhaps my mother, too, loved that peek into the perfect innocence of my sister's trust. And because it was a story she told with such love and absolute delight, I think I can see it, myself:

My sister, flipping from one side to the other. Me, asleep but riding waves of consciousness with each rustle, each exasperated sigh. Our mother, whispering to her little girl, a child full of faith, poised for a magical tale, a story made of just the right words. Waiting for them to drift over her in the darkness and lull her into dreaming.

Acorn Season

We recognize the arrival of acorn season even as the acorns still cling to the white oak growing just outside the bedroom window. They're green, but the squirrels are done with waiting. At dawn they sit in the branches of the magnificent oak and pluck the unripe nuts, taking a single bite before flinging the rejects to our roof: *BAM!* Then—*bam bam bam bam bam bam bam bam*—each one tumbles down the slope and—*BAM!*—slams into the gutter. One after another, a hailstorm of acorns, and all before the sun is up.

One morning I wake to the sound of the alarm, and I know the acorns are ripe. The squirrels are eating them now, passing over the green acorns and getting fat on the brown ones. They are all about acorns—eating them, caching them in the crooks of trees, planting them in the flower beds, in the pots on the deck, in the piles of pushed-up dirt around the mole runs. Squirrels are the Johnny Appleseeds of the oak forest, their tails bobbing up and down in an undulating arc that follows the motion of their thumbless hands, their canny fingers patting the soil gently around each acorn.

Lately the squirrels have been planting acorns in our house. Cooler nights have finally arrived, and the attic above our bedroom is the home they've chosen for winter, an alcove that can't be reached by any human. Before the alarm goes off, I lie in our room below their room and hear them running. What is the rush? They are so close I can hear them stop to scratch their fleas, but they are tucked away where I can't harm them.

They'll chew the wires and burn down your house, someone says. They carry diseases, someone says. No one says which diseases. But there is plenty of advice: poison that makes them so thirsty they'll flee, looking for water but finding instead a place to die; humane catch-and-release traps; humane traps that kill instantly. I don't want to cut a hole in my house to set a trap, and I don't want to kill them—or, worse, turn them into a slow, stumbling poison-delivery system for owls and hawks. I don't want to catch them at all. I want them to move away.

Sometimes I don't even want them to move away. I lie in bed before light and listen to the sound of their feet skittering across my ceiling, and the sound of the acorns they're rolling across it, storing food for winter. They are old friends. Their busy life above my dark room is a lullaby.

Faith

BIRMINGHAM, 1970

In church, under incandescent lights that make the brass candlesticks take on a golden luster, that make the polished pews gleam as though fashioned of marble, I sit between my mother and my great-grandmother, heavy bored by incense and holy water and the swishing of the priest's vestments and the clicking of his hard shoes on the hard floor. "Truly, I say to you," he intones from the ambo, "whoever says to this mountain, 'Be taken up and thrown into the sea,' and does not doubt in his heart, but believes that what he says will come to pass, it will be done for him."

I take my mother's hand and point it toward the lights. I twist it to make the light catch each facet of the diamond on fire. It is an absurd ring for someone like my mother, someone living in an apartment where the rent is paid in exchange for her trouble—for calling the plumber or the electrician whenever another tenant complains, for scheduling the grass cutters, for testing the chlorine level in the pool. The ring belonged to my father's mother, the grandmother I am named for but never met, the one my mother never met, but it has always been on her hand, and I have always played with it in church under a hundred blazing lights.

My great-grandmother's ring is not nearly so grand or so gleaming, but there is another game I play in church with Mother Ollie's hand. I take it in my own and pat it smooth, running my finger across its impossible softness, marveling at the way it ripples under my finger, as yielding as water. My great-grandmother's skin is an echo of her old Bible, the pages tissue-thin, the corners worn to soft felt. I gently pinch the skin above her middle knuckle, and then I let it go. I count to myself, checking to see how many seconds it can stand upright, like a mountain ridge made by a glacier in an age long before mine. Slowly, slowly it disappears. Slowly, slowly it throws itself into the sea.

RIVER

River Light

I try to imagine what it must have been like for the first human beings who moved through this dark forest: to glimpse a flare of light on moving water, to step out of the shadows of the close trees and see the sun flashing on a broad river. To see air and water and light conjoined in a magnificent blaze. That first instant must have felt the way waking into darkness feels—not knowing at first if your eyes are open or closed.

In that instant, the river is not a life-giving source of water and fish and passage. In that instant, it is not the roiling fury that can swallow whole any land-walking, air-breathing creature. It is only itself, unlike any other thing. It was here long before we were here, and it will be here after we are gone. It will erase all trace of us—without malice, without even recognition. And when we are gone to ground and all our structures have crumbled back to dust, the river will become again just the place where light and water and sky find each other among the trees.

Red Dirt Roads

LOWER ALABAMA, 1972

I was eleven, my brother and our cousin ten, and we were old enough to go anywhere our legs could take us: the pecan orchard, the blackberry patch, the cemetery next to the church, the community house next to the cemetery, the store with the gas pump outside and the penny candy display just within its swinging doors. If the adults were worried about the bull a neighbor sometimes pastured among the pecan trees, or the rattlesnakes coiled under the blackberry canes, or the fire ant mounds dotting the cemetery like miniature monuments to another natural order, no one said a word to us, even though my cousin's other grandfather was killed by a rattlesnake decades before we were all born.

Surely someone gave us boundaries of some kind, marked out the territory where our wanderings had to end, but if anyone did I have no recollection of it. I don't remember whose idea it was to turn down a red dirt road between two of our grandfather's fields, a road we'd never been down before, not on foot or on the neighbor's horses. I don't remember how we decided just how far to walk before turning around and heading back to the blacktop road where our grandparents lived. Perhaps it was only the monotony of the peanuts, row after row after row. Maybe we were hot and tired, or maybe that vast, silent expanse of agriculture—uniform, blank, impersonal—began to feel alien and unwelcoming to us. We knew all the varieties of pecans by name, could gather and sort them for market unerringly, ten cents a pound, but we'd not had any hand in the peanut harvest and felt no connection to those fields.

We had already turned around, were already on the way back to our grandparents' house, when the gun appeared. That much we all agree on; that much we all remember the same way. I don't remember the feel of dust in my throat. I don't remember the red sand ringing my toenails, ground into the cuticles, though surely it must have been, for we were always barefoot—it was too hot for shoes, and sandals were useless in the actual sand. But I remember, just as my brother and my cousin remember, the sound of a truck careening down the road behind us in the silence.

Without any sense of trepidation, we moved to the side of the road to let the truck pass. I was in front, my cousin and my brother single file just behind me, though they both stepped farther off the road and drifted to my right when the truck slowed to an idle. Even before I saw the shotgun resting on the frame of the open passenger window, before I realized it was pointed straight at my head, I saw the woman's angry face peering at me from the cab. My brother and my cousin must have seen the gun first. Or perhaps they saw only the baying dogs in the bed of the truck—dogs who could have been over that tailgate in an instant.

"You got no business here," the woman said. "You got no business hanging around this road with my menfolk so close by."

I stopped walking and turned toward her. My brother or my cousin, one of them, tried to push me forward, to make me keep walking, to make me pick up speed. "This is our grand-daddy's land," I said. "We got as much business here as anybody. More than you."

"I'll not have no city girls stealing my menfolk," she said.

I laughed out loud. *Stealing her menfolk?*

Did we hear her cock the shotgun, or did we only imagine the sound? Did I stop talking then? When my brother and my cousin tell this story, they remember being afraid my back talk would get us all shot, but I don't remember a feeling of fear. I only remember thinking it was so funny, the very idea that three children—one of them a boy, though it was the 1970s, and his hair was collar length—might pose a threat to anyone old enough to drive a car or shoot a gun unsupervised.

That's what I remember: the comedy of it, the ludicrous mismatch between the visible reality of the world and some crazy grown-up's inexplicable fears.

Somehow it ended, and the woman roared off in a shower of red dirt, the dogs lurching in the truck bed before finding their footing again.

When we got home we said nothing. We only turned back to hose off our feet when Eola pointed toward the door. No one got shot. No one got bitten by a rattlesnake or gored by a bull. No harm ever came to us, though we were patently in harm's way. It was years before I understood that I was never safe, not even there.

Different

The autumnal equinox comes and goes, but you would never know it by the weather in Tennessee. Most years the temperatures remain in the nineties. The English daisies, which normally bloom in spring, come back for a second, more subdued round of greetings. My mother carried daisies in her bridal bouquet, and when they bloom I always think of her lifelong joy in their sunny faces.

One fall, a daisy sent up a bloom unlike all the others. Instead of a golden disk surrounded by an array of white petals opened mostly flat and facing toward the sun, the flower had a globe-shaped center, and the petals ringing it were perpendicular to the ground. The bees showed no preference for the ordinary daisies in my garden that year, but we humans are acutely attuned to difference and tend to prize any rare variation from the norm. We believe a four-leaf clover brings good luck. A wild crow adopts an abandoned kitten, and the video goes viral. For us, an oddly shaped daisy is cause for surprise, and then for investigation, and ultimately for delight.

With other human beings, though, we aren't so understanding. Children with any sort of physical or cognitive or emotional difference are invariably bullied, and mental illness carries such a stigma that my mother would never speak of her bouts of depression, even after I'd wrestled with depression myself.

And yet, despite our capacity for brutality, human beings are an empathetic species. In 2007, the fossil remains of a severely disabled prehistoric man were uncovered in what is now Vietnam. The skeleton revealed the fused vertebrae and weak bones characteristic of a congenital disease called Klippel-Feil syndrome. The man was a quadriplegic, unable to feed himself or keep himself clean, and yet he survived to adulthood—during the Stone Age, mind you—because others in his community took care of him.

In 1988, during one stop on our honeymoon, my husband and I visited the San Diego Museum of Man. On display at the time was an exhibit of ancient clay figures. The human figures were all visibly different in some way: people with dwarfism, people missing a limb, people with severely curved spines or extra fingers. An informational placard explained that these figures had been fashioned by members of a tribe who revered physical difference. What we call a disability they had considered a blessing: God had entrusted to the care of their community a rare treasure, and even in their art they strove to be worthy of that trust.

Be a Weed

Sometimes, when I haven't slept or the news of the world, already bad, suddenly becomes much worse, the weight of belonging here is a heaviness I can't shake. But then I think of the glister of a particular morning in springtime. I think of standing in the sunshine and watering the butterfly garden, which is mostly cultivated weeds punctuated by the uncultivated kind that come back despite my pinching and tugging. I think of the caterpillars on the milkweed plants, unperturbed by the overspray, and the resident red-tailed hawk gliding overhead, chased by a mockingbird and three angry crows, and the bluebird standing on the top of the nest box protecting his mate, who is inside laying an egg. I think of that morning—not even a morning, not even an hour—and I say to myself, *Be an egg. Be a mockingbird. Be a weed.*

TOMATO

The Imperfect-Family Beatitudes

B lessed is the weary mother who rises before daybreak for no project or prayer book, for no reason but the solace of a sleeping house and a tepid cup of instant coffee and a fat dog curled on her lap. Hers is the fleeting kingdom of heaven.

Blessed is the suburban father whose camping gear includes two hundred yards of orange extension cord and a box fan, a pancake griddle, a weather radio, a miniature grainy-screened TV with full-sized rabbit ears, and another box fan. He shall keep peace in the menopausal marriage.

Blessed is the farm-born mother, gripped by a longing for homegrown tomatoes, who nails old roller skates to the bottom of a wooden pallet, installs barrels of soil and seeds on top, and twice a day tows it through the grass to the bright spots, following slivers of sun across the shady yard. She shall taste God.

Blessed is the fatherless father who surrenders his Saturdays to papier-mâché models of the Saturn V rocket or sugar-cube igloos or Popsicle-stick replicas of Fort Ticonderoga, and always to scale. In comforting he shall be comforted.

Blessed is the mother whose laugh is a carillon, a choir, an intoxication filling every room in the house and every dollar-movie theater and every school-play performance, even when no one else gets the joke. She will be called a child of God.

Blessed is the winking father who each day delivers his children to Catholic school with a kiss and the same advice: "Give 'em hell!" He will be summoned to few teacher conferences.

Blessed is the braless mother who arrives at the school pickup line wearing pink plastic curlers and stained house shoes, and who won't hesitate to get out of the car if she must. She will never be kept waiting.

Blessed are the parents whose final words on leaving—the house, the car, the least consequential phone call—are always "I love you." They will leave behind children who are lost and still found, broken and, somehow, still whole.

Night Walk

It's a crazy cartoon of a moon, over the top even by Hollywood standards. No one would ever believe this moon on a movie screen: the outrageous roundness of it, the deep gold hue, the way it's settled in the center of a soft nest of light against a warm black sky, above stark black branches. Gray clouds are rushing across it in a wind so high the moon winks and recovers as quickly as it would in a time-lapse film.

What a rebuke this weather has been to my own frequent claims that fall and spring are the seasons of change, that nothing much happens in winter. The last days have brought balmy, shirtsleeves sun and brutal, bone-tightening cold and this tree-bending wind. And now the wind is bearing in a cold rain, already sputtering down in horizontal pellets.

When the moon no longer emerges from the clouds and the rain picks up, the dark world closes. The screen goes black, and now the soundtrack is all that matters. A neighbor's wind chimes jangle, and then another's. A clatter of bare sycamore branches and a lighter rattle of seedpods in the dried trumpet vines climbing a power pole. The snapping fabric of a flag. A castanet of stiff leaves in an ancient magnolia standing unperturbed in the rush of air. Maple leaves scudding down the rough asphalt. A train whistle. A siren. A wary greeting from the three-legged dog behind her fence, warning me to come no closer in the dark.

Every Time We Say Goodbye

"Every time we say goodbye, I die a little," Ella Fitzgerald is singing while my parents dance on an ordinary Tuesday afternoon. My mother is barefoot. My father is wearing his work shoes, but my mother's toes are in no danger. These steps are as familiar to them as their own heartbeats. As familiar as the words of this song.

I stand in the doorway and watch, embarrassed by something I can't even name. My father's arm is around my mother's waist. My mother is on tiptoe, her arm across his shoulders, her head tucked beneath his cheekbone. Their other hands are intertwined, held between their hearts. Their steps are so practiced, so perfectly in sync, not a single inch opens between them as they spin.

Gall

At a dinner party, I ran into another writer whose subject is often backyard nature—a writer who lives in the same town, though we'd never met in real life before. "So you're a trained naturalist?" she asked. I had to confess I'm more of a Googler. I grew up playing in the woods, and all my life I've turned to woodland paths when the world is too much with me, but I am no scientist. It took a lot of nerve for someone so ignorant of true wilderness to fashion herself as a nature writer, but the flip side of ignorance is astonishment, and I am good at astonishment.

One spring I was standing at our bedroom window with my camera, using the zoom lens to search for a house wren I could hear but couldn't see, when I noticed something odd on a branch of the oak tree that grows just outside the window. A spongy white pod, about the size of a golf ball, protruded from the very tip of a thin branch. I had never seen one before and couldn't guess what it was. A cancerous growth? A cocoon? The seedpod of a parasitic plant? And what search-engine terms could possibly yield an answer?

"Puffy white ball on the end of an oak twig" finally turned up an image that matched the object on my own oak tree. It was a growth called a gall. There are many different kinds of galls, but this one was made by the wool sower gall wasp, a small black insect that lays its eggs in winter at the tender ends of young branches. The eggs hatch in springtime, just as the twig begins to put on new growth. Then the larvae produce a chemical secretion that forces the tree to form a gall, a protective woolly home where they can live until they are ready to take to the air.

The transformation of any sort of grub into any sort of winged being is a metamorphosis I will rearrange my life to witness, so I checked on the woolly gall every day, many times a day, hoping to be on hand the precise moment the young wasps emerged into the light of springtime.

The oak, meanwhile, was not ready to surrender its own purposes: instead of wool sower gall wasps, what emerged from the gall was a pair of perfectly formed but apparently dwarfed leaves. In time these leaves began to stretch out languidly, not exactly like but also not entirely unlike a typical oak leaf. The gall was taking on the appearance of something pregnant with an alien life-form, and that alien fully intended to hatch.

More than a month passed with no sign of the wasps. I continued to peer at the gall through my bedroom window, if less and less often throughout the day. By the time another month passed, the gall had begun to shrivel and collapse in on itself. Clearly, I had missed the emergence of the wasps, but I kept going to the window to look at the gall anyway, out of a vague remaining curiosity, and possibly out of habit, too.

What I wanted, I think, was some sort of closure, some reckoning of what it means when a thing in nature makes what it needs from only what it has on hand. But as with all other matters in nature and in life, I entered this story in medias res: unaware of its beginning and owed no right to witness its end.

The Honeymoon

The day I started my first period, my father invited me for a walk after supper. It was a typical walk, a familiar habit, until he spoke: "Your mother tells me you became a woman today," he said.

He was holding my hand—at thirteen I was still holding my father's hand with half my body even as I was bleeding with the other half—and reflexively I pulled away. Are there any words more appalling to a girl savoring the privacy of new transformation? If a volcano had erupted below my feet in the heart of Alabama, I would gladly have gone up in ash.

My mother had offered nothing beyond the pragmatics: instructions on how to work the straps to the belt that came with the box of pads she'd pulled down from her closet shelf. How often to change the pad. How to wrap it up and take it to the kitchen trash can, which the family dachshund could not reach. The absolute, unvarying importance of that trash can.

I never knew if she had asked my father to broach the subject, or if she had merely passed along the day's news over the glass of whiskey they always shared before supper, a relic of postwar civility in the chaotic days of Watergate and Vietnam and never enough money in our hollow-doored apartment outside town.

Catholics aren't squeamish about sexuality, and my education at Our Lady of Sorrows School had already included a unit on human reproduction, including a poster-sized diagram of the female reproductive system and a teacher armed with a pointer stick and a holler-it-out insistence on correct pronunci-ation: fa-*loh*-pee-an, *oh*-va-ry, en-do-*mee*-tree-um, *clit*-or-is. All in the context of a religion-class unit on family life and the moral implications of sexuality.

It would take more than a year for Mom to make her own half-hearted attempt at The Talk. I laughed out loud before she'd gotten a whole sentence out of her mouth, and that was the end of the subject. In all the years afterward, I never heard her make even a veiled reference to her own sexual life or to mine. My mother, I decided, was something of a prude.

I don't remember when I found the lone honeymoon photo in my father's sock drawer. It was a black-and-white Polaroid of Mom wearing a frothy gown-and-peignoir set. She's stand-ing in a doorway, her hair freshly brushed, and the corner of a bed is visible in the foreground. Her smile is open, utterly guileless, happy.

"Where's this?"

"I took it on our wedding night," my father said, taking the photo from me and peering at it. It was a picture of Mom moments before she joined him in bed for the first time—a pic-ture of a woman who was not suffering even a hint of shyness.

As a child I would ask my mother, "But why did you wait so long to get married?"

Sometimes she would cite, obliquely, the Catholic prohi-bition against birth control: "We couldn't afford to have a fam-ily yet." Sometimes she would say, "We loved to dance. Once we got married and the babies came along, there wouldn't be many chances to go dancing."

No money for children. No money for a sitter. *I* was the reason they had waited so long. I, who lived nestled in their love like a world-sized cradle. I, who had always felt so sub-limely like the center of their universe. They hadn't wanted me to join them yet. They had wanted to keep dancing.

After my mother's death, I found the rest of the honey-moon pictures in a box that had sat in an Alabama attic for more than fifty years. In the one I think of as the morning-after companion to the wedding-night picture, Mom is the photographer, and Dad is the subject, standing before the mirror in a motel bathroom, shaving. But it's Mom I like to imagine. I think I can see her, barefoot in the doorway to the bedroom, relishing the intimacy of life with her new husband, the man who had not yet become my father.

In Which My Grandmother Tells the Story

of Her Brother's Death

LOWER ALABAMA, 1976

I've left out when Wilfred died, haven't I? Well, in May—no, in June—of 1976, he was down to go with us to the church reunion, and he had Joseph with him, his first grandchild, and was so proud of him. And Mother went home with them that Sunday, to be there with them the next Sunday, which would be Father's Day. Wilfred left for a business trip on Tuesday. And of course he kissed them goodbye, and on Thursday they called to say they had found him dead in a motel room where he had gone back to take some medicine, some blood pressure medicine. Well, it upset us terribly because we had just seen him so well.

Mother, of course, was brokenhearted because she had lost a child. When she went to the casket to see him the first time, she stood there and looked at him and said, "Why couldn't it have been me?" And she sobbed, and that's the only time she cried. When they brought her to our house on the day of the funeral, I went out and hugged her. And she had a few little tears but not much. She was real composed. And so he was buried on Saturday before the Father's Day that she was to spend with him.

Squirrel-Proof Finch Feeder,

Lifetime Warranty

The steel grommets around the miniature openings, fit only for conical beaks, cannot be chewed open by even the most persistent rodent. Both the top and the bottom of the feeder detach for ease in filling and cleaning, but the pegged fittings can't be managed by thumbless hands. The seed is black niger—a feast for goldfinches, distasteful to squirrels. So say the experts at the bird supply store.

The experts have not met this squirrel. He takes the feeder by the perches, one in each hand, pulling it to his mouth like an ear of sweet corn at a Fourth of July potluck. He makes his own mouth small to match the cleft mouth of the feeder, and he licks the seeds out, one by one. This is an embrace, a kiss that goes on for hours. Seed by seed, he fills his belly. He has nothing but time, and the squirrel-proof finch feeder, impervious to fury and force, is undone by patience and time. He knows I am at my desk barely more than an arm's reach from the window, but I do not concern him. I am only watching through the window, and I do not in any way concern him.

There Always Must Be Children

At the end of our great-uncle's funeral, our great-aunt stopped the pallbearers as they carried him out of church. She fell upon the casket, trying to reach with her frail arms all the way around it and wailing like one whose own life was ending. All five of us, my brother and sister and both cousins, watched from the front pew, entirely untouched by devastating loss. Our parents and grandparents went to our aunt and surrounded her and held her up when her legs could no longer bear her weight.

We looked at each other. What would happen next? And what would we ourselves be called upon to do? Our favorite aunt, howling with uncontainable grief, resembled no human being we had ever seen.

When the next-youngest child coughed to disguise a laugh, the rest of us collapsed between the pews. We huddled together on the board floor and buried our faces in our arms, strangled by swallowed laughter.

Tracks

Walking around the neighborhood soon after we moved to the house that decades later he would die in, my father tapped his toe against the place on the side of the road where rusted trolley-car tracks emerged from the asphalt. "Every day I would wait right here for my father to get home from work," he said. "Every day he got off the trolley and asked, 'Have you been a good boy?' And every day I would have to tell him no." He hadn't minded his mother, or he'd fought with his brother, or he'd bothered the chickens. And then the grandfather I never met would walk home with the little boy who grew up to be my perfect father, and he would spank that child with a belt.

My grandfather died in a car accident when my father was five years old, and my father remembered almost nothing about him except one thing: that every day when he was a boy he would meet his father at the trolley stop and walk home with him for a beating.

In Which My Grandmother Tells the Story

of My Grandfather's Death

LOWER ALABAMA, 1977

*L*et me see, it was on the Thursday before Christmas. I brought him home from the hospital, and he seemed so happy, and I was happy. I'd had him a chair moved in—I bought a chair and had them to bring it. I said, "Be sure to have it there by ten o'clock," so they had. The hospital had one that he could sit in and press himself up. He had said, "I want a chair like this," just offhandedly, so that was the kind it was.

In the car I could see him observing the trees and where things had been planted and just everything. He was very alert. And we drove into the yard, and Max Junior was there under the pecan tree. So we got Max out with his walker, and he walked around the front of the car, and we got the door open, and he got just inside the door. And I said, "You see your Christmas gift over there?" and he nodded his head.

And that was it. His feet began slipping out, and I held him until he got to the floor, and Max Junior and I did all we could. Neither one of us knew much about resuscitation. And Nina called down to the store, and there wasn't but one man there and he came, but she also called the paramedics. And everybody worked on him. I don't think he ever breathed again.

We got to the hospital, and the doctor came out and said, "It was just too late."

"No," I said. "Is he gone?"

And he said, "Yes. It was just too late."

Well, Max Junior and I both just almost collapsed. The doctor got hold of us and he said, "If I had been right there I couldn't have done anything." Said, "Everything about him just quit at once."

And we went back and called Olivia, and of course all of you were there by morning. Now that was on Friday, you see. Well, we had to bury him on Christmas Eve. And the day of his funeral it was just pouring rain, and I remember very distinctly how many people came anyhow, even if it was Christmas Eve and raining like it was.

And when we got back to the house I went to bed, and all five of y'all came in there quietly—I wasn't asleep, but you came in there very quietly—and said, "Mimi, will it be all right for us to fix a Christmas tree?" I said, "Sure you can." I said, "Granddaddy would want you to."

MARIGOLD

My Mother Pulls Weeds

The kitchen can be full of unwashed dishes, both counters covered in granules of spilled sugar and puddles of congealed milk. The tops of the curtains can be dusted with droppings from the cockatiel who screeches his sorrow so plaintively that she cannot bear to cage him for long. The chairs in the living room can be piled high with laundry, and magazines dated years earlier, and junk mail still leaved together with the unpaid bills, and my sister's forgotten schoolwork, the manifold worksheets of a child still in elementary school. My mother's need for order has nothing to do with the chaos of a life with too little space and too little money and almost no chance to make something beautiful of it all. The chance to create loveliness is always waiting just past the door of our matchbox rental.

She never prepares for gardening—no special gloves, no rubber garden clogs, no stiff canvas apron with pockets for tools. No tools, most of the time. She steps out of the house—or the car, setting her bags down before she even makes it to the door—and puts her hands in the soil, tugging out the green things that don't belong among the green things that do. Now another bare square of ground appears, and there is room for marigold seeds, the ones she saved when last year's ruffled yellow blooms turned brown and dried to fragile likenesses of themselves. The light bill might be under the covers at the foot of her bed, the unsigned report card somewhere in the mess of papers on the mantel, but she can always put her hands on last year's seeds. And later, in the summer, the very ground she walks on will be covered in gold.

Fly Away

BIRMINGHAM, 1978

His face was ridiculous: the rouged cheeks of Raggedy Andy, an elaborate Kabuki crest. He had the run of the house, swooping from curtain rod to curtain rod and door top to door top, joyfully shredding the newspaper and nibbling the spines of my books, his round gray tongue probing at the bindings, searching for glue. Though he knew a few human words, he spoke mostly in his own inscrutable language, muttering conspiracies to my sister's toys, shuffling among the stuffed animals and attempting to incite a riot. Claiming a teddy bear for his mate, he hissed at my sister, his yellow crest flattened, if she tried to take it away.

When I called, he flew to me, but he bit my lip at least as often as he held still for a kiss. He loved to be scratched, offering up each angle of his face to my fingers, and his trust thrilled me. I rubbed behind his crest, under his white-ringed eyes, beneath his gray beak. I could feel the hot skin beneath his feathers and the swift pulse just beneath the skin. When new feathers came in, he would present himself for preening, waiting as I unfurled each one, rolling them between my fingers. The powdery new feathers smelled earthy and alien at once.

He came to harm at times—singed feathers when he flew too close to an open flame on the gas range, an entire toenail lost to a slammed door—but he complained so bitterly in his cage, pacing the wooden perch, biting the bars, clutching the closed door with both feet and screeching, that we always gave in to his demand for freedom. The bounded freedom of our 1,300-square-foot house.

Inevitably, he flew away. Propping the storm door open with her hip one day, my mother stooped to pick up a bag of groceries, and he landed on her head before launching himself into the sky. He lingered in a tall pine, waddling along one branch and hopping to another as I stood below, holding my finger in the air and calling. Soon I couldn't see him in the gathering gloom, but I followed the sound of his voice as he talked to himself: "Pretty bird. Kiss, kiss, kiss." I didn't see him leave the pine.

Days later, more than a week, a miracle: my father woke me on Sunday morning, newspaper in hand. There, in full color, perched on an old man's finger, was our wayward cockatiel. We knew him instantly by the missing nail on his crooked gray toe. My father called the paper and somehow reached the photographer, who gave vague directions and a general description of the house.

We made the drive past factories and industrial parks to a part of town that couldn't rightly be called "town" anymore, with dirt driveways, bunched trailers and clapboard shacks, and lots overgrown with struggling saplings. A world I couldn't reconcile with the world.

We knew the house by the broken-down car out front, a cinder block where one of its wheels should have been, and the peeling red paint. It was some time before the old man from the photograph answered our knock. Opening the door, he stepped back, and my father stepped back too, explaining. The man pointed at the car. "No window screens here at the house," he explained.

I took the steps two at a time. The bird was lying on the back seat, his feet curled, his body still warm—from the heat of the closed car, perhaps, or because he'd died even as we stood on that porch asking for him. I held him in my hands and wept, pressing him to my face. All I remember for sure of that moment is his familiar smell. And the sight of my father and the old man standing together, side by side, at the bottom of the crumbling steps.

Church of Christ

O ne day my father picked me up from the children's shoe store where I worked after school and pulled into the Church of Christ parking lot around the corner from our house. Then he shut off the car and said, "Your mother's been crying all day. She thinks you don't love her."

I looked at him. I had no idea what he was talking about. "Why would she even *think* that?"

"She says you had an argument this morning. She wouldn't tell me what it was about or what you said to her. What could you have possibly said to your mother to make her cry all day?"

I was seventeen. I had given no thought to my mother that day. I gave hardly any thought to either of them on any day at all. Even prompted in the dark church parking lot, I could not recall a single conversation that might have made my mother cry.

I said, "I don't remember having a fight with Mom before school."

Migrants

Every spring my bird-watching neighbor across the street tells me she is waiting for the rose-breasted grosbeaks to return to her feeders for a day or two during their long, long migration, and every spring they turn up, right on time, to feast on the safflower seeds she puts out especially for them. I keep a safflower feeder up all the time—primarily to discourage visits from European starlings, who dislike safflower seeds—and so I started looking for the rose-breasted grosbeaks every spring, too. I was always disappointed.

Then, one year, I had grosbeaks every day for two solid weeks. At first they were skittish, heading into the trees as soon as I stepped out the door, but they got to know me. I could walk around the deck, watering plants, sweeping, and they would peer at me from the back side of the feeder for a few moments before going back to their meal. All day long they lined up for a turn, it seemed, waiting on the nearest branches until a perch opened up at the feeder.

Tennessee is just a way station for the grosbeaks, who spend winter deep in the rain forests of Central and South America but mate and rear their young primarily in the northernmost reaches of the United States and Canada. Appalachia appeals to them too, and my neighbor is sure that our guests are headed to the mountains of northern Georgia. And why not? Her guess seems as good as any.

But guessing is getting harder to do as the songbird migration is complicated by the effects of climate change. The timing of spring has shifted, and migratory songbirds, leaving the equatorial jungles at the usual time, arrive in North America too late for the food sources they expect to encounter along the way. For thousands and thousands of years, the path of the migrating songbird has been synced to the growing season of plants that now bloom and fade out of their once typical seasons. What will the birds eat if the berries they rely on have long since withered by the time they arrive? Is that why the grosbeaks—one of the species most affected by changing climate patterns—finally came to my feeder? Why they came and stayed and stayed and stayed?

Wherever they have been, and wherever they are going, it's the birds only passing through our region that excite the most interest from serious birders. I am not myself a serious birder, but I still feel a thrill when I notice a new face at the feeder, a stranger at the birdbath. I treasure these glimpses of the exotic, this sense of having traveled to distant lands, and hearing, however briefly, their strange, foreign songs. One evening I looked out, and there in the growing twilight was a male scarlet tanager taking a drink. I had never seen one in this yard before, and I have not seen one since. But I think often of that beautiful bird, of the few seconds I could stand at my window and watch him taking drink of water in the gloaming. To me he looked like a blood-red, hollow-boned embodiment of grace.

Prairie Lights

Even in a land-yacht station wagon, we were piled in too tight: in the back seat, my high school boyfriend and his angry sister, with me between them so their skin never touched in the heat; their parents up front; the little brothers ricocheting around in the wayback with all the suitcases. When we were halfway across the endless Midwest, moving fifty-five miles an hour through towering forests of corn and sunflowers, the car's anemic air-conditioning went out entirely and with it any cheer that could be produced by an I Spy game or a lunchroom carton of chocolate milk from the cooler on the front seat.

When we got to the tidy town on the plains of Colorado, all the aunts and uncles and cousins poured out of the grandmother's house, a great constellation of kindness come to meet us and welcome the family home. Someone mentioned that the Perseids would be putting on a fine display the following night, and someone else offered to bring blankets to the clan's usual spot on the prairie, and my boyfriend's father explained that I, a child of the damp, congealed air of Alabama, had never seen a night full of stars like the one I would see that night in the high, thin air above the plains of Colorado.

Though it was August, we had to put on sweaters when they woke us deep in the night, and though we were all still so tired from two days of driving in the heat, my boyfriend and his sister didn't quarrel, laughing instead to remember another childhood trip to see another meteor shower, and when we turned off the road onto the grass, the soil of the prairie was not at all flat and smooth but jarred us till our heads bumped the roof of the station wagon. Everything surprised me. I understood that I understood nothing at all.

And, oh, the stars were like the stars in a fairy tale, a profligate pouring of stars that reached across the sky from the edge of the world to the edge of the world to the edge of the world. Even before the first meteor winked at the corner of my eye, I tilted my head back and felt the whole planet spinning, and instantly I dropped to the ground and hunted for something to hold fast to before the prairie tilted and tossed me into the black void that holds this tiny blue world.

In silence the family lay together, quilts set edge to edge. Across the grass I could hear the mother still trying to coax one of the younger boys out of the car, telling him she would hold him tight, but he would not budge. "I'm too little," he said. "It's too big, and I'm too little."

ECLIPSE

A Ring of Fire

In the winter of 1991, my brother read Annie Dillard's ecstatic essay about watching a total eclipse, decided then and there to see it for himself, and looked up his next chance to see one in the continental United States. When that date turned out to be impossibly far in the future—not till 2017—he and my sister-in-law made plans to view another eclipse from a mountain in rural Mexico, the nearest possible place to see the shadow of the moon obscure the sun.

There is some disagreement now about what they actually saw. My sister-in-law remembers a wall of darkness hurtling toward her across the Mexican valley, just as Annie Dillard describes. My brother only remembers reading about it. Did they see the shadow of the moon traveling across the land at 1,800 miles an hour, or did they conflate the experience of reading about an eclipse with actually seeing one? Could it have happened so fast that an ill-timed blink meant my brother missed what my sister-in-law saw?

I wanted to see this exceedingly rare phenomenon too, but I didn't want to see it in some distant, unfamiliar part of the world. I wanted to see it in my own country, in the company of blue jays. I wanted to see splintered light glinting on all the intricate webs that our own micrathena spiders had strung across narrow footpaths in the night. I wanted to see sun parings wink through the wild rose of Sharon flowers—an effect of the partial eclipse that turns a forest into a great pinhole camera, projecting images of the waning sun onto the ground and leaving moon-shaped holes in all the shadows.

In 2017, I had my chance. I arrived at a nearby field in a

public park to find it already ringed by people speculating about exactly when each known effect would take place. When would the color of the sky deepen? When would the air begin to shimmer, as though lighted by some other planet's sun? When would the birds fly into the trees to roost?

Then there was my own unvoiced question: When it's all over, will I know what I saw? Will I be able to tell the difference between what I saw and what I had merely been primed to see?

I still don't know. I know only that something ineffable, something beyond the reach of my own language, happened in the ordinary sky. The air turned blue and then silver. A dog barked. A bird whose song I don't know began to sing and then abruptly fell silent. The air cooled, and suddenly Venus was gleaming in the midnight-blue pitch of the sky. The people under the trees at the edges of the meadow had moved into the darkness of the open field. By the time I looked down again, they had gathered a sheen that made them all look like angels.

And at the center of everything was a ring of fire in the sky, a thin sliver of flame that burned as brightly as the sun but was nothing like the sun. It was nothing like anything else I have ever seen, but I recognized it anyway because it was exactly like something I have heard. In Nashville, you can hear it wafting from the open door of any honky-tonk: a song about love, about desire. Like desire, it burned, burned, burned, and it made me feel puny and insignificant but also ablaze with life. The ancients believed an eclipse would bring the end of the world, but the end of the world did not come for me.

I didn't wait for the sun to wax full again before heading home. I had to get out of there without talking to any of my fellow mortals, without hearing any of their earthly concerns. I had to leave while the air was still full silver. And all the way home, tiny crescents bespeckled the road, a path of fractured light that led me back to my own place in the world, right to my very door.

Once Again, the Brandenburgs

By the spring of our senior year, we knew our teacher was dying. In truth she had been dying for some time, since the winter we were juniors, but her faith was unshakable, and she had young children at home, and so she believed this cancer, like the one that had claimed her breasts when she was only a teenager, was just a blackberry winter—an out-of-season cold snap that will not last or cause permanent damage. We believed, too, because how could we not? We were children. Death had no hold on us.

Spring came to Alabama, but it did not come to our teacher, whose hair was gone by then, her voice barely more than a whisper. She had long since ceased to lead the class in any conventional way. On good days a family member would drive her to school and help her to our classroom, but most days were not good by then, and she would send someone from home to collect our work or give us another task. Assignments came through her wavering voice played back on a cassette tape—notes on what to look for in our reading, assignments for our presentations on Shakespearean tragedy or the Romantic poets or the novels of Thomas Hardy. I remember so much about those books and plays and poems, the kinds of details I remember from no other high school class. I still know great chunks of *King Lear* by heart.

Of all the memorable moments of that memorable year, the one that has held me through my own calamities is a story we read the spring we realized our teacher was dying. She came into class carrying a thin box of records and a sheaf of photo-copied papers, and behind her came her stepfather, pushing a cart from the library that held a record player.

But here the recollection comes undone. Picturing that day now, I'm suddenly not sure about those papers I think I see stacked on top of the box of records in her arms. Maybe she didn't hand out the story as copies; maybe it was bound instead in the textbook we had hardly opened all year. All these images are absolutely clear, but I know better than to trust them. I have turned them over so often the edges have become soft and worn, their contours wholly unreliable.

I know it was the story of a man during wartime who sat in the back of a boxcar and closed his eyes and removed himself from the massacre by playing Bach's Brandenburg Concertos in his mind. And after we had read it, our teacher opened the top of the record player, carefully removed an LP from its sleeve, and placed it on the turntable. When she set the needle down, the sound of Brandenburg Concerto no. 1 filled that windowless, cinder-block room.

I could not believe that something so beautiful, so otherworldly, had been conceived by a human mind and brought to life by human hands. So many of the other details of that day have fallen away—surely there was a class discussion, though I don't recall it—but that high, haunting violin in the second movement of Bach's Brandenburg Concerto no. 1 in F Major is something I will remember till I die.

It has been decades since the English class that burned itself into me and the death of the teacher whom I will always love. As grief has piled on grief in that way of time, I think I've come to understand why a soldier would find solace in such timeless music, which I have heard since then in recordings and on the radio more times than I can count. But when I heard it live for the first time, when I sat and listened to an orchestra play all six Brandenburg concertos, all I could think of, in the midst of that unfathomable beauty, was a line from *Lear*: "Why should a dog, a horse, a rat, have life, / And thou no breath at all?"

While I Slept

I was dreaming about babies in cages, and while I slept it began to snow. Piled deep, hushed and hushing, it rounded the rough edges of the world in a way I'd seen before only in picture books and movies. I came downstairs in the unfamiliar house to peer from the windows in the kitchen. In the stillness before dawn the room seemed full of light, though all I could see outside were shades of sepia and iron, ocher and ash. The gray was muffled, giving way to whiteness.

I was visiting a friend at his childhood home, a prewar infirmary on the grounds of an orphanage. The tour he'd given me only hours before already seemed like a dream summoned by the bewilderment of travel. But it was not a dream. Abandoned children still lived in the dormitory buildings just across the way. My friend's father ran the orphanage, and the infirmary had been refitted for him and his family. Their bedrooms were in the old nurses' quarters on ground level. The ancient clinics were below in the basement. The operating room—its instrument trays and enamel tables left behind, thick with dust— was on the second floor, where I was sleeping. Most forsaken of all was the dormered attic that once served as a nursery: metal cribs still lined the walls.

I stood at the window in the dim kitchen and watched the snow pour from the sky. I don't know how long I stood there before something just outside the window began to take shape in the dawn light, something alive with movement and still somehow immobile. Finally a bird feeder untangled itself from the limb of a hackberry tree, and all around it cardinals were jostling for space. The snow was falling, and they were falling too, and rising again—a blur of movement within movement against the still backdrop of fallen snow and black branches, a scarlet tumult reeling from feeder to spilled seed and back, again and again and again. I stood in the window and watched. I watched until I knew I could keep them with me, until I believed I would dream that night of wings.

PIEBALD FAWN

Seeing

I have poor vision, the result of an uncorrected lazy eye. In some babies born with amblyopia, the lazy eye wanders, but my eyes had no noticeable misalignment, so no one knew I was seeing with only one eye. The way to improve a lazy eye is to patch the dominant eye, but the window for correction is small. By the time I finally went to an ophthalmologist, I was nearly thirty years old—decades past the age when a patch would do any good.

Because the part of the brain that develops in conjunction with the eyes did not receive sufficient input during those early years, I still see mainly through one eye and always imperfectly, even with glasses. I was born into a strong family history of blindness—my grandmother went blind from glaucoma, my mother had macular degeneration, her brother suffered blood clots in both eyes—and I take no day with vision for granted. I am filled with gratitude for the sight I have.

And yet I can't help but wish I could see better. I look forward every spring and fall to the songbird migration, but I have only rarely seen the tiny traveling wrens and warblers. Binoculars are of limited help when the brain doesn't develop in a way that produces binocular vision—although if someone says to me, "Look!" and points in the right direction, binoculars can give me a good idea of what's there. To see the smallest creatures truly, I rely on a camera with a zoom lens, and even then I have to upload the images to my computer and look at them on a larger screen to know for sure what I've photographed.

One of the nicest things about the lake where I like to walk is that there is nearly always someone on the trail saying, "Look!"

Thanks to that natural human urge to share something wonderful, even with a stranger, I have learned this lake's terrain over the years and know where to look for the well-disguised secrets I would miss on an unfamiliar path. I know that a barred owl frequently perches in a dead tree near a particular bridge. I know that a great blue heron often stands as still as a photograph on a submerged log in one cove. I know the rise where wild turkeys drag their wing feathers on the ground and blend in with the leaf litter, and I know the bank where beavers climb soundlessly out of the lake. One summer I knew where to look for a hidden hummingbird's nest because of a stranger with better eyes than mine.

I also knew where to look for a piebald fawn who was born in these woods late one spring, but knowing where to look is not the same thing as seeing what you're looking for. Walking around the lake with my niece that fall, I mentioned that I'd long been hoping to see the white fawn, and half a minute later she said, "Look! There it is!" And there the fawn surely was, coming through the trees, her mother and twin right beside her.

That fawn was a sight to behold, glowing among the shadows, picking her way through the white snakeroot grown nearly as tall as she was. At one spot, following her mother, she seemed to encounter an obstacle too large to step over and took a sudden leap into the air. For an instant her delicate hooves flashed in the late afternoon light. If I'd had a camera, and if I'd clicked the shutter at just that moment, she would have looked as though she were taking flight.

The trail was busy—the trail is always busy on weekend afternoons in pretty weather—and all around us people were saying to each other, "Look!" and stopping to watch the piebald fawn walking along the deer path. Parents were picking up their children and holding them high: "Look!"

Farther down the trail, my beautiful niece, whose eyes see twenty-twenty even without glasses, paused before a fallen tree covered with shelf fungi. She pointed to a ladybug nearly hidden in the folds. "When I was hiking in Colorado, I saw a whole bunch of ladybugs, so I checked Google to see if there's a name for a group that gathers in one place," she said. "It's called a 'loveliness.'"

In Which My Grandmother Tells the Story

of Her Mother's Death

LOWER ALABAMA, 1982

Well, sometime after that, then, Mother broke her hip. After we got her out of the hospital, we thought we were going to bathe her, but she wouldn't let us bathe her. There's a place in the Bible that says the children should not look on their parents uncovered, or something like that. I don't remember the words, but she was a firm believer of that. She'd let Eola bathe her, though.

She continued walking with her walker, but was having terrible pain. She was real touchy on her hip. And so we went back to the doctor, and he made X-rays. And he said, "The pins have slipped." Said, "They're going into the flesh is the reason you're having so much pain." And said, "Now, I can take them out right here in the office and give you relief, but you won't ever walk anymore." But said, "We can go to surgery, and I can put in a ball." And so she said that's what she wanted to do.

The surgery went great, and it don't seem like it was very many days before they began taking her to therapy. And she came in one time, and she was just smiling. And she says, "I took a few steps today." And so we were all just so pleased.

But she didn't want to eat, and I was trying to get her to eat. And I said, "Oh, Mother, don't do like that!" when I was trying to feed her. And she looked at me, you know, so strange, and she said, "You don't usually talk to me like that." I was scolding her.

The next morning, I reckon it was, I was in the room with her, and I got up and walked over to Mother and put my hands on her arm, and it was just burning up. So about that time the doctor walked in, and I said, "Doctor, she is just burning up with fever." He switched right around and went to the desk, and he called the other doctor, and they got me out of the room and they did a spinal tap, and she was all the time saying, "Mildred, don't let them do this." And you know I couldn't do anything about it, and Mother never did talk anymore after that.

When Olivia called that time, she said, "Mother, you want me to come?"

And I said, "Well, why don't you wait until we go home."

And she said, "I'm coming for you, not for Mother Ollie."

The next morning they said, "She's become a medical problem now," and they moved us up to the next floor. I always will feel angry toward them. Because they knew she was dying.

They got her in this room, and she laid just as quiet, didn't move a muscle. I had gotten my cot in, and Olivia was sitting in the big chair, and she was where she could see Mother Ollie, you know. And finally she said, "Mother Ollie's not breathing." And she was gone just like that.

Redbird, Sundown

Everywhere else, in every other place where the wide sky reaches, the space beyond the trees is still blue, the black branches spread out on a flat plane as if cut from construction paper, as if pasted in delicate tracery on an azure scrim. The pure, blinding blue that reaches from treetop to treetop in the east is the only sign that this is not a sepia world made entirely of brown grass and rustling beech leaves, pale as dawn light, and the dormant hydrangea's dry ghost petals and the white scaling of the sycamore.

The earth has faded, but the sky will not give up its right to color, doubling down in the west with reds and oranges and yellows. The light catches in the bare branches of the maple and clothes it in a fleeting dream of autumn, all pink and auburn and gold. The cardinal perched near the top of the tree bursts into radiance, into flame, and for that moment nothing matters at all—not the still soil nor the clattering branches nor the way this redbird will fall to the ground in time, a cold stone, and I too will grow cold, and all my line.

Never mind. Mind only this tree in winter and this redbird, this tiny god, all fiery light leading to him and gathered in him, this lord of the sunset, this greeter of the coming dark.

Twilight

I went to a land-grant university, a rural school that students at the rival institution dismissed as a cow college, though I was a junior before I ever saw a single cow there. For someone who had spent her childhood almost entirely outdoors, my college life was unacceptably enclosed. Every day I followed the same brick path from crowded dorm to crowded class to crowded office to crowded cafeteria, and then back to the dorm again. A gentler terrain of fields and ponds and piney woods existed less than a mile from the liberal arts high-rise, but I had no time for idle exploring, for poking about in the scaled-down universe where forestry and agriculture students learned their trade.

One afternoon late in the fall of my junior year, I broke. I had stopped at the cafeteria to grab a sandwich before the dinner crowd hit, hoping for a few minutes of quiet in which to read my literature assignment, the poems of Gerard Manley Hopkins, before my evening shift at the dorm desk. But even with few students present, there was nothing resembling quiet in that cavernous room. The loudspeaker blasted John Cougar's ditty about Jack and Diane, and I pressed my fingers into my ears and hunched low over my book. The sound of my own urgent blood thumping through my veins quarreled with the magnificent sprung rhythm of the poem as thoroughly as Jack and Diane did, and I finally snapped the book closed. My heart was still pounding as I stepped into the dorm lobby, ditched my pack, and started walking. I was headed *out*.

It was a delight to be moving, to feel my body expanding into the larger gestures of the outdoors. What a relief to feel my walk lengthening into a stride and my lungs taking in air by the gulp. I kept walking—past the football stadium, past the sororities—until I came to the red dirt lanes of the agriculture program's experimental fields. Brindled cows turned their unsurprised faces toward me in pastures dotted with hay bales that looked like giant spools of golden thread. The empty bluebird boxes nailed to the fence posts were shining in the slanted light. A red-tailed hawk—the only kind I could name—glided past, calling into the sky.

I caught my breath and walked on, with a rising sense that glory was all around me. Only at twilight can an ordinary mortal walk in light and dark at once—feet plodding through night, eyes turned up toward bright day. It is a glimpse into eternity, that bewildering notion of endless time, where light and dark exist simultaneously.

When the fields gave way to the experimental forest, the wind had picked up, and dogwood leaves were lifting and falling in the light. There are few sights lovelier than leaves being carried on wind. Though that sight was surely common on the campus quad, I had somehow failed to register it. And the swifts wheeling in the sky as evening came on—they would be visible to anyone standing on the sidewalk outside Haley Center, yet I had missed them, too.

There, in that forest, I heard the sound of trees giving themselves over to night. Long after I turned in my paper on Hopkins, long after I was gone myself, this goldengrove unleaving would be releasing its bounty to the wind.

In Which My Grandmother Tells the Story

of the Day She Was Shot

LOWER ALABAMA, 1982

*I*t was the twenty-ninth day of November. I had been sewing and
became tired and bored. This was like many days since Mother
died in September. She had been such a comfort to me when my
husband died in 1977. Now it seemed I had no anchor.

I decided to drive down to our little country store, where I
was sure I would find my best friend and her son, who owned it. I
had been there about ten minutes when a man came to the door
and asked about some oil for his car. Thomas asked him whether
he wanted the can with the red label or the can with the green.
The man went out to his car and came back with a rifle.

I was sitting in a rocking chair just inside the door to his
left. When I looked up, he was pointing the gun at Thomas to his
right. I yelled, "Thomas!" The man turned on me and fired into
my chest. This gave Thomas time to get his own handgun. He
fired twice at the man, killing him instantly.

It seemed ages before anyone could call an ambulance. They
also called the sheriff and the coroner. All the way to the hospital I was conscious and in terrific pain. After surgery I had the
strangest feeling that there was a ring around me holding me up
or protecting me. I'm sure now it was the Lord's presence. I was
on all kinds of life supports—breathing machine, heart machine,
oxygen, IV, catheter, etc. But I had no thought that I might not live.

I left the hospital on December 23. When the doctors or others would say, "It's a miracle that you're alive," I always replied, "I know it is a miracle because my God answers prayer."

All the time during my husband's last illness and then my mother's, I prayed to be strong for them. I wanted to look after them. Then, when they were gone, I thought, Nobody else needs me. Now I know the Lord wants me for something else, and I'm praying for him to show me what it is.

Babel

PHILADELPHIA, 1984

I thought I had escaped the beautiful, benighted South for good when I left Alabama for graduate school in Philadelphia in 1984, though now I can't imagine how this delusion ever took root. At the age of twenty-two, I had never set foot any farther north than Chattanooga, Tennessee. By the time I got to Philadelphia, I was so poorly traveled—and so geographically illiterate—I could not pick out the state of Pennsylvania on an unlabeled weather map on the evening news.

I can't even say why I thought I should get a doctorate in English. The questions that occupy scholars—details of textuality, previously unnoted formative influences, nuances of historical context—held no interest for me. Why hadn't I applied to writing programs instead? Some vague idea about employability, maybe.

When I tell people, if it ever comes up, that I once spent a semester in Philadelphia, a knot instantly forms in the back of my throat, a reminder across thirty years of the panic and despair I felt with every step I took on those grimy sidewalks, with every breath of that heavy, exhaust-burdened air. I had moved into a walkup on a main artery of West Philly, and I lay awake that first sweltering night with the windows open to catch what passed for a breeze, waiting for the sounds of traffic to die down. They never did. All night long, the gears of delivery trucks ground at the traffic light on the corner; four floors down, strangers muttered and swore in the darkness.

Everywhere in the City of Brotherly Love were metaphors

for my own dislocation: a homeless woman squatting in the grocery store parking lot, indifferent to the puddle spreading below her; the sparrows and pigeons, all sepia and brown, that replaced the scolding blue jays and scarlet cardinals I'd left behind; even deep snow, which all my life I had longed to see, was flecked with soot when it finally arrived. I was so homesick for the natural world that I tamed a mouse who lived in my wall, carefully placing stale Cheetos on the floor beyond me, just to feel the creature's delicate feet skittering across my own bare toes.

If I was misplaced in the city, sick with longing for the hidebound landscape I had just stomped away from, shaking its caked red dirt from my sandals, oh, how much more disrupted I felt in my actual classes. The dead languages I was studying—Old English and Latin—were more relevant to my notions of literature than anything I heard in the literary theory course. The aim of the course, at least so far as I could discern it, was to liberate literature from both authorial intent and any claim of independent meaning achieved by close reading. "The text can't mean anything independent of the reader," the professor, a luminary of the field, announced. "Even the word 'mean' doesn't mean anything."

To a person who has wanted since the age of fourteen to be a poet, a classroom in which all the words of the English language have been made bereft of the power to create meaning, or at least a meaning that can be reliably communicated to others, is not a natural home. I was young, both fearful and arrogant, and perhaps I had been praised too often for an inclination to argue on behalf of a cause.

"The word 'mean' doesn't mean anything"—these were fighting words to me. I raised my hand. "Pretend we're in the library, and you're standing on a ladder above me, eye-level with a shelf that holds *King Lear* and *Jane Fonda's Workout*

Book," I said, red-faced and stammering, sounding far less assured than I felt. "If I say, 'Hand me down that tragedy,' which book do you reach for?"

The other students in the class, young scholars already versed in the fundamental ideas behind post-structuralist literary theories, must have thought they were listening to Elly May Clampett. They laughed out loud. I never raised my hand again.

Once, not long after I arrived in Philadelphia, a thundering car crash splintered the relative calm of a Sunday afternoon outside my apartment, and the building emptied itself onto the sidewalk as everyone came out to see what happened. I'm not speaking in metaphors when I say that my neighbors were surely as lost as I was: mostly immigrants from somewhere much farther away than Alabama, they couldn't communicate with each other or with me—not because we couldn't agree on the meaning of the words, but because none of the words we knew belonged to the same language.

Bare Ruin'd Choirs

The miserable heat of summer lingered and lingered and lingered, and the drought deepened and deepened and deepened, from moderate to severe to extreme. Most leaves simply curled up from the edges, fading from green to brown before dropping to the ground with hardly a flare of color to remind us that the world is turning, that the world is only a great blue ball rolling down a great glass hill, gaining speed with each rotation.

My favorite season is spring—until fall arrives, and then my favorite season is fall: the seasons of change, the seasons that tell me to wake up, to remember that every passing moment of every careening day is always the last moment, always the very last time, always the only instant I will ever take that precise breath or watch that exact cloud scud across that particular blue of the sky.

How foolish it is for a mortal being to need such reminders, but oh how much easier it is to pay attention when the world beckons, when the world holds out its cupped hands and says, "Lean close. Look at *this*!" This leaf will never again be exactly this shade of crimson. The nestlings in the euonymus just beyond the window will never again be this bald or this blind. Nothing gold can stay.

And yet in winter the bare limbs of the sycamore reveal the mockingbird nest it sheltered all summer, unseen barely a foot above my head, and the night sky spreads out its stars so profusely that the streetlights are only a nuisance, and the red-tailed hawk fluffs her feathers over her cold yellow feet and surveys the earth with such stillness I could swear it wasn't turning at all.

Thanksgiving

Winter break came so early in December that it made no sense to go home for Thanksgiving, no matter how homesick I was. But as the dark nights grew longer and the cold winds blew colder, I wavered. Was it too late? Could I still change my mind?

It was too late. Of course. It was far, far too late. And I had papers to write. I had papers to grade. Also, I had no car, and forget booking a plane ticket so close to the holiday, even if I'd had money to spare for a plane ticket, which on a graduate student's stipend I definitely did not. Amtrak was sold out, and the long, long bus ride seemed too daunting. I would be spending Thanksgiving in Philadelphia, a thousand miles from home.

"I don't think I can stand it here," I said during the weekly call to my parents that Sunday. "I don't know if I can do this."

"Just come home," my father said.

"It's too late." I was crying by then. "It's way too late."

"You can always come home, Sweet," he said. "Even if you marry a bastard, you can always leave him and come on home."

My father intended no irony in making this point. He had never read Thomas Wolfe—might never have heard of Thomas Wolfe. These were words of loving reassurance from a parent to his child, a reminder that as long as he and my mother were alive, there would always be a place in the world for me, a place where I would always belong, even if I didn't always believe I belonged there.

But I wonder now, decades later, if my father's words were

more than a reminder of my everlasting place in the family. I wonder now if they were also an expression of his own longing for the days when all his chicks were still in the nest, when the circle was still closed and the family that he and my mother had made was complete. I was the first child to leave home, but I had given no thought to my parents' own loneliness as they pulled away from the curb in front of my apartment in Philadelphia, an empty U-Haul rattling behind Dad's ancient panel van, for the long drive back to Alabama without me.

I gave no thought to it then, but I think of it all the time now. I think of my father's words across a bad landline connection in 1984 that reached my homesick heart in cold Philadelphia. I think of the twenty-six-hour bus ride into the heart of Greyhound darkness that followed, a desperate journey that got me home in time for the squash casserole and the cranberry relish. I think most of my own happiness, of all the years with a good man and the family we have made together and the absorbing work—everything that followed a single season of loss, and only because I listened to my father. Because I came home.

BLUEBIRD

The Unpeaceable Kingdom

In spring, I used to search for nests. I would part the branches of shrubs and low-limbed trees, peering into their depths for a clump of sticks and string and shredded plastic—the messy structure of a mockingbird's nest. I would squat and look upward for a cardinal's tidy brown bowl. I scanned the ivy climbing the bricks, searching for a hammock tucked into the leaves by house finches. I checked the hanging fern for the vortex tunnel built by a Carolina wren. I watched at my window for blue jays flying into and out of the tree canopy and tried to pinpoint the exact Y-crook in the branches where they'd hidden their young.

For ten years, this was my faithful nesting-season ritual because our little dog, Betty, a feist mix, was hell on fledglings. In her leaping, tree-climbing youth, I took down my feeders and emptied my birdbath, determined not to invite songbirds into the yard. They nested here anyway, perhaps because our lot backs up to a patch of sheltering woods, perhaps because birds will nest more or less anywhere.

I couldn't keep Betty in the house all spring and summer, but I could certainly keep her inside during the few days when new fliers are most vulnerable. But to do that I needed to know when the babies were likely to leave the nest, and to know *that* I needed to find the nests and keep watch over them. If I knew the species of bird on the nest, and I knew the day her eggs hatched, I could make a good guess about when her young would fledge.

The problem with knowing something is that I cannot un-know it. Knowing there are two eggs in the redbird nest means knowing not only an approximate fledge date for the redbird babies but also exactly how many eggs the rat snake ate between yesterday afternoon, when I checked on the mama bird, and this morning, when I found her nest empty. The loss you don't know about is no less a loss, but it costs you nothing and so it causes you no pain.

Human beings are storytelling creatures, craning to see the crumpled metal in the closed-off highway lane, working from the moment the traffic slows to construct a narrative from what's left behind. But our tales, even the most tragic ones, hinge on specificity. The story of one drowned Syrian boy washed up in the surf keeps us awake at night with grief. The story of four million refugees streaming out of Syria seems more like a math problem.

The grief of the failed nest echoes in an entirely different register, but it is still a grief. In Tennessee it's common for cardinals to nest twice in a season, hatching between two and five eggs each time, but few of their young will survive. The world is not large enough to contain so many cardinals, and predators must eat, too, and feed their own young. It should not trouble me to know the sharp-eyed crow will feed its babies with any hatchlings it steals from the cardinals, but I have watched day after day as the careful redbird constructed a sturdy nest in the laurel, and I have calculated how many days and nights she has sat upon those eggs, how many trips she has made to the nest to feed the babies, how many times she has sheltered them through a downpour. Day after day after day.

After Betty died, I stopped checking my yard for nests in springtime, but my eyes are tuned now to the signs of nesting—to the male blue jay feeding the female on the limb just past my deck, to the tufted titmouse plucking loose fur from my surviving dog's haunches as he sleeps in the sun, to the chickadee gathering moss from the deepest shade at the back of the yard. And I can't unsee the nests they build.

It's wrongheaded to interfere in nature when something is neither unnatural nor likely to upset the natural order. I can't help myself. A crow lands too close to the redbird nest, and I rush outside with my broom. A red wasp chases a brooding bluebird from the nest box, and I rub soap into the wood of the birdhouse roof. It's humiliating, all the ways I've interfered.

In recent weeks I've watched a pair of Carolina chickadees building a nest in the bluebird box outside my office window. When a bluebird arrived and tried to evict them, I stood outside in the pouring rain and put up another nest box a few yards away. The bluebird gave it no notice, but he stopped pestering the chickadees, and all seemed well. Then a house wren showed up.

One year a wren killed a chickadee nestling on my watch, so when I heard the unmistakable trilling of a house wren calling for a mate, I looked reflexively toward the bluebird box where the chickadee was sitting on five speckled eggs. There was the brown wren, a feathered fusion of music and violence, perched right on the roof of the birdhouse and singing a song that could only be a territorial claim. The new nest box, empty and pristine, was ten paces away, but that one didn't interest him. I got up from my desk, went outside, and walked straight toward him until he flew away.

Two days later the chickadee was gone, her nest empty, and I watched from the window as two male bluebirds fought over the box, leaping into the air and knocking each other to the ground. In the underbrush at the edge of the yard, the wren was still singing.

March

I lived less than a hundred miles from Selma, Alabama, but I was three years old on the day in 1965 that came to be known as Bloody Sunday. Twenty years later I knew next to nothing still. I knew state troopers had clubbed six hundred peaceful African Americans as they knelt to pray for courage on the Edmund Pettus Bridge, but I had never heard of Jimmie Lee Jackson, murdered for believing in the right to vote. I didn't know that the idea for the march first took hold when someone said they should carry the body of Jimmie Lee Jackson to Montgomery and lay it on the capitol steps so George Wallace could see what preserving white supremacy actually looked like.

In 1985, knowing so very little, I walked in the commemorative march from Selma to Montgomery on the twentieth anniversary of Bloody Sunday. I wish I could claim it as a long-held plan, but I hadn't meant to march. I had driven south with two friends to join in the rally, to hear the speeches after the march was all over. But far outside town, just past Prattville and the sign warning travelers to GO TO CHURCH OR THE DEVIL WILL GET YOU, the northbound lanes of I-65 had been closed to automobiles and our side turned into a two-lane thruway. Drivers in both directions were confused, or just curious, and traffic was hood-to-trunk, hardly moving. Clearly we were never going to make it into Montgomery for the rally, so we pulled over and parked. Just then the first group of marchers arrived on the other side of the road, heading into the city.

They were exuberant, singing and laughing, walking hand in hand or with their arms around each other's necks. Some of them looked across the median blooming with crimson clover and saw us leaning against our car. We waved. They waved back.

Then a handful of them were beckoning, and without even pausing to look at one another, my friends and I were dodging between the slow-moving cars and heading across the median. Seeing us coming, the entire group sent up a cheer; several of them—those closest to the spot where we joined the line—hugged us, draping their arms across our shoulders and singing at the top of their lungs the words to a song I'd never heard before.

More than three decades later, I can still exactly recall the smile on one older woman's face as she reached out to grab my sleeve and pull me into the throng of marchers. I can still smell the damp clover in the median. I can still feel my burning cheeks and my thumping heart. But no matter how joyful, how hopeful, I suddenly felt—no matter how desperately I wanted to—they were singing a song I didn't recognize, and I couldn't add my voice to theirs. I could not sing along.

Still

I pause to check the milkweed, and a caterpillar halts mid-bite, its face still lowered to the leaf.

I walk down my driveway at dusk, and the cottontail under the pine tree freezes, not a single twitch of ear or nose.

On the roadside, the doe stands immobile, as still as the trees that rise above her. My car passes; her soft nose doesn't quiver. Her soft flanks don't rise or fall. A current of air stirs only the hairs at the very tip of her tail.

I peek between the branches of the holly bush, and the redbird nestling looks straight at me, motionless, unblinking.

—

Every day the world is teaching me what I need to know to be in the world.

—

In the stir of too much motion:
  Hold still.
  Be quiet.
  Listen.

Homesick

I left Philadelphia, but in between the determination and the act were many humiliations: endless weeping, an illness I couldn't seem to shake, incompletes in all my courses. I actually went back to Philadelphia in January, determined to start all over again, but forty-eight hours later I bought a ticket on a train heading south. When I lurched into the club car near midnight, I was not surprised to find a guy in back playing hobo songs on a harmonica. I had become the tragic heroine in a Willie Nelson movie.

I could have looked for more congenial courses, shifted the focus of my study. Instead I spent the semester as a typist for Kelly Girl, as a substitute teacher at my old high school, as the lone night clerk at a Catholic bookstore. On the way home from work, whatever "work" happened to be that day, I would stop at the video store and rent *Harold and Maude*. I always checked the new-release shelf just in case anything more appealing had come in, but nothing ever did. Night after night it was *Harold and Maude*.

I pretended to everyone, including myself, that I would be going back to school; as soon as I felt better, I would complete the final papers I owed my first-semester professors and be ready to start again in the fall. My parents held their tongues. On the way to the kitchen late at night, my father would walk through the dark living room, pause a moment, and ask, "Whatcha watching, Sweet?"

"*Harold and Maude.*"

"Ah."

Clearly I was going nowhere, least of all to Philadelphia.

In June, back at my old college for my brother's graduation, I hid from the professors who had written my graduate school recommendations, the ones who had been so pleased to aid my escape. But walking through the experimental fields I'd stalked in despair only two years earlier, I ran into my former Latin teacher, the kind of old-school professor who teaches an overload unpaid—convening class at seven in the morning, before any other classes began, five mornings a week, for more than two years—because the university wouldn't sched-ule a Latin literature course for only four students. I ended up sitting on his porch for an hour, lamenting the failure of self-knowledge that had led to my miserable fate.

"Don't go back," he said. "Go with Billy to South Carolina instead. Get your master's in writing while he gets his in art. Write poems instead of papers."

Sitting on that front porch in the heat of an Alabama sum-mer, with grasshoppers buzzing in the ag fields just across the road and bluebirds swooping off the fence posts to snatch them up, I considered the alternate future he was laying be-fore me: a life of poems. It was a lifeline to a life.

Revelation

The fog comes on little cat feet, as everyone knows, but the fog does not sit on silent haunches except in poems. In the world, the fog is busy. It hides stalking cat and scratching sparrow alike. It blunts sharp branches, unbends crooked twigs, makes of every tree a gentler shape in a felted shade of green. Deep in the forest, it wakes the hidden webs into a landscape of dreams, laying jewels, one by one, along every tress and filament. The morning sun burns in the sky as it must, but the world belongs to the fog for now, and the fog is busy masking and unmasking, shrouding what we know and offering to our eyes what we have failed to see.

FIG

Nature Abhors a Vacuum

In South Carolina I found my way back to myself. All it took was an ant swarm on a glittering chain-link fence, thousands of new wings glinting like silver in the sun. An escaped hawk trailing its zoo leash, joyfully killing pigeons on the state capitol steps. The heart-tripping sight of a brown water snake coiled in a tree in the Congaree swamp. The sulfurous scent of a dogwood tree outside my window split in half by a lightning bolt. The whinny of a screech owl in the dark. The taste of fresh figs.

Two by Two

In springtime the chickadees bring bits of moss to the nest box; and the redbird feeds his mate, seed by seed; and the bluebird carefully inspects every nest site her suitor escorts her to, hoping one will meet her standards; and the red-tailed hawks circle the sky on opposite sides of the same arc; and the bachelor mockingbird sings all night long. He will keep on singing until someone accepts his song.

The Kiss

The bench was hard, curved and flat in all the wrong places. The grass was too damp to lie in, and the night swarmed with mosquitoes the likes of which can be found only in a river basin in South Carolina—large and insistent and more numerous even than the roaches. The slippery Skin So Soft I'd applied hours earlier in lieu of DEET was sticky by then and doing nothing to repel mosquitoes, despite my own best organic intentions. My favorite teaching skirt was getting ruined—hopelessly wrinkled, flecked with flaking green paint, and smeared with bird droppings. None of these things registered with me.

But they must have registered somehow, at some point, because decades later I recall them all perfectly—the feel of the bunched fabric of that long cotton skirt, the salty-sweet smell of Skin So Soft mingled with human blood from slapped mosquitoes, the wet grass licking at our ankles and pooling at our feet, the way the seat of the bench was too deep and cut off circulation to my knees. I was Edith Ann in the old *Laugh-In* skit, my legs sticking out, too short to touch the ground. I was also nothing like a child.

We were alone in the back of an unlighted pocket park, hardly more than a vacant lot with a rusty swing set in the middle, located somewhere between the attic apartment where I lived with my brother and the classroom where I was teaching undergraduates to write. It was already getting dark when a man in my graduate program—a friend who might be on the verge of becoming something more than a friend, although who can ever say for sure about a thing like that so early on, when the question first forms itself into a question?—had offered to walk me home.

We hadn't walked far before suddenly neither of us was in any hurry to get me there. I don't remember how we drifted from the sidewalk to the bench, or how we even knew the bench was there in the dark, or whether we wandered over to it while there was still light in the lengthening April day and simply stayed till the light ran out. I don't remember where I set the tapestry bag my mother had made to carry all those ungraded papers back and forth on my long walk to class. I don't remember taking off my shoes, or hitching up my skirt, or whether I was hungry, or how we started kissing. All I remember is the kiss that lasted for hours in the dark, a kiss that ended only when the darkness had gone from black to almost gray and was moving on toward dawn.

I Didn't Choose

The night after my husband and I brought our first child home from the hospital, my mother and father cooked a celebratory meal. I looked around the festive table, happy to be home. I was grateful for the loving man I had married, for the loving parents who had raised me, for the new little person who had come into the world in the midst of all that love.

Hot tears welled up so suddenly my eyes blurred. One drop fell onto my plate and quivered in the candlelight: a miniature dome of inexplicable sadness.

My husband noticed first. "Honey!" he said. "What is it?"

"I don't know." The tears poured down.

Maybe it was hormones at first, but weeks passed and still I cried. I cried because it hurt to nurse. I cried because I had no instinct for baby talk and felt foolish trying. I cried because I missed myself. I would look at my puffy face in the mirror. *What has happened to me?*

What happened to me: depression, mastitis—raging infections over and over again—loneliness, a baby who needed to be held all the time, and it never crossed my mind that he was simply cold. It was January, and the world was full of microbes. The pediatrician told me not to take him out until his immune system was stronger, so I fed him, and I held him, and everything else fell away. We moved from bed to sofa and back again, day after day after day. I smelled of sour milk and vomit. My hair hung limp in my eyes because I was too tired to lift a hand and push it behind my ears.

At the baby's eight-week checkup, the pediatrician looked at her clipboard. "Are you still nursing?"

My throat closed up. By the time she looked at me an instant later, tears were falling onto the baby's head, one fat drop after another. She put the clipboard down. "Tell me about it," she said.

I told her about the midnight trips to the emergency room, my breasts on fire, my teeth chattering from fever. I told her my baby was always, always hungry. I told her I did nothing all day but feed him. I had to bite a dry washrag to keep from crying out.

The doctor leaned forward and put her hand on my arm. "The best mother is a happy mother," she said. "Give that baby a bottle."

Overnight my baby stopped crying, surfeited for the first time in his hungry life. He would drop off to sleep, his whole body at ease, arms and legs as limp as a rag doll's. He slept and slept. The days grew warmer and longer. I pushed his stroller to the park, and we watched the older children play. All day long he smiled at me with a look of love so rapturous I felt unworthy. No one had ever loved me that purely. As a girl, I was as wholly loved as any child on earth, and I was sure this baby loved me even more than that. And the love he felt for me was nothing at all to my love for him.

But I missed my teaching job. I missed having people to talk to. I missed spending my days considering the greatest literature produced in my language. My baby slept and slept, and I was restless. Finally I buckled his tiny self into the car with an absurd amount of gear and drove home to Birmingham.

"You loved your job, too," I said to my mother, who had once been a home-demonstration agent with the county extension service. Before I was born, she had traveled the back roads of Lower Alabama carrying pattern books in her trunk, stopping at community houses and church fellowship halls to show the rural women gathered there what the latest fashions looked like, to teach them the latest sewing techniques. Later, she had chafed so much at the monotony of life with young children that her frustration was clear to me even as a child. "You talk about that job all the time. Why did you decide to stay home?"

"I didn't *decide*," she said instantly, with a bitterness I had never heard in her voice before. "I didn't *choose*." She had been forced to resign as soon as she was visibly pregnant with me. By law the mothers of children too young for school could not work for the state of Alabama.

I remembered, then, a time when my mother went to work in my father's office, though she could neither type nor take dictation—and suddenly it made sense to me. My mother had chosen work, even work she was not qualified to do, over staying home with her children. I thought of how desperate I felt during my seemingly endless maternity leave. If staying home was this hard for me, with an end point in sight, supported by my very culture, how much harder must it have been for her in 1961?

In another age, or in another place, my wildly creative mother might have been very different. She was a woman who designed and made her own clothes, who loved to jitterbug, whose laugh was so infectious even strangers turned, searching for the source of her joy. Perhaps she would have gone to art school, thrown ecstatic parties. Perhaps she would have been happier in even a small-town life, instead of retreating every afternoon into a darkened room, curtains closed against the heat. Perhaps she wouldn't have needed her little girl to tiptoe in with a blue pill and a glass of water in the gloom.

In Bruegel's *Icarus*, for Instance

GULF SHORES, 1993

It was our son's first trip to the beach, and I had dressed him in a swimsuit for children who cannot swim: it reached from his throat to his knees, blocks of buoyant foam sewn into pockets circling his chest and belly—the soft toddler belly that swelled with each breath. "He looks like a suicide bomber," my husband said. In those days we still joked about suicide bombers here, where such creatures seemed almost imaginary, dwelling on the other side of the world.

"I don't want him to be afraid of the ocean," I said.

"He's not afraid," my husband said. "You're afraid."

So I settled our boy on my hip and carried him straight into the water—ankle-deep, knee-deep, hip-deep, waist-deep. He kicked his fat feet and his squat toes. I turned to look at my husband, triumphant. He was already striding toward us from shore, his long legs pushing through the waves.

I never saw the one that rose up behind me, the one that crashed over my head, knocked me over, and snatched our baby from my arms. I remember clearly the sudden silence beneath the brown water, though surely a churning ocean could not have been silent. I remember my own hair dragging the sand through that murk—however improbably, decades later, I still see my hair swaying against the floor of the sea.

When I finally found my feet, when I finally pushed my streaming hair away from my face and wiped the stinging water from my eyes, the absurd swimsuit had done its job, if poorly: our boy had risen, too, but yards away, bobbing upside down on the surface of the spent wave as it pulled back from shore, his white legs scissoring the air.

My husband reached him first, swim-team strokes of decades past closing the gap in a moment, and scooped our baby up and carried him to shore, those small lungs coughing out all the water in the world.

By the time I reached them on the sand, they were smiling. No tragedy had touched us, no catastrophe but the near loss I still carry—the shadow that, even now, I cannot set down.

All Birds?

NASHVILLE, 1999

Except for the splayed wing feathers, the robin in the street was unrecognizable. "What dis?" my three-year-old asked, squatting to peer at it.

"That's a bird," I said.

Toddlers are severe enforcers of norms, and my middle child was not having this explanation. "Dat not a bird," he said. "It not flying."

"It's a dead bird," I said. "It can't fly anymore because a car ran over it."

"Dat bird dead," he repeated. "Have a little trouble flying."

Every day, for nearly a week, we had to walk down the street to look at the tatters of this unlucky robin. My boy was clearly trying to work something out, but he didn't ask any more questions. He just looked at the bird for a bit and then walked on. "You dead," he whispered once, squatting in front of the bird. "You dead. You not a bird."

Then one day he looked at me. A new thought had come to him: "All birds die?" he asked.

I tried to put the best possible face on a hard truth about this lovely world. "All birds die, but first they build a nest and lay eggs and feed their babies worms and fly and fly and fly."

"All birds die," he repeated. His eyes filled up with tears.

A few days later he was lying on the floor beside our dog. "Scout will die?" he asked, almost absently. I told him Scout would die one day, too. The next question came immediately: .

"All dogs die?" And then he was off. Every day became a crash course in the reach of mortality:

"All fish die?"

"All squirrels die?"

"All teachers die?"

"All dese people in the grocery store die?"

"All mommies die?"

I answered his questions without hedging. I didn't want my three-year-old staring into the abyss, but I wouldn't lie to him either. But then he asked the question that made me want to lie and lie again and keep lying forever: "I will die?" he said, his voice quavering. "I will be dead?"

HONEYSUCKLE

Metastatic

A starling lifts itself from the wire, and a thousand starlings follow, spiraling into the sky. They are pouring in from the treetops, from the roofline—the sky is roiling with wheeling birds, each one an animate cell.

In spring the bush honeysuckle shelters the bluebird fledglings and the brown wrens. In summer the honeysuckle flowers open to the eager bees. In fall the honeysuckle feeds the cedar waxwings, who cling to the bending stems and pass the berries to flock mates who cannot reach. In winter the honeysuckle waits, gathering itself to spring forth, to wrap its roots around what rightly belongs. To choke it out.

Behold the fearsome lionfish, its spines fanning out like a mane, its stripes an underwater circus act, its translucent fins an exotic veil. Behold the gorgeous lionfish floating unmolested in foreign waters, passing near the small creatures at home here and gulping them down, whole.

The lymph nodes are clusters of grapes, ripe, though there will be no wine. They swell and swell with cancer, malignant cells spilling over and spreading, clinging and growing, spilling and spreading and clinging and growing and spilling and spreading and spreading and spreading.

Death-Defying Acts

Terminal illness was perched on the house like a vulture. We walked beneath its hunched presence as though it weren't there, the way you try not to make eye contact with a stranger who's openly staring.

Need governed our days. My father needed help, and my mother needed help with the helping, and I needed to help in a way that allowed me to do my work and also take care of my family. Dad had chemotherapy every other Wednesday. On Thursday, Mom would pack the car and drive them to my house, 182 miles away. My oldest son would sleep on the futon in my office, my husband and I would sleep in our son's double bed, and my parents would sleep in our room, the only room in the house with its own bathroom. Twelve days later, Mom would drive them home. They would sleep in their own bed and wake up in time to head to the clinic for another round of chemo. The next day it was back to my house again.

During one of those visits, Dad suddenly remembered that the circus was coming to town. Not to Nashville, the town where I live, but to Birmingham, the town where he lived.

"You know, I've always wanted to go to the circus," he said one day, out of nowhere.

"You should go, Dad," I said. "Of course."

"The boys would love the circus," Dad said. "You know how much they would love the circus."

Oh.

This wasn't part of the last-chance bucket list at all. This was another trope, one that involved indelible images of grand-fatherly largesse. It was a hedge against oblivion, a way to be remembered.

I spent much of my father's final illness in a state of exhausted resignation, but the flip side of resignation is fury, and fury sometimes found its way through the cracks in my splintered life. My husband, my children, my parents, my siblings—they were the entire bounded universe to me, and one of them was being pulled away forever. But lying under the covers in my own bed, the bed I almost never slept in, I knew my beloved father was asking me to give up two of the only four days every month when I had my own little family to myself. He was asking me to give up my only near respite from cancer.

"No." I said it flatly, a belligerent word left over from toddlerhood or the year I was thirteen. "I'm sorry, Dad. We can't go to Birmingham to see the circus two days from now. We have stuff to do here. We have plans."

"Oh," he said, sounding slightly surprised. "Oh." Then, recovering, not quite pleading but trying one more time: "You know the kids would love the circus."

"I know they would, Dad, but I wouldn't," I said.

I was forty years old—a writer, a wife, a parent—but I still thought of my father's love, of his unshakable belief in me, as the surest protection against my own inconsequence. "You can always come home," he had said. "Even if you marry a bastard, you can always leave him and come on home." But that home had long since ceased to exist, reduced to a sour-smelling shell holding whole shelves of medication and a trash can for my father to cough into as phlegm built in his throat. Becoming responsible for his care and my mother's equilibrium probably meant I had been hauled into a new kind of adulthood unaware, even if I wasn't behaving like an adult. "No," I said. "I don't want to go to the circus."

At the time, I still thought I could find a way to bear the idea of a world without my father in it. What I couldn't bear was any more suffering. I wanted my father to act like my father, damn it, even to the end. Was that my reason for refusing to let him take my children to the circus? By acting like a child myself, was I trying to force him to become my vibrant father again and not a frightened old man who wanted only to be remembered as a hero by his grandsons?

"Well, put it on the calendar for next time then," he said, backing down. "The circus comes back in two years, and I want to take the boys next time."

Next time.

For my terminally ill father, there would be no next time, and I knew it. And he knew I knew it. We were going to the circus.

In Praise of the Unlovely World

Teetering between despair and terror, alarmed by the perils that threaten the planet, defeated in imagining any real way to help, I'm tempted to turn away, to focus on what is lovely in a broken world: moonlight on still water, the full-body embrace of bumblebees in the milkweed flowers, the first dance of the newlyweds, whose eyes never leave each other in all their turnings on the gleaming floor.

But even destruction can remind us of all the ways the world has found of working itself out. Someone steps on a cockroach on the dark sidewalk, and by morning the ants have arrived to carry it off, infinitesimal bit by bit. A car hits a doe on a country road, and the flies share it with the glossy vultures. A beer can tossed carelessly from the car window glints like treasure in the sunlight. Even in its shining, it is already in the long grip of corrosion—eighty years, a hundred—that will take it down to fertile soil.

Chokecherry

When I think of the first time my heart broke, the summer I was fourteen, I don't think at all of the boy who broke it. I think of walking around and around our block, desolate among the ubiquitous dogwoods, weeping as though I had invented heartbreak all by myself. I think of my father, standing at the end of the driveway, cracked where a chokecherry root had pushed up the concrete so it buckled like a fault line, waiting for me to come home. Each time I passed, still crying, he would kick his toe against the break and try to look as though he were considering the maintenance problem at hand. He'd smile at me, and though I couldn't have known it then, it was the smile of someone whose own heart was breaking too.

On the night my father died, he was lying in the big bed in the corner room where he had slept for thirty years. Listing beside him was a slanting bookcase he had built himself, and on one of its shelves—right at eye level—was a picture of my mother on their wedding day, and one of me in my First Communion gown, and pictures of my brother and sister, of the commonplace life of our family. All through the long night it took my dying father to die, I lay beside him, holding his hand and looking at those pictures.

He was long past seeing by then, and each breath was a gasp that shook his whole body, but still the breaths kept coming. *Please die*, I thought, every time there was a pause between the shuddering exhale and the next desperate, grasping breath. *Please die. Please let this be the last one. Please die.*

I didn't see it when the last breath finally came, when my strong, sheltering father ceased for the first time in my lucky life to be my father. I didn't see it because I had lifted my eyes from his face just once, turned for only a moment to the window on the other side of the room, wondering when the light would come.

RABBIT

He Is Not Here

One year, helping me in the garden in early spring, my middle son inadvertently uncovered a cottontail nest tucked beneath the rosemary. The baby rabbits seemed hopelessly vulnerable: thumb-sized creatures, eyes still closed, without any shelter from the cold March rains.

And yet their nest under the rosemary plant was a snug nursery. Their mother had scooped out a shallow hollow in the soil and lined it thickly with her own fur; more fur lay on top of the babies; and on top of that was a final layer of leaves and pine straw and dried rosemary needles. It was impossible to distinguish the nest from the jumble of dead vegetation that had piled up during fall and winter. And as my son pointed out, the location of the nest was ideal: to predators it would smell exactly like rosemary and not at all like rabbit. We tucked the babies in again and left the bed unweeded till they were safely out of the nest and on their own.

I've been desultory about weeding in springtime ever since. Spring is the time, Gerard Manley Hopkins noted, "when weeds, in wheels, shoot long and lovely and lush," and there's another reason for waiting to clear out my flower beds: the neighborhood bees are busy among the flowering weeds long before the perennials bloom. Who can resist the names of wildflowers—fleabane and henbit and purple deadnettle and creeping Charlie?

Finally, though, the day comes when there can be no more waiting or the weeds will choke out all the flowers I planted on purpose. That day came one long Easter weekend. My reliable garden helper was away in college, and

I worked alone, gingerly, careful to watch for signs of a nest. There was nothing beneath the rosemary but mock strawberry vines. Moving from bed to bed, I hauled away weeds by the wheelbarrow-load.

Then, in the next-to-last bed, I tugged up some purple deadnettle growing around the fragrant skeleton of last year's oregano, and what came away in my hand was a tuft of rabbit fur. The nest was empty but so newly vacated as to be entirely intact, an absence exactly shaped to denote an ineffable presence.

Hypochondria

On another day I wouldn't have noticed the lump. My breasts have always been bumpy, and my doctor has never seemed concerned—"busy breasts," she calls them. I didn't even bother checking them in the shower: If everything's a lump, then what's the point?

That day I was anxious but also bored. We were waiting for the test results that would tell us whether a hellish bout of radiation and chemo had killed the cancer growing in my father's esophagus. Pacing the oncology hallway, I picked up a plastic card that explained how to do a breast self-exam, and I was still holding that card when the doctor came into the examining room and clipped some scans onto a light board. He pointed to a cluster of ghostly white orbs that were swollen lymph nodes. He pointed to a dark spot on my father's liver. The cancer wasn't gone. The cancer was spreading.

Being in the presence of death can transform otherwise reasonable people into augurs, bargaining with the cosmos: "If I stop being blasé about my health, will you promise not to kill me?" Holding that card, I vowed to call for an appointment the moment I got home. If I didn't want my own children to face the agony of losing a parent too soon, it was time to let a medical professional decide which of the myriad lumps in my breasts were normal and which were not.

The nurse practitioner was kind. As she gently rubbed and prodded and kneaded, I told her about my father's illness. Dad had always been the one person who could make me feel both completely protected and certain of my own strength. It was hard to separate what was happening to him from what was happening to me. I was surely wasting her time, I said, but I wanted to be safe.

She nodded. Then she said, "Oops, there's a mass."

A word like "mass"—just by itself, not even to mention the dying father taking up the dread chambers of the mind—has a way of stripping all logic from a conversation. The nurse told me, repeatedly, that this mass did not feel to her like cancer, that 80 percent of breast lumps, even suspicious ones, turn out to be nothing, that it was not time to start planning my funeral.

To a person with a mass in her breast, a word like "funeral" is a dirty bomb, exploding into cutting fragments that lodge deep in the reptilian brain. By the time I'd had a mammogram and an ultrasound and a biopsy, by the time I'd met with the cheerful surgeon who said he wasn't worried but still wanted to see me again in three months, I knew I was dying.

Over and over again during my father's illness and for more than a year after his death, the pattern was both primitive and modern: a lump, an inconclusive test, more doctors, more tests. Each time the mammogram was stable, the ultrasound fine, the biopsy normal. I was not relieved. I would brood about the cancer they didn't catch. My father was dying, and I was surely dying too.

When decorations went on sale after the holidays, I would think, *I might not live to see next Christmas*, and buy nothing. Every headache was a tumor, every bout of indigestion stomach cancer. Stress and grief colluded to produce ever more symptoms, and each new symptom required a test: ultrasound, colonoscopy, endoscopy, colposcopy, EKG, blood test after blood test after blood test. They all turned out fine, but I knew I wasn't fine. I was dying.

When I didn't die, however, and then didn't die some more, I came one day to understand: I wasn't dying; I was grieving. I wasn't dying. Not yet.

The Shape the Wreckage Takes

Barefoot and still in her nightgown, my mother comes into my kitchen at lunchtime and looks down the steps to the family room. Her eyes are swollen and red, as they have been for all the weeks since my father's death. My four-year-old, the youngest, is playing on the wooden floor alone. He is pushing small metal cars off the bottom step and watching them crash into each other. This game requires all his concentration. He seems to have some plan for the shape the wreckage must take. He does not hear, or at least does not acknowledge, his grandmother. "Hi, honey," she says.

"Hi, Wibby," he says, not looking up. Then, "Granddaddy played cars with me."

Whenever my mother told this story in the years to come, it was meant to be an example of how God had made a terrible mistake. It was another reason in the long list of reasons she always marshaled for why, if she and my father could not have gone into the next world together, then at least she should have been the one to go first. Confirmation that a bad bargain had somehow been struck.

But my four-year-old's remark was not a rebuke. It had nothing to do with her. He was a little boy, and he was still finding out all the places where his grandfather had been but would be no longer. This new absence was a missing tooth, the hole he couldn't help probing with his tongue. His grandfather had played cars with him. His grandfather had read books to him. His grandfather had walked around the block with him, holding his hand.

Witches' Broom

My great-grandfather ordered a sprig of the Dr. Van Fleet rambling rose shortly after it was introduced in 1910. When my grandparents married in 1930, my grandmother brought a rooted cutting to her new home a few miles down the road. Years later, when we moved to Birmingham, my mother brought a cutting with us, and later still, I brought one to Nashville.

I don't grow roses because of all the spraying invariably involved, but the Dr. Van Fleet is an absurdly hardy exception. For almost two decades, ours withstood countless droughts and Nashville cold snaps, needed no chemicals at all, and seemed impervious to insects. Every year it sheltered at least one cardinal's nest, and those baby birds always made it safely into the world. (A bird's nest built among the thorny canes of an antique rambling rose is about as predator-proof as a nest can be.)

Then my Dr. Van Fleet contracted rose rosette virus, a fatal and incurable disease. First discovered among wild roses in 1941, it is now widespread in the United States. The virus is carried on the wind by mites, and the popularity of Knock Out roses, which are particularly vulnerable to RRV, seems to have hastened its spread.

The telltale sign of this disease is the witches' broom— stems of disfigured new growth clustered at the end of a rose cane. With a rambling rose, if you know what you're looking for, you can sometimes see the beginnings of a classic witches'-broom formation in time to dig the diseased canes out, but I didn't know what I was looking for the year my rose first got sick. By the next spring, when only a few canes leafed out, there was almost nothing left of the Dr. Van Fleet but thorns.

Having no choice, we cut it down and dug up as many of the roots as possible, heartsick. All my beloved elders were gone, and the rose I had hoped to pass along to my children was gone now too.

Rambling roses are easy to propagate in springtime: to create a new rosebush, you place a pot of dirt beneath a cane and set a brick on top of the cane to hold it against the soil in the pot. Beneath the brick, the rose will put down roots. After a few weeks, you can remove the brick, cut the pot free from the main cane, and carry it to a new place in the yard. A rose propagated in this way is genetically identical to the original rose. In essence, you have only one rose, though it is growing in two different places. My own Dr. Van Fleet was the very same rose my great-grandfather first planted in 1910.

The year before I lost the Dr. Van Fleet, I had started a potted rose and forgotten about it beneath the tangle of canes. When I discovered it again in cutting down the rose, I assumed it too would be afflicted with the witches' broom. I kept it just in case I was wrong, but I set it far from any other flowers in my yard and never planted it. Still in its pot three years later, at age 107, it bloomed.

You Can't Go Home Again

LOWER ALABAMA, 2006

My grandfather was tired of being hot in the summertime and cold in the winter. Perhaps he was getting a bit muddled, too, but in 1970 my grandmother didn't try to stop him when he decided to sell the big house, the homeplace, where he had lived almost every year of his life. It was his house to sell if he wanted to, according to my grandmother, and he wanted to: "I have carried in wood and carried out ashes all my life, and I'm tired of it," he said. "I'd like to get a place we can heat and cool."

The man who bought the big house promptly sold the timber off the back acreage for more than he'd paid my grandfather for the whole place, and then he sold the house for yet again more money than he'd paid. My heartbroken mother could hardly bring herself to forgive her father, old though he was and so feeble. He had given away her family home, a safe place for the generations, and all for a cinder-block double-wide with a concrete driveway and central air.

By the time my grandmother died in 2006, she had been with my mother in Birmingham for more than ten years and blind for longer than that, and I hope she never saw the changes in the big house, though they unfolded barely half a mile down the road from the tiny house my grandfather had built for their old age. Her rose border: gone, including the Dr. Van Fleet she'd brought from her childhood home. The floorboards of the front porch: gone, replaced with a concrete slab. The gnarled old tree that grew plums swollen and almost black with juice: gone. And gone, too: all the red wasps drunk on plum juice fermenting in the Alabama sun.

We brought our grandmother back home to Lower Alabama in a box. After the church funeral, my brother and sister and I left our mother at the potluck in the old schoolhouse where our grandmother had once taught and walked over to look at the big house. The first thing we noticed was how small it was.

Ashes, Part One

For a long time, Mom wouldn't tell us where she kept Dad's ashes. "That's between your father and me," she would say. Given her unconventional taxonomies, we knew she might have stashed them anywhere. And given her tendency toward hoarding, we also knew they would be hard to tell from detritus. Once, trying to restore order on a trip home, I found the urn in a box under the old claw-foot table. It was surrounded by mouse droppings, junk mail, outdated newspapers, and garage-sale rolls of fabric that my mother had left on the dining room floor. The next time I went home, the urn was gone.

Years later, after Mom had moved to Nashville and we finally talked her into putting the Birmingham house on the market, it dawned on my sister that she might have accidentally sold the urn at our own garage sale, the one designed to unload all of Mom's geegaws. I didn't think it was possible, but how could we be sure? It wasn't like we could say, "Hey, Mom, we can't find Dad, and there's a chance Lori just sold him to a stranger. Thoughts?"

On a road trip to Lower Alabama to bury our aunt, my sister tried again: "Don't you think it's time to do something about Dad's ashes?"

"That's none of your business," Mom said. "I have a plan for us both, but it's just between Daddy and me."

My sister saw an opening: "But after you die, won't we need to know where Dad is to make this plan work?"

Mom gave in: "OK, he's on the bottom shelf of the guest room closet."

"Great. Now, what's the plan?"

"The family plot is full, but y'all can take a posthole digger down there in the middle of the night and stick me and Daddy in the ground near Mimi and Granddaddy," she said. "I want to go home."

Be Not Afraid

Early in their courtship, my parents knew a little girl who could not pronounce my mother's given name, Olivia, and called her Wibby instead. Wibby became my father's pet name for her, the shorthand he used to summon their days of flirtation. Even during hardships, times of deep worry or sorrow, there was always that echo of their early romance passing back and forth between them. Whenever he heard her laughing— even from another room, having no idea of what had amused her—he couldn't help laughing too. After she started a floral business, he would help with the big orders by copying every move she made: if she added a daisy to the center right of her arrangement, he would add a daisy to the center right of his. When Dad brought home a midlife motorcycle, Mom bought a leather jacket and climbed on back.

During the two and a half years Dad was sick with cancer, Mom left his side only long enough to walk from their room to the kitchen for anything he thought, however fretfully, might settle his churning stomach, and when he died she was lost. Her children, her friends, her church, her flower beds, her sewing projects—none of them offered comfort in the face of cavernous grief.

She had grown up during the Depression on a peanut farm in Lower Alabama, miles from the nearest library. For the first seventy-one years of her life, she had no feeling at all for stories as a source of pleasure or solace, and I never saw her read a book. Then, months after my father died, she went to the library to check out Jane Austen's *Pride and Prejudice* because she'd seen the BBC miniseries a dozen times already and had fallen in love with Mr. Darcy. And that's how, overnight it seemed, she also fell in love with reading. In Regency England she found an entire absorbing world, a grand love story she recognized, though she had never been to Great Britain—had, in fact, rarely left Alabama.

After that it was *Emma*, and *Sense and Sensibility*, and the rest of Austen. Then came other books from the same period and love stories from any era, until finally it was almost anything. During the nine years she lived beyond my father, Mom read comic novels and mysteries, romances and tragedies, and every knockoff Jane Austen novel she could find, no matter how scandalous with twenty-first-century details. ("I couldn't believe it when Mr. Darcy took Elizabeth on the *dining room table!*" she once said.) For Mom, alone in a silent house, these characters must at times have seemed more real to her than even family. In her last years, she lived across the street from my family, and I often checked in midmorning to find her still asleep. "My book was getting so good I had to stay up all night to finish," she would say.

Just before she died, I took her to the emergency room for what was clearly a kidney stone. She had suffered kidney stones before, and the symptoms this time were obvious, but the nurse could give her nothing for the pain until a doctor saw her, and the only doctor there that day was busy with other patients. For more than two hours, the nurse would check in, Mom would ask for pain medicine, and the nurse would apologize: no, narcotics could make certain conditions much worse, or complicate any needed surgery. "I'm not afraid of dying," Mom told her. "I'm afraid of *hurting*, but I'm not afraid of dying. My husband died nine years ago, and every night I tell God I'm ready to see him again."

Four days later, with no warning at all, she got her wish.

Stroke

NASHVILLE, 2012

Earth and air won't cease their quarrel. Tornadoes take up their form in the Midwest, a writhing cone of soil and breath and bite.

Hurricanes shoulder and churn off the Gulf Coast, each one a gray ferocity, a roaring violence of roiling water.

Volcanic ash rises in the Philippines. Air becomes mass; dust becomes rock; the sky is raining fire, and no hissing rain will come to cool it.

The ocean floor cracks open in the Pacific, heaving waves of nausea across the surface of the sea.

A scar down the middle of the Mississippi River unzips and fills the world with livid water.

In Nashville, a brain breaks open.

In the universe, a star folds in on itself.

And God said, *Let there be darkness.*

Dust to Dust

She left in a state much larger than herself—two fire trucks, an ambulance, a rolling stretcher pushed by big men. The neighbors waited in their doorways to see which of us would emerge on the stretcher. I texted my friend standing quietly across the street, one arm around her older daughter: "Mom fell. Maybe a stroke. Probably not too bad—she's still talking, and we'll be at the hospital in plenty of time."

Lights swirling, sirens wailing—that is how she left. She came back in a black box marked with her name and the day she died and the day they burned her body. Inside the box was a plastic bag of ashes, closed with a twist tie, like a loaf of bread.

Lexicon

NASHVILLE, 2012

Words my mother permitted me to say in childhood:
Damn.
Shit.
Fuck.
Piss.
Hell.

—

Words my mother did not permit me to say in childhood:
Snot.

—

The last words of my father's favorite joke:
Oh, shit. I stepped in the dog doo-doo.

—

The first words of my father's favorite poem:
It was Saturday evening,
The guests were all leaving,
O'Malley was closing the bar,
When he turned and he said
To the lady in red,
"Get out; you can't stay where you are."

—

The last words my mother ever spoke:
>Thank you.

⁓

The last words my father ever spoke:
>Stop it.

⁓

The words I spoke in the rooms where my parents were dying:
>I love you.
>It's OK.
>Don't worry.
>It's OK.
>I love you.

⁓

The words I couldn't say in the rooms where my parents were dying:
>Damn. Shit. Fuck. Piss. Oh, hell.

Drought

"Nothing is plumb, level, or square," Alan Dugan writes in "Love Song: I and Thou," a meditation on the persecutions of marriage. My own marriage is full of joy, but all day long I walk through this drought-plagued landscape thinking that nothing in the world is plumb, level, or square. Inside, wooden doors hang crooked in their frames; the hot wind blows them open. Outside, the land has tightened and contracted. To the east, forests are on fire.

The earth is cracked, constricted, a bloodless sore. Leaves that should be a hundred different colors are dusty and faded. In the garden, the soil is powder; brown stems lift from it as though they'd never had roots, as though they were formed by heat and air.

For months the land has been pulling away from the edges of the world. A day of rain weeks ago was not enough—hardly more than spit from a parched mouth. Nothing fills the cracks in the dry ground; nothing rises from the roots to hold up a flower.

Everyone is talking about the drought; everyone is worried, even in this town with a deep river running through it and all the water we can pay for only a twist of the faucet away. Every morning I drag the hose out and fill the birdbath with water. The desperate robins hardly wait for me to turn away before they crowd the edges of the shallow dish to drink and drink and drink.

WARBLER

Insomnia

All her tricks have failed, all the gentle seductions: the warm bath, the quiet book, the perfect sex, the cool sheets on the cool side of the bed, even the first unpanicked Benadryl and then the desperate second. She surrenders to it now, hoping only to live with it in peace, side by side, like an animal she has invited into the yard never expecting to tame. After a lifetime spent conjoined with sleep like a twin, like the truest friend, she is bereft, abandoned. So many hours in the night! She had no idea.

She will not think of the unworried man, the rebuke of his tranquil sleeping, or of their children, grown now, the ones who first taught her how to sleep lightly, tuned to the slightest infant sound. She will not think of her parents, who welcomed her between them after dreams she was too young to know were dreams. She will not think of how she misunderstood her mother's last fall, how she felt so sure it was a simple accident, a broken hip, perhaps a little stroke, wholly reversible in that early window after the ambulance arrived. She will not think of the way she sat in the front seat of the ambulance, obedient, when she ought to have insisted on a place in the back, a place where she could hold a still but still-warm hand.

She will not think of the troubles of the ones she loves, or of her own troubles. The night is long, but the days are rushing by, gone gone surely gone, and she thinks to remember what she might otherwise forget except for the gift of this endless night. She lists to herself the names of flowers that will bring butterflies to her yard next spring, and she tries to name the New World warblers, thirty-seven in all, that rest in her honeysuckle tangles on their migratory journey, and she considers the miracle that happens when afternoon light in summer becomes the afternoon light of early fall.

At last, somewhere between the magnolia warbler and the Tennessee, she feels in the back of her neck the click that sometimes signals the first moving gear in the great machine of sleep, and she turns on her side and settles the covers, just in case.

How to Make a Birthday Cake

NASHVILLE, 2012

Remember that one of your children won't eat buttercream icing and one won't eat cream cheese icing and one will eat only the layers and leave every morsel of icing absolutely untouched, a giant F-shaped slice of butter and cream. On his plate it's the Second Coming, but only the cake is raptured, leaving behind a skeleton of powdered sugar sin.

The no-icing kid prefers the brown sugar pound cake, remember, not the cream cheese pound cake or the sour cream pound cake. Remember that your grandmother's recipe for brown sugar pound cake is on a card labeled "Caramel Pound Cake" though there is not a hint of caramel in it. Remember how your grandmother always said "caramel" as though it rhymed with "carousel." Remember when your grandmother's handwriting was sure and strong and she could still see to copy out a receipt, as she sometimes called it, and remember when she was too weak and blind to bake but still knew the receipt for care-a-mel cake by heart.

Remember that the card is tucked into your mother's recipe box between the card for cranberry Jell-O mold and the card for brandied fruit. Wonder for the first time why she filed a cake recipe between two fruit recipes (or, really, two "fruit" recipes) until it finally comes to you: this must be the Thanksgiving section of the recipe box. There was always some taxonomy behind your mother's inscrutable systems, and her brown sugar pound cake recipe would of course be grouped with the squash soufflé and the pecan pie, too, because it goes without saying that there will be no pumpkin pie recipe in any Thanksgiving file created by your mother, who spent her childhood harvesting pecans in Lower Alabama.

When you pull out the eggs and the butter and the flour—plain, not self-rising; you will never make that mistake again—and the absurd quantities of sugar, remember to set the recipe card in a safe place. There are things you cannot keep safe, that you have already failed forever to keep safe, but you must remember to protect this one card written in your grandmother's hand and saved in your mother's recipe box. There's a child in your house who won't eat icing, and today is his birthday, and he will not always be a child, and you will not always keep him safe.

Homeward Bound

NASHVILLE, 2012

Every time my mother went to visit my sister or my brother, she would leave her brown dachshund with me. And for days afterward, the dog would sit before our back door and wait for her. This was the same door my mother used every night when she and the dog came over for supper, and its full-length window is the only one in our house that reaches low enough for a dachshund to see through. The dog would wait and wait and wait, and three days later—a week at most—my mother always came back to her.

Two weeks after Mom's funeral, the dog ran away. Dapple-colored, she was both willful and invisible: she had never once come when called, and she could disappear beneath the lowest bushes, behind the smallest fallen branch. Terrified, I turned that yard inside out looking for her. When I finally thought to check at my mother's house across the street, I found her at the back door, jumping up and scratching to be let in. She had been scratching so urgently, and for so long, that the paint was chipped away from the doorjamb.

What I Saved

I saved only one of your thirty-seven coffee mugs, the white one from the church in Birmingham with the massive pietà hanging behind the altar. I keep it in the back corner of the cupboard, next to the mug emblazoned with a troubling Bible verse that gets used only when all the other mugs are dirty.

I saved the nicest of the towels filling two closets but none of the fabric remnants piled in the guest room, and none of the garish rhinestone brooches from the fifties, and none of the Jane Austen fan fiction, and none of the *Southern Living* magazines from the eighties, and none of the Hallmark Channel DVDs. The retirement home, the one you almost moved into, was grateful to have the DVDs. The retirement home, you would be glad to know, has finally gotten rid of the bedbugs.

I saved all five giant boxes of OxiClean, and oh my God why did you never tell me about OxiClean? At 156 loads per box, our socks have been white for all the years you've been gone.

I saved three lipsticks in a shade of pink I will never wear, but I threw away two dozen more, along with bottle after bottle of expired vitamins, and don't even get me started on the expired boxes and cans in the pantry. I wish I had known how much you loved blueberry muffins. I wish I had made you blueberry muffins every day of your life.

I saved miles and miles of Christmas ribbon and boxes of note cards. Even after the funeral thank-you notes, there were enough cards left for all my correspondence for years to come.

I saved your nice wooden coat hangers, and I wish I'd saved the gorgeous red raincoat that was too big for me when you died but would fit perfectly now.

Naturally I saved the baptismal gown with the handmade lace and the impossibly dainty white-on-white embroidery, half a century old by the time I found it in your sock drawer, and I saved the socks, too, or at least the ones with mates.

I saved all the photos and all the love letters, and the recipe cards that can be dated, like ancient trees, by layers of butter stains. I saved your wedding ring and the pearl pendant with the diamond chip that Dad gave you, promising a lifetime of diamonds and pearls, though there was never any money for diamonds or pearls. I saved what was left of your wedding gown and the gown you wore on your wedding night. I saved Aunt Fidelis's silver vanity set with mermaids embossed on the Victorian hair receiver. Before I threw away your brush, I saved your snow-white hair, too. The pale, thin strands are almost invisible in the cut-glass jar where the mermaids keep watch.

I saved the empty bird feeders and the empty pots in the garage and even the nearly dead holly fern you dug up from our old yard and carried here in a plastic bag but didn't live to plant. I filled the feeders with seeds, and I filled the pots with flowers, and I planted the dry roots of the holly fern, and now my yard is filled with birds and blossoms. I saved all these things. But what I couldn't save weighs on my heart like a stone.

When My Mother Returns to Me in Dreams

NASHVILLE, 2012

I had wanted the story to be a gift, a tribute to the house my mother loved long past the time when love could save it. Mom was still refusing to leave, and I struggled to understand her fondness for a place that was tumbling into ruins around her. But as I was writing the essay, I began to grasp her deep-rooted reasons for staying, and why my arguments carried no weight against them. In trying to fathom my mother's love for that house, I came around to remembering my love for it, too. That would be my gift to her: understanding. The story was set to appear in a magazine my mother often read, and it would be illustrated with pictures of the house and our family's life in it—a photo of me in my First Communion gown, a picture of Mom in her wedding dress—and I planned to wrap up a copy for Mother's Day.

But my brother had his doubts: "It might make her feel bad for strangers to read about how terrible the house looks," he said. "She might be embarrassed." So I never said a word.

By the time the essay finally appeared in print, Mom had moved to Nashville, but it was months before she ever saw it. One day she banged open the door of my office and slammed a copy of the magazine down on the desk. "What is *this*?" she yelled, her face so flushed the scalp showed pink beneath her clean white hair.

I could see how it had happened. She sits down beneath the dryer at the beauty shop to flip through an old magazine. Suddenly she comes to a full-page picture from her own wedding album. There she is, standing with Dad on the church steps, squinting into the Lower Alabama sun, in the dress she'd designed and made by hand.

"Mom, listen," I started.

"No, *you* listen. What made you think it was OK to publish my picture in a magazine without even *asking* me?"

"I wanted it to be a surprise," I said. "I was planning to wrap it up for Mother's Day, but Billy thought it might hurt your feelings to read about how bad the house looks."

The air whooshed out of her. "Oh," she said. "Oh." She picked up the magazine and looked at the picture again. "Well, that's OK, then."

When Mom returns to me in dreams, she's always heartbreakingly herself, not some otherworldly haint or visible expression of my own grief. Whenever she appears, my first reaction is always relief. *Oh, thank God. It was just a misunderstanding. You're alive.* And Mom is always puzzled, always surprised when I grab her and hold her tight, when I say again and again, "You're here. You're back. Thank God."

And when I find her somewhere else, in an unfamiliar dream landscape, it's always somehow recognizably ordinary—not paradise at all but a cinder-block house with knotty-pine paneling and worn floral curtains. I walked into a strange house once and found Mom sitting with my father and my grandparents, and my father's godmother, and they all looked up when I opened the door, but they were no gladder to see me than if I had merely stepped outside to check the weather. My dead don't seem to know they're dead.

In one dream Mom was annoyed to discover her coat hangers in the closet next to our front door. "But why would you take *all* my nice wooden hangers?" she said.

"Because you died, Mom," I said. "You were dead."

"Oh," she said. "That's OK, then."

CICADA

Carapace

Hush. Be quiet. The long summer day is coming to a close, spooling up its lovely light, but there is nothing to fear from the night. There is nothing to fear from life giving way to death, for that matter, or from any dark thing. Stand in the shadows under the trees for only a moment, for half a moment, and a dozen fallen things will reveal themselves to you.

Last year's sassafras leaf, clinging still to a bit of its yellow luster, has gone gorgeous in lace, and the cicada, dwelling in the black soil for all those years, has climbed out of its shell and taken to the trees and begun to sing, has become the song of summer evenings, and the sweet-gum ball has lost its spiky armor and released its seeds into the generations, and the acorn, too, has shed its shell and sent roots into the earth, and the dead sycamore at the edge of the quiet lake's lapping water has leapt into flame as it does every single evening, and then the red-winged blackbird, the bright badge on his wing a flare of incandescence in the light at the end of the day, settles on a branch and sings the nighttime home.

Resurrection

A dozen monarch caterpillars arrive in the mail, tender, unprotected, but I am ready. I've set out an entire flat of native milkweed plants, new additions to a bed I planted earlier but that so far has not attracted a single breeding pair. I've enclosed the butterfly garden with a sturdy wire border covered by mosquito netting, to protect the caterpillars from birds and spiders and wasps and parasitic flies and praying mantises and the hundred other predators waiting outside. Even inside the enclosure, all manner of calamity could befall them: various diseases, poorly timed shifts in the weather, hungry animals with claws or beaks too sharp for mosquito netting to repel.

Within a day, sure enough, some other living thing has unfastened the netting from where I've pinned it tightly to the soil, pushed past it, and gulped down two of the caterpillars. Monarch larvae subsist entirely on poisonous milkweed leaves and are therefore toxic themselves, but they are not toxic enough to prevent all predation. A hungry bird will devour almost any insect, no matter how distasteful. My husband once plucked a large stinkbug from the driveway and tossed it out of harm's way. The instant it took to the air, a robin swept out of a tree and caught it mid-flight. This is a predator-friendly yard: I have set up nine feeding stations to welcome birds, and never mind the opossums and the raccoons and the rat snake that winters under the garden shed.

A day later, another two or three or four are gone, though their enclosure appears intact this time. Exactly how many are missing I am no longer sure, for despite their jaunty yellow and black stripes, monarch caterpillars are surprisingly good at hiding and instinctively freeze as soon as they see me approach. Possibly they are somewhere else in the garden altogether, for now I find a flaw in my rigged-together enclosure: the netting is not so tightly fastened to the ground as I had thought. A few old bricks solve that problem, but already I am waiting for the next problem to arise.

Very few caterpillars survive to become butterflies—perhaps as few as 1 percent—and nature responds with profligacy: a female monarch lays around four hundred eggs during her brief reproductive life. Before the widespread use of herbicides, this reproduction rate was enough to keep North America dense with butterflies. Now the monarchs are dying out, and I am invested in trying to save them.

How literally am I invested? I try not to count up the costs for milkweed, fencing, mosquito nets, the caterpillars themselves. But I find myself doing the math each time a caterpillar goes missing, recalculating what I will end up having paid for each monarch that ultimately survives. I know I am fast approaching the butterfly equivalent of what my country friend calls the forty-dollar homegrown tomato.

For a while—an hour, two—all seems well, but when I check again, a caterpillar has crawled onto the net and stopped moving. I'm not worried at first, and I'm only slightly worried a few hours later, but by morning something seems terribly wrong: for at least seventeen hours, this caterpillar has not moved at all, and creatures who eat for twenty-four hours each day should not remain so wholly still.

When I check again, for now I am checking obsessively, a black blob extends from its hind end, a sticky film of some kind, too large to be excrement. I think of the pet rabbit who died in my arms in childhood, how it gave a single kick and then fell limp, filling my lap with urine. Is this the way a monarch caterpillar surrenders its life, hanging upside down and spooling out a thread of thick black tar?

It's useless to return to my desk—there's no way I'll be able to work. I squat and wait. The internet urges monarch stewards to remove diseased caterpillars from their enclosures, but how can I be sure I know life from death in the odd demiworld of this garden, this mesh-enclosed anteway I have fashioned between the mailbox and the sky?

The caterpillar stirs, and finally I see: this is not a death at all but only a pause before another stage of life, splitting the skin it has outgrown and crawling away from what it no longer needs. It is a new creature. Even before it begins again, it begins again.

In Darkness

Early autumn is the heyday of the orb weaver spiders. A spider's egg sac bursts open in spring, and the infinitesimal hatchlings spend all summer growing and hiding from predators. By fall, they are large enough to emerge from their secret places and spin their marvelous webs. Every night the female makes an intricate trap for flying insects, and every evening she eats up the tatters of last night's web before starting in again on something new and perfect.

By September, our house always looks as though nature has decorated early for Halloween, but I can't bring myself to sweep the webs from the windows or out from under the eaves. I know the spiders are there, the few who survived the long, hot summer. They are crouched in corners, waiting for nightfall, when they will again commence to wring a miracle from the world. For beauty, what tidy window ever matched a spider's web glistening in the lamplight?

One year I watched an orb weaver spider at uncommonly close range. She had set up housekeeping by stringing her web from our basketball backboard to the corner of the house. Just above the eave on that corner is a floodlight that's triggered by motion. Every night that September I carried my late mother's lame old dachshund out for her last sniff around, and every night the light blinked on, catching the spider mid-miracle. While the ancient dog did her business, I stood in the shadows just beyond the reach of the light and watched the spider carrying on her urgent work. If I held still enough, she would keep spinning, and I could watch something unfold that normally takes place entirely in the dark. But whenever she saw me studying her, she would rush up the lifeline she'd spun for herself and squat behind the Christmas lights that dangle from the eaves, the ones that wink all day and warn birds who might otherwise crash into the windows when the slant of light changes in autumn.

Human beings are creatures made for joy. Against all evidence, we tell ourselves that grief and loneliness and despair are tragedies, unwelcome variations from the pleasure and calm and safety that in the right way of the world would form the firm ground of our being. In the fairy tale we tell ourselves, darkness holds nothing resembling a gift.

What we feel always contains its own truth, but it is not the only truth, and darkness almost always harbors some bit of goodness tucked out of sight, waiting for an unexpected light to shine, to reveal it in its deepest hiding place.

No Exit

"Marry an orphan," my mother used to say, "and you can always come home for Christmas." What she should have said: "Marry an orphan, or you'll have *four* parents to nurse through every torment life doles out on the long, long path to the grave." But I married the opposite of an orphan—the son and grandson of people who live deep into old age despite diseases that commonly fell others: cancer, sepsis, heart failure, emphysema, you name it. My husband's elders get sick, and then they get sicker, but for years they persevere.

My own father died of cancer five days shy of his seventy-fifth birthday. Mom dropped dead of a hemorrhagic stroke at eighty. When I checked on her the night before her death, she was eating a cookie and watching a rerun of *JAG*. I almost pointed out that eating in bed is a choking hazard, but for once I let it go. She was in good health, but she needed my help in countless annoying ways—annoying to her and annoying to me—and she was heartily sick of being told what to do. I take some comfort now in knowing I skipped that one last chance to boss her around.

There's an art to helping people without making them feel bad about needing help. It's an art I was learning but hadn't wholly mastered with Mom. "I would've died if my mother had done this to me when I was your age," she said when she moved in across the street, but by the time she actually died three years later, we had both adjusted: "I know I can be a bitch sometimes, but you can be a bitch sometimes too," she would say. "I figure it all works out in the wash."

I saw my mother at least twice a day and talked with her more often than that. But as close as we were, I sometimes found myself despairing her long-lived genes. My great-grandmother lived to be ninety-six despite spending the bulk of her life without antibiotics or vaccines. My grandmother lived to be ninety-seven despite being shot in her seventies by a crazed stranger. I knew my kids would one day leave for lives of their own, but Mom's needs would just keep growing. By the time my nest was truly empty, I thought, there would be precious little left of me.

When she died so suddenly, still issuing hilarious pronouncements and taking our teenagers' side in generational disputes, I felt as if a madman had blown a hole through my own heart. Unmoored, I could not stop weeping. Caring for elders is like parenting toddlers—there's a scan running in the background of every thought and every act, a scan that's tuned to possible trouble. And there's no way to shut it down when the worst trouble, irrecoverable trouble, comes.

A year later, before we'd even settled the question of where Mom's keepsakes should go, my husband's parents moved across several state lines to an assisted-living facility five minutes from our house. Physically frail—he from heart failure, she from Parkinson's disease—they needed far more help than my mother ever did, but I figured their new living arrangements would surely make up the difference. After cooking for Mom, driving her to appointments, managing her medications, paying her bills, and washing her clothes, I looked forward to having parents nearby who needed only our love and our company.

Years earlier, when we told people Mom was moving to Nashville, men would look at my husband incredulously: "You let your mother-in-law move in *next door*?" After my in-laws arrived, my friends said much the same thing to me. But clichés have no place in this story: my husband loved my parents, and I loved his.

My mother-in-law was in every way a divergence from the stereotype: preternaturally patient, radiant with love, alert for ways to support and approve of her children, including those who had joined her family by marriage. Soon after our wedding, I heard my husband griping in the next room about how much money I spent on toiletries. "I just don't see how anyone can drop thirty dollars in a drugstore without buying a single drug," he said. And I was astonished to hear my deeply traditional mother-in-law take my side: "Son, Margaret works hard. If she wants to take her money and stamp it into the mud, you can't say a thing about it."

So when my in-laws moved to Nashville, only my sister's objection struck home with me: "But you know how all this will end."

In fact, my father-in-law collapsed three days after arriving and had to be hospitalized, and the stress of the move dramatically worsened my mother-in-law's Parkinson's symptoms. One crisis followed another: infections, head injuries, broken bones, even a fire. And each disaster meant the need for more help from us, plus a constant stream of houseguests as my husband's far-flung siblings put their own lives on hold to pitch in. Back on the caregiving roller coaster, I struggled to remember the lesson I had just learned so painfully with Mom: the end of caregiving isn't freedom. The end of caregiving is grief.

Even as he recovered from open-heart surgery himself, my father-in-law continued to coordinate my mother-in-law's care. Once, overwhelmed by those responsibilities, he reminded my husband that in the old days families took their elders in. My husband reminded his father that in the old days people with heart failure and Parkinson's disease didn't live long enough to need the kind of help they already needed, never mind the inevitable disasters the future would bring.

My own mother could not afford assisted living, and we always understood that one day she would move in with us. But Mom wanted to be independent for as long as possible, and I had my own reasons for keeping at least a lawn between us: I work from a home office, and it would be nearly impossible to conduct my professional life with a needy elder in the very next room. The dilemma never had to be resolved with Mom, but it came up again once my mother-in-law entered hospice care. It broke my heart to imagine my beloved father-in-law living alone in that assisted-living facility after sixty years of happy marriage.

"But your dad would be lonely here too," I said to my husband. "If he moves in with us, I'd have to rent an apartment. Wouldn't it be better if he stayed in assisted living, where there are people around all day, and came over here for supper every night the way Mom did?"

My husband looked at me. "You mean an *office*, right?" he finally said. "If Dad moves in, you'd need to rent an office?"

I laughed. I meant an office, but for a moment he wasn't absolutely sure. And in the end, my father-in-law stayed put.

Of course, my father-in-law had a point: families once worked in a very different way. During the Depression, when my mother's childhood house burned to the ground, her whole family moved in with my great-grandparents. A few years later, my other great-grandmother moved in too. I was in college myself before the last of that generation passed away. "I've been taking care of people my whole life," my grandmother wondered. "What will I do with myself now?" As my mother-in-law entered the last stage of a savage disease, when just getting through the days was a dreadful challenge for her and for all of us who loved her, I constantly reminded myself of my grandmother's plaintive question.

Then we lost my beautiful mother-in-law too. I think of her, and of my parents, every single day. They are an absence made palpably present, as though their most vivid traits—my father's unshakable optimism, my mother's irreverent wit, my mother-in-law's profound gentleness—had formed a thin membrane between me and the world: because they are gone, I see everything differently.

No Such Thing as a Clean Getaway

One great-uncle fell from a third-floor window, possibly pushed by his wife. Another fell asleep before an unscreened fire and was burned to a black crisp, sitting in his armchair. Still another succumbed to a gas leak while sitting on the toilet. Amazingly, he was not the only uncle to meet his end in the bathroom, but circumstances are less clear with the other: Was his early death brought on by a heart condition, long known, or did he simply fall in a drunken haze and hit his head, the trouble with drink also being long known? No way to say: these are not family stories that get passed down in precise detail.

I remember well the difficult great-aunt whose stroke left her with a scrambled vocabulary but no fewer demands. Unsure what might come out of her mouth, she compensated, attaching every attempt to communicate with a declarative prefix. Her order at the diner: "It's true I want crayons." Her request to go home: "It's true I got to pee."

And what to tell the children about their ancestor, tiny but severe, who entered her dotage so sublimely unaware of social constraints that she was banned from community meals for masturbating in the dining room? Or the beloved elders who pulled back at the very end, no longer loving in their last hours, no longer concerned in the least for those they would leave behind? "Stop it," said my mostly unconscious father when I adjusted the pillows that left his neck crooked at an awkward angle. "Don't do that," said my mother-in-law as I stroked her hand.

Oh, the lives we grieve in their going. Oh, the lives we grieve in their going on.

Ashes, Part Two

NASHVILLE, 2015

My father-in-law is poring over an image of the marker he has ordered for my mother-in-law's grave. It will be set over the shoebox-sized plot where her ashes were put to ground a month ago, her parents and her grandparents beside her. My father-in-law is not sure the spacing between the letters looks quite even. He is not sure the carved lettering is quite deep enough. He is not sure each word appears on the correct line—perhaps the dates should come last? My grieving father-in-law sits at our table and studies the image for a long time. He asks us each in turn to look at the photocopied page that came in the mail from a mortuary more than five hundred miles away. Do *we* think the lettering is right? It must be perfect. It is his job to see that it's perfect. In time, his own marker will stand beside hers, and he will not be here to set it right.

He looks at me: "Where are Bill and Olivia buried?" He has never thought to ask before, though my mother has been gone for more than two years, my father for more than a decade.

My husband coughs and turns away. Our sons look at me.

"We haven't buried them yet," I say.

My father-in-law looks startled: "Where are they then?"

A sound that isn't strictly a cough erupts from my husband. I look at the boys.

"They're in Dad's closet," one of them tells his grandfather.

MAPLE

Nevermore

The rains we've been waiting for, yearning for, have finally arrived in our part of Tennessee, and the maple leaves are falling now in great clots. Rain is falling and leaves are falling and my youngest son, like his brothers, has received his selective service card in the mail, and today I have returned to my house to find a lone black vulture standing in my front yard.

I am always grateful to vultures, that indefatigable cleanup crew doing such necessary work along the roadsides. Nevertheless, a vulture adopting an attitude of possession toward my own home does not exactly constitute a welcome autumn tableau, especially not during a melancholy week of rain in the window and inescapable images of war licking at the edges of a mother's mind.

We live on an unkempt lot in a neighborhood where most of the lawns are pristine, and vultures are not common visitors. Yet here is one standing a few feet from my front door. I idle in the driveway to watch. It is eating nothing. It is only standing there, looking at my house. Occasionally it dips its head and hunches, mantling its wings, but there appears to be nothing at its feet, no prey to protect from encroachers. Nor any encroachers, for that matter.

I drive around back, walk through the house, open the front door. The vulture turns its bald, black face to look at me in that peculiar side-eyed way of birds, and then it flaps heavily off, low across the yard and up and over the house where my mother lived. When I let our old dog out, he sniffs again and again at the spot where the vulture was standing but comes to no discernible conclusions.

There is a newly dead chipmunk in the street, seemingly unnoticed by the vulture. I think it must surely have registered the dead chipmunk's existence at some visceral level; surely the dead chipmunk is what has summoned this bird to my yard. The chipmunk has been a sort of housemate of mine, living in an elaborate tunnel system under our foundation, and I don't like to think of it lying unmourned in the rain-soaked street. I step back from the doorway and wait, hoping the vulture will come and claim its prize.

But these are willed thoughts, a hedge against an atavistic instinct to read omens and signs into a giant black vulture that has staked out my home on a day when the federal government has announced its intention to claim my child. I think of myself as a rational person. I am not a reader of portents or horoscopes. I greet the promises of fortune cookies with wry hope at best, but there was a time, more than two decades ago, when I hand-delivered twenty copies of a chain letter on the last day before bad luck was supposed to descend on anyone who dared to break the chain. I was not in my right mind: I had recently suffered two devastating miscarriages and was precariously pregnant again with a child that no one expected to live. I stuck a bunch of chain letters in the mailboxes of people I did not know, just to be safe.

That child registered for the selective service two years ago, and now it is his younger brother's turn. If a simple card in the mail can cast me back into the ancient reach of augury, I can only imagine the dread that claws at the heart of a mother whose child is serving in a part of the world where dangers are real and not merely imagined—where fear is of a piece with sacrifice and not of superstition.

I know a vulture is only a bird, only a bird and not an omen, no matter the temptation to turn it into the equivalent of Poe's raven. Arriving shrouded in widow's weeds and standing in solitary magnificence to stare at me with one unblinking eye, it is still only a bird, a big, black bird entirely indifferent to the workings of the human realm. Unaware of the workings of the human heart.

When I leave to walk the old dog after dark, the unlucky chipmunk is still lying in the road where it met its end. The next morning I wake up late. When I finally sit down at my desk and look out the window, there's not one trace of the former chipmunk clinging to the asphalt, not one glossy black feather resting on the grass.

History

"Your hand feels just like your mother's hand," my father tells me as we walk hand in hand. I am twelve. I pull my hand back, hold it out before me: dirty fingernails, torn cuticles, no ring. It is not my mother's hand. It is nothing like my mother's hand. It is only my hand.

—

Mom finishes hemming the confirmation dress while I'm at school. The dress has two hems, really—one for the yellow foundation, and one for the gauzy filament of see-through daisies that floats on top. When I try it on, it is just barely too long. It touches the floor, and the daisies are too fragile to be dragged across the asphalt parking lot—the gauze will be rags by the time I'm called to the altar. There's no time to rip out the hems, pin them up again, and make all those tiny stitches, so close together they can't be kicked out by an eighth-grader walking in a floor-length dress. "Wear these," Mom says. My first heels, all of one inch high. My feet settle into the slight indentations my mother's heels have made, where the balls of my mother's feet bend, where my mother's toes spread out. The shoes fit perfectly.

—

The wedding gown has spent twenty-eight years in an Alabama attic. "There's bound to be nothing left of it," I say. What dry rot hasn't ruined, the moths have surely long since eaten.

"We'll see," my mother says, kneeling beside the bathroom tub, squeezing baby shampoo through the stained Chantilly lace she sewed seed pearls into so many years before, through the shot silk she ordered from England for the gown she'd designed herself. Half a dozen soakings in the tub, half a dozen mornings spread out on a sheet in a sunny backyard, and the dress is white again. Days more with the finest-gauge thread, a magnifying glass hanging from a chain above patient fingers, and the torn bits are whole once more, the scallops at the collarbone perfectly rounded, the points at the wrists exactly centered. I step into its white tumult, slip my hands through a filigree of sleeves, and hold my breath while she zips. Not a single seam needs adjustment.

—

My mother had three children between thirty and thirty-six, and I had three children between thirty and thirty-six. Now my body is an exact replica of her own. I see her in my own thickening waist. I watch as her feet propel me through the world. I feel her in the folds of my neck and the set of my brow and the slight curve of the finger where I wear the ring my father gave her. The ring she never took off but had to leave behind.

Ashes, Part Three

After her own death, I suddenly understood Mom's reluctance to consign Dad to the ground. At first it was just impossible; there was no way to drive so far, from Nashville to Lower Alabama, through streaming tears. Later, the logistics were daunting: How would we get permission to open the family plot by even a posthole digger's width when it was already accommodating as many of our dead as it could officially hold? We all agreed that driving in at midnight was out of the question: this was the deepest part of rural Alabama, where everyone is armed. Permission from the preacher would be required.

On the fifth anniversary of Mom's death, it came.

⟶

I am dreaming when the alarm goes off the morning my siblings and I leave to take our mother's ashes home. In the dream, some children and I are singing: "Ashes, ashes, we all fall down." One child stops the game and says severely, "We aren't supposed to have ashes in our pockets."

⟶

On I-65, just past Prattville, kudzu smothers every fencerow, and I strain to see the famous mill wheel, no longer turning, through the tangle of vines, but the GO TO CHURCH OR THE DEVIL WILL GET YOU sign is gone now. We turn off the interstate after Montgomery onto the blue highway that will take us home, to the place I still think of as home though I have not been there in years, not since my grandmother's death. The mimosas are in bloom. In the pastures that spread back from the road, egrets stand upon the dozing cows and pick at the edges of the ponds near the road.

We pass the last house our grandparents lived in—the one they built from cinder blocks when the big house became too much for them to keep up—and head straight for the church. In its cemetery, a mockingbird sings in a tree by the gate, competing with another mockingbird in the pines across the yard. Birdsong and wind are the only sounds in this corner of the universe.

My brother takes out the posthole digger, which I packed primarily as a symbol, a nod to the specificity of Mom's plan. I did not expect it to be useful, at least not compared to the long-blade shovel I also packed. But the posthole digger, it turns out, is the perfect tool. Decades after she left her birthplace for good, our mother still remembered the exact texture of its soil, a mixture made mostly of red sand and dust that yields to the blades with no resistance at all. Within only a minute or two, my brother has dug a hole large enough to hold our parents' ashes.

He opens the boxes, and then the boxes within the boxes, and then the plastic bags within those, and he shakes the ashes into the hole. It would be easy to scrape the leftover soil into the hole with only our feet, but we all seem to have a vague, unspoken sense that kicking dirt into a grave would be disrespectful, though neither of our parents had been the sort to stand on ceremony. My brother and sister and I each take up a handful of dirt to drop into the hole on top of the ashes. We look at each other. Should we sing? Say a few words of prayer? No one steps forward to lead, and so my brother finishes up with the shovel. The mockingbirds sing their own hymns, and we all step on the mounded dirt to pack the soil tight.

They are buried now in the graveyard between the church where Mom was baptized and the schoolhouse where she learned to read. They are buried now deep in the soil she sprang from, deep in the soil her parents sprang from, deep in the soil their parents sprang from. They are buried near all those who came before them, too far back for anyone to remember.

Masked

When they first appeared in the neighborhood, I assumed they were starlings. A flock of starlings is the bane of the bird feeder—a vast, clamoring mob of unmusical birds soiling the windshields and lawn furniture, muscling one another aside so violently that no other birds dare draw near the suet.

But this flock stayed high in the treetops, far from my feeders, too far away to recognize. Then a cold snap kept all the puddles frozen for days, and every bird in the zip code showed up at my heated birdbath to drink. That's how I finally got close enough to know them for what they were: cedar waxwings, the most exotic of all the backyard birds. They are here in Middle Tennessee only during late fall and winter, when the hollies and hackberries and Japanese honeysuckle are bearing fruit. Seeing the entire flock at my birdbath seemed like a miracle.

But there's a new slant of light in winter, and the trees surrounding the house are bare now, casting no shade. For birds, this combination can be deadly. Our windows have turned into mirrors, giving back the sky and making a solid plane look like an opening. I've made every adjustment I can—installed screens, put stickers on the glass door, hung icicle lights from the rafters—but migratory birds can be especially vulnerable to disorientation near unfamiliar buildings. The day after the waxwings appeared at my birdbath, I found one of them, its flock long gone, panting on the driveway below a corner of the house where two windows meet and form a mirage of trees and distances. When I stooped to look at the bird, it lay there quietly.

Though I could see no sign of injury, I knew it must be grievously hurt to sit so still as I gently cupped my hands around it to move it to a safer place in the yard. It made a listless effort to peck at my thumb, but it didn't struggle at all when my fingers closed around its wings, and I didn't know what to do. So much beauty is not meant to be held in human hands.

Those golden breast feathers fading upward to pale brown, and backward to gray, give the cedar waxwing a kind of borrowed glow, as though it were lit at all times by sunlight glancing off snow. Its pointed crest and dashing mask—a wraparound slash of black—sharpen its pale watercolors into a mien of fierceness. It's a tiny bandit with flamboyant red wingtips and a brash streak of yellow across the end of its tail feathers. An operatic aria of a bird. A flying jungle flower. A weightless coalescence of air and light and animation. It was a gift to hold that lovely, dying creature in my hands. It was wrong to feel its death as a gift.

I didn't know it was dying. I knew but didn't know. At least half of all birds who fly into windows will ultimately die of internal bleeding, even when they seem to recover and fly away, and this stunned cedar waxwing was in no shape to fly. Even so, my only thought in that moment was to set it high in a tree where our dog couldn't kill it with a curious sniff.

In any crisis I always seem to find myself suspended between knowing and not knowing, between information and comprehension. When my middle son was a toddler, he hit his head and briefly stopped breathing. I had been trained in CPR, but knowing exactly how to position a small body for help, knowing exactly how gently to puff into a baby's lungs, didn't figure into a scene in which my own child was in danger. I snatched him up and cradled him while his lips turned gray and my husband called the ambulance. In a contest between knowledge and instinct, instinct wins every time.

I should have taken that injured bird someplace safe and warm to die. Instead I took it to a cypress tree a few feet away and set it on a limb deep in the greenery. Its feet worked spastically for purchase but finally caught hold. It was clinging to the branch when I left it to go back inside. By the time I returned fifteen minutes later, it had tumbled into the soft ground cover below. One wing was spread out like a taxidermist's display, those waxy red tips stretched as far apart as fingers in a reaching hand. I didn't need to pick it up to know it was dead. I knew it was dead, but I hadn't known it was dying.

Why didn't I know? My mother died of a cerebral hemorrhage, and I have seen up close what it looks like when a living thing is dying because its brain is bleeding and there's nowhere for the pooled blood to go, no way to keep the blood from crowding out the living cells of thought, the living cells of self. "I love you," I said as we waited for the results of my mother's CT scan. "You're my good mama," I told her as her eyes closed. "Thank you," she said. I was waiting for the doctor to come and tell me what to do, and I didn't know that these would be her last words. I knew but didn't know.

I wish I had taken that soft brown miracle of a bird into a dark, warm room to die. I wish I hadn't noticed the way my mother's hand was already cooling when she took her last breath.

You'll Never Know How Much I Love You

I don't know exactly where it came from—this phrase of pure treacle, worse than cliché. My father kept the car radio tuned to the big band station, the oldies channel of his middle age, so I could have heard the words in a song sung long before my time. Perhaps I heard it on the transistor radio I kept clutched to my ear the year I was ten or eleven, that age when language sticks, when poems and song lyrics and incantatory prayers merge with the rush of blood in the veins. Now, more than forty years later, the songs on my transistor radio are playing on the oldies channel of my own middle age. I will never learn the new doxology.

Possibly I read it in a terrible novel, or the cropped version of a terrible novel. In those days they came bound five or six to a volume from *Reader's Digest*, blessedly pruned books by authors who felt no uneasiness about writing a sentence like "You will never know how much I love you."

Did someone say it to me once? In the desperate madness of mismatched love, did a boy whisper those very words into my very ear, where they found a place to latch, lingering decades longer than a love that now seems hardly more than a dream?

No matter. Somehow it worked its way into the sinews of my thinking, into the folds of my always unfolding memory. I hear it in my sleep; it comes to me while I'm washing dishes or watering the garden, snakes around my ears and slithers into my hair, settling like an invisible crown, too tight, on my skull.

I was six when I lost my first love, a boy whose family stayed across the road and up the hill while my own family left town. *You will never know how much I love you because I am too young for such words, because I am too young to be the vessel of longing and fury that I have become.* Did I already know, even then? Was I already so tuned to loss that a single line of pure banality could lodge in the reptilian brain?

A woman I thought of as a friend once said to me, "Your central motivation is fear of loss." It was not a description but an accusation. She meant I was a coward. She meant I was destined to go nowhere, accomplish nothing. It occurred to me to wonder if she had ever, even once, loved anyone enough to fear the possibility of loss, but that thought was as ugly as her own, and in any case she was not wrong.

What makes a little girl walk into her parents' room in the middle of the night and lay her hand on each in turn, a touch too light to wake them, just to be sure they're still breathing? My hand rises and falls with each breath they take. I turn to leave. They will never know I've been there. They will never know how much I love them.

ROBIN

Separation Anxiety

It is dusk in August, and the voices of robins fill the air, surrendering daylight with one last call-and-response song against the darkness. All spring I watched these birds building their nests and raising their nestlings, heard those sharp-eyed babies making their harsh, monosyllabic demands. All summer I watched the parents teaching their fledglings to flutter up from the ground and into the tree limbs, or at least the inner branches of a dense shrub, as quickly as they could. Now the young birds have grown past the one-note call of desperation, and the robins are all, young and old, singing the same song. At twilight it is a mournful sound—something less than heartbreaking, something more than melancholy.

Or maybe this edging sadness has nothing to do with robins. Summer is ending, and my younger sons—the only two still at home even part of the year—are heading back to college, and I can hardly bear to see them go. When my children were younger, the connection I felt to them was visceral. During those early days of carrying a child—whether in my body or in my arms—I came to feel like one-half of a symbiotic relationship. All these years later, motherhood still thrums within me like a pulse, and I catch myself swaying whenever I'm standing in a long line, soothing the ghost baby fussing in my arms. I look at my sons, all taller than six feet now, and sometimes I can't quite believe I'm not still carrying them around on my hip, not still feeling their damp fingers tangled in my hair or clutching the back of my blouse. Sometimes at supper, when one of them brings a glass to his lips, I can still imagine a sippy cup gripped in his fingers.

I haven't forgotten how exhausting it was to be the mother of young children or how often I was frustrated by the close rooms and constricted plans of those days, the way my boys were always in my arms or at my feet. I haven't forgotten how repetitive those days were, how I often felt unable to draw a deep breath.

And yet I sometimes let myself imagine what a gift it would be to start all over again with this man, with these children, to go back to the beginning and feel less restless this time, less eager to hurry my babies along. Why did I spend so much time watching for the next milestone when the next milestone never meant the freedom I expected? There will be years and years to sleep, I know now, but only the briefest weeks in which to smell a baby's neck as he nestles against my shoulder in the deepest night.

With my own nest emptying, metaphors of loss are everywhere. The limping old dog who was my sons' perfect childhood companion is gone now, and I take my after-supper walk alone. I watch the sun dropping behind my neighbors' houses, and I listen to the robins' song. It's too late in the day for most songbirds and too early for owls; the robins have the stage to themselves in this margin between light and dark. I listen with an edge of grief around my heart. Summer is going, and daylight is going, and now my children are on their way again as well.

Already they are packing the minivan we bought when the youngest was in second grade. The house that all summer has been loud with life will fall almost silent. My husband and I will drive them to their dorms on the other side of the state, take a few minutes to unload, and then turn around to head home again. I will lift a hand as we pull out, though I know they will already be turning away, turning toward their beckoning new life. It has been years since the last time they looked back after leaving a car. They long ago stopped waving goodbye.

Farewell

Again and again I have to teach myself the splendor of decay. The cerulean feathers drifting beneath the pine where the bluebird met the Cooper's hawk for the last time. The muddle of spent spikes on the butterfly bush, winter-dried to the palest rustle. The blighted rose, its tangled canes gone black and monstrous in death, baring now the fine architecture of the cardinal's nest it sheltered last summer. The gathered dust on the living room piano throwing off light like sparks in the waning day, and the cut lilies' petals, released in one long sigh.

Recompense

It's your birthday, which always seems to fall on the most splendid day of October. Even if it's a workday, you must find some time to set aside your whirring machines and your contentions. Maybe there is a creek that all summer was still and dry and now is wet and tumbling with twigs and leaves and sweet-gum balls. Maybe there is a field gone golden with weeds, with finches perched in the seed crowns. Maybe there is an old train track that hosts no trains but lays out a whole parade route of purple thistles, or a dirt road where the close pines have set down a thick carpet for your hurting feet. Maybe there is a lake where a bald eagle sometimes fishes, where you might chance to see it dive, to hear its wings rise up to break its fall, to watch its yellow feet pull a sleek brown fish from the green water.

And while you are walking, keeping your eyes turned to the sky, maybe the earth will pull you back to the path, back to the toddler holding up her hands to the drifting leaves; and to the floating meadow of duckweed the color of new grass in springtime; and to the lone frog calling with no response from the marshy backwater; and to all the sunning turtles lined up on their black logs like rosary beads; and to the crows and the blue jays conducting a bitter dispute high in the treetops; and to the young woman with a prosthetic arm sitting on a bench and telling a story with wild gesticulations while her sweetheart gazes at her, smiling, never lifting his eyes from hers. And maybe you will see two vultures, as beautiful on the wing as any eagle, circling the sky, and all the while the leaves will be letting go of their branches and falling down on you like blessings.

MONARCH

Late Migration

Every monarch in North America is hatched on the leaf of a milkweed plant, and almost all of them spend winter on fir-covered mountains in central Mexico, in clumps so thick that tree branches can crash to the forest floor from their weight. One recent March, a storm brought such shattering winds and rain to their Mexican wintering grounds that millions of butterflies died before they could head north to breed. And the milkweed that the survivors were looking for—once ubiquitous on American roadsides and in vacant lots and at the stubbled edges of farms—is mostly gone now too, a casualty of the herbicides that go hand in glove with genetically modified crops.

Twenty years ago, there were at least a billion monarch butterflies in North America. Now there are only ninety-three million. Once upon a time, even a loss of that magnitude might have caused me only a flicker of concern, the kind of thing I trusted scientists to straighten out. But I am old enough now to have buried many of my loved ones, and loss is too often something I can do nothing about. So I lie awake in the dark and plot solutions to the problems of the pollinators—the collapse of the honeybee hives and the destruction of monarch habitats—in the age of Roundup.

When it was time to put my garden to bed one fall, I pulled out the okra and squash and tomatoes and planted a pollinator garden: coreopsis and coneflower and sage and lavender and bee balm and a host of other wildflowers. Once spring came, I threw in a handful of zinnia seeds to fill in when the perennials were bloomed out. The crowning glory of the garden that first year was a flat of native milkweed plants. I know this scruffy half-acre lot is no match for what ails the pollinators, especially not in suburbia, where lawn services dispense poisons from tanks the size of pickup trucks. Around here I think I might be the only one losing sleep over the bees and the butterflies.

Our feist mix, Betty, was always in intense pursuit of moles. In a spray of dirt like something from a Road Runner cartoon, she could dig up a mole run in a matter of minutes, leaving a system of open trenches crisscrossing the yard. Once the mole was dead or had taken refuge under the roadbed, I would rake the mounds of dirt smooth again, cover the turned soil with white clover, and water it down.

"Rye?" a neighbor asked, watching me scatter seeds.

"Clover," I said.

She looked at me. "You're *planting* clover?"

"For the honeybees," I said.

"Last summer there was a big ball of bees up in the crepe myrtle next to my garbage cans," she told me. "It took a whole can of Raid to kill them."

Spring brought a nice crop of clover that year and the first blooms in the butterfly garden. The native bumblebees loved the new flowers, crawling into them with a fervor that explains how they got all mixed up in a metaphor for sex in the first place. But I never saw more than one honeybee, and the monarchs apparently never noticed the milkweed plants with their rangy stalks full of vibrant orange flowers. Oh, there were other butterflies: cabbage whites and clouded sulfurs and Gulf fritillaries with their deceptive orange wings. But the milkweed bloomed and faded without a single monarch arriving in the nursery I had built for them.

There will be another summer, I told myself.

That fall, with temperatures still unseasonably warm for Middle Tennessee, I watered the butterfly garden through a profound drought that lasted for more than two months. Only the zinnias were still blooming, and I debated with myself the right way to approach the weeks of unexpected flowers. Cut the spent blooms back and force the plants to keep making new flowers for any butterflies still on the wing? Or let the zinnias go to seed for goldfinches to harvest?

As with most quandaries, I came to an inadvertent compromise: cutting the dead blooms when I thought to, ignoring them when I didn't. So the goldfinches had their zinnias, and the Gulf fritillaries had theirs, too.

And then, a miracle. Walking to the mailbox on a sunny November afternoon, I spied a flash of orange in the flower bed. I was a step or two on before I saw it: a monarch, riding a hot-pink zinnia nodding in the wind. I walked closer, and there on a yellow zinnia was another. And on the red one too—and on the orange, the white, the peach ones. Monarch after monarch after monarch was gathering nectar from the flowers. All that mild afternoon, my butterfly garden was a resting place for monarchs making a very late migration to Mexico.

Monarchs migrate as birds do, but it takes the monarch four generations, sometimes five, to complete the cycle each year: no single butterfly lives to make the full round-trip from Mexico to their northern breeding grounds and back. Entomologists don't yet understand what makes successive generations follow the same route their ancestors took, and I can only hope that the descendants of these monarchs will find respite in my garden, too. Every year will always find me planting zinnias, just in case.

After the Fall

This talk of making peace with it. Of feeling it and then find-ing a way through. Of closure. It's all nonsense.

Here is what no one told me about grief: you inhabit it like a skin. Everywhere you go, you wear grief under your clothes. Everything you see, you see through it, like a film.

It is not a hidden hair shirt of suffering. It is only you, the thing you are, the cells that cling to each other in your shape, the muscles that are doing your work in the world. And like your other skin, your other eyes, your other muscles, it too will change in time. It will change so slowly you won't even see it happening. No matter how you scrutinize it, no matter how you poke at it with a worried finger, you will not see it chang-ing. Time claims you: your belly softens, your hair grays, the skin on the top of your hand goes loose as a grandmother's, and the skin of your grief, too, will loosen, soften, forgive your sharp edges, drape your hard bones.

You are waking into a new shape. You are waking into an old self.

What I mean is, time offers your old self a new shape.

What I mean is, you are the old, ungrieving you, and you are also the new, ruined you.

You are both, and you will always be both.

There is nothing to fear. There is nothing at all to fear. Walk out into the springtime, and look: the birds welcome you with a chorus. The flowers turn their faces to your face. The last of last year's leaves, still damp in the shadows, smell ripe and faintly of fall.

Holy, Holy, Holy

On the morning after my mother's sudden death, before I was up, someone brought a basket of muffins, good coffee beans, and a bottle of cream—real cream, unwhipped—left them at the back door, and tiptoed away. I couldn't eat. The smell of coffee turned my stomach, but my head was pounding from all the tears and all the what-ifs playing across my mind all night long, and I thought perhaps the cream would make a cup of coffee count as breakfast if I could keep it down.

When I poured just a drip of cream into my cup, it erupted into volcanic bubbles in a hot spring, unspooling skeins of bridal lace, fireworks over a dark ocean, stars streaking across the night sky above a silent prairie.

And that's how I learned the world would go on. An irreplaceable life had winked out in an instant, but outside my window the world was flaring up in celebration. Someone was hearing, "It's benign." Someone was saying, "It's a boy." Someone was throwing out her arms and crying, "Thank you! Thank you! Oh, thank you!"

So much to do still, all of it praise.

DEREK WALCOTT

Works Cited

Not all allusions in *Late Migrations* are cited in the text. Here is a list of those that aren't:

p. 2: The title is a paraphrase of "Nature, red in tooth and claw" from "In Memoriam" by Alfred, Lord Tennyson.

p. 9: The phrase "Life piled on life" appears in "Ulysses" by Alfred, Lord Tennyson.

p. 30: The final two sentences of "The Snow Moon" are an echo of "mon semblable,—mon frère!" from Charles Baudelaire's *Les Fleurs du mal*.

p. 45: *Barney Beagle Plays Baseball*, a beginning reader by Jean Bethell, was first published in 1963.

p. 51: "Operation Apache Snow" was a US offensive launched on May 10, 1969, against the North Vietnamese that resulted in massive casualties on both sides.

p. 54: The title is a quotation from the poem "Tell Me a Story" by Robert Penn Warren.

p. 58: In the first sentence, "heavy bored" is an allusion to "Dream Song 14" by John Berryman.

p. 58: The Bible passage that closes the first paragraph is Mark 11:23.

p. 69: The "Beatitudes" commonly refers to a set of teachings delivered by Jesus in the Sermon on the Mount.

p. 72: "Ev'ry Time We Say Goodbye" is a song written by Cole Porter and recorded by Ella Fitzgerald, among others.

p. 78: "The world is too much with us" is an allusion to William Wordsworth's sonnet of the same title.

p. 80: The title of this essay alludes to a line from W. H. Auden's poem "Musée des Beaux Arts."

p. 85: The description of my mother as someone who never prepared for gardening is an echo of E. B. White's description of his wife, Katharine S. White, in an introduction to her book, *Onward and Upward in the Garden*.

p. 95: Annie Dillard's essay is "Total Eclipse," first published in 1982.

p. 96: The song I mention in the penultimate paragraph of this essay is "Ring of Fire," written by June Carter and Merle Kilgore and made famous by Johnny Cash.

p. 98: The short story we read in class, I later learned, is "Brandenburg Concerto" by Lawrence Dorr.

p. 110: In the final paragraph, "goldengrove unleaving" is an allusion to "Spring and Fall," a poem by Gerard Manley Hopkins.

p. 114: "Shaking the caked red dirt from my sandals" is an echo of Matthew 10:14.

p. 116: The title of this essay is an allusion to a line from William Shakespeare's "Sonnet LXXIII."

p. 116: "Nothing gold can stay" is an allusion to Robert Frost's poem of the same title.

p. 118: "Heart of Greyhound darkness" is an allusion to Joseph Conrad's novel *Heart of Darkness*.

p. 129: "The fog comes on little cat feet" is an allusion to "Fog" by Carl Sandburg.

p. 131: The title refers to an observation commonly attributed to Aristotle.

p. 132: "Two by Two" refers to the way the animals entered Noah's ark in Genesis 7:9.

p. 138: The title of this essay quotes a line from W. H. Auden's poem, "Musée des Beaux Arts."

p. 151: "He Is Not Here" is a quote from the Biblical Easter story.

p. 159: "You Can't Go Home Again" echoes the title of a novel by Thomas Wolfe.

p. 163: The title of this essay echoes repeated exhortations throughout the Bible.

p. 166: "Dust to Dust" echoes Ecclesiastes 3:20.

p. 175: "Homeward Bound" echoes the title of a 1993 film about three family pets making their way home after an unexpected separation from their people.

p. 187: "No Exit" echoes the title of a play by Jean-Paul Sartre.

p. 195: "Nevermore" is the word the bird repeats throughout Edgar Allan Poe's poem "The Raven."

p. 219: "Holy, Holy, Holy," is the title of a Christian hymn published in 1826 by Reginald Heber.

A final note: "In Which My Grandmother Tells the Story of the Day She Was Shot" is an edited version of an essay my grandmother wrote in 1983 that was never published. All the other essays in her voice are transcripts of interviews my brother conducted with her in 1990. The excerpts are faithful to the original recordings except where slight changes—adding names, for example, or omitting repetition—contribute significantly to understanding.

Publications

These essays appeared, often in significantly different form, in the following publications:

"Separation Anxiety" (as "Motherhood and the Back-to-College Blues")
The New York Times, August 20, 2018

"Gall" (as "What to Expect")
O, The Oprah Magazine, October 2018

"Homeward Bound" (as "What It Means to Be Loved by a Dog")
The New York Times, June 18, 2018

"Howl" (as "The Pain of Loving Old Dogs")
The New York Times, February 25, 2018

"Babel" and "Thanksgiving" (as "It's Thanksgiving. Come On Home")
The New York Times, November 23, 2017

"A Ring of Fire" (as "In Nashville's Sky, a Ring of Fire")
The New York Times, August 21, 2017

"Holy, Holy, Holy"
River Teeth, July 27, 2017

"The Unpeaceable Kingdom" (as "Springtime's Not-So-Peaceable Kingdom")
The New York Times, June 4, 2017

"Masked" (as "What Dying Looks Like")
The New York Times, February 26, 2017

"Late Migration"
Guernica, December 6, 2016

"Nevermore" (as "Quoth the Vulture 'Nevermore'")
The New York Times, October 31, 2016

"Recompense"
Proximity, September 13, 2016

"Red in Beak and Claw"
*The New York Time*s, July 31, 2016

"No Exit" (as "Caregiving: A Burden So Heavy, until It's Gone")
The New York Times, August 8, 2015

Acknowledgments

It takes a village to raise a child. It takes a multigenerational nation to publish a first book at the age of fifty-seven.

I am grateful to the writers who helped shape these essays from an embryonic stage: Ralph Bowden, Maria Browning, Susannah Felts, Carrington Fox, Faye Jones, Susan McDonald, Mary Laura Philpott, and Chris Scott. Extra thanks to Maria, who read the whole book—twice—while it was still trying to become a book.

I am unendingly thankful for the writers at *Chapter 16* and for the Tennessee authors, librarians, and independent booksellers whose work gives *Chapter 16* its mission. I will never find enough words of thanks for Serenity Gerbman and Tim Henderson at Humanities Tennessee. For ten years their flexibility and unflagging support made it possible for me to be both an editor and a writer.

At *The New York Times*, I'm profoundly grateful to Peter Catapano, whose genius makes my words better every single week, and to Clay Risen, whose offhand remark in a conversation at the Southern Festival of Books—"Would you ever want to write about that?"—led to the first essay I wrote for both the *Times* and this book.

Joey McGarvey plucked an incomplete manuscript of *Late Migrations* out of the slushpile at Milkweed Editions and somehow saw what it could become. Her gentle guidance and brilliant editing turned a jumble of essays into an actual book. And after it finally became a book, the rest of the team at Milkweed— Meagan Bachmayer, Jordan Bascom, Shannon Blackmer, Joanna Demkiewicz, Daley Farr, Allison Haberstroh, Daniel Slager, Mary Austin Speaker, Abby Travis, and Hans Weyandt— worked unceasingly to help it find its way. Thank you, all of you.

Writing *Late Migrations* has brought home to me how vast the literary ecosystem truly is. I send my heartfelt thanks to Kristyn Keene Benton of ICM Partners for her expansive understanding and expertise; to Carmen Toussaint of Rivendell Writers' Colony for building the haven where this book could grow; to Mary Grey James, who came out of retirement to help me understand the book business from a side I'd never seen before; and to Karen Hayes and everyone at Parnassus Books for creating a crucial "third place" for Nashville's readers and writers, and for believing in this book from the very beginning.

All my life I have been wholly fortunate in teachers and mentors, especially Ruth Brittin, James Dickey, John Egerton, Sharyn Gaston, Ann Granberry, and R.T. Smith. Most of them didn't live to read this book, but their influence can be found in every paragraph. Teachers everywhere, thank you. You are planting seeds for the ages.

In eighth grade, having exhibited no competence in middle school biology, I abandoned my plan to be a large-animal veterinarian. When I told my parents I'd decided to be a writer instead, they bought an ancient manual typewriter at a garage sale and brought it home. I wrote all my high school, college, and grad school papers on that Underwood Noiseless Portable, and probably a thousand poems, too. That's the kind of parents I had.

It's the kind of family I still have: part safety net and part trampoline. I am grateful to Shannon Weems Anderson and Max Weems III, the cousins who shared so much of my childhood. I am grateful to our Nashville family—the Hills, the Baileys, the Michaels, the Tarkingtons, and all the dear friends who make our entire neighborhood a home. I am grateful to my brilliant siblings, Billy Renkl and Lori Renkl, who are my constant inspiration. I am grateful to Sam Moxley, Henry

Moxley, and Joe Moxley, the greatest gifts of my life. Most of all, I am grateful to Haywood Moxley, who is life itself to me.

In the end, this book is for my people. For my parents and my grandparents and my great-grandparents. For my husband and our children and, someday, for the families our children will make. For my brother and my sister. For my husband's parents and siblings. For all our beloved nieces and nephews on both sides. If there's anything that living in a family has taught me, it's that we belong to one another. Outward and outward and outward, in ripples that extend in either direction, we belong to one another. And also to this green and gorgeous world.

A Conversation with Margaret Renkl

and Sally Wizik Wills, June 2019

SALLY WIZIK WILLS is a co-owner of Beagle and Wolf Books & Bindery, located in Park Rapids, Minnesota. This conversation appears courtesy of *Bookselling This Week*, a publication of the American Booksellers Association.

SALLY WIZIK WILLS: After reading *Late Migrations*, I can be sure you're never far from the outdoors. What do you see when you look out your kitchen window, and how does that nourish your life and your writing?

MARGARET RENKL: Because we've added onto this house willy-nilly over the years, my kitchen window actually looks into our family room, not into the outdoors. But I have a small home office whose window overlooks a part of the yard where I've put up a birdbath, a mealworm feeder, and a nest box. The office is where I answer emails and do research, and that window makes for an excellent opportunity for procrastination when work gets tedious. On the other side of the house, in the family room itself, there's a long table beneath a bank of windows, and that's where I actually write. Those windows overlook another birdbath and feeding station, as well as my pollinator garden. Even during winter, something is always happening out there—squirrels looking for nuts they buried in the fall, songbirds picking through dead foliage for bugs, hawks looking for squirrels and songbirds.

Our yard is only half an acre. It's nothing like the woods and fields I played in as a child, but it's teeming with life anyway. It reminds me that I'm part of a cycle that's much larger than my own life. Most people are nourished by encounters with nature, whether or not they had access to long stretches of unsupervised time in the natural world as a child, but for me those encounters are truly essential. They help me remember who I am. They remind me of what really matters.

SWW: What advice do you have for people who would like to see the natural world more deeply? Are there disciplines a person can cultivate to become more keenly observant of the world around them?

MR: I'm sure there must be, but I'm not an expert in the how-to of this kind of observation. I grew up in a time when parents expected children to show up for meals and didn't bother too much about where they spent the rest of their time, and one of the great gifts of a free-range childhood was the opportunity to indulge my own curiosity. I learned very young that the way to study a wild creature is to be very still and very quiet and very patient.

These aren't skills that our own age rewards. Now that everyone carries the ultimate distraction device in their pockets, boredom sets in much sooner than it used to. But the trick is still to be very still and very quiet and very patient. If you can resist the impulse to check email (or your social media feeds, or the weather, or the headlines), nature will always unfold for you, no pollinator garden required.

Sit still on a bench on a busy city street and wait. Soon you'll see the house sparrows collecting crumbs. Follow them with your eyes as they fly away, and you'll likely see the crevice in a nearby building where they've hidden their nest.

Move to a closer bench and listen, and you'll hear the baby birds crying out when their parents return with food. You'll notice the timbre of their voices deepening day by day, and when they begin to sound like their parents, you'll know it's almost time for them to leave the nest. If you aren't checking your phone when it happens, you might even be lucky enough to see their maiden flight.

SWW: Your brother Billy's illustrations are a beautiful and sensitive accompaniment to your words. Tell us about your collaboration on the book.

MR: Billy and I are only a year and a half apart in age, and we've been collaborating on some kind of project or other since we were very small—we often worked together on little books for our parents and grandparents and friends. In high school, Billy was the art director for the student newspaper when I was the editor, and in college he was the art director of the student magazine I edited. Even now, all these years later, our interests often overlap: his artwork frequently features the backyard world of birds and insects and flowers. So I knew from the very beginning that I wanted this book about our family to be his book about our family, too.

I had already written all the essays in the book before Billy started working on the art, but one day I'd love to try it the other way around—it would be fun to let him make a set of collages that I later "illustrate" with words.

SWW: I live in Minnesota, and this spring the birding has been spectacular. Unusually large numbers of Baltimore orioles have been at backyard feeders and the usually hard-to-spot scarlet tanagers have flaunted themselves in yards across the state. The scientific explanation of the latter is that climate change has disrupted normal patterns of migration. On a deeper level, how do unusual occurrences in nature help us understand ourselves and the world in which we live in different ways?

MR: Climate change has become a political issue, but it didn't begin as one; for years, politicians on both sides of the aisle accepted the reality of climate change and the role human beings play in it. (I highly recommend Nathaniel Rich's book, *Losing Earth: A Recent History*, for an explanation of how oil-company marketing executives managed to hijack the conversation.) But one beautiful thing about the natural world is that it stubbornly insists on responding to reality, not spin, and it is showing us the enormity of this calamity.

People who are paying attention, even just a cursory kind of attention, are beginning to ask questions. How is it possible to go for a long drive in the dark and come home with almost no bugs smashed against the windshield? Where are the bees that should be crowding the magnolia blossoms? Why are the secretive scarlet tanagers suddenly coming down from the treetops? Where are the tree frogs that ought to be filling the summer nights with song?

Asking questions like that is the first step toward understanding what's happening to the earth. And the next question is usually "How can I help?" I think most people truly want to help, and helping is how we begin to understand ourselves as creatures—not separate from the earth but part of it.

SWW: In *Late Migrations*, your observations of the natural world and of your family are braided together. Is it possible for you to tease them apart? Which comes first for you, and what are the ways in which they inform one another?

MR: For a long, long time, I thought I was writing two completely different kinds of essays—I didn't think of them as braided together at all. I was writing the family essays in response to the grief of losing my mother, and I was writing the nature essays in response to my grief over what was happening to the world.

But the more I wrote, the closer the two threads came together, and the more clearly I saw them as connected. In part that's because I spent so much of my childhood outdoors, so my family memories are shot through with a deep engagement with nature. And in part it's because the more I wrote about the natural world, the more I realized that the creatures who share my yard feel almost like family members. It's always a mistake to anthropomorphize nature—we miss the true majesty of the natural world when we try to domesticate it—but seeing myself as part of that world, not alien at all, is one of my chief sources of comfort. For me there's no distinction anymore. The nature essays *are* family essays.

Ultimately, I think, that feeling may be our greatest chance to save the planet. If we can come to understand at a deep emotional level that what is happening to the earth is also happening to *us*, that our fate is inextricably entwined with the fate of the natural world, then we might finally be inspired to do something about it.

Questions and Topics for Discussion

1. *Late Migrations* begins with the story of the birth of Margaret Renkl's mother, and it ends with her death. Ask each person to share the story of the birth of their own mother. If they don't know that story, ask them to share someone else's birth story—perhaps their own.

2. As a child, Renkl roamed the landscape of Alabama, where she developed keen observational skills within the natural world. Have you—as a child or as an adult—had the opportunity to closely watch the natural world around you? Talk about one such experience.

3. Renkl also closely observed the adults in her family. She clearly felt loved and protected, but she didn't always understand what she saw. Talk about the references to her mother's depression in these essays: "The Monster in the Window," "Swept Away," "Things I Didn't Know When I Was Six," and "I Didn't Choose." In what ways are Renkl's mother's experiences a reflection of the time in which she lived? Share an example of something you observed as a child but didn't understand.

4. Each essay in *Late Migrations* is titled. How did you respond to these titles? Did any of these titles surprise you? Make you laugh or make you sad? Did any influence or change your response to its accompanying essay?

5. In the essay "Let Us Pause to Consider What a Happy Ending Actually Looks Like," Renkl writes, "But the shadow side of love is always loss, and grief is only love's

own twin." How do you react to this statement? In your experience, has it been true? Give an example to illustrate your response.

6. Ask each person to pick one illustration in the book at random and to reread the essay it accompanies. How do the writing and the image inform each other?

7. In the essay "What I Saved," Renkl lists both the belongings she kept after her mother's death—her wedding ring and gown, but also a mug, laundry detergent, coat hangers—and those she threw away. Do you own anything that reminds you of a departed loved one, whether special or seemingly ordinary?

8. Reread the book's epigraphs: "Well, dear, life is a casting off. It's always that way" (Arthur Miller, *Death of a Salesman*) and "Therefore all poems are elegies" (George Barker). In what ways do they illuminate the book (or not)? How about the quote that follows the final essay: "So much to do still, all of it praise" (Derek Walcott)?

9. In her conversation with Sally Wizik Wills at the end of this book, Renkl says of climate change, "People who are paying attention, even just a cursory kind of attention, are beginning to ask questions." What changes have you noticed in the natural world around you?

10. Ask each person to select a favorite essay or quote from *Late Migrations* and to share their response with the group.

Heidi Ross

MARGARET RENKL is a contributing opinion writer for *The New York Times*, where her essays appear weekly. Her work has also appeared in *Guernica, Literary Hub, Proximity,* and *River Teeth,* among others. She was the founding editor of *Chapter 16,* the daily literary publication of Humanities Tennessee, and is a graduate of Auburn University and the University of South Carolina. She lives in Nashville.

Interior design by Mary Austin Speaker
Text typeset in Century; display set in Filosofia.

Century is a Scotch typeface originally cut by Linn Boyd Benton for master printer Theodore Low De Vinne for use in *Century* magazine. Later and more widely used iterations of Century were redesigned by Benton's son, Morris Fuller Benton, who devised the invention of type families.

Filosofia was designed by Zuzana Ličko for Emigre in 1996 as a contemporary interpretation of Bodoni.

milkweed
editions

Founded as a nonprofit organization in 1980, Milkweed Editions is an independent publisher. Our mission is to identify, nurture and publish transformative literature, and build an engaged community around it.

Milkweed Editions is based in Bdé Óta Othúŋwe (Minneapolis) within Mni Sota Makhóčhe, the traditional homeland of the Dakhóta people. Residing here since time immemorial, Dakhóta people still call Mni Sota Makhóčhe home, with four federally recognized Dakhóta nations and many more Dakhóta people residing in what is now the state of Minnesota. Due to continued legacies of colonization, genocide, and forced removal, generations of Dakhóta people remain disenfranchised from their traditional homeland. Presently, Mni Sota Makhóčhe has become a refuge and home for many Indigenous nations and peoples, including seven federally recognized Ojibwe nations. We humbly encourage readers to reflect upon the historical legacies held in the lands they occupy.

We are aided in this mission by generous individuals who make a gift to underwrite books on our list. Special underwriting for *Late Migrations* was provided by Mary and Keith Bednarowski.

milkweed.org